Eden Phillpotts was born in India in 1862. His father was political officer for two Indian States. Coming of Devonshire stock, he sent his son back to school at Plymouth. Afterwards Eden Phillpotts spent some time at a dramatic school and then went into an insurance company.

He began to write in 1890 and from then until his death in 1960, at the age of 92, he produced a prodigious flow of novels, plays, fairy stories, poetry, reminiscence, gardening books, and books about Devon. At the height of his success Eden Phillpotts was publishing two or three books a year, and sometimes more; and in a sense he paid the critical price both for his industry and the popular acclaim that went with it. In a celebrated remark, made in a letter of 1913, D. H. Lawrence said 'It is amazing how narrowly Phillpotts shaves it, and *just* misses, always.' Phillpotts might not have recognized the uncompromising standards which Lawrence thrust on fellow writers, as much as on himself. But he knew very well how to achieve his effects; how to weave character, and plot, and landscape into a satisfying whole.

Nowhere is this more apparent than in the *Dartmoor Cycle* of novels. Numbering eighteen books in all these are the books by which Eden Phillpotts will be remembered and which deserve to find a new readership. *Widecombe Fair* is the best-known but *The River, The Thief of Virtue, Children of the Mist* and *The Virgin in Judgement* are all books of uncommon power and quality. From the wild and beautiful Dartmoor country, which he knew down to the finest topographical detail, Phillpotts wrung a canon of ??? which do honour to Devon and to the Devon charact???

THE DEVON LIBRARY

Following the warm welcome which has greeted *The Cornish Library* we have felt emboldened to cross the Tamar and explore the literary heritage of its neighbour, Devon. Both counties have outstanding and varied scenic beauty. Both have a powerful maritime tradition and each has a strongly marked local character. There the similarities might seem to cease. But Devon has a literature every bit as robust and distinguished as the Cornish. *The Devon Library* will seek to do justice to this and to present the best of Devonian fiction and non-fiction in attractive paperback editions.

Titles in print or shortly to be published:

A Devon Anthology	*Jack Simmons*
Widecombe Fair	*Eden Phillpotts*
Devon	*S. Baring-Gould*
Mrs. Beer's House	*Patricia Beer*
The Initials in the Heart	*Laurence Whistler*
Diary of a Provincial Lady	*E. M. Delafield*
Father and Son	*Edmund Gosse*
The Thief of Virtue	*Eden Phillpotts*
Dewer Rides	*L. A. G. Strong*
Crossing's Dartmoor Worker	*W. A. J. Crossing*
Lorna Doone	*R. D. Blackmore*
The Old Stag	*Henry Williamson*
Westward Ho!	*Charles Kingsley*
On the Moor of a Night	*Jan Stewer*
Devon Short Stories	Ed. *Wendy Monk*
The Hound of the Baskervilles	*Arthur Conan Doyle*

All the books in *The Devon Library* are numbered to encourage collectors. If you would like more information, or you would care to suggest other books that you think should appear in the series, please write to me at the following address: Anthony Mott, The Devon Library, 50 Stile Hall Gardens, London W4 3BU.

THE DEVON LIBRARY
NUMBER TWO

Widecombe Fair
EDEN PHILLPOTTS

ANTHONY
MOTT
LTD

LONDON

Published by Anthony Mott Limited 1983
50 Stile Hall Gardens, London W4 3BU

First published by John Murray 1913

First published in this edition 1921

ISBN 0 907746 21 7

Printed in Great Britain by
Richard Clay (The Chaucer Press) Ltd

To
JAMES MATTHEW BARRIE
In Friendship

Widecombe Fair

CHAPTER I

ACROSS the brightness of afternoon sunshine, a west wind blew bannerets of smoke from the brows of many hills. These vans of vapour were purple in earth's shadow, but grey under the shadow of the clouds above them; and where the low sunshine burnt upon their streamers, they shone a dazzling silver.

It was February; swaling had begun, and Dartmoor's annual cleansing by fire liberated this splendid mass of matter, to fill the lower chambers of the air. With many aerial arches, rolling waves, and glimmering crests, the smoke spanned the depth beneath, where spread the Vale of Widecombe, within its granite cincture of great hills—a dimple on the face of the earth, a cradle under a many-coloured quilt of little fields.

Over the shoulders of Hameldon, the sunshine came slanting amid great shadows, that fell, wine-coloured, from the hills. Light began to ascend and wing out of this deep cup, until only the pinnacles of the church still flamed and flashed rosily above the gathering gloom.

North of the Vale the ground climbed abruptly to the wild heights of Honeybag Tor, Chinkwell Tor, Bel Tor; and upon a lower slope of the last, with their faces turned to the valley, sat a man and a young girl. Upon their left stood the pile of granite known as Bone Hill Rocks, and beneath them, separated from the Moor by a wood of pine and larch, lay Bone Hill Farm, a dwelling with a cheerful face that turned towards the south.

Forth from the trees with busy chatter came a flight of jackdaws. Like stars they sailed out, for the light flashed from their polished wings, and did not reveal their colour.

" Oh, the pretty birds ! " cried the girl. " And how happy they are ! And so they ought to be in such a place."

But the man hardly shared her enthusiasm.

" A desolate, uninhabited sort of a spot," he said. " This is what they call a rural district, Tryphena. I hope you won't find it very dull and dismal after the bustle and stir of Exeter."

He was a lawyer's clerk engaged in the duty of bringing an orphan child to her new home.

" I shall be happy, Mr. Blatchford, if the people are kind people," she answered.

" They are your mother's people, and will certainly be friendly to you. You read your uncle's letter—Mr. William Coaker, of Southcombe Farm. I wonder if we can see your future home from here."

" There's little houses dotted about on the hills, Mr. Blatchford."

" And each with its fields around it. But the loneliness, Tryphena ! How strange it must be to live in a house a mile away from everybody else ! "

They had walked from Bovey, by which action Mr. Blatchford, whose expenses were paid, stood to save ten shillings in cab hire. But he was weary now, for he had not guessed at the distance.

" We will go down into the valley and have a meat-tea at the inn," he declared. " Then they can tell us which is Southcombe. Your box will be sent for."

" I'm terribly hungry, Mr. Blatchford."

" So am I, my dear."

Tryphena Harvey rose and displayed herself as a girl tall for her age, with a face rather pale, red-lipped, grey-eyed, and wistful. There was a twinkle about it, and a suggestion of intelligence. Her black dress and her black hat suited her fairness. Her hair was down, and hung in a good mane of rippled straw-colour. Her dress was short, and revealed a pair of well-shaped legs in black stockings. She wore a jacket of dark-blue cloth, too short in the arms. An inch of white wrist separated the coat-sleeve from her black-thread gloves.

The clerk was elderly and bald. He carried a leather bag for his papers, and a large umbrella. He was not dressed for the country, and his trousers were muddy, his boots causing him pain.

They descended into the valley past Bone Hill Farm, whose white-washed face smiled with cheerful aspect beneath its grove. Somewhat farther down the hill a single house stood, of a character very different from its surroundings. It displayed a red-tiled roof, a prim garden, and a little conservatory. A lawn extended before the front windows, and a small flagstaff arose upon it. An araucaria guarded the door, and the front gate was painted green. Along the topmost bar appeared the words " Genoa Villa." In all its prim, suburban perfection this dwelling lay amid the fields, farms, and farm roads. But Mr. Blatchford's city soul welcomed this glimpse of a higher civilisation, and rejoiced to see it.

" Dear me! " he exclaimed. " To think that a modern house has sprung up here! One would never have expected such a thing."

As he spoke a woman came briskly up the lane and raised the latch of the green gate. She was short, grey, and of a square build. Her face was full and florid, and its apparent breadth had been increased by an old-fashioned arrangement of little curls, like grey wood-shavings, that sprouted from under her bonnet on either side. Her eyes were round and bright. She wore a plum-coloured dress, short over very tiny shoes, and a coat of tawny fur with the collar turned up. She carried a string bag, and when Mr. Blatchford addressed her, answered in clear-cut accents with some affectation of culture.

" Pardon me, madam, but which would be the way to Widecombe? " inquired Mr. Blatchford, lifting his top hat from his bald brow.

" You cannot mistake it," was the answer. " If you pursue this road till you reach a bridge over the river and then proceed to your right over the bridge, you will arrive in the village."

" Thank you very much. I was just venturing to admire this house. It is a surprise to see such a dwelling on Dartmoor."

The lady exhibited pleasure.

" Yes," she said, lifting her eyes fondly to her home. " It is a villa residence. People are astonished to see it. Tourists stand still and look at it."

" A good example to the country-side, I'm sure."

" It is—indeed. My father, who built it, was accustomed to use those very words; but example is thrown away here, I'm afraid."

" Seed on stony ground, madam—seed on stony ground. And may I ask which of these farms round the valley is Southcombe? "

She surveyed Mr. Blatchford with interest, and then turned her eyes to Tryphena. It was clear that the mention of Southcombe had conveyed some meaning to her. She knew their business.

" You proceed through Widecombe, and, about three hundred yards further on, will observe a steep lane extending up the hill on your right. If followed it will take you to Southcombe Farm, the residence of the Coaker family."

She spoke with her eyes on the orphan's face.

" I thank you," answered Mr. Blatchford; then he opened the lady's gate for her. She bowed and passed in.

" Evidently a maiden lady of pretty good means," he said.

" And such funny round eyes," replied the girl. " But a kind sort of old face."

" Not old, my dear," answered Mr. Blatchford, who lacked imagination—" not old by any means. If you said fifty you'd be within the mark, I believe. Fifty-three at the outside."

They tramped on and reached the village.

CHAPTER II

CROSSING the village green upon the northern side of the church, Tryphena Harvey and her companion found themselves at the centre of Widecombe. Upon one side of the space wherein they stood rose a lichgate, and springing from it extended an ancient Church House—partly used as dwellings for the needy and partly as a school. Before it ran a heavy porch on granite pillars above cobblestone pavement; beside it lay Widecombe's treasure, a fragment of the village stocks. In the midst of the central square a yew-tree stood, perched on a triple row of granite steps, while westerly appeared the smithy behind a formidable frieze of ploughs and harrows, and the " Old Inn," a comfortable and ancient house, whose entrance was beneath the level of the road.

Here Arthur Pierce was licensed to sell beer and spirits, tobacco and snuff.

" Food! food! " cried Mr. Blatchford. " Positively I can go no farther, Tryphena, until we have eaten and drunk."

A thin, smooth-faced man led the travellers to a little parlour that faced west, and still harboured a beam of setting sunshine. The man had a long, lean countenance with a pointed chin and feeble mouth. He was very loose-limbed, and of an invertebrate and nervous temperament. Instinctively patronising this poor-spirited person, Mr. Blatchford ordered ham and eggs, tea for Tryphena, and a glass of brandy and water for himself. The landlord, who spoke in an anxious, hurried voice, fell in with these suggestions, and began to explain that the house was short-handed. He displayed a great vagueness of opinion and indecision of action. At length he met with an accident, and broke a pink glass vase which stood in the middle of the table. This catastrophe unmanned him. He gazed with alarm at the fragments, then, murmuring some words about his wife, fluttered from the room.

Tryphena laughed softly, rose from a black, horsehair sofa in the corner, and cleared the table of the ruined ornament.

" What a helpless sort of man ! " she said—" for all the world like a daddy-long-legs."

" I think he's slightly wanting," declared the lawyer's clerk. " I hope he won't forget the order."

A woman entered the room as he spoke—a full-bosomed, black-eyed woman of sturdy proportions, with her sleeves rolled up to the elbows.

" Good evening. Mr. Pierce have broke a vawse, he tells me. Not man's work laying a tablecloth, of course, but we're in trouble along of a drunken cook. Mr. Pierce be all nerves, as I dare say you noticed."

" In a publican that is an awkward thing," said Mr. Blatchford.

" So it is, then, but he wasn't always so, poor wretch ! He had a breakdown along of his being very near drowned, and it have left him a mere shadow."

"Did he tell you about the ham and eggs? " asked Mr. Blatchford.

" He did; you can hear 'em," she answered. " The cook's gone, thank God—a drunken baggage. But Mr. Pierce be doing your food. Quite a cook in his way. Only he will get so excited."

" He'll grow stronger in time, we'll hope."

" Not him. The nerves be gone—rotted away at the roots, I believe. Us have tried to build him up with every mortal thing. The cream and milk that man let's down would keep a dairy. But there he is—so thin as a new come snipe, and his voice be sunk to a bleat."

" I'm sure I'm very sorry for you," said Mr. Blatchford.

" So's everybody. You ask the people what they think of Mabel Pierce, and they'll tell you. Mr. Gurney—that's the blacksmith next door but one—he says that the church martyrs were in clover compared to me."

A sound of trouble ascended the passage, and Mrs. Pierce shouted down it from the door :

" I'm coming, Arthur."

Then she spoke again.

" Human creatures he simply can't face—especially them he's never seen afore. 'Tis a great strain for a female, and there's times when I say in my heart, ' Oh for a man ! ' "

She departed, and returned presently with Mr. Blatchford's brandy and water.

" Too dashing a walk of life for Mr. Pierce since his great misfortune," she went on. " He didn't ought to have been a publican no more after that, for it throws a man in the public eye. He don't even dare to take round the dish in church any more, for his nerves won't suffer it."

She withdrew, and returned with the meal. She spoke at length about the difficulty of getting servants, and related her experiments.

" The worst of all was when I tried sisters. Ah, that's a mistake—a far-reaching mistake with consequences. Don't you never have sisters, master. The toads back each other up, and one's always egging on t'other. The old sort of honest, hard-working girls, as came to larn their business, and didn't worry about money, they be all gone now. The Board Schools ruined 'em body and soul. I catched a chambermaid playing on that pianer the second day she was here ! "

Mr. Blatchford soon paid his bill, expressed hopes that the landlord's shattered system would in time recover tone, and then again inquiring the road to Southcombe, started on his way. He was very stiff, and began to wonder whether his legs would carry him back to Bovey.

Tryphena had left him after tea, and when he reappeared before the inn, he found the girl listening to music.

Under the yew-tree by the lichgate, on the lowest granite step that surrounded it, sat a small man on a little folding stool, and beside him stood a woman. The man was squat and squarely built ; he revealed great power in his arms and shoulders; but he was blind. Out of a dogged, underhung face stared his sightless, blue eyes. His hair was grizzled, and descended, thick and close-cropped, to his low brow; his nose was upturned, and beneath it bristled a short grey moustache. His chin was shorn. A brutal pugnacity marked his countenance, and he displayed broad hands, with short, stubby fingers. His mild occupation assorted ill with the ferocious and grim character of his face and frame. For he played on an accordion, and from his fighting mouth, in guttural accents, there came a hymn. The woman beside him was like a ferret, sharp-nosed, red-eyed, swift in her motions—a predatory thing. Her brow was wrinkled and keen: her temper was as fierce as the man's. Nicky and Nanny Glubb were fighters both and beggars both.

When Nanny saw a stranger appearing, she had called to her husband, who had been wrangling at the time with an almsman hard by. She had then drawn him quickly to his stool and set the accordion in his hand. Now Nicky Glubb sang while Tryphena, with a fine lack of self-consciousness proper to her, stood beside him, fixed her grey eyes upon him, and solemnly listened to the music.

Within the porch of the almshouses an old man in white corduroys sat and scowled. He was known as " Gaffer Bell." During a pause in the hymn, the pensioner shouted to Tryphena :

" Don't you give him nothing, miss. He's a wicked old humbug, and the disgrace of Widecombe! "

Then appeared Mr. Blatchford, with his bag and umbrella, and joined the blind man's audience.

> " Rock of Ages, cleft for me,
> Let me hide myself in Thee! "

sang Nicky, while Nanny produced a sea-shell, whose concavity was coated with mother-o'-pearl, and extended it to Tryphena that she might subscribe.

" I haven't got any money," she said, " but perhaps this gentleman——? "

" No, no," declared the lawyer's clerk. " It does them no good and—— "

" Then why did you listen? Why did you listen, you long-legged young scamp? " cried Nanny to Tryphena, and Nicky abandoned his hymn and accordion.

" Get along with you! " he said. " You're the sort would steal the bread of the poor, and let the blind work for nothing! Damn you, if I had my claws on your face you'd soon want a piece of plaister! "

" Come away! " said Mr. Blatchford. " He's a dangerous character, and oughtn't to be allowed."

Then Nicky put down his accordion and got up.

" Lead me to him! Lead me to him, Nanny! " he shouted; and she, nothing loath, prepared to do so; but Mr. Blatchford made great haste, while husband and wife cried abuse after him. Then Nanny turned Nicky round again and brought him to his stool. They were breathless with their exertions. Gaffer Bell laughed aloud from the almshouse porch, and Nicky vented his anger upon him.

" All your fault, you living death! " he screamed out. " Who be you to dare to speak when I'm singing? I'll play at your funeral yet, you worm-eaten bag o' bones—yes, I will then—play at your burying and dance on your grave! "

Elsewhere T·yphena and her escort climbed the steep lane to Southcombe, and arrived at the farm. A black-and-white sheep-dog, with different coloured eyes, welcomed them, and such was his amiability that the girl loved him from the moment of meeting. At the porch of the little farm stood a man and woman, and they greeted the travellers with friendship. Mrs. Grace Coaker kissed Tryphena, and William Coaker, her husband, shook hands with Mr. Blatchford.

The woman spoke first.

" I'm your Aunt Grace, my dear," she said, " and this is Uncle William, and, my word! but you be terrible like your dear mother about the eyes! "

" She's like you, too," said Mr. Coaker, " and her mother was like you if I call her home."

" No, she weren't," answered his wife. " Tryphena's mother was a bowerly woman wi' grey eyes and a lot taller than me. And you'll be the same, and very near so pretty as her, I doubt not, when we've fatted you a bit. Come in. I'm sorry to say as your box haven't yet arrived, but your cousin, Elias, be going to drive into Bovey for it after he's took his tea."

This news inspired Mr. Blatchford.

" If anybody drives back to Bovey," he said, " I should think it a merciful thing to give me a lift."

" Of course—nothing simpler," answered William Coaker. " In a word, my son Elias shall drive you to Bovey and pick up Tryphena's box at the ' Dolphin.' "

The Coakers were a comfortable and happy couple, with one son. Their life prospered, and they were content. Then came a challenge to their days. Mrs. Coaker's only sister perished suddenly with her husband at sea, and their daughter, Tryphena, was left an orphan. The Harveys were returning from Australia with their children when death overtook them. A boy and a girl also perished, but their elder daughter had been saved.

Mr. Blatchford sat in Southcombe parlour presently, sipped a glass of sloe gin, and explained the position to Tryphena's uncle, while her aunt took the girl into the kitchen to see her cousin Elias, the son of the family.

From his bag Mr. Blatchford produced certain documents, and expounded the situation with respect to Tryphena.

" You must pardon me if my learning goes a little beyond you, farmer," he began. " We lawyers are so used to language that we forget that what seems simple to us may be difficult to the lay mind. Now when I speak of the Greek law of Charondas, that, of course, means nothing to you. You know less about it than I do about the way to treat new-born lambs. Yet what better plan has been devised for the guardianship of orphans? By this law their care is very wisely distributed between the relations on both sides, so that the father's people look after the fortune, if there is any, and the mother's people look after the body of the child. You see in a moment how just is this arrangement. The money is committed to the presumptive heirs, who have the greatest interest in increasing it and administering it to the best purpose; while the life and health and education of the orphaned little one is entrusted to those who would have no dark motive to injure it."

" Good powers ! " said Mr. Coaker, " 'tis a creepy thought ! "

" To an honest mind like yours, no doubt it is," answered the clerk. " But law is concerned with all sorts and conditions, and we know, only too well, that many an innocent child has paid a terrible penalty for the accident of being rich. In this case, however, the estate will probably prove of doubtful worth. The Harveys are a humble folk."

" Cordwainers to Exeter. Bachelors and very honest men, I believe."

" They are. We do their little business for the brothers. Tryphena's father had meant to return to Exeter and live near them. There will doubtless be a certain amount of cash; but he had directed them to find him a house at forty pounds a year for his wife, himself, and three children. This would argue modest means. You will hear as to that in due course. He owned land near Sydney, and grew oranges in the Paramatta district—a business which makes few fortunes, I understand."

" Us be very glad to have the maiden, money or not," said Mr. Coaker. " My wife always wanted a darter, and was terrible jealous when her sister got two. ' If the Lord had wanted for you to have had a darter, a darter you'd have had,' I said to Grace Coaker. But it took me ten years to drive home that simple fact, though you'd think a religious-minded woman like my wife would have been the first to see it. However, she'll take this fine young thing to her bosom and treat her just as if she was her very own."

In the kitchen Elias and his cousin regarded each other with interest. He was twenty-one—a mighty, raw-boned youth a foot taller than his father. His hair was red and curly, his face freckled. He felt a little nervous under the new-comer's steady grey eyes; but he liked her voice, with its sunny colonial accent. Then he used a folk-word, and she laughed as at a friend, because often she had heard her mother use it.

Tryphena spoke gently, and with sorrow of her parents. When Elias had driven Mr. Blatchford away, her aunt took her up to the little room that was to be her own, and left her there. Dusk had come down, and Tryphena saw from her chicket window a great sloping field with tall hedges round about. Smudges of dim, pearly light occurred against the gloom of the meadow, where mother ewes lay with their lambs snuggled beside them. The girl marked these, and some accidental synthesis awoke emotion in her mind. She wept for a while, and then dried her eyes and looked round the little chamber.

CHAPTER III

When sunshine passed from the eastern face of Widecombe church tower, labourers aloft on the eastern moors knew that it was time to stop work and eat their dinner. A dozen farms lay spread upon the hills round the village, and one might see Southcombe, Kingshead, Woodhayes, and Bag Park, dotted beneath the rolling heights of Hameldon, while in the valley stood Chittleford, Venton, and Lower Dunstone, and aloft, where now three men worked at the erection of a new gate, spread in an extended chain, Higher Dunstone, with Tunhill, Blackslade, Southway, Northway, and Bone Hill. All these homesteads were akin; they resembled each other in their general scheme of utility; they differed in their endowments of beauty, site, elevation and disposition.

The labourers aloft in a field of Tunhill Farm perceived that the time had come for food. They abandoned their work, therefore, found a flat granite boulder amid the fallen fern of last year, and reclined together with their eyes on the Vale. To them the scene, so strange to the lawyer's clerk and Tryphena, was the page of a familiar book, and they amused themselves now by enumerating each dwelling and the fellow-creatures who called it home.

The three men were known respectively as Young Harry Hawke, Birkett Johnson, and Pancras Widecombe. The first, a stout, muscular man of thirty, with brown hair and a very brown face, was called young to distinguish him from his father—a farmer of the same name, known always as ' old.' They dwelt at Woodhayes. Birkett Johnson was an elderly, serious soul, of a hatchet build with respect to his facial angle. He had grey hair, a wrinkled forehead, and a puzzled eye. He was headman at Tunhill Farm—a homestead that lay directly below the party on the hillside. The third labourer, named Pancras, after the boy saint of Widecombe church, and surnamed after the village itself, was a foundling. Pancras possessed a soaring and flamboyant soul, and it had served well to fortify him against the handicap of life. This man was fair and florid, with sandy hair and bright, pale, grey eyes. He lodged at a room in a little inn. His unconquerable hope and power of exaggeration made all men laugh, but it was his natural bent of mind.

Now, in the examination of their environment each of the assembled three displayed his character and mental outlook.

Young Harry Hawke's mind was commonplace and concerned only with things; Johnson, from his experience of five-and-fifty years therein, looked at the world with a spark of imagination; while Widecombe saw it illuminated by the light of his own sanguine spirit.

" You can see the place throwed out like a school-map from up here," said Pancras. " I reckon I shall be shamed to bide in such a little hole much longer."

But his contemplative elder challenged him.

" Size be nought," declared Birkett Johnson regarding the Vale. " 'Tis a busy, bustling place, and, for my part, I always feel glad that my lot fell in a church town, where there is such a deal doing."

But Pancras laughed aloud and denied it.

" That depends on the size of your head, Birkett. 'Tis stuff you tell! I've sucked Widecombe so dry as an empty egg-shell. I know all about it, and all that be going on, and what the people hope and fear. I sum 'em all up."

" You silly man! There's things happening under every roof within sight as you don't know and never will—good things and bad. And as to summing up—who be the folks to tell a rattle-pate like you their secrets, or what they hope or fear, and what they want and what they don't want? "

But Pancras was not discouraged.

" They tell me more'n they'd tell you, Birkett; because I've got a lot of understanding. You'm dumb as a newt, and 'tis uncomfortable work talking to you. Look around—where be the place I ban't welcome in? "

" I was just telling over the people," said young Harry Hawke. " And I was surprising myself a good bit to find what a lot of 'em be known to me."

" I'll run 'em over," said Pancras Widecombe, " and you'll see I shan't leave out one among 'em. First there's Southcombe yonder from t'other side. Bill Coaker, his wife, Grace Coaker; his son, my friend, Elias; and the two men—they brothers Webber. So much for that."

" Wrong," said Johnson quietly, " you come a cropper at the very first farm."

" Never, Birkett! "

" Wrong, I say."

" There's the kitchen girl, Susy Tope—I didn't count her."

" Wrong still."

" You don't mean as the new-comer, Mrs. Coaker's niece, have arrived? "

" Arrived a week ago."

" And I didn't know it—fancy that! "

" Fancy that! " echoed young Harry Hawke.

Unabashed, the mason proceeded.

" Then there's Kingshead, where Widow Windeatt bides to, with her three men; and Woodhayes, where you and your father live, Harry, and his wife and your wife."

" And my wife's going to have a babby in June," declared young Harry Hawke.

" Us'll drink good health to mother and child to-night," said Pancras Widecombe; then he enumerated other farms and the folk of them.

" There's Bone Hill with Peter Smerdon, your father-in-law, Harry, and his wife, and their long family; and Bone Hill Cottages, with that bad old rip, Reep and his wife and darter in one—and him dying—and they Mogridges, father and son, in t'other. Then there's Tunhill down there, where you be to, Birkett. And there'll soon be one less there also, I suppose."

" Yes," said the head man of Tunhill. " Mrs. Sweetland's at death's door. And master wishes she'd go. He's got to that high pitch now, along of her sufferings, that he wishes she'd go. I met Miss Sweetland, master's sister, this morning. 'Tis even a matter of hours, she reckons."

" They come and they go," commented young Harry Hawke.

" Then there's Blackslade," continued Pancras, pursuing his perambulation. " That strange widow-man, Gabriel Shillingford, and his two queer-named darters—Petronell and

Sibley. He's of great havage, and be always dreaming of his forebears."

" And in sight of the workhouse, if they tell truth," added Hawke.

" You mustn't say that, Young Harry. 'Tisn't true. He pays everybody, and is a high character."

It was Johnson who spoke; but Pancras had proceeded.

" Then Venton, with Uncle Tom Cobleigh and Christian, his son, and Mary Gay, his widowed darter; and then Chittleford, with Mr. Valiant Dunnybrig, and Jane, his wife, and Araminta Dench and four men; and then there's the Gurneys of Dunstone, and the Hearns at the post-office, and Tom Gurney at the smithy, and Parson Brown at the Vicarage, and the ' Old ' Inn, with Mrs. Pierce and that poor reed, her husband—a reed shaken with the wind, I call him, for he says that all his food turns to air in his stomach ! "

They continued the survey, and were presently interrupted by the arrival of two among those they had named. Gabriel Shillingford, the master of Blackslade in the valley beneath, came climbing up by a hill-path, and beside him walked his daughter Sibley. The farmer was broad and solidly built. His hair was black, and his eyes were dark brown. His eyes declared a dreamer, rather than a man of action, and, indeed, his life was largely a dream, and his ambition a futility. His daughter much resembled him, but did not share in his ruminant nature.

Of Shillingford it might be said that he was that uncommon thing, a reflecting man—a sort rare on every plane of human life, but as frequent among the uneducated as any other class.

Mr. Shillingford knew that Johnson was of kindred pattern, and now he stopped a moment and addressed him, while Sibley spoke to Young Harry Hawke.

" Changes everywhere, neighbour," said Gabriel.

" Sure enough, farmer. Here's my mistress, Mrs. Sweetland, dying, and that old poacher to Bone Hill—Dan Reep, I mean—he's going, too. And against them you can set the little maiden that have arrived at Southcombe, Mrs. Coaker's niece, and a child that be going to be born in June to Young Harry Hawke here."

" A child coming to Woodhayes, eh? " asked Shillingford. " Well, Young Harry, Woodhayes dates from ancient times, you know. 'Tis in the manor of Widecombe proper, and belonged to my ancestors, the knightly family of Fitz-Ralph. They took the surname of Shillingford afterwards, and my race has sprung from 'em. I'll grant you leave to call your

son ' Fitz-Ralph,' Young Harry Hawke, and 'twould be a good
thing to revive the name there, in my opinion."

Sibley laughed at her father, but he had no sense of humour,
and seldom even smiled.

" Suppose it should happen to be a cheel, your honour? "
asked Young Harry.

" A girl? Of course that might be."

Then he recollected himself, and addressed Birkett Johnson.

" For a moment it had escaped me, but your mistress is
dead."

" Dead, father! " cried Sibley. " You never told me that,
and yet you must have known it an hour ago! "

" True; but the actual event loosed a train of thought, and
I forgot the starting-place.   Mrs. Sweetland was a good
woman, and a Cornford of sound stock . . . the Cornfords—
yes."

" I must be gone," said Johnson. " Master will be wanting
me."

He picked up a frail and strode off to the valley, while
Gabriel Shillingford and his daughter also went their way
where Blackslade Farm nestled half a mile beneath.   Then
Pancras Widecombe and the other labourer were left together.

CHAPTER IV

MR. DANIEL REEP lay dying, but there was life in the tough
body yet; his mind continued clear, and his physical discomfort
did not prevent him from thought and speech. His daughter
Margery sat beside him; his wife, Joyce, had gone into Widecombe. Daniel was a bearded veteran of sixty-eight, and now
he reviewed his wasted life with complete satisfaction.

" 'Twas just the accident of being poor as made me a
poacher. 'Twas in my blood to shed blood, you might say,
Margery."

" Ess, faither."

" I held a day ill spent when I hadn't put an end to bird,
beast, or fish; and if I'd been rich, no doubt I'd have been a
very famous sportsman, and a fine old English gentleman, and
all that."

" Ess, faither."

Margery was a thin, flat maiden, poorly clad. Her hair was untidy and harsh; her colourless eyes were dim with long night watches.

"But," continued the reprobate, "being so poor as a coot, I was counted just a baggering, old, worthless poacher, a disgrace to Widecombe. Yet I was a very clever chap, Margery, and I shan't be forgot."

He spoke of himself in the past tense.

"Never, faither. Scores o' dozens of kind things you've done."

"I wasn't much of a father and husband, along of my great passion for letting blood. And I can't say as I was a one woman man ezacally. To be honest, I was a bit of a love-hunter, Margery."

His daughter didn't answer.

"But a steady man," continued Daniel. "Steady as time where drink was concerned—a self-denying sort of man in that matter. None ever saw me bosky-eyed or even market merry."

"No, faither."

"Mend the fire. I can't catch heat. When I be gone, you might see Pancras Widecombe, Margery. He's a stonemason, not a stonecutter; but such is the cleverness of the man that there's little he can't do if he tries. You see him and ax him to make a stone for friendship's sake. He'll do it cheap."

"I will, faither."

He turned and sighed.

"And spring coming and all. How cruel well I know how 'tis all happening! The plovers be running about so saucy, down among the rushes in the water meadows; and the trout be moving and the frogs hollering. And the tassels are twinkling, like the lambs' tails, on hazel and aller, and Farmer Coaker be breaking into his great store of roots—the mound he buildeth under the lew hedge. I know it all; but I shan't see, nor hear, nor smell none of it no more—damn it!"

"Don't talk; it makes you weak."

"Give me them primroses," he said, and Margery brought a jam-jar with primroses in it. He shut his eyes and smelt to them. Then he spoke.

"There's one thing: if they can't put me where I will to go, Margery, you take care as I don't lie on the north side of the tower. I'd like to think the greybirds was hopping above me; but on the sunless side they wants* have got in the ground something shocking, and I wouldn't have 'em burrowing round about me, and me at their mercy down there!"

* *Wants*—moles.

" You shan't go there, faither, if me and mother can help it."

" There's strange powers in Nature, and much hid from man's knowledge," said Mr. Reep; " and they might know about the scores o' dozens of their kind I'd catched to make moleskin waistcoats and suchlike."

She took the flowers from him, fed him, and gave him some drink. For awhile he relapsed into silence; then the stimulant affected him. He moved restlessly, and spoke again.

" Oh, Lord, Margery, how terribly much I should like to kill something afore I die! " he exclaimed suddenly.

The proposition startled Margery.

" Don't you worry about things like that no more, my old dear."

" Get my gun," he said, " and mind, for 'tis loaded. I must just touch the old devil again."

" Faither! "

" Get it, and be slippy! "

Two minutes later the gun was beside its owner.

" Lift me a bit," he said.

" The poultice will slip, faither."

" Let it slip to hell. Prop me up, I say."

" 'Tis death, faither! "

" So I want it to be—for ummat. The elm be right afore the winder in a straight line. With a bit of luck a starling or something will pitch there."

He was alive and alert. His weakness made him shake; but he had strength to lift the gun and fire, and he knew it. Margery, in tears, opened the little leaded window as far as it would go, and exposed a square space into the air. The chamber was small, and the foot of Mr. Reep's bed was but three feet from the aperture; the muzzle of his gun, but five feet. In the line of fire rose an elm, its branches glimmering carmine with inflorescence. Sunshine lit them.

" If by good hap something do light in the elm—prop me a thought higher and keep clear."

He lay gasping with his gun at full cock, and his daughter cried :

" 'Twill kill you, faither—'twill kill you to fire it."

" No matter if it do," he said. " A very brave death for the likes of me."

But further grief lay in store for Margery. There came a hurtle of wings, a flash of bright feathers, and a great pigeon with slate-grey plumage and a neck, bright as an opal, lit on a swaying finial of the elm. It shone there like a jewel, and Reep instantly raised his gun.

" For God's sake, faither! 'Tis Mr. Mogridge's famous carrier——"

But Margery was too late. The dying man fired; the pigeon at such close range was simply huddled into a heap of feathers, and the shock flung it a yard into the air before it fell. The crash and bellow of the gun shook the chamber and filled it with smoke; while Mr. Reep fell back and nearly perished.

" Carrier or no carrier," he gurgled, " it didn't carry so fast as my gun. I've shot un! You run down and fetch un up for me to handle. And throw ope the door, else the smoke will finish me off."

He groaned, and she obeyed.

" Now I can die in peace," he said, when she returned with the mangled bird. " 'Twas a Providence—for I be level with that Alfred Mogridge now. Two birds wi' one stone—and them laugh best that laugh last."

But Margery did not laugh. She cried noisily while her father stroked the pigeon.

" 'Tis all up with me now—all up with me and Jack," she said. " You've done for us. Mr. Mogridge won't never let Jack marry me now, faither."

" Mogridge needn't never hear tell about this."

" He has heard tell," answered Margery. " Little Walter Smerdon was passing under the tree when you fired, and thicky pigeon very near fell on top of his head. And he knew the famous creature, and ran straight off into the Bone Hill garden where Mr. Mogridge be to work."

Daniel Reep was about to speak when there came a loud shout from below, and his blood tingled with satisfaction to hear the wrath of his neighbour. Margery hastened downstairs just in time to prevent Mr. Mogridge from coming up. Alfred Mogridge bawled up the staircase behind her :

" You've killed my prize bird, you anointed rascal—my prize bird you've killed, and 'twas worth five pounds, and I'll have it out of your widow, if I have to wait till Judgment for it. She shall pay after you be dead and rotten, and I'm right glad you be going to die—thankful to God, same as every other respectable person be! "

Mr. Reep heard and grinned with joy. He longed to retort, but was unable. When the furious gardener stormed himself away, and Margery returned to her father, he appeared to be better, and was obviously happy.

" Don't you pay the man a penny for it, when I be gone. You ban't responsible for my doings. Oh, Lord, lift me up— I'm choking for air! "

His daughter tended him, and grumbled bitterly while she did so.

" 'Tis all very well for you, faither; you'm going out of it; but mother and me be left to face him. And the man was never known to forgive; and so sure as death he won't let Jack marry me now—he never will."

" No loss neither," he answered. " Jack Mogridge ban't good enough for you, and never was. He's under his father's heel, and Alfred don't think no more of him than the worm he cuts in half with his spade."

A noise came to their ears, and the harsh voice of their neighbour rose again from the door below.

" There's mother, and Mr. Mogridge be on to her ! " said Margery.

She descended to support a little, worn, grey-headed woman who had just returned from Widecombe with a few parcels. Mr. Mogridge was raving, and Mrs. Reep, who as yet knew nothing of her husband's achievement, stared helplessly at him.

" Don't you let him think he's going to escape, because he ban't. I've got witnesses—'tis clear as daylight—a felony and a slaughter; and if he lives he'll go to gaol for it, where he'd have been many a long year ago but for the Dowl, his master."

Margery explained, and drew her mother into the cottage.

" 'Tis no good answering the man," she said. " He's got right on his side, and we shall have to pay for faither's cruel fun, as we've had to afore, times without count. He's shot Mr. Mogridge's far-famed carrier—blowed un to ribbons, you might say—would do it out o' the winder."

Joyce Reep hastened to her husband. He was weak, but triumphant.

" With my dying breath I bid you not to pay the toad a penny," he said.

Mrs. Reep brought bad news from Widecombe.

" Mrs. Sweetland have gone—went two days ago, I hear. I met Mr. Birkett Johnson to the post-office."

Mr. Reep was much vexed at this information.

" Cuss the woman ! Cuss all women ! They never do the sporting thing. They all die when you want 'em to live, and live when you want 'em to die. Now she'll go in under the sycamore—just where I'd set my heart."

" Don't you take on, Daniel; I'll speak to the Reverend Brown, my dear. He's a very kind and reasonable man."

" No, he ban't—not with me. He've always had his knife into me. He'll put me down along with the moles—just for spite he'll do it—'cause I never went to church. Be damned if I'll die at all now! I'll live, so you'd better hot up some poultices and get to work at me."

CHAPTER V

A FORTNIGHT after his bereavement the widowed master of Tunhill Farm sat with his sister and debated a delicate subject, destined to occupy his highest energies in the time to come.

Mr. Samuel Sweetland was a full-bodied, sheep-faced man of fifty-one. He had lofty eyebrows, a bald head, a long upper lip, a fat rosy mouth, and a very receding chin. His eyes were large and lustrous and short-sighted; their colour was uncertain. He was a man of religious principles and generous heart; but life had plotted to hide from him much of the truth concerning himself. His lines had fallen easily; his plans had prospered; and two adoring women had for five-and-twenty years concealed from Samuel the peculiarities and defects of his character.

They sat in the kitchen of Tunhill, and Miss Sweetland altered a dress of her dead sister-in-law's to suit her own more generous frame.

" Little she thought, poor darling, when she bought black for her Uncle Tozer, that another would wear it for her. And yet such was her sense, she'd have been the first to say 'twas right and proper."

Samuel nodded.

" So she would, then. And when I lie awake with the intellects working, I feel that a man of my loving and fiery nature ban't built to live on memory, Harriet. I shan't shock you I know if I speak of such things, for you understand me too well for that."

" You'll never shock me, Samuel. And 'tis only right and proper to look ahead. I can face any choice you are likely to make, with a trusting spirit."

" Marriage be a holy ordinance, ordained for such men as me, and to wed again, in my opinion, be a compliment to a good wife, and not the contrary, as some maintain."

" Of course you're right, Samuel. Would our darling have come between you and happiness? Wasn't it very near her last word? "

" It was," answered Mr. Sweetland. " She didn't name no

names—too wise for that, because you can't dictate even to your own husband in such a delicate matter, but 'twas her expressed wish—and Nurse Maine will bear me out—that I should take another when I found myself equal to doing it."

" You'll be the prey of every free woman in Widecombe, Samuel; but I needn't tell you that."

He smiled and looked at a photograph of his wife which stood on the mantelshelf.

" She knew women and read their hearts."

" And so can I. They hide little from me, for where you are concerned I can do most anything. Don't think I haven't run 'em over, though I dare say in your tender, bruised mind you couldn't bear to think of any other—save just in a vague and general way. But the thing have got to be faced."

" They can't propose to me, however," said Mr. Sweetland. " But to be frank, I have thought in the long night watches about who have got to be the second. 'Twas no disrespect to my darling Tibby, Harriet."

" On the contrary, Samuel, 'twas her own dying gasp that you should do so."

" She knew me. Yes, it must be done. Nature calls for it —and a torn and suffering heart. Not that you ban't my guardian angel and my salvation and the noblest woman that ever chose to bide single out of sacred love for a brother— not that you ban't all that and more, Harriet; but marriage is marriage, and—well, I've run over the possibles more than once. Fetch a piece of paper and set down a name or two that be floating round my mind. You know my great modesty of nature. I can't suppose that the first I may seek out will take me—nor yet, perhaps, even the second."

Then Samuel blew his nose, and she wiped her spectacles.

" Mrs. John Windeatt, of Kingshead, be in your mind, Samuel."

" You've guessed her! Louisa Windeatt first. A proper woman—strong—sensible, and childless, like me."

" Yes—perhaps a little too sporting and self-opinionated—if if I may say so."

" Not a bit—and that well preserved. She must be forty-five if a day."

" Nearer fifty."

" Yet, who'd think it? Her back view's not a day more than twenty-five."

" You'll live with her front view, however."

" I hope so—I'm such a humble sort of man where the women are concerned."

" Of course, she'll take you gladly enough. And she'll be a lucky woman. She'll know real happiness at last."

" She was happy enough with Windeatt for that matter. Then for the second string, I'm a good bit inclined towards Nelly Gurney. She's a maid, 'tis true; but she's forty-three, if a day, and got a large experience, owing to the youth and silliness of her stepmother."

" The Gurneys of Dunstone be a feeble folk," declared Miss Sweetland. " For Abel Gurney to marry again was a very foolish thing. I'm not saying that Nelly is not a good, sensible, hard-working, and God-fearing creature, and keeps Dunstone together for that matter. Her stepmother's a feather-headed fool, and so's her father, Abel. She's a great friend of Araminta Dench—Nelly is, I mean—and, in my opinion, Araminta be the likelier one."

" No," declared Mr. Sweetland. " Araminta's too young for me. She might have children, and that's not to be thought upon. Valiant Dunnybrig's niece is a fine girl—I grant that; but she's too young, and she's too sly. I shouldn't feel happy with her out of my sight. Put down Nelly Gurney. There's two more—both spinsters—but I don't know which to put third and which to put fourth. My mind lies open between 'em."

" No need to set down more, Samuel. If Mrs. Windeatt, by any queer chance, didn't take you, of course Nelly will jump at you."

" Two more I have in sight, however," returned her brother, " and I leave the order to you. There's Mary Hearn, at the post-office, and your own friend, ' T. T.' Ah! I thought you'd jump. But I mean it. Between them two, though their gifts are different, I can't make up my mind for third place. Mary's a fine woman, with ladylike ways, though a thought excitable, yet she might be a comfort, and good at figures, though poor herself; while Thirza Tapper, though a regular, right down old maid, to the casual eye, and very near so old as I am, have got a mind and a lot of saved money. She's a dignified piece, and, of course, a lady born—far ahead of all the others in that respect."

" You'll never come to her. 'Tis merely a question when you'll begin courting Mrs. Windeatt."

" I'll do it so gradual as the falling dew upon the neece," he said. " I shall go up over and call in, and ax for a glass of milk or cider. Then she'll express sorrow for my loss, and I shall thank her, and just drop a witty word or two. I shall talk about me and her both knowing what 'tis to be happily married, and losing a blessed partner, and so forth."

" I shouldn't do that, if I may advise you."

" But she cared a great deal for him, I tell you. 'Tis safe to praise him to her. Her memory has dropped the little details, and just kept the main idea of him, as a bright, laughing, sporting sort of man."

" You know best, Samuel. Of course no spinster can pretend to read the mind of a married woman. But she had dreadful times, by all accounts."

" So do all we married people," confessed Mr. Sweetland. " There are concerns happen in every home, where there's a husband and wife, that seem, while they be going on, so terrible tragic you'd think neither the man nor the woman could ever be the same after. They say things, and do things, and even think things, that you'd fear must throw the house out of windows, and wreck the home for evermore. Yet the human character in marriage be such an elastic contrivance and bends such a lot afore it will break, that you'll find after the storm goes down and you be looking about for the wrecks, that married pair bob up again all trim and taut, and no sign of the fearful tempest. 'Tis a daily miracle all the world over."

Mr. Sweetland, whose voice had failed him, took another jujube.

" There's no eye, after God's own, will be more anxious to see how I get on than my dead Tibby's," he declared.

CHAPTER VI

Six different manors comprise the parish of Widecombe, and of these Dunstone is the smallest in area save one. Besides the name hamlet, where dwelt the race of the Gurneys, this manor included certain important homesteads. At Venton dwelt Uncle Tom Cobleigh and his son and daughter; Mr. Valiant Dunnybrig, his wife, and his niece inhabited Chittleford; at Tunhill reigned the widowed Samuel Sweetland; and Blackslade was the abode of Gabriel Shillingford and his daughters.

Blackslade stood near a mile from the church in a sheltered and woody nook, flanked by good tilth and crowned with granite, where Whittaburrow clustered against the east. The dwelling was highly distinguished in its austere reserve and severity. The master, a yeoman of long descent, occupied much leisure with efforts to link his family into one of noble blood; he was sensitive to its present humble state, and felt himself to be made of different stuff from the folk; but he allowed his knowledge to take no positive form of aggression or patronage. Instead, he regarded himself as under obligations. Life proved difficult, for the man was poor, and made himself poorer by struggling to maintain a dignity and preserve a state in keeping with his pride rather than his pocket. Gabriel was kind-hearted and generous. None came to him in vain, but his own servants, of whom he kept more than the farm demanded, often grumbled at the delay in paying their wages. Some people laughed at him, and the rising generation refused him homage. The farmers themselves were friendly, and, if they laughed a little behind Gabriel Shillingford's back, treated him with courtesy and deference to his face. He had quarrelled with but one man in Widecombe— the clergyman. When a new vicar arrived—the son of a tailor —the young man had patronised Mr. Shillingford. Whereupon Gabriel resigned his appointment of vicar's churchwarden, turned his back upon St. Pancras, and henceforth drove his daughters to Buckland weekly that they might worship there. This caused them acute inconvenience, and Sibley resented it; but Petronell thought and felt as her father thought and felt.

Sibley was practical, and controlled the home. She laboured under no delusions, and while aware of a certain shadowy distinction belonging to her race, also perceived that money in the pocket is more useful than ancestors in the grave. Moreover, even the ancestors were doubtful. There existed certain parentheses in the family archives, and as yet, despite much patient examination and research, the master of Blackslade had failed to establish beyond possibility of doubt his right of connection with the noble Shillingfords of the past. His search had extended over many years, and Sibley secretly hoped that the hiatus would not be bridged or the remaining links forged, for did that happen her father's occupation would be gone. She had, indeed, other ideas for him. He was still a man in his prime, and she hoped that he might marry again when she and her sister were disposed in matrimony.

To a husband Sibley looked forward with certainty. It only remained to assist Petronell, because she herself might marry when she chose, and had a devoted lover. In her busy, bustling way she planned everything—even to the widow who waited for Mr. Shillingford. And meantime the more romantic

Petronell was also arranging for her own life's future and keeping her own secrets Both girls resembled their father, and both enjoyed a measure of beauty; but while Sibley's good looks were obvious, and her black, flashing eyes, high colour, and fine bosom challenged the spectator, Petronell was cast in a lighter mould; her figure was tall and delicately modelled; her face was of an olive tone, inclined towards sallowness; her eyes dreamed rather than sparkled. She talked little and reflected much.

As his house, Gabriel was distinguished, reserved, and modest. While Blackslade concealed its pride behind an ivy cloak, and allowed the dark green leaves to hide the date of 1652 graven on the lintel, so did he dwell within himself, make no open claim, and utter no despondent protest.

There came a Sunday when certain guests arrived at Blackslade to drink tea with the Shillingfords. Of his few personal friends, Gabriel counted the master of Southcombe as the closest, and now arrived William Coaker with Grace, his wife, Elias, his son, and Tryphena Harvey—the new-comer. Another also called—expected by one alone. There existed a secret friendship between Sibley and Whitelock Smerdon. They were, indeed, betrothed, but none knew it, and to their young spirits half the joy of the situation lay in its secrecy. Now came Whitelock Smerdon, ostensibly from his father on an errand to Mr. Shillingford; but Sibley knew very well that he was there as a guest privately invited to the unusual entertainment.

There was not much soul in Whitelock Smerdon, but his good-looking face, his vitality, his masculine love-making appealed to Mr. Shillingford's elder daughter.

The company sat about a 'high' tea, with Sibley at the teapot and her father and William Coaker on each side of her. Whitelock—a tall man with broad, high shoulders, shrewd eyes, and a heavy black moustache—chattered to Mrs. Coaker.

" And how do your young lady like Widecombe? " he asked, gazing with frank admiration into Tryphena's face.

" She's took to the country something wonderful, the dear, and be ever so useful, ban't you, Tryphena? " asked her aunt.

The girl, however, doubted. She smiled and shook her head.

" 'Tis kind of Aunt Grace to say I'm useful, but I'm not much good, not yet—except with the chickens. I'm getting handy with them."

" And the cleverness! " declared Elias Coaker. " For book-reading she'll be a second Miss Petronell, I do believe. Try have read every page of print us have got to Southcombe, and be crying out for more books, like a lamb for its mother."

They regarded the prodigy with interest, and Mr. Shilling-ford spoke :

" We want more scholars in Widecombe, and, so far as I can see, school don't make 'em."

" 'Tis a very true word," said William Coaker. " ' School don't make scholars ' is a very true word—look at Elias."

His son admitted the reflection with laughter.

" I be clever enough to see cleverness in other people," he said, looking at Petronell. " Not but what I've got a few fine things from somebody here and there, and shall get many more. And a bit of book-larning for all father says, haven't I, Try?"

" Yes, you have," said Tryphena. " You know a lot of very fine old fairy stories, Cousin Elias."

Gabriel Shillingford spoke to Tryphena.

" You must come and see me and my daughter," he said. " Petronell is a very clever girl, and full of stories; and I have more books than any man in Widecombe—haven't I, William? "

" Certainly you have, Gabriel. 'Tis well known that your collection beats Parson Brown's hollow."

" Touching him, least said soonest mended. The learned clerks were of small account when my ancestors reigned in these parts. Now 'tis a password to good company to be a parson, and so the common, rich men put their rich sons in. I say nothing against that. A man is just as good as himself, and no better and no worse. It doesn't lift him to be a clergy-man if he's low-minded, and it doesn't lower him to be a stone-breaker if he's high-minded."

" True, Gabriel. But these be too deep subjects for a meal. Is anybody going to ax me to eat another sausage? I see there's four going begging yet."

The party sorted itself out anon, and, when tea was done, William Coaker went into the yard to see some calves, while his friend took Tryphena to a room he delighted to call his library. The grey eyes of Tryphena glittered, for she had never seen so many books. The farmer watched her, and she reminded him of Petronell in the past. But Petronell read less than of yore.

" Now, I'll tell you what I'll do, Tryphena," said Mr. Shillingford. " I see by your hands and eyes that you under-stand the greatness of books, and so I'll make you free of my library! You shall come and go, when your aunt can spare you, and you shall borrow one book at a time."

She was greatly obliged to him; her face grew hot with pleasure, and she thanked him sincerely.

" 'Twill be a fine thing for me, Mr. Shillingford, sir," she said.

" So it will, then, and you must tell me about Australia, and all that. 'Tis the curious way of things that to prove kinship with the great is often difficult, while kinship with rascals be the surest and easiest thing in the world. For why? Because the great are rare, but rascals are common as blackberries. I say this because I found, six months ago, that a Shillingford was sent to Botany Bay for sheep-stealing in the year of the Lord, eighteen hundred and thirty. Did you ever hear the name there? "

Tryphena never had.

" As to the name of Harvey," he continued, " 'tis a good old English name, and it has been borne by some very famous men indeed. However, if you would like for me to inquire into your family tree, and have any data, I will do so."

Tryphena was much impressed. None had ever treated her in this grown-up fashion before.

" 'Tis truly kind," she said, " but all my folk be dead, save my two uncles in Exeter. I don't think we was of great account."

She selected a book presently, and went into the little garden, where some " Darwin " tulips and polyanthus primroses made a bright light in the evening sunshine.   Mr. Shillingford left her presently, and joined William Coaker—to find him with another man.

" Where has everybody got to? " asked Gabriel. " Where are my girls? "

" Where they should be—with the boys," answered William. " They've gone a-walking to take the air. 'Tis springtime. And here's Birkett Johnson from Tunhill—well met, as I tell him—for a cleverer chap don't breathe in this parish—after yourself."

Mr. Johnson wore Sunday black, and was on his way home. He touched his hat to Shillingford, according to his custom, and Gabriel returned the salute.

" A strange world," he said. " I've just been up in Bagworthy, and I fell in with a man or two, and they say that Alfred Mogridge, of Bone Hill Cottages, have refused his son to wed the late Daniel Reep's darter, because Daniel shot his carrier-pigeon in a last flash of sport just afore he died! "

" Mogridge would sink to that," declared Mr. Coaker. " A terrible narrow-minded varmint he is."

" A strange world, as you say," commented Shillingford. " Miss Thirza Tapper it was who told me that Reep took on terribly before his death, because Mrs. Sweetland died first, and so had the grave-plot he wanted. Now, that's a curious side of the human mind."

" As to that," answered William Coaker, " they put Daniel between young Mrs. Caunter, who died three years ago of pewmonia, and that doubtful widow, Jane Page—pretty women and fine women both; and if poor Reep could have known, I'm sure he'd have been very well content to bide the Trump in such company."

Elsewhere, Sibley and Whitelock Smerdon sat aloft at Moor edge in the stone crater of an old beacon on Whittaburrow.

Now, it appeared that their relations were very much more intimate than others guessed. Indeed, the plump Sibley was invited to sit upon Whitelock's knee, and she crowned that perch without any hesitation. The high-shouldered man closed his eyes, put his arms round his burden, and rubbed his cheek gently against his sweetheart's. But she was a little uneasy.

" Which way did Elias and my sister go? " she asked. " We should look a pair of zanies if they was to pop their heads over the stones."

" No, we shouldn't," declared young Smerdon. " A woman never looks better than she do on her lover's knee, in my opinion."

" 'Tisn't that. But we don't want 'em to know yet. Only your mother knows. I'm waiting for just the right moment, and then I'm going to tell father."

" Rub my mother into him. She once had a doctor in her family. 'Tis true he's been dead about a hundred years, and he was only a horse-doctor; but you needn't explain."

Sibley laughed.

" You simple thing! You little know father. If 'tis told that we are going to wed, he'll turn up his books and ferret out everything about the Smerdons, and trace 'em back to Adam, if he can."

" Does he know about your sister and Elias Coaker? "

" Not he, and Petronell thinks I don't know neither."

" How d'you like Elias? " he asked, and Sibley shrugged her shoulders.

" I know he's a friend of yours; but he's not my sort—too masterful. There must be give and take—as you and I know. But Master Elias wants all his own way, and be like to trample rough-shod on a gentle dreamer such as my sister."

" I wish we could put our hands on a Smerdon or two back along as had done something," said Whitelock; " but, to tell truth, we cannot. I was coaxing father to speak about his father and grandfather afore him; but he only knew they was very respectable men and had no luck with their wives. In fact, so far as he can tell, father's the fust that ever did have."

" He won't be the last, however."

" No. By Gor, he won't ! "

Sibley was squeezed and cuddled, and they began personalities. She accused him of putting too much pomatum on his hair, and he retorted by declaring that she was getting heavier very quickly.

" My mother says that your mother was a mountain of flesh before she went," said Whitelock, with genial pleasantry; " and if you be going to grow the same, just you say so, and we'll break it off while there's yet time."

They wandered homeward presently as the shadows began to fall, and met Elias and Petronell returning from Blackslade Wood.

They went back together and found another visitor.

Mrs. Louisa Windeatt, of Kingshead, had called to see the sisters, and was waiting for their return.

CHAPTER VII

Mrs. Louisa Windeatt stood high in the esteem of Gabriel Shillingford. To begin with, her husband's pedigree was adequate, and her own even superior to his. Her ancestors had been broken in the wars of the Commonwealth, and not only did the lustre of this circumstance surround her like an aura, but Mrs. Windeatt herself was blessed with personal charms of mind and body. She was handsome, and she was humorous, and sensible, as humorous people often are. Aged forty-five—yet many years younger than her age, even in the eyes of the least gallant—Louisa Windeatt was a childless widow, who inherited her husband's freehold farm of Kingshead on Hameldon side. She loved work, and understood cattle, and was prosperous. She rode to hounds, and mixed with her fellow-creatures cheerfully. Mrs. Windeatt enjoyed freedom, yet would have ceded it in one quarter; she was fond of masculine society, but quarrelled not with the women. She had called at Blackslade about a servant, and greeted the

Coakers, who were just taking their leave. Tryphena already knew her, and secretly liked the slight-built, wiry widow better than anybody in Widecombe.

Now it was Tryphena who won Mrs. Windeatt's caress and got a kiss from her.

" She's a dear," declared Louisa, when the party from Southcombe had set out. " I wish she was mine—a dinky girl, and her eyes go through one."

" They be very like your own, Mrs. Windeatt," said Whitelock Smerdon, but she would not allow this.

" Nonsense! Mine are small to hers, and screwed up through riding in the open air, with the wind always blowing in my face."

" Your heart looks out of your eyes, and that's all anybody wants to see," said Mr. Shillingford.

" You dear man," she said impulsively, putting her brown hard hand on his arm. " How terrible nice of you! That's the way to say pretty things, Whitelock Smerdon."

Young Smerdon's eyes sought Sibley's.

" I must larn from Mr. Shillingford," he said, while Gabriel, somewhat astonished at Mrs. Windeatt's praise, laughed nervously.

" 'Twas only a figure of speech," he declared, and his daughter reproved him, while Louisa made a face.

" There now, you've spoilt it, father," said Petronell.

She went to get Mrs. Windeatt a cup of tea and a slice of cake. Sibley saw Whitelock Smerdon as far as the gate.

" Was thinking of your late husband yesterday," declared Gabriel, when they were alone. " They called him haughty, but I liked him for that. He was much above the herd in mind—same as you are, and same as I am."

" Yet never stuck up. Just a working farmer. And I'm a working farmer, and you ought to be."

" You know very well I am, Mrs. Windeatt."

Cupid dwelt in the widow's eyes, but he did not go there to sleep. He peeped for ever, wide awake, from the brightness of them.

" Not you," she answered. " You play at it. You *think* you work and keep up with the day, but you find the old times much too interesting to bother about the new."

He stared, but the force of the criticism was much lessened by her voice and her expression, and the look of frank regard she cast upon him.

" I understand you, Gabriel Shillingford, better than you understand yourself, belike. 'Twasn't for nothing that you used to come up over to Kingshead, and sit there with poor

John, maundering away about dead bones, and setting the world right. I'll tell your daughters all about you some day."

" You're that quick-witted that the male mind toils after you in vain," he answered. " And as for my girls, Sibley's full of common sense; while as for Petronell, she's like me, a bit of a dreamer. We understand each other very well."

" She understands you; you don't understand her. You never understood a woman in your life, and never will. Your bent of mind throws you back so far that only the dead are alive to you. Now, if you had a ghost at Blackslade, I doubt not you'd get as thick as thieves."

He laughed.

" We have," declared he, " and in my opinion 'tis a sign of age and worth for a rumour like that to hang over a place."

" Even a bad ghost—eh? Some rascal who murdered his grandmother for her diamond ring. You'd make a fine fuss over him, I'll warrant! "

" My great-great-uncle is the man," explained Mr. Shillingford. " He owned this place, and was a famous miser in his day. 'Tis rumoured that he buried his treasure here, and still walks to show where 'tis."

" And well we could do with it," said Sibley, who had returned from the outer gate.

Then Petronell brought in a little meal upon a tray.

They sat round Mrs. Windeatt while she ate and drank, and remembered her errand.

" Didn't you have a girl called Sally Turtle here once? She's the daughter of old Turtle of Rugglestone Inn."

" Yes," said Sibley, " we did. And she left us to go to Miss Tapper. A good enough girl."

" Some mistresses always think their places are the best in the kingdom," answered Louisa Windeatt, " and Miss Tapper is one of them. She is doubtful what is going to happen to the world just now, because Sally has given her warning; and the result of that is that her attitude to Sally Turtle is just a little bit severe. So I thought I'd get a second opinion."

" She was a good cook, and clean as a new pin. You take her, Louisa."

" Miss Tapper's father was in the merchant marine," declared Mr. Shillingford. " The Tappers are an undistinguished race. She's too fond of calling herself a lady. One leaves a matter of that sort for other people to discover."

Mrs. Windeatt laughed.

" I suppose the woman who tells you she is a lady generally feels doubtful whether you'll find it out," she said.

Louisa stayed for an hour; then Mr. Shillingford himself brought her horse round from the stable, and she mounted and rode away.

CHAPTER VIII

MRS. JOYCE REEP, while preserving the outward forms of woe upon her husband's death, could not pretend to her heart that even this shattering event lacked compensations. But she was staunch to his memory, and would willingly hear no harsh word against him.

There came a day, however, when harsh words were spoken, and Joyce was forced to listen. Her husband's liabilities proved considerable. From the Rugglestone Inn, which he was wont to patronise, appeared a bill for two pounds, with which came an assurance from Timothy Turtle, the landlord, that he had reduced the total by one-half out of respect for Mrs. Reep. Other lesser accounts fell in from unexpected sources, but Daniel's dying adventure, in the shape of his neighbour's carrier-pigeon, represented the most serious call on the widow's slender purse.

For Alfred Mogridge declared that the bird was worth five pounds, and that he meant to have that sum. He had, indeed, gone further, and explained that in the light of this last outrage, a proposed union between the houses of Mogridge and Reep should be broken off for ever.

Joyce Reep now sought him upon this theme, and the question of the carrier-pigeon was also considered.

Alfred Mogridge was a man so narrow in the shoulders that his bush of a beard almost reached to them. He shaved round his mouth only, though that might well have been concealed, for it was ugly, heavy-lipped, and set with a broken hedge of yellow teeth. A habitual frown set upon his features; distrust housed in his eyes, and, like most suspicious people, he was bad tempered. His work of sexton and jobbing gardener filled his time, and his son was similarly employed. They were equally ignorant, and conducted horticultural operations in a garden plot with similar brutality; but while Alfred, from his three score years of rule of thumb, believed himself unusually skilled and would brook no criticism, Jack, a slight man of thirty, with little brains and no courage, hesitated not at all times to plead ignorance under censure. His feebleness made him a thorn in his father's side, and Alfred continued to treat his son like a child.

Mr. Mogridge was working in his own garden patch when Mrs. Joyce Reep approached a party-wall that separated their domains, and begged for speech. His hard eyes regarded Joyce, and he perceived that the grey widow was nervous, but he did not pity her.

" You be come," he said, " and none too soon. There's things have got to be put on a proper footing between us."

" Me and Margery can't work miracles. Every penny shall be paid, if it takes us a lifetime; but it have got to be done by degrees."

" Five pounds you owe me. You can ax the secretary of the West of England Pigeon Fanciers if you disbelieve it."

" I don't doubt that."

" You're a handmaid of the Lord, we all know," declared Mr. Mogridge, though his tone was not that of admiration, " and you married a limb of Satan and why you done it lies hidden between you and your Maker. However, distance throws dust into the mind and smothers the truth. I dare say you'll be telling the people he was a good husband ten years hence."

" So he was."

" Ah, exactly so! How is it, then, that you be putting on flesh since he went, and look ten year younger a'ready? "

" I'll thank you to leave my flesh alone," answered Mrs. Reep. " People what live next door to a man like you ban't likely to put on flesh, and I don't care who hears me say so ! "

At this defiant challenge a curtain in Mrs. Reep's window shivered, for there sat her daughter Margery, and the girl's emotion was imparted to the rag that concealed her. Her mother seldom flared out in this fashion, and she had chosen a most unhappy occasion for temper from Margery's point of view. This fact, indeed, Joyce Reep herself now appreciated, and prepared to escape from the reach of her daughter's ear.

" Come in your house, please. The sun be striking on my niddick.* I don't want to quarrel, however—least of all with you, and very well you know it. I'm here to have your opinion on two things, and first there's the pigeon. Me and Margery have made very careful plans for the future, and of course charing be the backbone of our wages. Well, will seven shillings a month satisfy you? "

" There must be interest, then," answered Mr. Mogridge, leading the way into his kitchen. " You must add three-

* *Niddick*—nape of neck.

pence over and above the seven shillings each month—
for interest."

Mrs. Reep considered this. Her arithmetic was sound, for
the poor are quick at figures.

"Three twelves be thirty-six, and three twos be six. That's
three-and-six for interest on five pound then. I call that a
cruel lot."

"You wouldn't if you understood such things."

She remembered her other business, and conceded the point.

"Be it as you will, then. And next Saturday you shall
have your first bit. And now about your boy and my girl,
Alfred Mogridge."

"Now 'tis my turn," he answered, "and I tell you, Widow
Reep, that I won't have no truck with your family at all.
Daniel was addicted to a lot of bad things, and no respecter of
persons or property; and blood's thicker than water."

"My Margery takes after me, however. You know that
very well. She's a tireless church-goer, and so good as gold,
and so humble as a worm; and she wouldn't take what didn't
belong to her any more than she'd fly over the moon."

"Well, my Jack don't belong to her, and never shall."

"In a manner of speaking he do belong to her, Alfred
Mogridge. How would you have liked it if somebody had
come between you and your late missis?"

"You ask a very awkward question for yourself," he
answered, "because, as a matter of honest truth, though I
might not have been pleased at the time, if anybody had thrust
me away from the late Joanna Mogridge, I can see very well,
looking back, what a terrible blessed thing it would have been.
I shouldn't have had her stuffy company for thirty year; and
I shouldn't have her silly eyes looking out of my son's
head to-day; and I shouldn't hear him fret me hourly with
his knock-kneed talk—simpleton that he is!"

"If my Margery was in your house, you'd know what comfort meant once again; whereas an understanding person have
only to look round this kitchen to see you're a stranger to it."

"You can buy comfort too dear," he answered. "And a
pair like that—what'll they breed? Ax yourself, Widow Reep;
and if you ban't brave enough to answer, I will for you.
Fools. My Jack, if he marries at all, did ought to find a
woman with a nerve of iron and a backbone of steel—a
courageous, high-minded, fear-nought sort of a thing as would
look the whole world in the eyes and tramp the road of life
flat for her doddering husband to walk upon. And since that
sort of fine thing would no more lower her eyes to my poor,

go-by-the-ground son than she'd wed a badger, then he's got to bide single. And there's an end of it."

She considered before answering :

"I didn't count to influence you much. You're the sort no woman could change from your opinions; but it ban't going to rest here, and I warn you of that."

"Don't you think to bully me," he answered; "I'm near seventy year old, and if a man ban't satisfied with his own reasons at that age, and ain't waterproof against the drip of other people's ideas—then more fool him. So there 'tis, and now I must go to work. Little enough time I get for my own patch, and if my son was worthy of the name, he'd see I wasn't called upon to rack my ancient bones like I be. I put in this afternoon at Miss Tapper's—'tis one of my restful jobs at ' Genoa Villa,' thank God, for I've got the place in such tilth that there's nought to do nowadays but chop the grass and cut back the bushes now and again."

"I be going there to sew this minute. She offered me work when my husband died—a good friend to the poor."

Mrs. Reep went to her work, and Alfred Mogridge returned to his digging.

The famous villa residence of Miss Tapper was not far off, and the widow, presenting herself at the back door, was admitted by Thirza herself.

"My new servant arrives from Newton Abbot in the course of the evening," she said. "I will ask you, therefore, Mrs. Reep, to turn your attention to the kitchen instead of the sewing, though I have reason to believe that Sally Turtle left everything decent and in order."

"You can trust Timothy Turtle's daughter in that matter," said Joyce. "A neater-handed and nicer creature don't live, and I'm sorry you have lost her."

"There are as good fish in the sea as ever came out of it, I believe," answered Miss Tapper, "and the character with my new ' general ' is quite stupendous, so to say. Sally was feather-brained—I say feather-brained deliberately, though to many it may seem a strong word."

"She's handsome, and that sort hankers for change, miss. 'Tis no good being handsome if you ban't admired—so they think."

"The admiration that is won by a fine skin and a mound of yellow hair should weigh very little with a thinking creature," declared Miss Tapper. "If I could have made her feel that it is better to bear the ills you have than fly to others that you know not of, no doubt she would have stopped at the villa.

And, as a matter of fact, you know what a unique place this is."

" Indeed I do, miss; and I wish to heaven that my Margery had been woman enough to fill it."

" She was not," answered Miss Tapper, " and in any case her home would have been too near. But when I think of the wages, the liberty, the freedom of access to myself—when I think of the room they have, facing west, and the utensils and conveniences——"

" 'Tis cruel wonderful they should want to leave, I'm sure."

" Of course, gratitude is a thing of the past. However, you will never hear me give an expression of opinion, Joyce. My own judgment I have, and I do not find it makes many mistakes; but, as my father used to say, ' A still tongue makes a wise head.' I speak but little and permit myself few confidential friends. Others, indeed, come to me with their secrets —I suppose there is something about me—but they get no secrets in exchange."

" They know you be safe and understanding, miss."

" Yes, I am that. I can throw light. True, it is only a borrowed light; but still I can throw it into the chambers of the heart. It comes—this remarkable gift of mine—it comes from living alone and thinking much and speaking little. Here, in my villa residence, lifted up all alone, like a hermit on a mountain, Mrs. Reep, I look down upon the entire life of the village and know everybody's business—in a Christian sense, of course."

" You're that large-hearted and charitable, I'm sure, miss."

" One does one's duty, I hope; but I never let the left hand know what the right hand doeth. I have to thank my father for everything. He taught me how to be both just and generous. Few people have the art to be both. One or other is common; but it is very rare to find anybody who is both."

CHAPTER IX

BEHIND St. Pancras Church a road ran away south-east of Widecombe to Venton, Chittleford and Blackslade under the hills. The way crossed Webburn river at a little bridge, where the stream on her journey through the Vale meandered amid meadows lighted now with the kingcup and cuckoo-flower. A few lengths of granite carried the road across the water, and a handrail of iron protected it. A freshet had lately shaken the foundations of this bridge, and Pancras Widecombe, the stonemason, was working upon it and whistling as he worked. Having passed the bridge, bright Webburn wound through rush flats, amid furze brakes and among little fields to the southern neck of the valley. Thence it plunged into the woods of Lizwell, where larches already glimmered emerald bright against the budding boughs of oak and ash.

It was the silent and lonely hour of midday, when men cease work and women are busy in their houses. Pancras had not spoken to a soul all the morning, and now he felt in doubt whether to return to the " Rugglestone Inn," where he lodged, that he might eat his dinner in company and hear his own voice, or stop where he was. The work on the bridge neared completion, and, as usual, since it was the last thing he had done, Pancras felt that it was the best. A large tract of green mortar challenged some sort of decoration, and the flamboyant man, feeling that nothing better than the craftsman's signature might adorn this space, now scratched his initials with a fine flourish, and added the date thereto. He ate a brown pasty of mutton and potato while engaged in this manner, and he had just walked back along Webburn's bank for a few yards to judge of his work, when a bright object showed itself upon the road, and a young woman appeared, walking from Widecombe. The mason was delighted, for he knew Sally Turtle very well, and had, indeed, been expecting her for an hour.

" Three cheers for you! " he cried. " And feeling pretty clever by the look of you. How d'you find Kingshead, Sally, and your new missis? "

Sally was a handsome, blonde girl, and she showed a decision of will and strength of character rare in a maiden of three-and-twenty. She admired Pancras and they were good friends.

" Mrs. Windeatt have gone over to Two Bridges for Belliver Hunt Week," she said, " and I've got leave till Saturday. She's a proper sort, and wonderful large-minded. I shall bide there very well content for a year no doubt. How's father? "

" Never better. Pitch here along with me for a bit and have some of my pasty."

" I can't pitch : I'm in my best gown," she answered.

" Then come down here a minute and then I'll carry your parcel back for 'e. I've just been fixing up the bridge that was shook abroad in the flood a month ago."

She descended, and laughed to see his sign.

" You vain thing! One would think you'd done something clever."

" So I have—a lot cleverer than you can see. The best be out of sight. There's work behind that mortar as would surprise you, Sally."

" Us'll hope the river won't surprise it," she answered. " Time to talk after Webburn's been up again once or twice."

" I want for it to hap," he answered her; " I'd like for a proper wall of water to come down and bury all; and when it had run fine again you'd see my bridge—' my bridge,' I call it, for 'tis very near as good as mine now—you'd see it come forth fresh as paint, without a stone stirred or a course sprung. Mind be the thing, Sally. 'Tis mind that makes me join stone and stone together, closer than a married couple, and mind that makes you cook every other girl out of sight. That's why you and me have both got a great future before us."

" That's all right," she said. " Ah, here's father coming to meet me! "

Mr. Timothy Turtle—a white-headed man with a straight back, a Roman nose, and blue eyes like his daughter's— approached, and she put her arms round his neck and kissed him. Pancras beamed upon this greeting, and then, leaving his tools by the river, took Sally's parcel from her and walked by her side.

" She's ever so happy," he said to Mr. Turtle, " and she thinks a lot of Mrs. Windeatt, as I foreknew she would."

The innkeeper nodded. He was a man of few words; but now he had a question to ask.

" Didst hear any more of that row to Pierce's? " he inquired.

" I did," answered Widecombe. Then, for the girl's benefit, he explained.

" You must know, Sally, that matters go from bad to worse at the ' Old Inn,' and naturally us at the ' Rugglestone ' be over and above interested, for there's only two pubs all told, and them that don't drink at Pierce's drink along with us. Well, there's a split at the ' Old,' and it's going to be a very serious thing, in my opinion. Of course, I go to both in my large way, and I hear everything; and this I do know, that the regulars at Pierce's house begin to take sides. I mean between him and his wife. Most of the men stick up for him, I fancy —anyway, Nicky Glubb do, and he's a power among 'em; and I do; and Birkett Johnson and Whitelock Smerdon and Elias Coaker; but Old Harry Hawke and Young Harry, and of course Tom Gurney and a good few other men be on the side of Mrs. Pierce."

" Why d'you say ' of course Tom Gurney '? " asked Miss Turtle.

" Because the blacksmith be terribly addicted to Mrs. Pierce," answered Pancras. " I'm among friends, or I wouldn't venture such a strong expression; but Tom Gurney thinks the world of her, and don't hesitate to say openly in company that Mabel Pierce drawed a cruel blank when she took Arthur."

" So she did," said Sally. " He's a worm, and no man—everybody knows that."

" And she knew it when she took him," answered the mason. " She knew the poor nerves of the man—didn't she offer marriage herself, and do the man's work? "

But Sally appeared to be on the other side.

" I don't know," she said. " It must be pretty poor fun to have a husband like Arthur Pierce."

Then Timothy Turtle took up the matter, in a voice very slow.

" Whether or not, if there's a split, us be the gainers. Them as leave the ' Old ' will come to the ' Rugglestone.' "

" Why should they leave the ' Old ' because Arthur Pierce is sat upon by his wife? " asked Sally.

" There's much more in it than that," Pancras assured her. " You women ban't no use at politics, and 'twould take a month of Sundays to explain all the ins and outs. 'Tis pretty well allowed by the far-seeing—for that matter I was the first to point it out—that a public won't go suent if the master and missis be always sparring. 'Tisn't even as if they sparred in private; but things be at such a pass that they'll quarrel in a full bar while mugs be lying empty. So what it will come to will be that they Pierces part; and that means new people at the ' Old Inn.' I'm sorry for Arthur; but the custom is the thing, and when that totters, 'twill soon be all over. The man will be glad and thankful to go and drop no more money. The woman wants to stop. His side will conquer, however, because I be on it, not to name Nicky and Coaker and Smerdon and the rising generation."

Sally laughed.

" Tom Gurney's stronger than all you noisy fellows put together," she said. " And he's rich, too."

" What can he do? " asked Pancras. " He's only one, and we are many. He'd like to run away with her; but that wouldn't pay him—a public man like him. And if he did, 'tis all right for the ' Rugglestone,' anyway; because, if Mabel

Pierce fled from Arthur, Arthur would be a lost lamb, and very like have to go in the asylum. At any rate, he'd stop work. And then, while the ' Old ' was waiting for another tenant, the people would get the habit of coming to the ' Rugglestone,' and habit be stronger than death, as we all know."

" 'Twill never go so far as that, and I don't expect it," declared Mr. Turtle. " Tom Gurney have got a very fine business, and 'tisn't likely he's going to throw it to the dogs for another man's wife."

The " Rugglestone Inn " now appeared before them.

The pride of Mr. Turtle's heart was his strain of Buff Orpington poultry. The birds were everywhere in the road and fields round about the inn. The impress of their claws was upon the mire in wet weather; in dry, their dust baths were scraped about the roads and hedges. They were a source of profit, and the huckster who called weekly at the " Rugglestone " generally took eggs and a pair of the birds to market.

The " Rugglestone " was a mean building set by the highway, but the taproom was large and the liquor good. Sally entered now, to find dinner ready, and Pancras Widecombe, having drunk a glass of beer, returned to his work at the bridge. It was ten minutes past one when he went back to the river. He made a note of this, and laboured ten minutes beyond the hour for finishing his day's work. Such honesty was rewarded, as he knew it would be, and Sally Turtle reappeared on her way to the village as he cleaned his mortar-board.

He walked with her then, and they came to Widecombe, met acquaintance and dawdled a little.

CHAPTER X

MR. VALIANT DUNNYBRIG lived at the large farm of Chittleford with his wife and niece. It was said of him that he pretended to a preposterous familiarity with the ways and purposes of a Creator fashioned on Old Testament models. He was as certain of this Supreme Spirit as a Jew, and as clear in his mind concerning the genesis of all things as a Hottentot. He never doubted; no " melancholy mark of interrogation " ever blotted his triumphant affirmation of Jehovah's principle and practice. Nothing had happened to shake his foundations;

indeed, only one doubt ever darkened his mind. He felt like a patriarch of Juda among the folk, and conducted his life in a large measure upon patriarchal models.

Chittleford, with its adjacencies, was itself almost a hamlet, and Valiant Dunnybrig ruled here—a sort of shepherd-king. He was, however, childless, and in that fact lay the farmer's sole uncertainty already recorded. He seldom found himself puzzled by anything that happened; but that he should have been denied the crown of parentage was a mystery beyond his power to solve.

He was a large, exceedingly handsome man, with a bush of a beard, still brown, a big voice, fine dark eyes, a broad brow, and spacious gestures. Though sixty years of age, he looked younger; his virility was not shaken, and physical work he rejoiced to do. He mowed with a scythe in the old fashion, and he threshed his grain with a flail.

Jane Dunnybrig thought she understood him, and was uneasily proud of him; but she knew far more about him than anybody else, and watched him closely. In his religious fervour Mr. Dunnybrig sometimes suffered a mental excitation that shadowed physical disaster. He was a fanatic, and once or twice a fervour of Old Testament enthusiasm had made him ill. There were dangers lurking ahead of Mrs. Dunnybrig, but she possessed powers to meet them. Under an impassive exterior, strong character was latent. She did not exercise it, and seldom intruded herself upon the picturesque existence of Valiant. But she was ready. She knew that he deceived himself a little in certain directions, and she had long since become aware that absolute adherence to the patriarchal rule was quite out of the question for Mr. Dunnybrig or anybody else. She was wise, and never interfered with her husband in public. Only at secret times—generally when she had gone to bed—did she seek to modify his purposes. Sometimes she succeeded, and sometimes she did not.

Araminta Dench was their niece, a woman of thirty, who knew the exact relations between husband and wife, earned her living with them, and kept her own counsel. She was a pale, silent woman, penniless and obsessed with the phantom of poverty, the need of means at any cost. Young men, however, were not tempted, because, while not ill-favoured of face and body, Araminta's tongue was keen. She ridiculed the nebulous opinions of her own generation, and admired Valiant Dunnybrig; but her aunt she did not like, though for both aunt and uncle, as the arbiters of her future, she entertained profound respect. She was sly and calculating, but Valiant thought very highly of her.

The man moved in an atmosphere somewhat unreal. His mind was grandiose in its conceptions; he felt the veil between him and a future life was thinner than that which separated his fellow-creatures in time from eternity. He saw through it in visions. He would have founded a sect and conducted a new schism with a little encouragement. It happened, however, that the clergyman of a neighbouring Nonconformist chapel suited Mr. Dunnybrig exactly, and allowed him some liberty of speech and action in connection with the conduct of the services.

Mr. Dunnybrig affected one book beside the Bible, and he read in it aloud to his wife and niece on an evening of early spring. He was long-sighted, and held the book before the candle almost at arm's length. Not only under conditions of stress, and by way of penance and privation did the farmer come to this gloomy volume; he used it also to chasten himself and his circle when things appeared to be going too well. To-day he had inherited an unexpected legacy of five hundred pounds, and everybody was very happy about it. So now, with supper done, he read John Hayward.

The full title of the book was the contents in a lurid sentence : " Horrors and Terrors of the Hour of Death and Day of Judgment that seize upon all Impenitent and Unbelieving Sinners, to which are added Sundry Examples of God's dreadful Judgments against violent Breakers of His Holy Commandments."

Valiant Dunnybrig had a certain inflexion of voice which he reserved entirely for this book. He read now until it was too dark to see, then bade Araminta fetch a candle that he might finish a passage. To her, money being the first consideration of life, the addition of five hundred pounds to the store of Mr. Dunnybrig was a solemn delight—quite beyond any power of " Horrors and Terrors " to abate. She speculated often as to the future disposal of Valiant's wealth, for he had no near relations, and was more than well disposed towards her. He interested her profoundly, and she never quite knew what he would do next. But she did not enjoy his confidence, or, rather, she shared it with the world, for Mr. Dunnybrig had no secrets. Of his solitary sorrow he had made no secret, and everybody was aware that Valiant Dunnybrig desired above all things to possess children.

When Araminta returned with a candle she found that a visitor had called. It was Gabriel Shillingford, and Mrs. Dunnybrig, who liked him, begged that he would stop to supper.

" Nay," he said, " my girls would wonder where I am. I

have been away all day at Exeter, and they will wait supper for me. But I heard the good news, and felt 'twas a neighbour's part to say that I am heartily glad."

"Come in, Shillingford," said the master; "you're welcome, and I thank you; but I'm in the midst of a sentence, and waiting for candle-teening to finish it. My eyes are hawk's yet, thank God. Here's Araminta."

Gabriel Shillingford sat down, and Valiant thundered to a finish. Then his wife and niece departed, leaving the men alone.

"You might be surprised to hear me reading from that book, and think a joy psalm of praise and thanksgiving was better fit after the good fortune of this five hundred pounds; but that's not my way," explained Mr. Dunnybrig. "'In the midst of life we are in death,' and I like to keep my eyes fixed on my latter end—not in fear or sorrow, but just in the same steady, long-sighted way as I look ahead in every other matter. The passing hour's a tyrant, Shillingford, and it's a strong man's place to get that tyrant under heel. I've even known a woman rise to do it here and there; though 'tis more wonderful in their case, for the passing hour's a proper terror to them most times. Their work's never done. It haunts their rising up and their going down. I read Hayward to steady me in joy and sorrow alike. Sit down and drink a drop of Araminta's slow gin. She's a clever girl at cordials."

"Ten minutes I'll stay with pleasure. I'd hoped to ask for your congratulations to-day, and not thought it would be the other way about."

"If you've had good fortune, I'll rejoice with you, neighbour Shillingford," said Valiant.

"Thank you for saying so. It lies still in doubt. I've been to Exeter upon the subject. In a word there is a thought to make me a Justice of the Peace, and I went up to see a man or two and let it be understood that I was willing to go on the bench."

Mr. Dunnybrig snorted.

"There's faults in you that make me terrible impatient," he said. "Answer me this : have you got time for it?"

"I can make time for a public office like that. And it is a seemly thing. Shillingfords have been justices for years and years."

"Well, you're wrong, Gabriel. You can't make time. No creature can make time. 'Tis God's work. He makes it and gives us each our portion; and if you be going to fritter you s away, messing about with the great unpaid, then I say you're wrong, and you're taking from one thing to give to another."

" You're frank, Dunnybrig, but you don't understand the claims of long descent in a man's veins. My blood cries out to be doing something besides farming."

" Then your blood's a fool," said Valiant. " And, since we're on it, and you know I love you, like I love all men, and only wish you well, I'll remind you, in the first place, that 'tis doubtful on your own showing, whether your blood runs straight from the great Shillingfords."

" Not doubtful in the least to me; but 'twould cost money to prove. The Heralds could prove it, if I could pay 'em to."

" Bah! " answered Mr. Dunnybrig. " Of course! They'd prove you was descended from the Pope of Rome—if you had money enough for 'em. And while you trouble to link your-self on to the great, you'll end by going bankrupt and finding yourself along with the least. It ban't worthy of a man wise in many directions, to let down his place like you do. Money's wanted everywhere, and if you'd put some of your money into gates instead of books, you'd be doing a kinder thing to Blackslade, and a fairer thing to your fine daughters."

Mr. Dunnybrig regarded a square parcel that Gabriel was carrying and shook his head at it. Then he continued :

" I ask you, man to man, what is the use of proving that your havage comes from the dead? Don't everybody's? Ban't we all kin? Why, I'm a greater man than Queen Victoria, Shillingford! Yes, I am, for I be nearer to Adam by a gener-ation than she is. So you get this bee out of your bonnet, my dear soul, for when all's done, and you've proved it up to the hilt, what then? It won't make the quality visit you. It won't make the bettermost—so to call 'em—trundle up to Blackslade. The fine folk don't come through broken-down gates, or marry penniless girls."

" But surely, surely, Dunnybrig, there be some left who take pride in a noble name, and honour a man for the sake of his ancestors, if he can show 'em he's worthy of those ancestors? "

" Dreams you be dreaming. 'Tis only God who harbours these high opinions nowadays—and maybe a few broken, high-born, poverty-ridden folk such as yourself. I'll give you all credit. You be just the sort of self-conscious, fidgety, proud sort of person that we'd expect to have had fine relations. Only the time be gone for what you want. The poison of worship of cash have got into the children, and the young generation touch their hats to a man's coat and hoss, not his name."

" You are good physic for one like me, I suppose," answered

the other. " 'Tis difficult to argue about it without—well, I might hurt your feelings, Dunnybrig."

" Not you, Shillingford. The man wasn't born to hurt my feelings. 'Tis only God can do that. And there's no harm in hurting a man's feelings when all's said. They may want it. We did ought to doctor each other."

" Well, you've just hurt mine—no doubt you thought in your way it would be good for Blackslade if you told me I was a fool. But you must allow for character, Dunnybrig; you must grant that there are natures hidden from you, with twists of mind, and an outlook on life what you can't understand or fathom."

" No," answered Valiant. " I don't allow that, Shillingford. I'm a man of very extraordinary understanding, owing to my simple life. I've lived so near to God that 'tis with me as it was with Moses on the Mount : I've caught a bit of the Shine. Araminta tells me they say in Widecombe that I walk arm-in-arm with God. Doubtless they didn't mean it kindly, but a fool's mouth will often tell truth. And true it is. I do. I've been properly amazed to find how often I catch myself seeing eye to eye with the Almighty."

Valiant's countenance blazed, and the master of Blackslade, scenting a sermon, rose to depart.

" Good-bye for the present. And, again, I'm glad of your good fortune. We don't think alike in many things, but we think alike in wishing each other well."

CHAPTER XI

THE tragic night of the schism at the " Old Inn " opened quietly, and few guessed that it was big with the fate of Arthur Pierce and his wife.

The usual company played protagonists, and there were present Birkett Johnson from Tunhill, Nicky Glubb, Young Harry Hawke and his father, Old Harry, Whitelock Smerdon, the loved of Sibley Shillingford, and Pancras Widecombe.

Then Harry Hawke the elder, who was an ancient man of small intellect, began grumbling to Birkett Johnson on the subject of birds, but won little sympathy.

The old man's voice was beyond his control, and piped and

quavered as he narrated, almost with tears, how bullfinches had eaten the buds off his gooseberry-trees.

" And what I say is that 'tis a crying shame, and be enough to shake a man's faith," he declared. " Ess, Johnson, I say that. There's no justice in it, and I should like to hear what them baggering birds was ever created for. Here the Almighty goes and builds up a gooseberry bush, and fills it with promise of plenty, and then He sends along one of them blasted bud-hawks to tear the herb to pieces and scatter the promise of fruit on the ground. And how be you or any other man going to square that with sense, or say 'tis right? "

" I don't say 'tis right, and I don't say 'tis wrong," answered the metaphysical labourer. " But I do say 'tis natural. The bud was no more made for you than for the bird. 'Twas made for itself—to take its chance of success, like everything else."

" But 'twas me made it, you might say. 'Twas me, under God, for didn't I grow it and nurse it and prune it and feed it?"

" You did all that," admitted Birkett, " but you didn't net it, you see, and the Lord would say, if He gave the matter a thought, He'd say, ' Well, Old Harry Hawke, you very well knew there was bullfinches about, and you very well knew their manners and customs; and 'twas your place, as a think-ing and immortal creature, to outwit 'em. But you didn't, and so you won't get no gooseberries this year."

" Like your cheek, Johnson," cut in Pancras Widecombe. " Like your cheek, telling what the Lord would say and what he wouldn't. You're as bad as Farmer Dunnybrig."

" Arthur here won't have no religion talked, and he's quite right," answered Birkett. " And 'tis no use our axing why the Almighty makes this or that creation, Old Harry Hawke. The bird be His thought, and so 'tis a proper bird and sent in the world for a proper reason. So 'tis no good crying out against the creature and saying it didn't ought to be made. If the veil was lifted, there'd be amazing surprises, and we should see the reason for slugs and woodlice and stoats and hawks, and many another varmint that shall be nameless. 'Tis the great difference between Man and his Maker, that He never does anything without a reason, and we be always doing so."

" Should we find a reason for Nicky here? " asked Pancras, who delighted to sharpen swords with the blind man; but though the question was answered, Nicky's reply reached no ear. The clock struck nine, and, as it did so, others entered. There came Tom Gurney, the blacksmith, and Elias Coaker, from Southcombe.

It was the hour when Mabel Pierce relieved her exhausted husband; it was also the hour when Tom, Mrs. Pierce's most s.renuous supporter, was wont to arrive for his evening drinking. To-night, however, Mrs. Pierce failed to be punctual. She did not appear, and her husband showed evidences of distress. He was a feeble man, but he had more friends than his wife, for her scornful attitude towards him excited the anger of many among the customers. Once, indeed, a remonstrance had been raised by Birkett Johnson, and he had hinted to Mabel Pierce that she was unwise and unkind. But nothing came of it, save a fierce attack on Johnson from Tom Gurney, the lady's champion. And now Gurney and Johnson spoke together no more.

"Where's your wife, Arthur?" asked the blacksmith, in his usual insolent voice. He was florid, dark, black-eyed, and big-chested. He kept an ironmonger's shop hard by his smithy, and was a prosperous bachelor, very useful to a wide range of customers.

"She ban't in the bar yet, Gurney, though 'tis her time," answered the innkeeper.

"Which we all know, else Tom wouldn't be here," said Nicky.

"I hope, to be sure, she won't be long, for I'm terrible tired, and my legs be giving under me to-night."

"Nonsense," answered Gurney. "What for do your legs want to give under you?"

"I do all I can."

"So you do, Arthur," said Pancras Widecombe. "And we know it. Us all can't be built like cart-horses. You don't get a fair chance, in my opinion—such a nerve-ridden man as you."

"You'll do well to mind your own business, Widecombe," said Gurney.

"And so you will, Widecombe," added Young Harry Hawke.

"'Tis just as much his business as yours, you hectoring creature!" cried Nicky Glubb, to the blacksmith. "You always think to bully everybody by vartue of measuring more round your arms than the rest; but you shan't bully me—blind though I am—and I tell you that you be thrusting in between husband and wife something shameful here; and if there's much more of it, me and my friends will take t'other side; and Arthur Pierce can rely upon us; and if he wants to bitch up this place so as to get out of it and retire in peace, we'll damn soon help him."

"Nobody's more like to ruin a business than you, you blind

varmint," answered the blacksmith. " And your custom be little worth, anyhow, because 'tis only the drinks that other folk stand you, ever get paid for! "

" You dirty liar! Look at the slate and see if I owe. And if you was blind—and I wish you was—we'd hear what money you could earn! "

They clashed together and the forces were arranged for battle. In support of Arthur Pierce stood Johnson, Widecombe, Nicky Glubb, Whitelock Smerdon, and Jack Mogridge, while Mrs. Pierce had for her champions, Tom Gurney and the Hawkes, who were related to her by marriage. Elias Coaker took no side. He drank half a pint of beer and departed.

There appeared at this electrical moment two women. Nanny came for her husband, for it was her custom to lead him home when the inn closed, and to drink with him for a while before doing so; and Mrs. Pierce entered the bar from a door behind it. Mabel, who was flushed and somewhat the worse for liquor, found her husband in distress, mopping at his brow.

" You be late," he said. But she answered in no good temper.

" Don't grizzle at me to-night, for God's sake, because I can't stand it."

" There! " said Gurney. " Don't that show? The instant moment the woman comes in the bar, Arthur here must needs yelp at her, and her tired to death in Newton. And you men can sink to take sides against a woman! "

In the momentary silence, Mabel turned on her husband.

" At it again, you slack-twisted, worthless worm! And me—thank God I've got patience."

" Glory! You think you'm patient," shouted Nicky. " You don't know the meaning of it! "

" You shut your mouth till you're spoke to," she answered. " You come here, and a lot more trash, standing up for this man against me, and making my life a burden—as if I hadn't got enough to bear."

" Mabel! I won't have it, I won't have it—not afore the people," cried Mr. Pierce. " You've got the will and the strength, and my mind and body be less by a good bit than they might be along of the bad circulation of the blood I endure; but—but——"

He stopped, and went on again.

" Not afore the village like this. I can't suffer it. My nerves be all of a torment this evening. If you only knowed —if you only knowed! "

"Shut your mouth and get out of my sight," she said. "I don't want for my dirty linen to be washed in public every night in this bar."

"Then why do you do it, Mabel Pierce?" asked Johnson.

"'Tis your fault, and I tell you this: a good wife——"

"For God's sake no preaching," cried the blacksmith. "Go—clear out and take Glubb and that sandy-haired fool, Widecombe—go t'other shop—we be well rid of you."

"Peace—peace, neighbours," prayed the innkeeper. "'Tis almost too much I assure you. Mabel and me understand in private."

"No, we don't, and never shall," she answered.

"And right you are!" shouted Young Harry Hawke.

Arthur turned his frightened eyes on the new speaker.

"Good Lord! be that you, Young Harry? What have I done to you?"

"Don't you mind him, Arthur—he's only a silly mump-head," said Pancras, and in a moment Young Harry turned upon him. The voices grew louder; Old Harry began to scream against Nicky; Arthur Pierce, retreating before his wife, who had lost her self-control, found himself finally jambed into the corner of the bar with her fist in his face.

"Oh, my God, what have I done to deserve this?" he said; and Gurney answered:

"You've got yourself born—that's what you've done, and 'tis a pity you can't find pluck to undo it and go out of it, for you ban't no use on earth."

"You marry a drunkard and see how you get on," shrieked Nanny. "A fig for you, you bullocky fool! If you be so set on another man's wife, why for don't you run away with her and let Arthur have a bit of peace?"

"Good for you, Nanny! I poke my tongue at the fool," yelled Nicky.

Then the blacksmith answered. Nanny screamed atrocious things at him, and Arthur Pierce, huddled behind the counter, began to cry.

"There—there—look at it!" shouted his wife. "There's a fine thing—a man blubbing like a babby!"

Birkett Johnson spoke, and bawled his loudest to be heard.

"You go to bed, Arthur. Let him pass out of the bar, Mrs. Pierce, and listen to me."

Arthur crept under his wife's arm, swept the company with a dazed and hunted expression, and then disappeared. Where-upon, while Nicky and Nanny screamed like a pair of jays at the blacksmith, and Old Harry Hawke, and Young Harry and

Pancras stood nose to nose with fists fast clenched, Johnson
made himself clear to the innkeeper's wife.

" A good woman ought to keep her husband's weakness out
of sight, I tell you, and 'tis plain cruelty to badger the poor
man in this bar, with Gurney there to help bait him. As sure
as you come in at nine o'clock, you begin on him and send
him to his bed chap-fallen and wretched. And even on the
rare nights when the man is in better spirits, what do you do?
Why, pour out your spite and——"

Mrs. Pierce heard no more, but cried out for succour. She
was leaning back, red-faced, against the bottles, and her big
bosom heaved and fell as she panted.

" Here, Tom, leave them jackdaws and help me against
this chap. He's blackguarding me up hill and down dale, and
who be he—a common labourer—to talk like this to me? "

" Cuss if you like, but listen," continued Johnson. " And
Gurney won't be the worse neither, for 'tis half his fault that
you be driving your husband daft. Look at it—Providence
turns out this man weak as water, though good as gold.
And another man may be hard as the nether millstone and bad
to the heart. And the weak man have hell all his life, and the
strong man gets his way, and justice don't come into it at all.
'Tis just cause and effect, and Providence——"

" Shut up you ! " said Gurney. " What the hell's the use
of talking? If you was a man, you'd take the woman's part
and not bleat about Providence. Where's Providence in it?
All the pity's her side, and them that take the woman's——"

" Call her a woman ! " cried Nanny. " She's a cat-a-
mountain—good for nought to man or beast. I'd——"

" You scarecrow ! You to talk—you as be only fitted to
lie and thieve for that drunken rip you pretend to be your
husband ! "

Thus spoke the blacksmith, and the argument terminated
there.

" Lead me to him ! Lead me to him, Nanny ! " yelled Mr.
Glubb. He foamed at the mouth; his grey hair bristled; his
sightless eyes stuck out of his head. And Nanny endeavoured
with all her might to do as he bade her; but she was prevented, and Nicky battered madly into the first person he felt,
who proved to be a friend. The din was dreadful, and arrested
the attention of a few passers-by. They hastened in with a
policeman, to see Mrs. Pierce rolling in fits of hysterical
laughter behind the bar, Tom Gurney and Young Harry
Hawke supporting her, and Pancras striving to calm Nicky,
who poured a flood of profanity on the head of the blacksmith.

The policeman protested. He had friends on both sides, and was not prepared to take any strong measures.

"Come!" he said. "'Tis very near closing-time. You'd best to go home, Nicky Glubb. There's a lot too much noise going on in here."

"You're right, Adam Saunders," answered Mr. Johnson. "There's a lot too much noise; but the 'Old Inn' will be a good bit more peaceful after to-night. Come on, boys! I've done what I could, and only got hard words for soft ones. We be o' Pierce's side, and the kindest thing for us to do will be to ruin the business, so far as it lies in our power, by going elsewhere, and leading others to do the like. And I hope Arthur will seek a strong friend or two to help him get free of that woman."

Old Harry Hawke, who had taken the least part in this stormy scene, was the principal sufferer, for Nicky, while struggling in the hands of Pancras, had kicked the ancient man on the leg. Now, groaning and threatening a summons, he went his way with his son, while the adverse faction departed together, leaving Tom Gurney alone with Mrs. Pierce.

Peace returned to the "Old Inn"; but, ten minutes before closing time, the little drinking-house known as the "Ruggle-stone," was inforced by important new customers, and Timothy Turtle, jumping up from the barrel whereon he had been drowsing, was greeted by the triumphant Pancras.

"We be come, Turtle!" he cried, "and us all drink here in future for evermore. We'll never go in the 'Old' again till them Pierces be gone, and Arthur's at peace."

Mr. Turtle bestirred himself, lighted another lamp, drew beer, and listened to the news of the night.

"Valiant Dunnybrig and Uncle Tom Cobleigh be only just gone," he said. "'Tis a great pity as they didn't stop to hear such an adventure."

"They'll hear of it fast enough," declared Pancras. "Why, man alive, Dartmoor will ring with it to-morrow. The place will never hold together against it—you mark me."

"Never—not with that woman," said Johnson. "'Tis doomed to fail. Us can only hope that Arthur's relations will come forward and take him away from her."

"He ain't got none; that's the mischief of it," explained Widecombe. "He's an orphan, like me, and she only took him for his money."

Then he held his hand to his face.

"Lord, Nicky," he said, "you did give me a proper smack on the nib."

CHAPTER XII

PETRONELL SHILLINGFORD and Elias Coaker sat together in a favourite tryst on Whittaburrow. Autumn had come again, and, while he spoke, young Coaker strained his ears and divided his thoughts, for the sound of a hunter's horn faintly rose and fell from afar. The wind shouted over the rocky cairn that crowned this height and whistled in the great heaps of granite piled there. A dark haze hung over the valley and shrouded the breast of Hameldon, until the mighty hill sulked the colour of lead, and Widecombe lay beneath the lovers, buried in gloom.

The restlessness of the hour influenced the young people who now made holiday. In secret they were here, for as yet their romance had been guessed by Sibley alone. They loved one another, but they knew very little about one another; and to-day they happened to enlarge their knowledge in a manner most shattering and unexpected.

Elias Coaker did not resemble his parents. He was a youth with red hair, blue eyes, and a finely moulded but heavily freckled countenance. That he had a fierce temper, Petronell knew, and he was aware that she suffered from the same incubus; but they enjoyed too much else in common to fear this danger. They both unconsciously felt the need of mystery in life, and found their secret betrothal supply this need. He excelled in plots and plans, and she rejoiced in them. They intrigued without the least necessity, and feigned that their understanding would set the world by the ears if it were known. But it was unlikely that anyone would have raised the least objection, save on the rational score of young Coaker's position. He worked for his father, and was not as yet able to consider a cottage of his own. So he dreamed of a castle.

In thought they played like children, but reality was no great part of their lives. Sometimes they amused each other, sometimes bored each other. In feats of imagination, Petronell was first; but when it came to action, Elias showed greater resolution and resolve. He declared that he meant to run away with Petronell some day, and she was delighted at the idea. Mr. Shillingford was elevated into the grand difficulty.

This fine power of make-believe often follows a boy into manhood, but very seldom can live in the soul of a grown girl. Petronell, however, possessed it, and since there was none other to exalt into dragon or ogre, her placid father filled that high office.

To-day Elias was restless, and wanted to be on foot. They had played their game of castles in the air for an hour; but it seemed that there were other things in the air also. They had differed, and Petronell had conquered in an argument. Now Elias rose.

" I give you best," he said. " You understand books and reading, and all that. Now let's get up over, I want——" He broke off. He wanted to reach a point from which it was probable he would see the hounds, whose music came fitfully upon the wind; but Petronell loathed sport—it was the one great subject upon which they had never agreed.

" We'll go across to Hennesbury Gate," he said, " and see what's doing."

" We'll go to Seven Lords' Lands," she answered. " We can sit in the midst of the stones unseen from the road; and you can keep watch."

Seven Lords' Lands was the local name for a neolithic hut-circle a mile from Whittaburrow; and hither now the young folk came—to a spot where a stone man's prehistoric home, on lofty ground all tinged with tors, marked a modern boundary and stood at the meeting-place of seven manors.

" 'Tis strange," mused Petronell, " to think that just here such a lot of estates come together. I wonder how many belonged to the Fitz-Ralphs of North Hall—they who changed their name to Shillingford in the reign of Edward the First. All Widecombe Manor belonged to them then. There was John Shillingford, Mayor of Exeter—a very wise and wonderful man; and his picture is much like father."

But Elias had heard all this before. His mind was on the hounds, and as he rose from a seat by Petronell in the hut-circle, he leapt, for, not two hundred yards distant, he viewed a hunted fox. Moved by the thrill of the sight, Elias did an unwise thing, and called his sweetheart's attention to reynard; but Petronell was sentimental in these matters. She took the sufferings of animals deeply to heart, and detested the slaughter or hunting of bird or beast. Now she saw a fox going very slowly with his brush down and his tongue out. The lovers viewed this spectacle from different standpoints. Both became instantly excited and both showed unreason.

Petronell thought of the fox; Elias considered the hunt.

" They're off the scent," he said. " I'll just run up to the top of the hill. They ban't far off—down in Grey Goose Nest bog by the sound."

" What! " she cried. " You'd help them against him!

Look at him—nearly dead, and nothing but his own cleverness has saved him."

The fox was slipping along through withered fern.

" Don't be childish, Petronell," cried Elias.   " 'Tis every man's right and duty to help a hunt if he can."

" 'Tis you who are childish, and all those grown-up idiots on horses yonder.   They're not clever enough to catch him, nor yet the hounds.   He's fairly foxed them, and if you put them on him again you'll be a coward," thus she spoke hotly; but his blood was up, too.

" Take care who you call names, and mind your own business, Petronell.   As a man, 'tis mine to give a view holloa, and I'm going to do it.   We'll argue afterwards."

" I forbid you!   I forbid you! " she cried.   " You hear me. I forbid you, Elias! "

But he was up and away.   He ran to the ledge of the hills southerly and saw the huntsmen, three parts of a mile distant, casting without success in the bog called Grey Goose Nest. He waved his hat, danced on the hill-top to attract attention, and screamed loudly.

Petronell, gone from hot to cold, watched him with hard eyes and thought what a fool he looked.

Her heart heaved in her bosom and she was terribly enraged. The castles in the air were forgot; the hopes and dreams huddled below the horizon of her soul before this grim reality. She knew that sport was a passion with Elias, but her views on the subject had always been made clear, and, until now, he had respected them.   The hounds rippled over the hill; the huntsmen followed young Coaker's direction, and Petronell saw the Master give Elias a nod and heard him shout his thanks.   Twenty men and women on horseback trailed by, and with them came Mrs. Louisa Windeatt.   She was clad in dark green and sat a great black hunter, on which she looked a tiny woman.   She saw Petronell in the hut-circle and kissed her whip-hand as she galloped past.   Others were there familiar to the girl.   Young men in pink went by and an old man or two in black.   Among the grey heads was Mr. Smerdon of Bone Hill, in corduroy, on a Dartmoor pony; and to see a grandfather thus racing after a fox stirred Petronell's deepest contempt.

Soon, having swept into the valley northwards, they were lost in the falling rain and the noise and bustle of them ceased. Then Elias came back quietly.   He anticipated some little explosion, but was quite unprepared for its gravity and extent.

" Young Christian Cobleigh was out, too," said Elias.   " He borrowed a pony at Chittleford, and it has fallen down and hurt its knee. He's walking it home. There's a good many on foot up over that went to the meet, and a few will walk back this way, so we'd better be gone before the rain gets heavy."

He considered that he had done nothing worthy of further mention; but she undeceived him.

"Be gone as soon as you like," she said. "I don't want you."

"Come, come, my dearie, don't make a fuss for nought. We've always had two opinions about sporting and always shall."

"Yes—and if you weren't blind, and as big a fool as you looked just now on the hill, dancing and screaming, you'd see that those two opinions are going to divide us once for all. Yes—you needn't put on that scared look. I asked you to be commonly decent—no more. I asked you to be the sportsman you pretend to be. A poor, clever creature, fighting for its life, outwits a lot of hounds and men, trained to catch and kill it. 'Twas too clever for 'em, and threw 'em off, and no doubt thanked God in its own foxy way that it had escaped; and then, instead of keeping your mouth shut and minding your own business, like any other outsider, you give it away and thrust your oar in against the creature, and call that a sporting thing to do!"

He laughed, but he made a mistake to do so.

"One would think that the fox was a friend of yours," he said.

"You may cackle. But I tell you you're a mean coward, and I *hate* you to-day—hate you properly. You'd best to go. I can't stand the sound of your voice no more. Clear out and let me get calm, else I'll say something I'll be sorry for."

"'Tis I that am sorry," he said. "And I never should have thought you could have took such a line, Petronell. A big-minded girl like you!"

"Go!" she answered. "I mean it. I've got no use for you just at present. I'll need to think of this. 'Tis less the actual thing than what it stands for. I ask you to favour me in a small matter—as clear as words could speak I asked it—and you refused me."

"I was excited."

"Yes, you were—and a pretty figure you cut."

"If you're going to make personal remarks, Petronell, I'll go."

"That's what I've asked you to do a score of times," she answered. "And I'd like to see a pack of hounds running after you, Elias, and hear what you thought of it when they caught you."

At this insult the man turned red, and made as though to speak; but he did not. Instead he left her abruptly and strode away over the heath in the direction whence they had come. They had walked towards Widecombe again aftei this incident, and now Petronell, from the heights, watched her lover march off. He soon sank into the valley, and as he did so looked back several times; but she stood still among the rocks, sacred to many a tryst. The thought touched Elias : he slowed down, turned slowly, and began to climb back to her. The rain fell sharply now, and his anger was quite gone. He returned to express very frank sorrow for the thing that he had done. But Fate was against him. A moment after he arrived beside her, and ventured to turn up the collar of her coat, the sound of pattering feet and a galloping horse reached their ears from the other side of the rock pile. The hounds were back, trotting beside the huntsman; the whipper-in followed, and at his saddle-bow grinned the mask of the fox.

" Thanks to you, Coaker," shouted the man. " We was just in time—ran into him two hundred yards from the stone heaps under Hey Tor. Mrs. Windeatt, from up over, got the brush."

They were gone, but they had done their work, and any possibility of a reconciliation vanished.

The girl turned white with passion now.

" Cruel devils ! " she said. " And you—all your work. And you can go and never see me again. God's my judge if I don't mean it ! If you refuse me the life of a poor fox while we're courting, what will you refuse me after we're married? And so I'll refuse you everything—everything—and dare you to speak to me again ! "

" Listen to reason, Petronell."

" Not from you—never from you ! I'd only listen to cowardice from you ! My father was right. 'Tis a fool's trick to marry beneath your station, and I won't do it."

Now he flamed in his turn.

" No ! You wait for a royal prince to come along. You're a damned, silly, sulky, little, headstrong brute—that's what you are—and you haven't got the sense of a mouse. You've insulted me a dozen times to-day, and I'm not the sort to take that and come whimpering up and licking your hand after. Please God, you'll never hear my voice again."

" So much the better for me," she said. " I've heard it once too often. The man who would betray a dumb animal would betray anybody."

She moved down the hill and he went in another direction. It was now growing dusk and pouring with rain. Sheets of grey vapour scudded across the hills, and the ponies turned their backs to it.

On the high road not far distant a dozen members of the hunt trotted by the Master, whose coat turned purple at the buffet of the rain. All were happy and cheerful at the success of their sport. Elsewhere Mrs. Windeatt, the richer for a fine brush, went her way to Kingshead.

Only the hearts of Petronell and Elias were dark. In silent gloom he returned home, while she, chilled through by rain and sorrow, crept to her chamber and wept while she changed her clothes.

She could not keep her secret griefs to herself, and spent half the night in Sibley's bed being kissed and consoled. The recital was long, since Sibley had to pretend she did not even know of the engagement; but when she heard the tragic particulars, when their beautiful dreams and secrets and private postbox and various adventures, extending over more than a twelvemonth, were poured into Sibley's ear, she could not fail to realise the dreadful nature of the day's work, or sympathise very heartily with her forlorn sister.

" 'Tis always uncertain with them red-haired men, and I dare say you're well out of it, though you may not think so for the minute," she said. " They will sport, you know; 'tis in the blood of the silly things. You'll have to overlook it— if not in him, then in another. The sportsmen be the best sort, sister—you'll find that. The chaps that ain't sportsmen may have more brains; but they've got different failings. Men are always unfinished things, compared with us; and yet nothing's more unfinished than us—without them. You must wait for another. You be far, far too fine for a Coaker."

" I know it," said Petronell, recovering slowly. " I know it, and I told him so; and he admitted it, though he was got in a towering passion by that time. And he looked a lot properer man in a rage than when he was yowling and throwing up his hat to make the hunters see. I wonder if he's awake now."

" I'll lay he is," answered Sibley. " Tramping his chamber and tearing his hair. Be sure of that. 'Tis a comfort, or should be, to think what a ragged-tailed, tousled, red-eyed wretch he'll look to-morrow."

CHAPTER XIII

TEN months were passed since Mr. Sweetland of Tunhill Farm lost his wife, and during these days of mourning he had not been idle. Agreeably to the spirit that set down the names of various women on a piece of paper, and decided that all were eligible in different degrees, Samuel Sweetland, as he told his sister, Harriet, kept in touch with each lady and endeavoured, so far as a newly-made widower might decently do so, to interest and attract not only Mrs. Windeatt of Kingshead, and Nelly Gurney of Dunstone, but also Miss Tapper of " Genoa Villa," Miss Mary Hearn at the post-office, and even Araminta Dench, as a remote possibility.

He wanted a wife badly, and was unhappy without one. His temper suffered, and his sister also suffered. Therefore, when there came a day upon which Samuel decided that he might set forth, Harriet was glad, congratulated him on his immense patience and self-control, and herself put a finishing touch or two to his toilet.

" 'Tis time and more than time," she said. " Your disposition is sweet as sugar by nature, but it have been called to undergo a dreadful strain without a doubt. 'Twas bad enough to wait, let alone the dead set made on you."

" I wouldn't say that."

" You're too modest, where the females are concerned, to see it; but I see it. You couldn't say ' good morning ' to Nelly Gurney, or send a brace of birds to Widow Windeatt, or drop in at the post-office to ask Mary Hearn after her nerves—you couldn't do none of these things without waking a fire of hope in them. Such a one as you—with your power over females and fascinating ways and kindness of nature—why, you be oil to fire in the heart of a man-loving woman. They can't help it—I don't blame them; but there 'tis, and I'm glad for all their sakes you be going to settle on one. For my part I'll welcome Louisa Windeatt very gladly, and the sooner the better."

" We mustn't count our chickens afore they're hatched," answered Mr. Sweetland. " How do you like this here blue tie? Coming after wearing a black one so long, it struck on my sight as a thought too garish and dashing."

" Not at all," she declared, gazing fondly at him with sisterly love. " Blue's your colour, Samuel; it suits with your fair skin."

She put her hand to the breast-pocket of his coat and pulled up his white handkerchief so that it might appear.

"Good powers! 'Tis one of the mourning ones!" she cried. "That'll never do to-day. You don't want to thrust it down the woman's throat that you're a widower. That's there in the background, we all know; but it must be left in the background. I'll get a white one."

Mr. Sweetland wore his Sunday black, with a hard bowler hat and dark red leathern leggings. Now Birkett Johnson brought round his horse, and he mounted.

"Get me my jujubes, Harriet," he said. "I'm sure to want them."

Mr. Sweetland trotted through Widecombe, saluted the people here and there, nodded to Arthur Pierce, who stood at the door of the "Old Inn," and declared to Young Harry Hawke, at the entrance-gate of Woodhayes, that the days were getting shorter very fast. Then he climbed the steep hill to Kingshead Farm, aloft on the shoulder of Hameldon, took his horse into the yard, handed the bridle to a man, who ran forward touching his hat, and went to the door. From this uplifted spot a bird's-eye view of Widecombe might be obtained It stood highest of all the ring of farms, and the Moor rolled to its outer gate.

Mrs. Windeatt was at home and would see Mr. Sweetland. He took a jujube, wedged it into a hollow tooth, where it could melt in peace, and made his bow.

The widow was letting out a habit; she set down her work, rose, and shook his hand.

"Why, Mr. Sweetland!" she said, "'tis a month of Sundays since you were up over. Whatever brings you, I wonder?"

"Of course you wonder," he answered, "but I shall not keep you long in suspense."

"I'm putting on flesh," she declared frankly, "and 'twas high time hunting began for me. The South Devon has made a good start. Foxes are plentiful."

"So I hear. No doubt you get a 'Dartmoor Greyhound' among your poultry sometimes."

"Often and often. I believe the rascals know they're welcome here. If a duck or fowl helps 'em to stand before hounds, then who with a kind heart would deny it to 'em?"

Mr. Sweetland had an inspiration.

"There are foxes and foxes," he said. "There are four-legged foxes and two-legged foxes, and I dare say some of the two-legged sort come here oft enough to see what they can pick up."

" No, they don't.   We're out of the way of tramps and beggars."

But the farmer had not done with his figure.

" There's some sorts of thieves what locks and bars be useless against.   And I'm one of them."

" You ! "

" Don't be startled."

" I'm sure I should be startled to hear you were out after what didn't belong to you."

He sighed.

" You've got a wondrous nerve for a woman, and I don't want to cast you into hysterics, or nothing of that."

" What a man of mystery you are!   Hysterics?   Me!   My goodness no—I'm not of that sort.   You've come to take what don't belong to you?   But you're an open thief seemingly, and not ashamed of yourself, for you've put on your black and new leggings and a wonderful blue tie to do it in."

He smiled indulgently.

" 'Tis rather a way I've got of fogging the female mind. My dear Tibby often used to say that I soared above her intellects."

" 'Tis your voice perhaps more than the things you say. You talk quick, and when you are interested in a subject it runs up into your head, till it sounds more like an excited guinea-pig squeaking than anything."

He started and regarded Mrs. Windeatt with surprise; he even flushed a little.

" I—but let it pass, let it pass.   I'm sure you don't want for to hurt my feelings.   A guinea-pig—well, well! "

" Hurt your feelings, my dear man !   Not likely.   But haven't you noticed it yourself? "

" I can't say I have.   My voice sounds to my ear much like any other man's; and I'm sure I hope it don't sound like a guinea-pig's in your ear, Louisa Windeatt, because if it do. . . . I'm here about serious matters."

" So you are then—I can see that in your eyes—and I'm ever so sorry.   You tell what 'tis you want—and I lay you'll be very welcome to it as a willing gift."

" I think so, too," he said easily.   " A little bird has whispered to me that I shan't get ' no ' for an answer.   Still we lovers—go on with your work, Louisa—we lovers are kittle cattle and the finer sort, that is to say the modest sort—a man like me, in a word—though everything seems to smile and promise a fair answer, yet such is our humble nature and lowly stand before the sex of women, that somehow we can't take ' yes ' for granted."

She laughed kindly.

" I'm ever so glad. But why did you want to see me about it? "

" Who else should I want to see? "

" Well, I suppose you are aiming at a woman, and mean to marry again, and have come to tell me the secret."

" My word, Louisa! You be very near so modest as I am myself," he answered. " I see you think I've come to tell you I'm in love; so I have—so I have, Louisa. But I'm not a man to give confidences or let out secrets, and there's only one reason why I mean to tell you what's up. Only one. Keep steady—I mean it—in a word I've cast my eyes round Widecombe, I've fixed 'em on you, Louisa. I've chosen you out to sit on the throne at my right hand—so to speak. I know what you are—far above common women—full of sense and understanding. I shall be a lucky man—and I'm ready to own it afore everybody. You'll tell the people that you're a terribly lucky woman, and I shall tell 'em I'm a most fortunate man. 'Tis a very fair bit of give and take seemingly. You've had a husband and I've had a wife, and you mustn't let your bad luck come in the way; you mustn't compare me with John Windeatt."

" Don't fear that," she said quietly. Her manner had changed, and she was exceedingly calm. " My husband was a good bit misunderstood. He was hard, but he was a man —far above this knock-kneed generation, in my opinion. No, I don't compare anybody with him."

" Well, well, we won't disturb the dust of the dead, then. Life is knocking at the door. I have long felt that we were made for each other. We think alike in so many ways, and your female wit often lands you in just the same opinions that my reasoning powers land me. I said only three nights ago to Harriet, as I looked across the valley, I said, ' Louisa Windeatt and me are like twin stars shining over Widecombe—one o' one side the Vale and one the other ! ' She answered that I ought to put down my thoughts in writing for the people to read, and I dare say I ought. But the point is that these things spring out of my feelings for you, Louisa; and there's that in me, like a hammer hammering home the fixed opinion that you are of the same mind. In fact, if I hadn't known it, and been, as you may say, dead positive of it, I shouldn't be here at this instant moment bubbling— bubbling over for you."

He suited the action to the word. His alto pipe cracked, and he blew foam from his wet lips.

" There! " he said, when he got his breath again. " I'll

warrant John Windeatt never made fiercer love than that!"

"You poor rabbit!" she answered—to herself; but she still regarded him kindly and asked a question.

"You've talked this over with your sister, Miss Harriet?"

"No," he replied; "I wouldn't say I talked it over, because a man like me doesn't invite other people to consider his actions. I've told her, what she knew already, that you're the finest woman in Widecombe; and it followed, from such a high opinion, that since you are free, I should come to you to be my wife, when the hour had struck."

"Stop," she said. "I'm so sorry; but I couldn't."

"Couldn't what, Louisa?"

"I couldn't marry you. It's a great honour to have pleased you so much, but, indeed, you have held me far, far too high. I could never make the sort of wife you want, Mr. Sweetland. I'm too independent a sort—must go my own way and be free."

"Don't let that deter you. My will is iron, so Harriet tells me; but you'd only feel the velvet glove. I should break you in, like I did my dear Tibby; but you wouldn't know it."

"I'm not like your late wife. I feel dreadfully positive that you wouldn't be able to break me in, Mr. Sweetland. If John couldn't, how could a gentle creature like you?"

"I'm not so gentle as you might think," he answered, "and I don't like the way the conversation's going. I come here, in all my might and strength and widowhood, for a spouse, and 'tis for me, not for you, to judge what sort of spouse I ought to have. I've read your character closer than you've any idea for a year—yes, all a year and more. And so far as I'm concerned, 'tis all cut and dried, and I hope your native sense . . ."

She shook her head resolutely, put down her work, and rose.

"It cannot be, Mr. Sweetland. Nothing in the world seems to me less possible."

"Do I catch your meaning, or are you playing about?"

"You must catch my meaning, and I'm not playing about in the least, Mr. Sweetland. I don't love you an atom—I never could. You are not my sort. Some might suit me, but not you."

He regarded her with a mixture of bitterness and surprise. He was exceedingly annoyed. But he considered how to act that she might perceive he was not crushed. Again he had an inspiration, and took a jujube ostentatiously.

"Good-bye," she said. "Good-bye, and thank you for this great honour, Mr. Sweetland."

"If I say ' good-bye,' I mean ' good-bye,' " he answered.
"Don't think that I shall come up your hill again, Widow
Windeatt, because I shall not. And if you reckon that it's
a decent thing to let a man open his heart like what I have,
and then just fling him off like this, then all I can say is I'm
glad. I don't *want* you now. However, I'm not here to judge
you. You won't let this go any further—that's all I ask.
There's a right and a wrong in these things, and 'twould be
the last straw if you whispered a word to anybody else—man
or woman."

"Be quite sure I shan't. I promise absolute silence, of
course."

"Then I wish you ' good-bye,' and I wish you more sense
at the same time."

"Thank you, Mr. Sweetland; I'll try and be wiser."

"And don't you write to me that you've thought it over and
feel inclined to change your mind, nor nothing of that;
because 'twould be all in vain now."

"I promise faithfully I won't. I quite understand that this
is final."

"You've brought your doom on yourself, as far as I'm
concerned."

"I know I have."

Mr. Sweetland preserved his haughty mien until out of sight
of Kingshead; then, at a gate beside the way, he drew rein,
stood still, and drearily surveyed the gloaming gather over
Widecombe. He was much disappointed and very astonished.
He had not dreamed of failure; the thing was incredible. Only
an excess of modesty, as he believed, had ever led him to
suggest second and third strings to his bow. Here, however,
was a woman who didn't' want him in the least! Had she
desired no man, he might have escaped without loss of self-
esteem; but she said clearly that men existed who would suit
her. He racked his brains to conceive of the sort of husband
she would prefer to him. Then sharp anguish overtook him
when he looked ahead. It was necessary that he should return
home to acquaint his sister with his failure, and the prospect
tortured him. Could it be avoided? He stood at the gate
and looked between his horse's ears into the valley beneath.

"Is there any way out? " he said to himself. "I'm sure
'twill break her heart to hear of this."

Far beneath, but not far distant, he saw a dim red spot in
the gathering gloom—a point of russet set in evergreen from
which twilight fast sucked the colour. It was the roof of Miss
Tapper's villa residence.

"Why not? " he mused. "She was third on the list, but

that doesn't much matter. She's well-made and has education, and reads books, and is a thinking woman. After all, these fox-hunting women . . . And it can never come out. She'll have to keep silent for decency's sake. In fact, she promised to. But she'll smart to her dying day when she hears what I did the next minute."

He rode into the valley, crossed Webburn, and ascended to the iron gate of "Genoa Villa." Miss Tapper herself arrived from Widecombe as he dismounted, and was delighted to see him. One of the hosts of Smerdons, from Bone Hill, passed at the moment, and Mr. Sweetland promised him twopence if he would hold his horse for half an hour. Then he went in, and Miss Tapper rang for tea.

"I'm sure this is a great treat," she said. "You have not honoured my humble home for at least six weeks."

"But I've often wanted to come," he assured her, "and I knew that I should always be welcome when I did. Tibby thought a tremendous lot of you."

"And I of her," declared Miss Tapper. "She was a noble sufferer—a living Christian and a living lesson."

CHAPTER XIV

MR. SWEETLAND conducted his second campaign in a manner lacking diplomacy. It was an adventure undertaken with mingled motives on the spur of the moment. Regard for Miss Tapper may be said to have constituted the least ingredient. He wanted to talk about Mrs. Windeatt, for she was uppermost in his mind. Mr. Sweetland, in truth, permitted himself to be very vulgar now; but the vulgarity was hidden from his hostess, who did not know whence he had come or what he had been doing.

"You don't often hear me criticise anybody," he said. "My simple rule is to find the good in us all and leave the bad alone. But I'm bound to say that Louisa Windeatt is rather aggravating to serious-minded folk."

Miss Tapper nodded. She was pouring out the tea.

"She must be, I suppose. I often smile to think how different people are. Mrs. Windeatt can't be much younger than I am, yet, to look at us you'd think, so far as age is concerned, we might be mother and daughter."

"Not at all," declared Samuel. "Far from it. You grow old—I mean you get on in a quiet and dignified way. She tries to cheat time and goes fox-hunting and playing about like a girl. Give me a dignified woman."

"'Life is real, life is earnest,'" quoted Miss Tapper. "Life is a matter of intellect, Mr. Sweetland. Life, in fact, is all a question of what we put first. My father showed me what really mattered while I was still a child. He had great contempt for those who do not put away childish things."

"These new-fashioned ways, and running after pleasure, and dressing young, and so on—like a sheep pretending 'tis a lamb—I've no patience with 'em. But there's one thing I'll say to your face, Miss Thirza Tapper, and that is that them like you shine something amazing by contrast with the other sort. You put such feather-headed things as Louisa Windeatt in their proper place. In fact, compared with you, she's no more than a laughing-stock."

"There's no occasion to compare her with me," answered Miss Tapper. "She has a good heart, and she's a shrewd and clever creature. We were on a committee together once—the Committee of the Children's Hospital. She abounded in suggestions."

"Silly ones, no doubt."

"Not at all—not silly. They came from a warm heart."

"Perhaps I know her better than you do," said Samuel. "We'll leave her. She dyes her hair without a doubt."

"I don't think she does."

"She does, I tell you," snapped the farmer. "And no doubt she starves her waist of room and so on—like she does her feet."

"Really, Mr. Sweetland! To think a man should observe such things!"

"Bless you, I don't observe. I only hear all this mentioned. My precious Tibby was a very keen observer. She always put you first—above them all."

"She was a dear, good woman, and I miss her to this day, Mr. Sweetland. She said to me once that my choice of words was so wonderful. I often used words that she had never heard before, and when she was doubtful how to pronounce words, she came to me. I don't claim much for myself, however. It was all my father's work. He had a great grip of languages, and could speak French and Italian like a native. He traded to Genoa, and knew it as well as you know Newton Abbot."

"Miss Tapper," said the farmer, "I'm here this evening for a solemn purpose, and I'm not going without my answer

In a word, I want you to consider me in a new sort of way. We've been friends, and good friends, thank the Lord, for twenty years. But I've thought ceaselessly upon you since my wife went to another world, and it has grown up in me to be a sort of . . . in a word, I respect you something wonderful, and, if the word may be used without offence on this virgin soil, I love you. We're old-fashioned people, you and me, and none the worse for that, though no doubt your Widow Windeatt and such-like empty stuff might giggle. In a word, 'tis a sacred thing, and I kneel down. I kneel down here on this carpet in your presence and offer for you. I want to marry you, Thirza. I'm still in sight of fifty—you *look* forty-five, and if you wore your hair younger and left off they little indoor caps. . . . In fact, you've got old before your time. But there 'tis. I love you. I want you. And why the mischief not? "

None had ever proposed to Thirza Tapper before, and it was a secret grief to her that she had been passed over. She would never have married, but a proposal she had always desired. It was the crowning glory, and a sign that one stood with the conquerors. As there are women who seek motherhood—not for the children's sake, but merely that they may be as other women—so there are those who regard their lives as incomplete unless their sex challenge has been accepted. Miss Tapper was one of these. She had no wish to marry; but she had a strong wish to feel that she might have been married. And now the man bleating on his knees had gratified this whim; henceforth she had stood among the elect who had been offered man and declined him. She was enormously grateful to Mr. Sweetland. She regarded the incident as highly dramatic, and with delicate sense of proportion struck a theatrical note similar to his own in her reply. She lifted a hand over the lover's head, and said, " Rise, dear Samuel Sweetland! " as though she were knighting him.

For a moment he misunderstood, and thought that all was well. He helped himself up with the arm of her chair and attempted to kiss her hand. But she drew it away. Both were flushed and excited.

" I beg you—I beg you! " she said. " You must listen. It is a great honour—a very great honour to be singled out. I wish my dear father could have known—perhaps he does. Indeed, I'm sure he does. But I have long ago decided never to marry, dear Mr. Sweetland, though if I had ever thought of such a thing, I could have dreamed of no better, kinder, nobler husband."

He put his hands in his pockets, and stared at her. He panted.

"Good God Almighty! D'you mean 'no'?" he asked in thin, shrill syllables.

She came to herself somewhat quickly at this. It was not the words but the tone of voice that steadied her.

"I mean 'no,' and I don't think you ought to say it quite like that."

He was thinking and looking back. He laughed unpleasantly, and glanced round for his hat.

"At any rate, you say that I should have been the one you'd have chose if you *had* chose—that's something—cold comfort, but better than—somebody else's damned insolence. However, you've spoken, and I've heard. It's not my day out seemingly. If anybody had told me when I woke this morning that . . . But words are thrown away. I've wasted enough. Blest if I know what's happened to the world. You'll be sorry for this, Miss Tapper. Mark me: you'll regret it."

"I shall regret giving you pain," she answered. "I'm too refined, I hope, not to regret it in that sense. One never gives pain willingly. But I cannot pretend to regret that you cared for me. I am proud of that circumstance—exceedingly so."

"Then why the mischief——"

"That's different. It couldn't be. I'm too old, and I'm a spinster. I have the spinster habit. You have already been happily married, and, quite naturally, want to go into the state again. I say nothing against marriage. Only it is not for me. But I shall always be very grateful to think how I won your love—and quite unconsciously, I'm sure."

"All the same, I'll thank you not to let it out—not to a soul, least of all to a woman. I've paid you a great honour, and it would be a base and cowardly act to let it out."

Again she flushed at his hortatory tones.

"Don't spoil it," she said. "Don't forget that you speak to a woman with very good blood in her veins. These things happen to all sorts, I believe, and it is possible that common, mean creatures might boast of a conquest, and so on. But you have offered your hand in marriage to the daughter of the late Lindley Morris Tapper, of the Merchant Marine. The event, to a woman of my delicate feelings, is sacred. To God only shall I mention it in my prayers. I shall pray for you, dear Mr. Sweetland."

"I don't want you to pray for me, or anything of that sort. That's all silliness and moonshine. Put the incident out of your head. I dare say you're right. Probably you're not the sort to shine as a wife. Now I'm away. Good-bye to you.

Forget everything. I'm not myself this evening. It's all a mistake."

He bustled to the door, and in the narrow hall kicked against some large seashells—curios collected by Miss Tapper's father. He hurt his foot and swore.

" Why the devil do you stick this rubbish in the middle of the passage for everybody to bark their shins against? "

She was behind him, and answered on the doorstep.

" Nobody has ever run against them before. As you say, you're not yourself this evening, Mr. Sweetland."

" Oh, go in," he replied; " don't keep echoing. Let me get on my blessed horse and ride home."

Samuel mounted and rode home. The problem that awaited him was, in his judgment, the most difficult that he had ever been called upon to face. Pride rebelled at the confession he must now make to his sister. He hated the thought of it, and before he had got home he began to wonder whether the ordeal was necessary. He considered the problem from various points of view, weighed the safety of a lie, and came to the conclusion that a lie would meet the case and save his honour. The women were both silenced, and he was safe from them.

Harriet appeared to be one large question when he returned; but she did not speak, and waited for him to do so.

" Nothing has happened, after all," he said. " Or, rather, great things have happened—things of the spirit. I've had a sort of revelation—same as Paul the Apostle. A blinding light, you might say. It seemed as if something came between me and Kingshead—regularly stood in the way, and stopped the horse from going up the hill. I can't explain; but it was borne in upon me that, what with the fox-hunting, and light-mindedness in some directions, Louisa Windeatt wasn't the one to follow Tibby, after all. I felt suddenly that she couldn't do it, in fact. It wasn't for me to argue, for the light came from above. And then, standing still and wondering, the name of Thirza Tapper rose uppermost, and there again, in some mysterious way, the light put her out, too. I found that Miss Tapper had got suddenly to be quite out of the question—all in a flash, like. I'm sorry for the women, and sorry for myself; but these things are in Higher Hands. No man in his senses could afford to flout them. And so I've done nothing, and yet, in a manner of speaking, I've done a great deal."

" These things don't happen by chance to a prayerful and religious man," declared Miss Sweetland. " And you're dog-tired, I see. I'll get the whisky. I hope you're not cruelly disappointed, Samuel."

" I was; but a long ride and a lot of thinking has brought

me to see 'tis for the best. You can cross the two out of the list. And I shall want a good few days before I stir in the matter again."

CHAPTER XV

HER adventure cast a new colour over life for Thirza Tapper. Each day the significance of her achievement awoke with her as a fresh and lively verity, gave a zest to life, and a fillip to her sense of her place in the eternal scheme. Only one regret tinctured her mind : none could know of the triumph, since unwritten laws demanded that no woman should reveal a proposal for marriage, or the name of the man who made it. Such was her old-fashioned and distinguished sense of propriety and decorum.

The minor incidents of Mr. Sweetland's rudeness she forgot. Only the offer of marriage remained. There were, however, outward signs of her experience, though she guessed it not. She held her head higher than ever, became more sententious and choice in her phrases, and minced in her going, like a game hen. But her kindness increased. She was benignant and beaming, and let her cup of joy run over. People who observed and discussed her little affectations and pomposities, suspected that she had been left a legacy. Indeed, this was the case, and it might have been said that what the farmer had offered under stress of mind—a gift worthless enough on every real count—became enshrined as a master jewel and precious heirloom among the spiritual possessions of Thirza. A man had wanted her.

Miss Tapper was still moving in this exalted atmosphere when, on a winter morning, there came strange visitors, and two humble people, in the shape of Margery Reep and Jack Mogridge, desired to speak with her. The girl was looking very wretched; the man appeared anxious and troubled. Miss Tapper knew them both, and was aware, through Margery's mother, who did chores at " Genoa Villa," that the young couple entertained a great attachment, but that Mr. Alfred Mogridge, Jack's father, refused to sanction any engagement.

" Me and Margery thank you for seeing us, Miss Tapper, Jack spoke, and defined a tragic situation.

though we be much afeared you'll take a very dark view of us. In a word, we've took the law in our own hands, and tried to force faither's hand, and now, when 'tis all done, very clever and regular according to the laws of nature and such like, faither won't budge an inch. And, in a word, me and Margery want for to know what to do about it."

" You don't marshal your ideas, Jack Mogridge; you don't put your speech in order. You had better begin at the beginning, instead of the middle. Let Margery speak for you both."

" No, Miss," said the girl. " Not me. I was 'fraid of my life to come at all, and I won't tell about it—God's my judge. Jack wanted me to speak afore we ordained to ask you, but I wouldn't. ' No,' I said to him, ' 'tis your work we be going to tell about, and you be the man, and I'm the weaker vessel, and I ban't going to squeak.' Didn't I, Jack? "

" You did," answered her lover. " And I've screwed myself to the deed. And I'll start again, if us ban't wasting too much of Miss Tapper's precious time."

" Go on, then," said Thirza, " and begin at the beginning."

" The beginning was when me and Margery went courting, and faither forbade it; but manhood will out, and so us went walking together unbeknownst. Then come the tragic affair of faither's carrier-pigeon; and faither swore on the Book as none of his should ever take a Reep. I be terrible under faither's thumb, and I confess to it. Braver men might break loose from faither, but I ban't brave, and Margery knowed that when she took me. So us plotted in secret to do by cunning what us couldn't do by force, and the tip was to put faither in such a fix that he'd have to say ' yes,' willy-nilly. And now we've done it, and of course faither ought to see the position that he be in about it, as a religious sort of man. But he won't—and so 'tis us be in a fix, not him. And if I wasn't under his thumb, I'd scorn him; but I be; and he denies and defies me, and won't let me and Margery marry even now."

Miss Tapper sighed.

" You get so mixed up, Jack," she replied. " Do try and arrange your statement more lucidly—more lucidly, Jack Mogridge. Now, let me see. You and Margery have done something which you think ought to compel Mr. Mogridge to sanction your engagement. But he is proof against it. In his judgment, then, the course you have seen fit to take does not necessarily indicate an engagement, and, perhaps, still less, an alliance between the families. And what is that step, Jack? What is your plot? "

" 'Twas a manly thing, whether or no," answered young

Mogridge. " Just me and Margery—and she's in the family
way."

Thus he burst his news upon Miss Tapper, and saw shame
make her face rosy. Her curls trembled. She took a long
breath, and did not speak instantly.

" Our hope by in Mr. Mogridge being such a religious and
church-going man," explained Margery, who found herself
more composed now that the truth was revealed. " We said
that if we took a strong step like that, that Mr. Mogridge—
such a Christian man as him—wouldn't rest till us was axed
out in church and wedded. But now we be cruel cast down
to find he don't care at all, and be just as much against me
as ever he was. I should be sorry for a lady to hear what he
said to me."

Silence fell, and four eyes peered anxiously into Miss Tapper's
countenance. She cleared her throat, straightened her back,
and regarded Jack and Margery.

" You did evil that good might come," she said, " and good
has not come, and the rest of your days will be spent in all the
dust and ashes of dead sea fruit."

" Have a tell with Mr. Mogridge, Miss," said Margery.
" Us can't make him do right about it; but you might."

" ' Do right,' wretched girl? Who are you to try and make
people do right by doing wrong? Don't you understand that,
for your own petty purposes and plans and selfish affections,
you have broken the laws of God and man? "

" Us don't see it in that light," explained Jack. " We
want to be married in church, and what we say is that the
nation ought to see that we be married this instant moment.
And if I wasn't under my faither's thumb, I'd go and tell
parson to ax us out next Sunday. But there 'tis : I be like a
man with palsy afore faither, and he's said that I shan't be
married, in his hardest voice; and what next, Miss? "

Thirza Tapper considered her father and the past. He
had been large-minded in these cases.

" You have sinned through the depths of your ignorance,
doubtless You have substituted low cunning for manly self-
assertion—— Let me consider. Yes, one sees your muddled,
unintelligent reasoning. And your guile is being answered by
your father's brutality. Since you were man enough to do
what you have done, then you must also be man enough to—
in fact, between your earthly father and your heavenly Father,
Jack—— It lies 'ike that."

" If you'd only have a slap at my earthly faither, Miss, I'd
gladly go on my knees to God A'mighty," promised the youth.
" And so would Margery. We be a very prayer-making pair,

and us thanked Providence something wonderful when it happened, because we thought then for sure that the end of our trouble was in sight. And it came as a terrible ugly jar when faither laughed, and said he was level with the late Daniel Reep at last, and refused the marriage. You see, his view is to make Margery a bad character, and I say it ban't sporting, and hope that somebody will have the wit to get round faither."

" You are a wretched thing, Jack, and you ought not to need anybody to come between you and your father at this juncture —I say at this juncture, Jack. You are a poltroon. Your duty is here."

" So it is, and I know it," answered the youth. " But 'tis no good telling to me like that, because faither's put the evil eye on me and got me in his power. I be shamed to say it; but 'tis the naked truth, and Margery will tell you the same."

" He's like that," admitted the girl. " Nobody's more sorry for it than Jack himself; but so it stands. He can't act if his father forbids. 'Tis a very peculiar, unfortunate thing—like as if he was tied with ropes; but so 'tis with Jack, and his father knows it and does according."

" Very well," answered Thirza. " Then I act—Nature never holds her tongue. The thing must be known. It must be blazed abroad. Your father shall hear of this in quarters that will surprise him. First, you must go to the vicar."

" No," answered Jack firmly. " I don't do that. I'll go to him quick enough, but only with the altar rails between us. I know very well what the Reverend Brown will say. I get enough dressing down to home without him. What have to be done is this : faither's got to be took in hand, and made to understand that if he won't suffer me to marry, he'll be hit himself and punished. As a jobbing gardener he's a good bit at the mercy of his fellow-men, and if they be all o' my side, then they can soon make it clear to him in the only place where he'll understand it. And that's his pocket."

" Your idea is as mean as what you have permitted yourself to do," retorted Miss Tapper. " But I see your point. We must have no nonsense about you being under your father's thumb. You must assist me; and I shall enlist the aid—I shall enlist the aid, Jack, of certain of the better class—the God-fearing."

" Dad works for Mr. Dunnybrig, Tuesdays, and for Mrs. Windeatt, Thursdays," explained Jack; " and me and Margery both think that if they knew, they'd soon dismiss him, if he wouldn't budge."

" They probably would do so. Does he work for Mr. Sweetland of Tunhill?"

" No, Miss."

" We must be careful. Obstinacy is the chief peculiarity of Alfred Mogridge. I think I will see him myself first—without threats. Threats are very dangerous weapons with a character like his. I will appeal to his Christianity, and ascertain whether it be skin-deep or not."

" Of course it be," declared Jack; " he's a hateful, beastly toad at heart—a proper, spiteful, revengeful creature, and don't care a cuss for religion really. He only pretends."

" Well, he cannot pretend any more—that is something. He is now faced with a problem in which pretence will be impossible. He must do right or wrong; there is no middle road, and there can be no two opinions. And as for you and Margery, you'd better ask God to forgive you for taking His laws into your own hands—or, it would be truer to say, for breaking His laws. However, enough has been said. You'd better go. I shall do what I believe to be right."

They departed doubtfully, and when they left the outer gate of " Genoa Villa " they began to compare notes and opinions as to their idea of the interview.

Jack held it of little use, but Margery was more hopeful.

" She's a clever old thing, and thought a lot of, I believe, by them that don't laugh at her. She'll set about your hateful father, and if she takes his work away he'll jolly soon change his tune."

Left alone, Miss Tapper's thoughts turned to the eternal question of sex, and she considered it with interest, but no knowledge. " Passion is a terrible thing. I thank God I never felt it," she said to herself. " I have, however, seen it. It lighted Mr. Sweetland's eyes undoubtedly when he gazed upon me. It made his voice—— Yet I never feared him. I felt armed at all points with the shield of modesty. But he couldn't help his eyes, and I suppose he couldn't help losing his temper. No doubt to cherish a hope for a year and then to have to relinquish it—— We women little know what awful conflagrations we kindle. And when it comes to the poor and ignorant—like this unhappy boy and girl. Of course, without the sanction of religion, love is merely—one can't pursue it—— We must feel safe and snug within the pale of the Church, even to allow our thoughts to play upon that complicated and solemn subject. Of course, there is sacred love as well as the profane sort. But men——"

CHAPTER XVI

SIBLEY and Whitelock Smerdon made holiday together in the deep woods where Webburn meets with Webburn and the rivers foam joyously together after long journeyings from their cradles on Hameldon. A single larch sprang above watersmeet, and its delicate emerald spired upward through traceries of young golden oak-leaves, that flashed round about. The dingle was full of breaking green under a panoply of great trees.

" 'Tis a terrible purty spot, sure enough, and I seed a woodcock last time I came here," declared the man.

" Find a lew place for us to sit and eat our meat," she answered.

" You shall eat and you shall drink," he answered; " and not the river neither, as no doubt you thought 'twould be! I've carried two pint bottles of pale ale hid in my coat—one for you and one for me."

Greedy Sibley rejoiced.

" I'll give 'ee a hundred kisses for a glass of beer this minute ! " she said; " and let me have the beer first. I'm as dry as dust along of such a walk."

" Don't forget what a solemn day it is, however," he reminded her. " There's great matters in the wind for us, and we shall want all our sense and cleverness to decide about it."

She admitted this, but bade him postpone the problem.

" Leave all that till after lunch," she said.

" Bananas, too, I see ! You are a darling to me, Whitey ! " Whitelock smiled.

" 'Tis what I feel, and so I do according. Nought's a trouble for you, and what makes it a pleasure is that the things I do, you notice. That's the salt of 'em for me. Now, Elias Coaker, he confessed to me a bit back along—naming no names, of course—that there wasn't anything more confounded cruel in his opinion than taking a lot of thought for a maiden, and her never noticing it. Of course he confessed he was tokened once—long ago; but I'm not supposed to know who 'twas. But we know very well. Be they friends again? 'Tis half a year, very nigh, since they fell out over thicky fox."

Part of the joy of lovers lies in criticising other lovers. Sibley continued to be deeply interested in Petronell's tribulations; she had even offered herself as a peacemaker, but her sister would have none of it, and declared that she desired no reconciliation with Elias.

"Thank the Lord we don't go on wires, with all our claws out, like them two," she said. "And for my part I hope very heartily that they won't make it up. People such as them ought to marry their opposites. Now, you and me suit each other every way."

"Like the halves of a flail, Sib—one nought without t'other."

"So we do, then, you dear; but they belong to different breed. They scream at their bad luck, and think every man's hand's against them. I saw our cat in the garden yesterday. He'd just eaten a young thrush, and the mother bird was two feet off his head, on a bough, giving him all the law and the prophets about it. A proper tantara she made; but the cat blinked up at her, and licked his chops, and cleaned his face, and heaved a sigh of comfort, and then stretched himself out and went to sleep, peaceful as a sucking-child, while she and her neighbours sat above him and raised clatter enough to waken the dead."

"The very image of the way poor Petronell goes on against the world; and of course the world don't care a cuss. She must find a man as will be good and kind and regular in his habits—a man as will enlarge her mind, and not let her turn his hair grey or ruin his life. She's got nerves, without a doubt."

"And so have Elias, and surely a man with nerves be no good to anybody. Look at Arthur Pierce."

He nodded.

"There'll be gay doings in that quarter afore long. We've some reckless spirits among us, and Tom Gurney, the blacksmith, will get the surprise of his life afore he's six months older."

"Him and Mrs. Pierce, you mean? I was in the post-office a bit ago, and Mary Hearn said that Widecombe would soon be a byword."

"She's an old fool."

"A prying creature, too—always wanting to burrow into other people's business."

"Just her," declared Whitelock. "My mother says she expects everybody else to be open as day, while she bides close as wax herself. My mother hates her, and hates to think as her letters goes through that woman's hands. In fact, my mother thinks that she wouldn't be above opening 'em. All the same, she's right about Tom Gurney. She saw him in the field behind the 'Old Inn,' with his arm round Mabel Pierce. And of course she took care to mention it here and there."

Sibley sniffed.

" You men are a lot worse than women over a thing like that," she said. " 'Tis always said that we can't forgive it and you can; but, from what I see, the men here are just as nasty-minded, and busy about other folks' business, and quick to think evil, as the women. Don't you have nothing to do with that sort of thing. Be like my father, and take a high hand, and be too proud of yourself to mess about with dirty little gossips and scandals."

" Trust me," he answered. " Your father is a very good model, and a wonderful man, and nobody wants to pleasure him more than what I do."

" The time has come, anyway. He's got to be faced, and we'll go afore him together, or singly, just as you please. It would be more braver for you to tackle him single-handed, and he'd think better of you for doing so."

" Certainly," replied Whitelock. " This is man's work."

" Don't be too humble and don't be too proud," she said. " A good while ago—cunning and casual like—I asked about your family, and he said 'twas pretty old and highly respectable, and no black marks much against it. And he said that nowadays we couldn't look or expect more from the lower middle class."

" Faint praise. However, I must go afore him fearlessly."

" He'll talk about ' contracting an alliance,' and things like that. You mustn't mind. He's always reading and reading, and the book talk soaks into him till he gets running over with it. Then he tells like a book himself. Sometimes he'll say a thing just the same as you or me might, and then he'll correct himself and say it over again in fine words. But he's gentleness and kindness alive under it all. 'Tis no more than a bee in his bonnet, as they say; but it ban't a stinging bee."

They turned to each other and dismissed the stern needs of the future for a little while. They walked hand in hand through the spring wood, rejoiced to be alive, and felt themselves at the very heart's core of the rolling world.

CHAPTER XVII

THE problem of Jack Mogridge and Margery Reep was just such a one as Valiant Dunnybrig delighted to approach. Indeed, he paid all attention to Miss Tapper when, true to her word, she visited Chittleford Farm and placed the matter before him.

His wife was out at the time, and he was glad, but Thirza Tapper was sorry. She hesitated, and proposed calling again.

" There are things that happen which one cannot discuss with a member of the opposite sex unless a member of one's own sex is present," declared Miss Tapper.

" Are there? " inquired Valiant, stroking his patriarchal beard and smiling down upon the spinster. " To me, as you know, nothing is common or unclean if sanctified by the spirit in which we approach it. But I can very well understand that to the maiden mind—— In fact, don't go; I'll call my niece, Araminta. She is also unmarried, but she has a clear sight, and isn't easily shocked. I hate unreality, Miss Tapper. I like to be at grips with the truth about life. I wrestle with it naked, as Jacob wrestled with the angel."

" You are wonderful, Mr. Dunnybrig—quite wonderful, I'm sure. But do call Araminta."

He obeyed, and the sly, silent woman appeared.

"Araminta," said Valiant, " Miss Thirza comes on a subject that's rather too delicate to pour into the male ears alone. So she can talk to you and I can listen."

Araminta gave a little laugh and said nothing.

" It may not be news to you," began Thirza. " At any rate, one need take but few words to portray the sad fact. Your gardener, Alfred Mogridge, has a son called Jack, Mr. Dunnybrig, and that son has got a girl into trouble."

" Ah! " said the man. " When two people join to bring an immortal soul into the world without the sanction of the Church, we call it ' getting a woman into trouble '; when they do it otherwise, then——"

" Why, of course—common sense, surely. It is getting a woman into trouble, and there's nothing on earth more troublesome for a woman than to bear a child without the sanction of society. Put religion on one side, if you like, though you are the last to do that."

" I don't put religion aside—not for one instant," retorted Valiant. " I never put religion aside. I never look at any question, great or small, from any other standpoint but the religious. I don't cut hay—I don't draw swedes—I don't thresh wheat, without prayer; nor yet eat a meal, nor so much as teel a trap for a rat, without religion. And what's the result? I'm different from everybody else in Widecombe. Because religion be more to me than the air I breathe. And living so close to it as what I do—closer than my shirt to my body, you might say—I get a whole host of new ideas different from

other people's, and I see deeper, and understand better, and can
look God in the Eye same as Indian hunters can stare at the
sun. Marriage wasn't invented to make children legitimate :
it was invented to bring 'em into the world. But the world
being what it is, and property being what it is, the rights of
the unborn have to be considered. We make a cruel fuss if a
man or a woman's unkind to a babe; but the unkindness after
they are born is generally nought to the unkindness before. I'll
have it out with Mogridge. I'm all for the children—like the
Saviour before me. Leave it to me. I'll be ready for the man
next Tuesday, when he comes here to work."

They parted then, and in a few days, when Mr. Mogridge
with his tools arrived at Chittleford's noble entrance, there
stood up Valiant Dunnybrig and stopped him.

" List to me," said Valiant. " It hath come to my ears,
Alfred, that you won't suffer your son to wed his sweetheart,
though there's every reason why he should do so."

" Not every reason, by no means," answered the gardener.
" There's one damned good reason why he should not, and
that's a stronger reason than all the others put together. And
the reason is that I won't have it. Why for d'you stand in
your gate and keep me out, Valiant Dunnybrig? "

" Because, until I hear sense and decency from your lips, I
don't want you in. Set down your tools, Alfred, and use the
little wits that God has given you and list to me. Marriage
and giving in marriage must be taken in a large spirit, and
I'm not going to pretend that our laws and regulations on the
subject are all they should be. We've broke away from God's
rule and ordinance in that matter a good bit, and what He
smiled upon and allowed was right and proper, this generation
have dared to call wrong and improper. And it may be left for
me to throw a bit of light on that matter some day, because
practice is better than precept. But marriage is the first step
for single people who love each other, and without it a bachelor
and a spinster who come together be living in sin. So there it
lies. Your son and Mrs. Reep's daughter must wed at once."

" Why for? " asked Mr. Mogridge, thrusting forth his lower
jaw and putting down his tools. " Why for? "

" To save their souls alive in the first place, and to justify
the existence of the new-born child in the second place. The
child is everything—a new soul—a flame-new soul coined in the
mint of God and sent into this world for His Almighty purpose. Out of the least may come the greatest; out of the
dungheap may spring the lily. There's no end to the possibilities when a child's born, no matter how humble the parents.
Look at me. Who would have thought my poor father and

mother could have done it? But so God willed, and here I stand."

" And if you had childer, no doubt they'd be first cousins to the angels in heaven," sneered Alfred.

" Out of the mouths of fools cometh wisdom," answered Valiant. " You touch a subject that has long occupied me and my Maker. And it has pleased Him to make the purpose clear. But that is not the question between us. I say that your son shall marry Margery Reep as quickly as it is possible for him to do so."

" And I say he shan't."

" He is of age. It must be put to him."

" I say he shan't, don't I? That's enough for him. He's got no will away from me. He wouldn't eat his meat if I told him not to do it."

" Poor creature! And yet he has been allowed to take a hand in the next generation! That's a mystery. But, since it has happened so, it behoves us to do our part. I bid you take off this blighting control you have over your son. You would have been punished for a witch for such doings fifty years ago."

" You bid me! You can't bid me, Valiant Dunnybrig. Nobody can't bid me. I'm free, ban't I? I'm doing no wrong. I say that my feckless fool didn't ought to marry— least of all ancther fool. Do we want more fools—more and more? Fools breed like rabbits always—'tis a law of nature to keep the weak going against the strong. They have to take it out in numbers."

" I didn't expect any thinking powers in you, Alfred," answered Mr. Dunnybrig; " but I can meet you there willingly enough another time. Now we'll stick to the subject, which is that your Jack marries Margery Reep. There's a new soul on the way by God's will, and if it's a fool, as we have every reason to expect, that, too, is God's will; and if, after they're married, they bring a dozen more fools into the world, that also is God's will. Brains don't get a man into heaven; in fact, they're more likely to keep him out. In my experience, the cleverest men are the worst as a rule. God plans all—for the best. He plans everything. He don't ask you for your opinions, or want 'em. The fact remains that Jack ban't married to Margery, and God's quite clear about that. It must be done inside the month."

Mr. Mogridge retorted with blasphemy. He cursed Chittle-ford and Valiant Dunnybrig; he defied heaven and hell to shake his purpose. His son should not wed—upon that point he was absolutely determined—and not all Widecombe nor the United Kingdom would shake him.

" Daniel Reep don't get the laugh of me—not for a thousand gardens," he said. " 'Twould be like a cup of water to his lips, where he is, to hear tell about it; and never, never shall he—not for you or any other meddlesome fool. I've done with you, and I hope to God the canker and the caterpillar and the blight will spring up in their might and millions and show you what you've lost ! "

With that Mr. Mogridge shouldered his tools, spat upon the threshold of Chittleford, and departed from the farm, while the farmer stroked his beard and looked thoughtfully after him.

He read " Horrors and Terrors " that night to Mrs. Dunnybrig and Araminta Dench until the clock struck ten. He even gave Mr. Mogridge a quarter of an hour's grace. But Alfred did not come.

CHAPTER XVIII

WHITELOCK SMERDON chose to appear before Mr. Shillingford on his twenty-first birthday, and, happily for him, the master of Blackslade was in a good temper. For the day was Sunday, and Mrs. Windeatt had paid one of her visits. Her effect upon Gabriel Shillingford was always beneficent, and this his daughters knew; therefore they asked the widow to see them oftener than she held it possible to do so, though not oftener than she would have liked to come, because Shillingford attracted the huntress of Kingshead. They had no parity of tastes; their views seldom ran alike; their opinions differed; their outlook upon life varied in fundamental particulars; yet, for all that, Louisa Windeatt cared for the man, and knew it very well; while he, too, cared for her, and went the happier for her friendship, but did not know it. Her companionship, however, left its mark upon him, and those most interested were very quick to observe both the sedative and tonic effects produced thereby.

Young Smerdon arrived before Mrs. Windeatt departed, and then, when she took her leave and the girls were gone to see her off, he lost no time in coming to his business. He had rehearsed the exact words all night, and was letter perfect an hour before the interview; but when it came—when he sat before Mr. Shillingford, with his hat on the floor beside him, and a cup of untasted tea at his elbow, the fine phrases flew beyond recall.

Gabriel was calm and at ease. His simple mind could put aside anxieties on Sunday, and he looked to the day to soothe him and repair those ragged edges that life was apt to tear. He found himself more than usually driven for money just now, but pinned his hope on promising stock that would go to market in the autumn.

" I've got a bit of a startler for you, Mr. Shillingford— begging your pardon, I'm sure. And—and least said soonest mended."

Thus Whitelock heralded his news, and thrust his speech abruptly upon the farmer at the moment when the latter was discussing church observance, and had only paused a moment to take breath.

" A startler, Smerdon—a startler ! "

" There's no other word for the thing. It's grown gradual, and I couldn't help it, nor more couldn't she. We was in up to our necks afore we knew it, in a manner of speaking, and we found it out the same moment, and she said, ' Make sure, Whitelock—make dead sure before we do anything final '; and I said, ' So I will, then.' Such was our great sense and caution. And for a solid year, and more than that, we kept company and no more, and unfolded our feelings, and got to know each other inside out—in a manner of speaking, Mr. Shillingford. And then I said, ' Shall we be tokened? For I can't live without you, God's my judge.' And she said, ' Yes, we will; for I can't live without you, neither.' So there 'twas —a very perfect understanding. And there it is—and now you know it."

" I'm sure I congratulate you, Smerdon. And I hope that marriage will be all you think it. If the girl has sense and patience, and has been brought up in a good home by sensible parents, all ought to go well. But it is not a ' startler '—by no means, because I'm a student of character, and a great observer of the springs of human action. You are just the sort of young man who falls in love early. And, for my part, I never had any objection to early marriage. Its advantages——"

" Wait, wait, sir, I do beg you ! " cried the lover. " Blessed if I haven't left out the most important thing. Good Lord ! So full of her, I be, that I thought—silly gawk !—that her name must go without saying ! In a word, 'tis Sibley—your blessed Sibley, or, I should say, my blessed Sibley. Yes, mine, if you please. And God's my judge, I'll make her such a husband as was never known out of a story-book. I'm cruel poor, and ban't of much account, I'm afraid, and not worthy to tie a Shillingford's boot-string. I know all that afore you tell me; but there 'tis—love, a fierce and fearful sort o' love I've got for her, and 'twill move mountains come presently, if 'twill only move you first. And I beg you won't say ' No ' out of hand, Mr. Shillingford, for I bear you a wonderful deep respect, and honour for yourself, and more yet because you're Sibley's father."

" ' Miss Shillingford '; you should speak of ' Miss Shillingford,' Whitelock," corrected Gabriel feebly.

" Yes, I know that. Miss Shillingford she is to the nation, but Sibley to me—my own precious masterpiece of a Sibley. Good God! in high moments I've even called her ' Sib.' Scores and scores of times I've done it. You don't understand—and yet 'tis like my cheek to say that, for wasn't you a fine lover yourself in the distant past? In a word, there 'tis, and I come before you so humble as a worm, Mr. Shillingford—so humble as a worm and also so proud as a turkey-cock. I've won her fair and square against everybody. Single-handed I've done it, and you mustn't think 'twas easy. She have got a great pride, I'm sure; and her love of me never made her forget her father, or what was due to him. If I'd been low or common, or rude, or made love in a coarse sort of way, she'd very soon have sent me packing. But we couldn't do wrong in each other's eyes, in a manner of speaking, and I do beg and pray, dear sir, as you'll see 'twas one of these things arranged by Higher Hands."

Mr. Shillingford regarded the perspiring man, and watched him mop his face. He harked back to Whitelock's original warning.

" A ' startler '—yes, certainly a ' startler.' 'Tis a word I haven't met before. But a very good word for the thing. In fact, you want to ally yourself with my family? I must say you have a pretty cheerful conceit of yourself, Smerdon."

" It looks so, no doubt; and so it did to me a year ago. I was properly dazed to think I'd got such cheek. But that showed all the more 'twas the real thing, because nobody in Widecombe would offer for her unless they was uplifted far above themselves, same as I was."

Mr. Shillingford appeared to be stricken dumb. He gazed solemnly at the young man, then began thoughtfully to bite his thumb.

" A ' startler ' is certainly a very good word for it," he repeated.

" With her—with such a one as her—I should rise to great things without a doubt," declared Whitelock. " I should certainly lift myself higher and higher, because her quality would draw a man up. I know, only too terrible well, how it looks to you, and if 'twasn't for the great and rash love we've got to each other, 'twould be a ridiculous thing, and a very one-sided bargain, indeed; but love—at least, so I thought——"

" I had considered the chances of my daughters marrying above their station, and decided that was impossible," said Mr. Shillingford, " because the exact rank they ought to hold can't be proved. Nobody of nice feeling would deny it to them; but plenty of people have no nice feeling, and plenty are jealous and demand proofs, a sure sign of smallness of mind. Still, love, as you say, is stronger than long descent. In these cases a parent has to consider more than his child—the welfare of the next generation. Our branch of the Shillingford race will cease with me, but the traditions must be handed down, and my grandchildren must feel great reverence and respect for their mother's family."

" They shall ! " cried Whitelock. " God's my judge, they shall ! 'Tis the very first thing shall be drove into their little baby heads ! "

Sibley entered at this juncture. She had been listening outside the door, and felt this to be the proper moment for her appearance. She was on her father's breast instantly, with her arms round his neck.

They talked for a long time, and a most unexpected individual saved the situation.

" I yield," said Mr. Shillingford, " because perfect love will conquer. It overrides everything, and I perceive that it exists between my daughter and you. Love is to be seen in the eyes. Your eyes burn. It must go through, though I tell you frankly, Smerdon, that I had hoped for a man rather higher in the social scale than yourself. But there is a saving clause—your maternal grandmother. She was a Downe from Holdsworthy, never forget that. In Prince's ' Book of Devon Worthies ' you may read an account of John Jewel, Bishop of Salisbury, a North Devon man, born at Bowden, and a great pillar of the Church. ' A rich shop-full of all choice and precious knowledge,' had he, as Prince says; and he was a man greatly ski'led ' to polish such pearls as are found in the word of God.' Peter Martyr was his friend. He was exiled for four years, and returned to England again, and happily laboured in his own county of Devon to carry the light of the Reformation. A very great man, and I have every reason to believe that your grandmother was descended from his sister, Joan, married to

John Downe of Holdsworthy. Therefore, though many generations separate you, you may say that the blood of Bishop Jewel runs in your veins. I will look into the pedigree of the Downes again. There was, of course, John Downe, the son of Joan Jewel—a pious clergyman, and he lived to see his children's children. To him Death was but a drone without a sting. We will look into these relationships more thoroughly now. For the moment all that matters is your betrothal to my daughter Sibley. A very great thing for you and yours, Whitelock—a very great thing.''

Mr. Smerdon rejoiced above measure, and could have taken his lover in his arms and danced with her, singing praises to God and Gabriel the while. But he restrained himself, shook his future father-in-law's hand with respect, and thanked him with humility for accepting him—one in every way unworthy to be united to a Shillingford.

'' But I'll do my bestest,'' promised the young man. '' Night and day I'll work like a team of horses to lift up my head in the land, for 'tis the man himself that counts, and you shall live to be proud of me, I do assure you, Mr. Shillingford.''

'' The fortunes of my house are low at present,'' confessed Gabriel, without the least embarrassment. '' It would have been a joy to me to dower my Sibley in a manner becoming her name and herself; but I must warn you, Whitelock, that, though she will be wedded with all proper ceremony and in keeping with the traditions of the race, there will not be money to go with her. An heirloom or two—that is all at present. Blackslade, however, will descend to her when I am gone.''

'' Don't talk of such things, father,'' pleaded Sibley. '' D'you think my darling boy here wants money or anything of that? He's a worker, and good for thirty shilling a week —ain't you, Whitey? ''

'' All this must be gone into,'' declared Mr. Shillingford. '' I must have time to consider the future. You work for other people at present, Smerdon, do you not? ''

'' For Mr. Macfarlane, at Bag Park.''

'' Well, as my daughter's husband, the case is entirely altered. We must see. It might be better that you came to me. As my son-in-law it is very doubtful whether you could work for Mr. Macfarlane at a salary. You are translated now —at least you will be when you marry Sibley. A salary may not be seemly in future. However, we shall go into that presently. You had better tell your parents that I sanction the engagement in a large spirit, and that I feel sure the blood of Bishop Jewel never ran in the veins of a bad man, and that I hope the union between our two houses has been planned by

Providence to help the happiness of the world. Your father will wait upon me at his leisure, Smerdon; or, since he is a senior man, I will visit him."

Very grateful, yet thankful to be alone again with Sibley, Whitelock went out from the presence.

The lovers departed together to see a litter of convenient kittens in a loft; and there, cuddled close, they babbled their joy into each other's faces for a while. Whitelock blessed Mr. Shillingford with all his might, while Sibley apologised for him.

" The darling dear—he do mix himself up with the King of England sometimes," she said; " but you're that quick and clever—you understand his little ways."

CHAPTER XIX

THOUGH he did not himself appreciate the fact, it was Mr. Shillingford's habit to drift up to Kingshead when any matter of moment overtook him. The Widow Windeatt had long perceived this, nor were Gabriel's daughters ignorant of it; but himself it would have much surprised to learn of the unconscious custom.

He rode thither now, making thereby a detour from his path, for he was bound presently to Bone Hill that he might see Peter and Martha Smerdon, the parents of his future son-in-law.

Mr. Shillingford declared much astonishment to find that Louisa Windeatt knew all about the engagement.

" Good powers! And not forty-eight hours old! " he said.

" A thing goes round Widecombe in forty-eight seconds," she told him. " The Vale is a whispering gallery, or else the birds bring the news. I had it from little Teddy Smerdon who is working here; and I had it from Tryphena Harvey, who is often here from Southcombe; and I had it from Nelly Gurney of Dunstone. And I wish them joy. Sibley's a dear girl, and he's a very sensible young fellow."

" I'm going to pay a visit to his parents at this moment. They are worthy people, and it is not for me to stand in the way—though I don't mind confessing to you that I could have hoped better things. However, my circumstances are unhappily such that I cannot very well dictate."

" Of course not; and you would have been a great deal too wise to do any such thing, if you'd been a millionaire. They are beautifully matched, and I'm hoping that Whitelock will come to live with you; he's a practical farmer, and I know the Bag Park people already begin to fear he will leave them."

" The details will work themselves out. There is an inclination on their part to marry as soon as it can be done. They have been attached for a long time, it seems. But it took them some while to screw up their courage to approach me."

" Such an ogre of a man as you—of course ! "

" Do you know Valiant Dunnybrig? " he asked abruptly.

" Who can help it? He is what one understands by a personality. He always seems to me several sizes too large for Widecombe. I've often wondered what his wife thinks of him."

" He has that assertive, Nonconformist way which somehow always sends a shudder up my spine. It is very wrong, of course; but the Nonconformists make me creep. I respect Dunnybrig for a good and a brave man, however. We can learn from the least as well as the greatest if we are humble. I met him on the way and told him the news. He, too, had already heard it, curiously enough. Well, he listened, and said that it was good. We conversed, and he made this interesting remark. I have considered it all the way up your hill. It showed a breadth of vision. Perhaps it was one-sided, but I'm not prepared to say there is no truth in it. Dunnybrig abounds in these flashes of sense."

" You have not told me yet what he said that struck you," answered Mrs. Windeatt.

" He said that I think more where a person has come from than where they are going to. It isn't true; it isn't true at all; but I grant that there's a germ of truth in the accusation."

She nodded.

" Well, you must have a bright wedding, and you must ask everybody—at least——" She recollected that Mr. Shillingford's means were much restricted at present.

" Have no fear as to that," he answered. " There are times when the pecuniary resources of a house must not be considered, and the marriage of an eldest daughter is one of them. There must be an element of dignity."

" Better be jolly than dignified—it's cheaper. Don't you go and waste a lot of money, there's a wise man."

" We owe it to ourselves," he said. " These things are remembered. My position in Widecombe is such that I am expected to do a little more than others. There was a time—

however, that time is passed. But fifty pounds will go a good way if spent with judgment."

" Don't you do it! " she cried; " or, if you must, then let me help——"

He gasped.

" Good Heavens, whatever are you saying? From anybody else——"

She longed to kiss the big hand that lay on the table beside her.

" Oh, you silly blind thing! Don't you know how fond I am of Sibley? "

" I shall be very grateful for your help in details. You are the kindest woman, Louisa—and so generous! It is a trait peculiar to high minds. But the base sneer at it, and think it foolish. It is a dying virtue. I suppose the whole of Widecombe will make holiday. There is a report that the Smerdons have a medical man in their family. I did not know this."

They talked for some time; then Mrs. Windeatt reminded her visitor of his intentions.

" You'd best be off now, else you'll be late for tea at Bone Hill, and you may be sure they'll have arranged a great spread for you. They are simple creatures, and well worth knowing. Peter's a keen sportsman, and he and his old pony do marvels when hounds meet within reach of them."

He departed, rode into the valley, climbed to the home of the Smerdons, where a sunset smile lit the whitewashed front, and presently took his place amongst them at table. Here reticence was impossible, and reserve not understood. Homely and unsubtle folk were these. They lived in a frank atmosphere of children. Life was punctuated by children. Their birthdays stood for the seasons and commemorations of the year. They had bred children, thought children, worked for children, and fought for children through more than a quarter of a century. They knew not pride, but took from anybody who would give. They were not at all alarmed at Mr. Shillingford, and greeted him without self-consciousness or self-deprecation. Mrs. Martha Smerdon was a barrel-shaped woman, still pleasant of face. Not a line could live on her plump countenance. She was of a sanguine complexion, with bright golden hair, still long enough to sit on—as she was proud of declaring. Her husband was tall, high-shouldered, and loose cheeked. He began to grow bald, and his expression belied him, for it was anxious, whereas in truth care seldom sat on his pillow.

Five children were sitting at the tea-table, but a special place had been reserved for Mr. Shillingford, and the young people were walled off from it by a loaf, a large pot of blackberry jam, and a dish of home-made cakes.

" Us be all in a muck, same as ever, master," said Mrs. Smerdon genially; " but you won't mind that. ' Childer come first,' as granny says, ' for they'll have to do the work of the world when we'm past it.' "

" Us thought to see you a bit earlier in the afternoon," said Mr. Smerdon. " Have Whitelock took your hoss? He's been waiting around a good while."

" Our tea be thin after yours, I reckon; but you'll take us as you find us, I'm sure," declared the mistress of Bone Hill. " Of a Sunday, when I can, I put in a bit more; but when the home be holding ten mouths, and often twelve to sixteen, along o' goings and comings, us have got to count the tea-leaves, I do assure 'e."

Mr. Shillingford smiled upon the children, who went on eating regardless of him. He sipped his tea, took food, and marked the red evening light along the row of young heads.

The children were regarding the dish of cakes, and their round eyes sought their mother's.

" I've told the dears as they wasn't to have no goodies till you'd helped yourself," explained Martha Smerdon. " You see what obedient toads they be. Put a couple on your plate, master; then us'll give 'em the rest, and let 'em run off."

" I shan't want one," answered Gabriel.

The children had the cakes and departed. Mrs. Smerdon then enumerated their names, qualities, and distinctions.

" Our childer comed in two batches," she said. " Fust there was the grown-up lot, with Whitelock and Emma, as married Young Harry Hawke, and Jane, in service to Bag Park, and Ethel, the deaf one, to Plymouth, and Westover, the railway-engine stoker; and then I rested for five year— a most unheard-of thing, but a godsend to me, I'm sure. ' I was like a giant refreshed with wine,' so my husband said; and at it I went again, and these five come in nine years, not to name a pair of dead twins."

" They are nicely brought-up children. That thin boy's squint might be cured. The little girl is pretty—the blue-eyed one."

" Minnie—so she is, then, and Sibley likes her the best. But us have got no favourites, have we, father? "

Mr. Smerdon spoke.

" I like 'em on and off—according," he said. " Sometimes 'tis one pleases me special and sometimes 'tis another. They've all got a good slice of their mother in 'em. And what more should any child want? "

A thin voice quavered out of a dark corner behind a screen by the fire. It murmured something about the children, but Mr. Shillingford failed to catch the remark.

" 'Tis only my wife's mother," explained Peter. " You needn't take no count of her. She'm mostly tootlish."

But Gabriel was more interested in the grandmother than his host imagined. Through the grandmother came hope; by way of her existed a possibility of kinship with the great Doctor Jewel. He rose, looked round the screen, and found a venerable woman shrunk to skin and bone. She was wrapped up in a heap of odds and ends—a shawl, a blanket, a quilt. A black cap covered her head. Her face was small and brown and wrinkled. She was murmuring to herself.

" Dear mother will go dwaleing on and on like that by the hour," explained Mrs. Smerdon. " My Minnie minds her. 'Tis something surprising. She'll do what she's told like a lamb if Minnie tells her. But she'll fight against me and father."

They talked in a rambling, indecisive fashion, and at last Mr. Shillingford, feeling an increasing uneasiness, prepared to depart.

He looked at the window, where darkness gathered, and Martha understood him.

" You be finding it a thought stuffy in here, my dear? And so it is; but us have to keep the chamber emetically sealed for gran'mother. If a blast of fresh air reaches to her tubes, she coughs her soul up."

" Lives on peat smoke, you might almost say—my wife's mother do," said Peter Smerdon. " For five years she've bided in that chimbley corner, and only crawled out now and again of a summer noon. A regular, old bed-lier she'll be till she dies."

" Doctor says 'twill come as a thief in the night. But she's ready," said Mrs. Smerdon.

" I don't want to die," piped the ghostly voice from the corner.

Peter laughed.

" You see she can follow conversation quite clever like that, when you least expect it."

" She'll often chip in when we be talking about her. And then for days she'll be hidden from us in a cloud, and we don't know what she's dreaming about more'n the dead—may be not so well, for she'll often talk out loud to folk as have been long dust in their graves."

The physical and mental atmosphere of the Smerdons began to make Gabriel pant. He felt deeply concerned for the aged creature in the corner; he had not the imagination to enter into these lives; he desired heartily to be gone. He changed the conversation and said the thing that he had come to say.

" I hope this match will be a very happy and prosperous one. I think very well of Whitelock. He is an honourable and upright man. Time must decide what plans are made by me in the future. We shall see. My daughter, of course, inherits."

" Inherits what, master? " asked Mr. Smerdon. " What does she inherit? ' Inherit ' be a great word in the ears of a small man."

" She inherits my estates."

" Oh—Blackslade? Nought else? They do say there's a bit of a rope round Blackslade's neck—a mortgage, in fact. Perhaps it ban't true? "

The other flushed.

" I object to my private affairs being discussed, Mr. Smerdon. It is not seemly."

" God forgive me, then," answered Peter, " for 'tis the last thing I meant. I was only going on for to say that our Whitelock be a proper nipper over money, and can make sixpence do the work of a shilling. I thought perhaps 'twould cheer you to know that. For, by all accounts, you'm one of they open-handed heroes that forget you've spent your cash, till you look round for it and find it gone. Now, I can say in all sober honesty that us don't know the meaning of money here at Bone Hill. It comes into my right hand and goes out of my left. My gold and silver be my wife and family—and my wife's mother yonder."

A gurgle came from behind the screen.

" In a word," summed up Martha, smiling, " we be poor as birds, and very near as cheerful. We've helped on the human race something wonderful with five boys and girls, and we ban't in the least shamed to remind our fellow-creatures that 'tis their duty to reward us. And you be a poor man, too —to say it without offence, my dear? "

" With only two maids and Blackslade all your own, I should have thought as you could have put by a pinch for a rainy day, or a daughter's wedding," continued Peter, " but that's your business, of course. And as you say she'll have the farm when you be gathered in. And if you make a clean breast to Whitelock about what be owing, you'll never repent it. For he'll set to work to straighten the figures—and beg, borrow or steal you out of your fix."

" I'm *not* in a—good gracious, man—how can you say these indecent things? " gasped Gabriel.

The nakedness of the Smerdon mind was only equalled by its absolute sincerity. But Mr. Shillingford resented such artlessness with all his might. No air-drawn dreams made atmosphere for them; no visions, no comely if nebulous imaginings ever softened the stark reality of their lives. The master of Blackslade felt as one fallen among naked aborigines, who were stripping him of his clothes also. Their simple, innocent eyes went through him.

" ' Ondacent ' ! " echoed Mr. Smerdon. " Why for? I be only telling you that, though my Whitelock ain't got any more money than your Sibley, yet he's the sort that can be trusted to make it. I thought you and me was alike—just honest men, but no use to anybody where cash was the matter. I thought you muddled along up to Blackslade pretty much like I muddle on here to Bone Hill. I thought the only difference was that I'd managed to keep clear of debt, by living so hard as a fox lives, and that you, with your higher opinions, and bigger ideas, and famous havage, had outrun the constable a bit here and there. Of course, between friends I be talking—between men as will soon be relatives, you may say. God, He knows I wouldn't tell like this outside our own families. Close as adders be me and Martha to the outer world. And who thinks the worse of you or me for being hard up? 'Tis the state to which it has pleased God to call nine men out of ten."

" I must go," said Mr. Shillingford, rising almost wildly as one under an incubus. " You mean well—I grant that you mean well, Smerdon. But you don't understand. We must have a certain reserve—a certain—I hardly think that I can explain what I mean really. There are some things—— In fact, we look at life from rather a different standpoint."

" I'm sorry, I'm sure—too blunt and common for you, I'm fearing. We've got nought much to hide—me and Martha. Our little lot be out in the world."

" For all to see and admire," added Mrs. Smerdon.

" And we pay our rent, and only eight times in twenty-eight years have it been overdue," she added.

" We shall get to understand each other better, master," concluded Peter. " You mark me, we shall grow very good neighbours, and a tower of strength to each other."

" We be thinking about the fine clothes for the wedding a'ready," declared Mrs. Smerdon.

Her husband laughed.

" And we'm glad 'tis a boy and not a maid this time," he said. " For you've got to find the feast as best you can, neighbour. You'd bust your sides laughing if us told you how we was put to it when our Emma took Young Harry Hawke. And

Timothy Turtle, to the ' Rugglestone Inn,' gave us four bottles of brown sherry as a gift. And we took it in the spirit 'twas offered and we don't forget, though I dare say he has."

Gabriel almost staggered when he returned to his horse; and then Whitelock Smerdon appeared.

" How do you like them? I hope they used you civilly, and as became them, Mr. Shillingford," he said.

" Yes, yes—all will be well. They have a remarkable power of coming to essentials," declared his future father-in-law. " They are a type of our old yeomanry—the people who live face to face with Nature, and are not frightened of her. There is much to learn from them."

" Especially mother," declared Whitelock. " She's a wonderful witty creature under her weight of flesh. And so brave as she's fat. The more you know her, the more you'll like her. And she says that Sibley's just perfection, and far too good for the likes of me! "

Mr. Shillingford rode away. The night air cooled his forehead and calmed his mind. He drank deeply of it, and endeavoured to correct his perspective. He wondered why the Smerdons had caused him such exquisite discomfort, and perceived that the atmosphere of reality, which they breathed so easily, was far too sharp for him. " My Sibley is marrying into a family of honest savages," he said to himself. " But yet—never to have owed a penny, even at the cost of living like a pig! It has its majestic side, and I'm the last man to deny it. Only it is so easy for them. They are probably more comfortable living in that way than otherwise."

He marshalled his ideas, and thought of kind things to say, that he might give Sibley pleasure when they met at supper.

CHAPTER XX

MISS MARY HEARN, the postmistress of Widecombe, overcome by the stress and turmoil of life, had suffered from temporary breakdown of nervous energy and taken a holiday; but Thirza Tapper, and others who liked her little, did not hesitate to hint that it was not Mary's own business that occasioned the collapse.

" It is the prying and poking into other people's affairs that has exhausted her," declared Miss Tapper severely; and this criticism she uttered in the ear of Mr. Sweetland; but had the lady guessed what was in Samuel's mind at the time, the words would not have been spoken.

For the master of Tunhill Farm was still in search of a wife, and he had decided that Mary Hearn should next be honoured. She was a fine woman of fifty, with dark eyes, a voluble tongue, and a full habit. Her mastery of figures was proverbial, and her mastery of news. As an intelligencer none equalled her. Before Miss Hearn broke down and went to Exeter for a holiday, Mr. Sweetland had taken a few preliminary steps and found the buxom postmistress very friendly.

Now Samuel paid the lady a serious visit, and she called her old mother into the post-office, that she might retire to the parlour with her friend.

" Here's Mr. Sweetland come, mother! " she cried in manly tones. " And he'll be wanting to hear me tell my adventures. So go and sit in the office, please. And if there's any money orders wanted, you call me."

The farmer saluted Mrs. Hearn and her daughter. He scanned the latter with a familiar, almost loverly glance.

" You're better—far better. I see that much without your telling me," he said; and she thanked him, and admitted that it was so.

" You'll stop for a dish of tea come presently? " asked Mary. " And first, how's the world treating you, Mr. Sweetland? You're looking pretty clever to my eye."

" That's as may be," he said, sitting down upon a little redcovered sofa, and putting his hat and umbrella beside him. " We're none of us growing younger. Now, for once, I'll begin and give you the news, Mary, because since you've only been home forty-eight hours, you can't be well up in it."

" On the contrary," she answered, " I've heard all about everything—Sibley Shillingford's engagement, and Margery Reep's baby—though I didn't ought to mention that, I suppose. However, evil be to him that evil thinks. Well, leave that. There's other greater things. Mabel Pierce be carrying on with Tom Gurney beyond anything you'd believe or imagine. So a little bird tells me. There'll be a proper tantara presently. In fact, something is in the wind, and Widecombe will ring with it afore the end of the year. And Arthur Pierce—poor wretch. My heart goes out to him."

" Don't let it," urged Mr. Sweetland. " If your heart is to go out—however, there's a place for everything and everything in its place. Now tell me about yourself. How d'you like Exeter? "

" There's no *news* in Exeter—that's all I complain of against it," answered Miss Hearn. " A large and a whirling city, no doubt, but there's never nothing *doing,* so far as I could see, like there is in Widecombe. A place of strangers; but the organs are very fine in the cathedral. I often went into the House of God for the sake of the organs, Mr. Sweetland, and also owing to feeling so terribly lonely."

" Ah! we'm never lonely in the Lord's house—not if we be good Christians."

" The people where I lodged hadn't an idea beyond their own affairs. The ignorance even in a place like Exeter would surprise you."

" They cathedral towns be cruel narrow-minded—so I've heard."

" 'Tis true; but I gave 'em something to talk about," she said. " A great adventure, in fact. As you know, I got sadly run down—along of the strain of the dog licences and the new laws and regulations. I mastered 'em, and didn't make a single mistake. In fact, my books are a wonder—so I've been told. But there 'twas—the struggle got on my nerves, and I couldn't digest my food, and saw black specks in the air, and a buzzing at—well, the pit of the stomach, to be exact. Between friends one may mention the frame, I suppose."

" Certainly, certainly; 'tis a mark of friendship to be so open, a great compliment to me," assented Mr. Sweetland.

Mary sighed.

" And then the doctor, finding his cautcheries weren't doing no good, bade me up and away. I went, and turned my back on every thought of the post-office. I didn't even answer your letter—though I valued it a lot. I didn't answer—for why? Because the very sound of a pen brought back the symptoms, and set me whirling. All went well till, in a fatal and rash moment, I was urged to go and take a look at the big new post-office to Exeter. I didn't ought to have gone; 'twas flying in the face of Providence, you may say; but there, you know how one's own business draws anybody. So there 'twas —the post-office drawed me, and I went; and the moment I smelled the post-office smell—like nothing else in nature—and the moment I seed a young man tearing off penny stamps from a sheet, and heard the click of the telegraph, there comed a sort of black mist over my eyes at the horror of it all. 'Twas as if I'd seen my own life, like the drowning, and I just gave one piercing screech and dropped my reticule and parasol, and fell lumpus in a deadly faint."

" Good powers, you don't say that! " cried Mr. Sweetland.

In his emotion he held her hand, and in her excitement she suffered him to do so.

"Yes, I fainted dead away, and when I came to, there was the public four deep around me, and a policeman and a man from the chemist's, which, by God's goodness, was next door, else I mightn't be here now. And the whole course of business at a standstill! No doubt, 'twill never be forgot by them who saw it."

"Never, never!" he declared. "Thank Heaven there were understanding people there to be kind to you."

"I wouldn't say that. Just common humanity 'twas—no kindness in particular. They called a cab, but nobody offered to pay for it, nor yet to see me to my lodgings, nor yet to pay the chemist for his physic. Not that I grudged his fourpence."

"Such a thing ought to have been in the papers," he said. "If some silly fool picks a blackberry at Christmas, or sees a butterfly on New Year's Day, 'tis sure to be recorded; and yet a tragical thing like this—anyway, I didn't read it nowhere. And I'm glad I didn't for that matter; because I'd not have rested in my bed till I'd come up to see how you was."

She withdrew her hand.

"We Widecombe people stick together," she said. "We be a regular happy family, you might say, compared with the folk in towns. Not but what the husband of my landlady in Exeter didn't show a great deal of nice feeling. Too nice he was for his wife's peace of mind latterly, and I felt glad to be gone. Them roses, in the vawse there, was his parting gift, and nothing would do but I gave him one of my likenesses."

"Your likeness! I haven't heard about 'em."

"'Twas to please mother. She've got a great passion for likenesses, so I was photographed. The man took three—one sitting with a stuffed cat on my lap—a cosy sort of picture—and one opening the pages of an album—and one looking up listening to a canary in a cage."

"I'm all afire to see them," answered Samuel. "'Tis funny you should have been took, for Harriet's been on to me about being done for very near a year now."

Miss Hearn produced the photographs and permitted the farmer to choose one. Her volubility was infectious. They talked one against the other. Her voice was much deeper than his. She had only to lift it to drown his treble. He blew bubbles from his lips, and squeaked, and waved the photographs; she dwelt at immense length upon each.

"Mother likes the one with the cat in my lap," said Miss Hearn.

"So do I," declared Samuel. "The album be too haughty,

and that one with your head up listening : 'tis as if you was straining to catch the sound of the shop bell. You can't see the canary, or it might be different. But you be waiting to hear something, and 'tis unnatural, in my opinion. But this one—'tis life, and the figure comes out to great advantage, if I may say so.'

" It do," she admitted. " I can see that for myself. That's the one my landlady's husband took. He was an advanced sort of man, and no mock modesty, if you understand me. ' Lord, Miss Hearn,' he said, ' if 'twas only a babby on your lap, now, instead of that beastly cat, the picture would be fit for a Christmas number !' "

" We've heard about enough of him," declared Samuel. " Come back to yourself, Mary."

" We had a picnic, too," she went on—" him and his wife, and his sister-in-law and her young man—a brewer's traveller. A tanner by trade, my landlady's husband was—and a far-seeing creature. He'd married the wrong woman, however, for all his foresight; but he married for money, and had to pay in kind, as all have who do that. I've a way of understanding men—never having got mixed up along with them—and he found it out, and brought me his private troubles. A very good husband—I could see that—but she didn't understand him, and was too close with her cash. He's wrote to me twice a'ready."

" You've been going it, seemingly," said Mr. Sweetland. " I've never heard you talk so openly about a man before, Mary."

" Bless you, at my age—'tis silly to pretend we know nothing. That man said I was his second self ! He was at a loose end, as the saying is, for there'd come a moment when 'twas ' whichy should ' between him and her. They fought in a quiet way from breakfast till supper, and through the hours of night also, sometimes, for I heard 'em often. I could see how 'twas, of course, but I didn't take no sides, nor nothing like that. I just went my way, and pretended I didn't notice anything, as a lady should. Adolphus was his name."

Mr. Sweetland began to grow perturbed.

" Let him rest," he said. " I didn't come here to-day to talk about your new friends."

" He's more than a friend, and he's less than a friend," explained Miss Hearn. " Of course, being as he is, another woman's husband, there's no question of friendship—in the deeper meaning of the word; and yet, owing to understanding him so quick, and my sympathy with him in his difficulties, and so on—— Would you like to see his photograph? 'Exchange is no robbery,' I said to him, when he begged so hard for mine. And so I've got his. 'Twas took a bit back, however, afore he'd been married more'n ten year. He had happier eyes and more hair then than what he have got now. But a speaking brow still.''

The farmer restrained his growing impatience, and Miss Hearn rambled on.

"You shall see it. Of course, it never can come to anything, humanly speaking, since the man's married and we be both good Christians; but his wife's people be pretty near all dead of consumption—like flies they fell under it; and she's got a churchyard cough, and no great wish to live, if what she told me was true. But she's got the money, and she's close as a mousetrap, and very hard on Adolphus. Here he is.''

She produced the cabinet photograph of a fair man, with small, sly eyes, a bald forehead, and pale moustache waxed at the tips. Mr. Sweetland, now fired to say what he thought, spoke slightingly of the portrait.

"A mean-looking creature," he said. "He might be a bit of a knave, or he might be a bit of a fool, or he might be half and half. I don't like the look of him. 'Tis a nasty expression, and I lay his wife be right to keep her eye on him.''

"You oughtn't to judge like that, and I wish I hadn't showed him," answered Miss Hearn, reddening, and withdrawing Adolphus. "And if you heard the way that woman talks against the man, you'd be sorry you let yourself be so rude. A tongue of gall she hath, and flays the poor wretch alive. However, enough said. I won't trouble you with my friends no more, Mr. Sweetland.''

"Be reasonable, Mary. What can he be to me? I'm only saying what I think.''

"And I'm saying you think wrong, and oughtn't to think without more knowledge. Adolphus Dexter isn't half a knave nor yet half a fool. In fact, he's quite as clever and straight as some older men that I know about—if not more so. And because a fellow-creature has had misfortunes, and married a consumptive and childless wife, with a temper like Apollyon, that's no reason why people, who don't even know the man, should pour out their contempt upon him, and say he's shifty. And that's a lie, because he ain't. You ought to be ashamed——''

She broke off, and her massive bosom heaved with indignation.

"I'm sorry—I'm sorry," said Samuel; "but how the devil can you suppose I care a button about the man and his troubles? What can he be to me? I'd meant—however, as usual, I seem to—I'll be gone."

" If you'd listened about him in a different sort of spirit, I should have told you all his difficulties," answered Mary. " As a Christian, and a man a good ten years older than Mr. Dexter, you might have been able to help him—as our duty is to help everybody. I was going to read you one of his letters; but another day——"

Mr. Sweetland jumped up. His attitude to Mary Hearn had changed radically in the space of half an hour. A veil was withdrawn—her voice, her speech, her very physical appearance had altered. He disliked her; he almost detested her. She seemed coarse, clumsy, above all, silly. He hated her deep voice now, and to hear her rambling on in masculine tones about another woman's husband angered Mr. Sweetland. And when he grew angry with anybody, he invariably became insolent. He felt profoundly disappointed and incensed. He reflected on the amount of time that he had wasted in this quarter, and it opened his lips.

" Well, I must go," he said; " and, what is more, I shall not return. It is a pity that you went to Exeter, in my opinion. I don't like the line you are taking, and your mother wouldn't like it either. I should have thought you would have been above it—at your age."

" You surprise me," answered the lady. " I don't know what the mischief you're talking about."

" It isn't so much what I'm talking about as what I was going to talk about," he answered. " I came here to-day with an object. I came expecting to find you what I always thought you were—a woman of very high-minded character, and, above all—well—such a woman as I could look up to as a woman. But, so far as I can see, Exeter's been the ruin of you."

" How dare you say that! " she panted, and sat up in her chair. The chair creaked very loudly.

" I dare say it, because I've got the use of my ears, I believe. Out of your own mouth I judge you. Not to put too fine a point upon it, I come hither expecting to get a warm welcome, and full of a great project, and bursting with the beautiful thought of—of us. And what do I hear? I hear ' Adolphus,' and nothing but ' Adolphus.' Adolphus this and Adolphus that, and his trials, and his sufferings, and his wife, and his business, and how you poked your silly nose into it, and got on the blind side of the man and messed about with him—God knows what for. What was in your mind I shouldn't like to say; it shows a loose nature, and—you needn't make those noises, because I will be heard. I'm wounded—I'm smarting. You ought to have honoured the friendship of a man like me a very great deal more. You knew, if you had the sense of a woodlouse, what I was coming to. You'd only got to be patient and maidenly, and wait my time. I've dropped a hundred hints, and you might have seen very clear what I meant. And then you go and do this—at your age—and come to me—me of all people on earth—full of a wretched, bald-headed tanner—and him married. You properly amaze me, Mary Hearn. Where's your modesty? "

Still she panted. Her lip had fallen. She was staring at him with unblinking eyes that reflected very real distress.

" Is this a nightmare to hear you talking about me so? " she asked.

" No, it isn't? 'Tis for me to wonder if I'm awake, not you. Why was I here? Why was I here in my best clothes? Didn't your woman's heart tell you? Evidently it did not. Good God! I've been sent down the wind like a thing of no account! I'm nothing, of course—a Christian widow-man, respected and prosperous, and so on—I'm nothing against this rubbish with his rat's eyes and long nose. And him married!"

" This is terrible—terrible! " she said. " You're possessed. Something have got into you, Samuel Sweetland."

He laughed bitterly.

" You're right there; something have got into me, and it's showed me the ugly truth that I'd missed. I was like a moon-calf, like a gaby, like a know-nought gert fool when I thought upon you; and I lifted you up to a sort of saint. I came here to-day to offer myself as a husband. That was my solemn and lasting purpose. I was going to offer you the place of my late wife, and lift you up to Tunhill and be your proud and happy husband till the Lord called me."

Unconsciously he relapsed into what he had already committed to memory, and spoke in the present tense.

" You'll find me a man easy to lead, but hard to drive. I've got a large heart, and, where a woman like you is concerned, a soft one. Gentle as a child I am, yet with all a man's strength and power. I love you in no feeble boyish manner; but with the feelings of a strong man. And if——"

" Are you offering marriage? " she said, still staring at him out of her great round eyes.

" Certainly not," he answered. " Not now. I'm only telling you what I should have said—what I came to say—what you've lost. That's the man you might have had, Mary Hearn. But not now. It's off—and so will I be. I'm sorry for what you're feeling; but you've brought it on yourself, and you deserve it."

They rose simultaneously, and it was Mary's turn to laugh. She uttered a deep and equine sound. Her neigh meant irony.

"You needn't be sorry for me. You've made yourself very clear, and now, if you know how to be fair to a woman, you'd better hear me. Of course, I've been waiting and hoping and panting for this, haven't I? Of course, I've thanked God for sending such a man into my life, and dreamed dreams of Tunhill, haven't I? I'm that sort—a woman that runs a big post-office and have earned her own living since she was twenty-one!"

Her tone deepened. She indulged a withering scorn.

"You—you—a thing kept in cotton-wool by your wife and sister! I'm more of a man than what you are! And I wouldn't have married you—not if you'd offered for me twenty times on your bended knees."

"Bah!" he answered. "Go along with you! You say that *now*; but I know better. You were ready to jump, and have been, ever since I took to coming in here off and on. You've only got yourself to thank, and now you can see whether the memory of a hen-pecked tanner will take the place of——"

"Mother!" cried Mary, "for God's sake tell this here wretched old man to go. He's insulting me something shameful!"

Mrs. Hearn hastened in with terror on her face.

"Guy Fawkes and Angels! what be talking about! Farmer Sweetland insulting you?"

"I bandy no words—I shake the dust off my feet," said Samuel. "And don't you go about saying I offered you marriage and you refused, because nobody on God's earth would believe you if you did."

"If I had a man belonging to me, I'd make him knock your sheep's head off for this!" roared Mary, and then Mr. Sweetland swept away, while the postmistress collapsed ponderously in acute hysterics.

Dire sounds startled passers-by, and the frantic old mother rushed out to her neighbours for assistance.

By good chance she met Nicky and Nanny Glubb returning home to their cottage close at hand.

"There's that new young Doctor Grenville over to Woodhayes," cried Nanny. "You lead Nicky home and I'll run like lightning and fetch the man."

She was off at once, and Nicky bargained with Mrs. Hearn that his wife should have a shilling for her trouble when she returned. He went further, and suggested a course of treatment for the postmistress.

" Empt a bucket of ice-cold water from the spring on her head," he said. " It never fails. For a fallen horse or a fainting woman 'tis the first and best cure. I very near drowned my wife like that afore I lost my eyesight. And she never was took again."

CHAPTER XXI

TRYPHENA HARVEY, while making no great impression upon those with whom she now dwelt, yet left a mark on subtler minds. She was a kindly maiden, and the altruistic attitude to life, won hardly by conscientious people, to her belonged as a gift of nature.

Aunt Grace Coaker and Uncle William were pleased with Tryphena, and soon found her a precious addition to their small home circle. She was fond of work, and since her personal tastes could not be shared by the master and mistress of Southcombe, she did not intrude them. The charm of the girl attracted many to her, including Gabriel Shillingford. He liked to see her and talk with her. His daughter Petronell quickly loved her; while another friend was Mrs. Windeatt of Kingshead. Miss Tapper, too, welcomed her, and was pleased to show Tryphena the curiosities of nature that Captain Tapper had collected in his wanderings. Her red-haired cousin especially attracted the new-comer; indeed, none interested her more than he. Books and nature and Elias were the distractions of her mind; but she put Elias first. They had become close friends, and the young man found Tryphena a sympathetic confidante. In time he much rejoiced her by whispering the secret of his love-affairs, and Tryphena gained importance from her own point of view, as the recipient of such sacred things. She went under the weight of the great romance, and felt it a solemn and momentous matter. Indeed, she fell in love with Elias herself, and believed that no such rare spirit dwelt in Widecombe. She praised him often to Petronell; but then Elias broke to her the shattering news of his quarrel and rupture with his sweetheart, and Tryphena found life darkened. She suffered almost as much as the lovers, and strove her utmost to make Elias forgive Petronell and go back to her and make it up. She also prayed Petronell to take the first step; but neither would yield; the long-drawn difference persisted, and Tryphena became quite obsessed with such a tragedy. She was timid, but possessed a very active conscience; and now, as month followed month, and Elias moped and Petronell grew paler, the watcher began to tell herself that here was work for her. Its magnitude terrified her, but her conviction would not sleep. It returned and clamoured: she began to feel that she must do something, if only to recover her own peace of mind.

It was long before she ventured to meddle in the matter. Only by night did the enterprise appear reasonable; with daylight it always assumed impossible dimensions. But having convinced herself of the necessity, Tryphena could not evade her task, and in desperation she set out at last to see Petronell and plead for Elias.

Gabriel Shillingford's younger daughter was at home and alone, for Sibley had gone to Newton with Whitelock Smerdon. Thereupon, Tryphena, who felt happier in the open air than under a roof, declared that she had something solemn to say to Petronell, and begged her to come into the garden.

They walked together and talked of books; then they sat on an old rustic seat, under a laurel in full flower, and the younger approached her task. She delayed, however, until Petronell challenged her.

" And now what solemn thing have you got to say to me, you grey-eyed dear? " asked the elder suddenly. " You're in love, perhaps, or think you are. Or somebody's told you he loves you—is that it? Everybody's in love in Widecombe—but me—I do believe."

" And you, too—you, too, Petronell! Don't say you aren't —don't say you aren't! " cried the other. " It's a terrible deed; but I've come to try and make you happier."

" You funny girl—what d'you mean? "

" I mean Elias, of course. Oh, Petronell, you loved one another so beautifully. And love can't really die, can it? "

" Yes, it can, Tryphena—nothing easier. And once dead——"

" But if you'd only see him."

" I have, quite lately. He's all right. He's got over it."

" No, no, I'm sure he hasn't. He only pretends."

" He told me so, anyway. And you mustn't think that we older people have your tender little heart. We're harder. And you wanted to bring us together again—you brave dear! "

" But—but—— " cried Tryphena, " you take the words out of my mouth so! I'd thought of such a lot of fine things to say."

Petronell's eyes were misty. She kissed Tryphena.

" Be sure that we've thought of everything, too, and suffered horridly, and wished we were dead, and gone through countless pains and griefs. It was bad enough for us both, but it's over and done. I was talking to Elias not a week ago—quite calm and collected and cold."

" Oh dear, oh dear," sighed Tryphena, " how bitter sad! And perhaps if I'd tried to do something sooner, before this fearful coldness came to you, Petronell——"

" It never was like that," declared Petronell. " My love for Elias died the day the poor fox died. I suppose you know about it. He betrayed the poor fox, and from that hour I didn't only not love him, but I properly hated him. For months I hated him. And then I happened to read in one of father's books that we are what we must be, and that character is stronger than love. That explained Elias Coaker to me. He had to do what he did. So I stopped hating him—you might as soon hate a nettle for stinging : 'tis born to sting, and can't help it. Now, he's just like everybody else to me, and I'm just like everybody else to him."

Tryphena was much disappointed.

" You are *not* like everybody else to him, whatever he pretends, and I'm sure something might have been done about it," she said. " 'Tis a terrible sad pity—two such beautiful things as you and Elias; and Sibley going to be married and all."

" Don't you worry, you funny, soft-hearted dear. You'll have to begin worrying on your own account some day soon, for you're a lovely thing already. And don't you be in any hurry, and never, never believe what they say about themselves, any more than what they say about you. Love makes liars of everybody, so far as I can see. I shan't marry now, but just stay with father."

" I never heard such sad talk as this," declared Tryphena, " and Elias is just as bad. Bitter as a lemon about girls. All for dogs now—owing to their being so faithful. Terrible things he says, and Aunt Grace, little knowing how near the truth she was, cried out against him only a week ago. She said : ' Shut your mouth, Elias, and give over talking against the women, else we shall think you've been crossed in love! ' But he only laughed. ' No girl for me,' he said. ' Life's hard enough as it is without going out of your way to make it harder. I can do mighty well without 'em,' he said, ' and I mean to.' "

"That's the truth, Tryphena. We feel the same—Elias and me. I shall never fall in love again. Of course Elias will—a man's different. The best are shallow compared to us. He'll marry for certain—a fool, if he's wise. No woman of character will have any use for him. You're a good, little, precious creature, and I hope, if ever you find a husband, he'll be worthy of such a darling."

" 'Tis a terrible difficult subject seemingly, and you meet it all round you," said Tryphena. "It doesn't interest me much. I'm sure; but you can't get away from it. Only just now, coming up here, I met Mr. Gurney, the blacksmith, with Mrs. Pierce. They were creeping along together at the edge of the wood; and they didn't want to be seen, I suppose. But properly miserable they looked, for I saw their faces. They just passed the time of the day with me, and then, when I'd gone by, I heard Mr. Gurney say, ' Damn that girl, now all the world will know as I've been walking here in this wood with you ! ' But why shouldn't they go there? If you feel miserable, you naturally want to hide in a wood. Anyway, I always do. No doubt they're both sorry about poor Mr. Pierce, and Mr. Gurney was trying to cheer her up."

" No doubt," agreed Petronell. " And don't you mention it to anybody else. They are in hot water enough already— poor wretches. They are a lot of mean, back-biting creatures in this place. They say Mabel Pierce beat her husband with a whip two nights ago. She got into a passion with him, perhaps. She'd had too much drink, I expect. At any rate, she punished him before Young Harry Hawke and another man could get over the bar and stop her. To have a husband you can thrash—that must be disgusting."

" You'd never have thrashed Elias," declared Tryphena, and the other laughed.

" No; but perhaps he'd have thrashed me."

" I hope you'll find the right lover yet—such a beautiful woman as you," said the girl. " But 'tis a doubtful state, I'm sure. My uncle and aunt are happy enough, but even they sling hard words sometimes—only neither pays the least notice, so no harm's done. Then take Mr. and Mrs. Abel Gurney, at Lower Dunstone—they're always laughing."

" But Nelly—Abel's daughter by his first marriage—she isn't. Her stepmother is a year younger than herself. Poor Nelly does all the work, and Sarah, her stepmother, gets all the fun."

" Nelly promised her real mother never to leave her father, so she told me," said Tryphena.

" Yes, she did, and she'll keep her silly promise. You see, when the old Mrs. Gurney died, she made her husband swear never to marry again. And she made her daughter undertake to live with her father for ever. But Abel Gurney broke his oath and took another wife in eight months."

" And they're as happy as larks, I'm sure."

" They ought not to be," declared Petronell, " but they certainly are. That's the one thing that seems to make it almost worth while being a fool. You can be happy, whatever else you can't be."

They considered others, and Tryphena decided that there were more happy married folk than not, while Petronell refused to believe it.

" No," said the elder, " you can't judge by the outside, because most men and women are too proud to show they've made a mistake. They hide it all they can; and brave, clever ones hide it altogether, and go to their graves with it hid. But some can no more hide their troubles than a crow her nest. The Pierces can't. Now talk about something else."

" We'll talk about books, then," said Tryphena, " because they're the nicest things in the world—next to people."

" They're nicer than people," declared Petronell. " They're far cleverer, and pleasanter to manage. If we could only shut up people, when we were vexed or wearied with them, and put them on a shelf till we wanted them again! What a different world, Tryphena! "

" But perhaps we'd be the ones to be shut up and put on a shelf, Petronell. And how hateful that would be. And perhaps none would ever want to take us down any more. I'd die of shame, I do believe, if anybody was to shut me up."

" There's never no need to shut you up," answered the other. " You're like a robin in winter : everybody's well pleased to welcome you and hear you sing your little song."

CHAPTER XXII

A PARTY of familiars met at this season upon strange business. At the " Rugglestone Inn " did the faction opposed to Mabel Pierce assemble. The folk could not see themselves, or appreciate the aspect of this business viewed from outside; they only knew that the matter of the publican and his wife seemed exceedingly serious to them, and represented a great and difficult problem, crying to be solved for the credit of the Vale. But opinions differed as to what should be done, and while some of the frequenters of Mr. Turtle's inn proposed one course

of action, others advocated a very different line. There were
also a few who advised the rest to mind their own business, and
leave fate to deal with the tragic and eternal situation of
Arthur Pierce, Mabel Pierce, and Tom Gurney.

The ill wind of this inquiry had blown good to one, and while
the " Old Inn " was peaceful of nights, and only the Hawkes,
Gurney, and a sprinkling of other people patronised it, much
beer was drunk at the " Rugglestone," and Timothy Turtle
began to take himself more seriously. Pancras Widecombe,
his lodger, also participated in the improved fortune of the
house. Indeed, he claimed that he was largely responsible for
it, and Timothy, who esteemed him highly, and wanted him
for a son-in-law, gave the stonemason all the credit that he
desired.

By appointment a dozen men now met to consider the case
of the " Old Inn." Nearly everybody was conscious of a high
purpose, and though one or two were uneasy, none among
them felt mean.

Mr. Valiant Dunnybrig, who was actuated by the highest
motives in this matter, consented to preside. There were
assembled Nicky Glubb; Birkett Johnson from Tunhill; Uncle
Tom Cobleigh of Venton, and his son, Christian; Pancras
Widecombe, and Whitelock Smerdon. Jack Mogridge was
also there, with Bassett Gurney and his father, Abel, from
Dunstone Mill. The latter were relatives, though not friends,
of Tom Gurney, the blacksmith; but while Mr. Abel Gurney,
a futile, feather-headed wight, had only come to see the fun,
his more serious-minded son, Bassett, who hated his cousin,
Tom, felt hopeful that the farrier was to be publicly attacked.
Old Bell, the alms nan, and a couple of labourers from Tunhill,
completed the assembly, and Timothy Turtle waited upon them.

" I propose Mr. Dunnybrig go in the chair," said Birkett
Johnson; and since the rest were of one mind with him,
Valiant took the top of the table.

" I'll put the case so far as I've heard it from young Bassett
Gurney here," said the master of Chittleford, " and if anybody
else knows different, they can up and speak. Afore we do
anything, we must be satisfied of the truth; and if we do anything, we must do it in a large spirit and strike at the wrong-
doing, not the wrongdoers. In old times rough justice was
often measured out by the people, and a sharp lesson oft
rubbed home. A sort of mob-law, but it seldom miscarried.
And this may be a case for it, or it may not. But I want to hear
more than Bassett Gurney on the subject, because he spoke to
me with a bitter tongue, and I saw he'd got a personal grievance against Tom Gurney, and wanted to do him an injury.

So I'll call upon Johnson first, because he's a thoughtful man, and temperate in his opinions and fair-minded—so at least I've found him."

Then Johnson spoke.

"I'm along with you, Farmer Dunnybrig. 'Tis the wrong-doing must be punished. In my judgment, the wife of Arthur Pierce, to gain her own private ends, be treating her husband with cruelty, and 'tis against her that we ought to act. Not, of course, direct, but, as you say, there's old, valuable customs to reflect the opinion of the people and cast a sidelight at the erring parties. Mabel Pierce have struck her husband and knocked him about in public. 'Tis a fact none can doubt, and so I say that 'tis her that ought to be chastened in public—for her own good and Widecombe's credit. And if a lot of sensible men can show the woman her mistake and let her see herself as others see her, it might be a useful thing."

"So much for you, then," answered Valiant. "You think that we ought to aim at the woman. That's not a manly line, and for my part I'd rather do anything else; but I'm only in the chair, and here to get out the sense of the meeting. Now I'll ask you, Nicky Glubb, to say what you think; and don't you let any personal feeling cloud your judgment, Glubb. You be too well known for a fiery and passionate man."

"I ban't no more passionate than anybody else," said Nicky, "and in this matter, seeing the beastly woman's beat her husband with a whip and slapped his face a score of times afore witnesses, and seeing that she's always playing about with Tom Gurney, the blacksmith—as my wife and other clean-minded women will gladly testify—then I say that she's the party that wants a damned good rap over the knuckles; and if Arthur Pierce had the pluck of a louse, he'd have got rid of her once for all long ago. And you can take home what you said about me being a fiery and passionate man, Valiant Dunny-brig, else I'll have something to say to you."

"Order—order! and list to the chair," cried Valiant Dunny-brig. "The chair says this: we must vote. And the question is: 'Be man and woman both to be punished, or is it the woman to be punished and the man go free?' 'Tis that we've got to decide. Now, who be for punishing the woman only?"

Seven put up their hands, including Johnson, Nicky Glubb, Whitelock Smerdon, and Timothy Turtle.

"Man is what woman makes him," declared the last, "and if Mabel Pierce hadn't run after blacksmith, he wouldn't have messed himself up with her. He's a woman-hating man in general, and I don't hold him to blame."

Then Mr. Dunnybrig spoke again.

" And who wants the man to suffer too? Though I needn't say that he will suffer, whatever is done; because to punish the woman is to punish him. Five, I see. Then thus we stand : Arthur Pierce's wife have got to be held up to scorn; and how is it to be done in a decent and orderly way, that won't bring us to scorn ourselves? "

" You'd best call on Uncle Tom Cobleigh," said Pancras. " He's forgot more about such things than any of us ever knew."

" I ain't forgot nothing—nothing at all," declared the ancient. " I know all about it, and the ways of it, and the rhymes, and everything. There's ' Riding to Water ' that's one fine thing; and there's ' Mock Burial '—that's another; and there's ' Mock Execution '—that's another. And ' Skimmity Riding ' be a thing of yesterday—we all know what that means."

" That's what we ought to have done in my judgment," said Widecombe; " but since the sense of the meeting be against touching Gurney, it must be something else."

" Tell us all about these ancient goings on, Gaffer," directed Dunnybrig, and Uncle Cobleigh launched forth.

" ' Riding to Water,' " he began, " used to be done when a man and his wife was quarrelsome and always making a disturbance, and upsetting the neighbours, and disgracing the parish. A chap would dress himself up like the husband, and another would dress himself up like the wife, and they'd start riding together on a donkey, with all the village behind them to the din of marrowbones and cleavers. They'd both have a empty bladder on a string, and belabour each other and the ass and anybody else as come within distance; and then the procession would go to the river, or hoss-pond, and the two mummers would fall in off the donkey and souse the people round about. 'Twas a very pleasant way to spend an afternoon, and there's no better fun in the world, if the two fellows be properly funny and keep the ball rolling."

" That won't do in this case," declared Mr. Dunnybrig, " because the sense of the meeting is that the woman shall be chastised, but not the husband, because he's innocent."

" Then out Lydford way there was a merry game," continued Uncle, warming to his subject. " If 'twas thought a man or woman had tripped and forgot the rules of marriage, the people held a ' Stag Hunt.' Ess, a 'Stag Hunt ' they held, and a nimble youth put a pair of horns on his head, and dressed himself up so fantastic as you please; and then he galloped off on an appointed round and a good rally of neighbours and dogs and boys ran after him. 'Twas a noisy pursuit, but for frolic and laughter you couldn't beat it. And then, at the finish, the ' Stag ' was run down and catched in the garden of one of the sinners. Now, it might be a woman, and now, again it might be a man. Then blood was sprinkled over the cabbages and all the people yelled to express the fullness of their feelings. I mind a good few cases, when I was that side of the Moor in my boyhood. But folk be nicer in their manners nowadays, though there's just as much secret naughtiness in my opinion. But it ban't taken to heart like it was."

" That would be a very brave contrivance, and I say let Pancras Widecombe go for stag, and gallop all round the manors, and let the hunters run him down in Tom Gurney's garden," suggested Whitelock Smerdon. But Pancras objected.

" We can't do that. The case isn't proved against 'em, and it might be libellious," he said.

" Then we come back to the starting-point," declared the chairman. " A ' Stag Hunt ' would be a terrible blow to Gurney, but unless the stag was run down in the courtyard of the ' Old Inn,' the woman wouldn't be struck at, but only the blacksmith. And it has been agreed by the most of you that Mabel Pierce, and only her, is to be reproved. So you must think again, Gaffer Cobleigh."

" Wet your whistle, uncle," added Timothy.

The old man drank and considered.

"There's buryings of effigies; but that won't do, though 'twas revived, they tell me, not so long agone. And, lastly, there's the public execution—a very telling and dreadful judgment on anybody; and I've known it to send a man out of his mind once. And it nearly always sends 'em out of the parish. 'Tis done on a man if he's cruel and wicked to his wife; but I can't say as I've ever heard of it being done on a woman—though there's no reason against it—except the rhyme."

" How does it go, then? " asked Johnson.

" I remember the rhyme—I remember the rhyme! " cried Nicky Glubb. " I can sing it for that matter, and though it speaks of a man, there ain't no reason why it shouldn't be a woman."

" Be quiet, Nicky; we want to hear Uncle Cobleigh," said Mr. Turtle.

" I direct Uncle Cobleigh to tell us just how it went," added Mr. Dunnybrig.

" 'Twas a famous wife-beater," continued the old man, " and Nicky have a better memory for rhymes than me, because hymn-singing be his means of livelihood. So I'll leave the verses to him. Well, the man—he's dead now, so it don't

matter mentioning his name—was called Luke Parsons. And
being moved at his maltreatment of a very long-suffering wife
—a poor, draggle-tailed heart-broken wisp of a woman, and
flat as a board, she was—we rose up and built a figure of
Parsons, and assembled ourselves together in Lady Land
meadow and pretended 'twas an execution with funeral to
follow. First we hanged the image on a great gallows, and
while he swung above the crowd, twenty of us or more,
wi' lungs like church organs, shouted out the rhyme. Nicky
can say it, for he was there."

"And so I can," replied the blind man, "and no man
bellowed it louder than me while the figure of Parsons was
strung up. It went this way, and I'd dearly like for to sing
it again in public :—

> ' There is a man lives in this place
> Who beats his wife to a sad disgrace;
> He beats her black, and he beats her blue;
> He beats her till the blood runs through.'

"That's the first verse, and the second goes like this :—

> ' Now, if this man don't mend his manners,
> We'll have his skin and send to the tanners;
> And when the tanners have tanned it well,
> His hide shall be hung on the nail of hell! ' "

The company applauded Nicky, and Pancras pointed out that
it would be quite easy to alter the rhyme and fit it to the
culprit; but Valiant Dunnybrig showed lack of sympathy.

"Let's get through with the meeting so soon as we can,"
he said. "I'm tired of it, and I don't much like the turn
things are taking. Go on, Uncle."

"That's pretty near all," declared the ancient. "After the
hanging came the funeral, and, of course, the grave was dug
ready and everything in order. None interfered. The man had
no friends to fight for him."

"That's not all; you've missed the best part of the sport,
Uncle," declared Nicky. "Don't you mind how the ' clergyman '—Henry Smerdon 'twas, brother of Peter Smerdon of
Bone Hill—how he talked to the swinging effigy and told it
its sins and said how it was to reform afore it was too late.
He dressed the man down through the image; and 'twas all
spoilt, in my opinion, because there wasn't anybody to have
a row. But this will be different, because Tom Gurney and
his friends will get properly mad for certain, and there'll be
some good fighting, please God, and a bit of history made."

"That's just what I was coming to," declared Mr. Dunnybrig, "and, as chairman, I say at once that I'll be no party

to any vulgar disturbance. In fact, I don't approve of the idea at all. 'Tis a pity at this time of day if a lot of reasonable, God-fearing men can't show this mistaken woman her errors without making a breach of the peace."

" Get out of the chair, then ! " cried Nicky Glubb. " You'm a coward, for all your big voice and brimstone opinions. I propose that Valiant Dunnybrig do quit the chair."

" Nobody needn't trouble to second," answered the farmer. " Because I'm going to quit. I'm not vexed, nor nothing like that; I'm in a minority of one, and, as such, I can't do better than go home. And you'll be wise to leave Glubb out of any-thing you may do."

" I won't be left out," retorted the blind man. " And as to you, you be always weak where the females are concerned. 'Tis well known that you've got queer ideas about 'em."

But Dunnybrig, without paying the least attention, said " Good-night all," and withdrew. Old Bell, the almsman, went out with him. Meantime, Nicky's opinions were challenged.

" You'd look a tidy fool without your woman, anyway," said Abel Gurney. It was the first time that he had spoken, and several applauded him. " Yes," he added, " if your squint-eyed Nanny was to die, where'd you be? "

" I'd be mighty soon feeling out for another," answered Nicky. " And I'd mighty soon find one. And I wish Nanny was here at this moment to lead me to you, Abel, you slight, windy fool, for I'd send you home to your own silly wife so as she wouldn't know you. You to talk ! A man who sold his soul to a female twenty years younger than himself and very near as big a fool ! But if you ax me, I say that 'tis your down-trodden, overworked daughter, Nelly, as you should crow about, not your trollope of a wife."

" If you wasn't blind ! " shouted Mr. Gurney; and Glubb shouted back :

" You all say that—you bleating cowards ! If I wasn't blind, I'd crow over the whole pack of you, and well you know it; and even as 'tis you won't stand up to me. I'm as good as any two of you, blind though I am, and when we hang up that scarlet woman, Mabel Pierce——"

All the men began to talk at once, and Timothy Turtle cried out to Mr. Johnson : " Get in the chair, for mercy's sake, Birkett ! Us shan't have no peace till order be brought back !"

Anon the argument was resumed, and the majority favoured Uncle Cobleigh's last suggestion.

It was determined to hang and bury Mrs. Pierce in effigy as a husband-beater, and the rest of the evening was devoted to allotting the parts proper to the ceremony

" Us'll go one better than ever was gone afore," declared
Pancras Widecombe. " A proper old upstore us will have,
and it ban't no use your crying off, Johnson, same as Farmer
Dunnybrig, because you've sanctioned and upheld it. And
now it have got to take its course, like the law. We be doing
it all on account of Arthur Pierce, and I hope he'll have good
cause to bless the day—poor man."

But Johnson's mind misgave him.

Nicky chuckled to Nanny, who had just come to take him
home. He made her drink, and whispered to her of the
projected ceremony.

" The fools talk about it all going off as if 'twas a proper
funeral with a proper carpse! " he said. " But it shan't—not
if you and me be there! And Tom Gurney won't take it
lying down if I know him, nor yet that brass-bound female
neither. None can keep up her end of the stick better than
Mabel Pierce. And if we don't have a proper, furious, bloody
fight, and a rich lot of broken heads, and something to get
drunk about when all's over—then it won't be my fault for
one. There'll be music, so I've got to be there; but the best
tune I'm going to play be on somebody's earhole. I've got a
lot of grudges waiting to be paid off, and I hope to God I
shan't be put out of action till I've done my share."

While he spoke, the parts were being allotted. Everybody
wanted to do something, and Pancras proved fertile of imagination, for he invented several additions to the ceremony as
reported from old time.

A provisional date was fixed, and the company broke up in
the best of spirits.

CHAPTER XXIII

VALIANT DUNNYBRIG returned home in some concern at the
attitude of Widecombe with respect to the Pierces. He hated
pettiness, and this attack on a woman unhappily wedded
appeared to him exceedingly base.

And yet none held more stoutly to the old customs; none
preserved ancient rites with such ardour. At Yuletide, or on
May Day, Valiant Dunnybrig rejoiced in antiquated ceremonial;
he loved to feast the poor, to christen the apple-trees, to gather
the last corn-sheaf with song, to welcome the gleaners and
give generously at the festival of Harvest Home. He eyed
with favour likewise such venerable proceedings as Uncle
Cobleigh had described, and he saw no reason why sinners

should not be admonished, scolds bridled, or witches ducked. The Old Testament expressly declared that a witch should not be suffered to live, yet Valiant, in his earlier days, had known of notorious practitioners who prospered secretly and against whom no man ever dared to raise his hand.

In the case under notice, however, he was not convinced that Mabel Pierce had done anything to merit a rebuke so public and so grave. His private convictions and secret desires contributed in some measure to modify his judgment. Indeed, at this season, Valiant was entirely preoccupied with his own life. For years one great difficulty had dominated him until it had grown into an obsession. He was very uneasy and very concerned. The closest obedience to Old Testament tenets had more than once brought him into collision with his fellow-men, and from these encounters the farmer usually emerged triumphant; but now his cast of mind was leading him into a graver sort of difficulty and danger. Not with man, but with woman would he come in conflict soon; not with woman in general, but with his wife. And she was ready. By hints and opinions; by the expression of unusual views; by anxiety as to his Maker's will; and by a general patriarchal attitude to marriage, had Valiant Dunnybrig given rise to questioning in the heart of Jane. She was used to his ways, yet could never affirm that she was able to anticipate him. For he abounded in surprises; he did not crystalise into solidity as other men, but kept a fluid mind and changed his outlook from month to month. None could accuse him of self-seeking or dishonesty. Sometimes, indeed, a new standpoint might entail personal prosperity and accrued advantage; but as often a sudden conviction or suspicion that a previous attitude was not justified by his supreme exemplar, the Bible, would lead to actions that were opposed to his own temporal good. Thus he frequently astonished all who knew him, and in his fiery soul there also raged secret conflagrations that none ever discerned or suspected.

The nature of the great problem that now cried to be solved was revealed by a conversation which Valiant held with his niece, Araminta Dench. The woman lived at Chittleford, appreciated her uncle's great spirit and large generosity, planned to please him always, and looked to him for her future prosperity. She was content to believe as he believed; she was willing to trust her welfare to him in this world and in the next. For his part, he approved her character and regarded her as a precious addition to the home. His wife and Araminta were good friends, and as yet Mrs. Dunnybrig had found no occasion to quarrel with her niece. Araminta was sly—that her aunt had discovered, but the trait was unalterable and made no difference to Mrs. Dunnybrig. She uttered a warning, however, since, to Valiant, slyness was an objectionable vice. And now, Jane had gone to Newton for the day, and Araminta's uncle approached her upon a most sensational theme. From his point of view, as one contented to move and live and have his being under the aegis of Jehovah, there was nothing unseemly in his proposition; but since patriarchal living and its adjuncts strike harshly upon a Christian ear, Mr. Dunnybrig's views startled his niece not a little, albeit of his good faith there could be no question. He towered high above such small offences as impropriety. Such a word could not be brought against his megalomania. He was before all things impressed with the position to which it had pleased God to call him, and the endowments with which it had pleased God to bless him. He put his case loftily, and Araminta felt almost ashamed of herself for regarding it in a smaller and more cautious spirit than his own. Yet it was impossible that she could do otherwise, because her life and future were profoundly affected; her good name was flung into the world's balance.

Valiant submitted his proposal in the hayfield, where six scythes purred together, and the long swathes fell all silver-green on the shorn emerald of the meadows. He loved the work himself, and always took a share in it among the rest; but now his niece and a little girl came to the hayfield with great jars of cider, and prepared to carry away others that had been emptied. And seeing Araminta, the farmer ceased from his labour, turned down his sleeves, buttoned his shirt, and put on his coat.

"A crop so thin as an old man's hair," he said. "The drought have done it. 'Tis the Lord's will that we have no hay to name at Chittleford this year. Come hither. I want to speak to you, Araminta. Be sure that the things that I'm going to say weren't reached on the spur of a moment. 'Tis reversing the order of creation in a very wonderful manner—the Lord's doing, and marvellous in my eyes; though more often my Maker and I think alike to a shade. But the order's reversed, and while most times, in well-doing, the spirit be willing and the flesh weak, in this great matter, the spirit's weak and the flesh don't count. Pitch here and list to me."

They sat by the hedge, beyond earshot of the labourers, and Araminta watched the flash of the scythes and listened from time to time as hone hummed on steel, while still her uncle talked.

"I want to know, first, if there's anybody you care about in this world—anybody you walk out with, or think some day to be tokened to? "

" None at all," she answered. " You and Aunt Jane be the only people I care about in the world."

" Then I'll speak. Mind you, I know that I go on a lofty height above the folk. I'm nearer the Light; I've been well paid for my lifelong service, and can see what's hidden from most of us. So if you can't see as far as I can; if you find the earth and the people come between, I shall understand and think no worse of you. I must talk about marriage first, and what 'tis for. There's a people called the ' Perfectionists ' in America somewhere. I don't know how they thrive—none too well, I reckon, the world being what it is; but so far as I could read about 'em, they appeared to me a very high-minded sort, and almost so near to the Fountain of Wisdom as I have got myself. And they say that marriage is first and foremost an institution for the good of posterity, not the present; and the first thing we ought to enter the state for is the unborn. In their judgment, to be all wrapped up in your wife be a sinful respect of persons and a very improper frame of mind indeed. What you ought to feel is the sacred joy of bringing souls to the harvest. So they American people have stamped on love of women, and made love of offspring the grand thing. To marry a 'voman for her own sake is a sinful and selfish piece of work. 'Tis very little better than setting up an idol. And if you follow me that far, say so."

" How is it, then, as in your case, when a man ain't got no family? "

" Exactly! " said Dunnybrig. " The Lord put that question into your mouth without a doubt, because in the answer lies what I've got to say. Now it stands like this : God Almighty made me a very uncommon man. 'Twould be false modesty to pretend otherwise. I look round me with seeing eyes and feel terrible sorry there ain't more of my pattern scattered over the world. A little leaven leavens the whole lump, and you can see for yourself, and so can anybody, what I've done in Widecombe. My father was such another. Well, there it is; when I went into holy matrimony, my first purpose was to bring grist to the heavenly mill, and hand on my stamp and impress my character on the next generation of souls. I didn't take your aunt because I loved her; I took her because I respected her character and felt that she'd be a strong, wise mother and helpful to her offspring. She came of healthy stock, and her elder sisters—three in number— were all successful parents. But what happened? Man may plant, but only God gives the increase—as the swedes and mangolds will show afore long. 'Twas not given to Jane Dunnybrig to respond; and so I stand here now bitterly disappointed of a great desire to bring good human material into the world's market. A man of fine character and lofty mind be the best gift we can offer to the nation, and one like me—brimming over with rare qualities—the very qualities most lacking from my own generation and most useful to the next—a man like me has to think terrible serious before he lets go his right to fatherhood without a struggle. In a word, 'tis hiding my light under a bushel to have no children, Araminta; 'tis also escaping from the responsibility and duty and obligation—'tis a coward's act—and while I've sheltered thus long under the excuse that my wife ban't to be a mother, and that therefore my duty in the matter is at an end, I feel stronger and stronger of late that, for an Old Testament and Jehovah man, this is no excuse at all. There's the story of Abraham and Sarah staring me in the face; and how am I, as a righteous and honourable creature and the servant of the Most High, going to still my conscience now? "

His earne-tness was tremendous, and his honesty of purpose it had been impossible to question.

" I want a mother for my children; and I want you to be that mother, Araminta. Are you brave enough to rise to it and face the opinion of the world? There's no sin nor shame in it. If there was, then Abraham was a shamed and sinful man. I don't love you in the earthly sense; I never loved more than anybody else. If you love God as I do, then your love for your kind be just a placid, far-reaching, universal thing—like moonlight compared to the sunlight of your love for your Maker. I don't love you, but I find you placed here in my home, healthy, religious-minded, and not drawn to any man. You're free to do the Lord's will; you're the handmaid of your aunt, same as Rebecca to Sarah. Of course, my wife must always have the first place of honour; in fact, your children will be brought up at her knees. Widecombe will talk—and God will act. So there you are."

Araminta's brain whirled, but she had not lived with Mr. Dunnybrig ten years for nothing. Her values and ideas were largely tinctured by him. His attitude on this question did not shock or pain her. Her emotion centred in the profound alteration it must produce in her own life. She was practical now, and exhibited no sentiment.

" What about Aunt Jane? " she asked.

" A natural question, which I have put before myself long ago. Of course I had to ask your opinion first. That was more important than hers."

"I doubt it, Uncle Valiant. Your wife goes with you in your large ideas, as far as she dares; but women haven't got any use for the Old Testament nowadays, whatever they might have had once."

"She'll always be first and at my right hand, and held in highest honour; but I want to raise up seed afore the Lord of Hosts; and I can't see why she should feel any objection to that honourable wish. The world can hear my opinion. It has come to me in visions, and I've even been allowed to see my children in the spirit. Three boys and two girls—that's what would happen—and the boys would be called Abraham and Isaac and Jacob, and the girls would be called Ruth and Naomi."

"Your wife would go mad."

"We're talking about you, not her, yet. You call upon your God and ask Him what He's got to say, and the issue won't be long in doubt. Go with an open mind and pure spirit; don't be worldly; don't be nasty; don't be small-minded about the details. Trust me and trust your Maker."

"'Tis a terrible big thing."

"To be the mother of my children is a terrible big thing. I grant that. So much the prouder woman you."

Araminta's whole soul began to calculate; but she could not utter the thoughts that came into her mind. They would have shocked the man, for he had expressly ordered her to approach the problem in a pure and lofty spirit. Her instinct, however, forbade that. She naturally considered the subject from the point of view of her values. It meant her own place assured for ever, for she knew that Dunnybrig was absolutely honest and sincere. He would not treat her as Hagar was treated, or suffer any such thing. Yet, he might be out of his mind; there was that reasonable fear. If he became insane after the step was taken—where was Araminta then? Her instinct told her to leave him now as quickly as possible, before she betrayed herself. She rose, therefore, and prepared to depart.

"Go back to your mowing," she said, "and I'll be off. You've given me something to think about with a vengeance! I'll try to look at it from your point of view, and you must try to look at it from mine. There's the world to be thought upon. This is a bold step for a lonely woman. In most eyes I should be——"

She was going to say "ruined," but did not, for fear the word might anger him.

"'Tis better to be wrong in some eyes than right," he answered; "and when you be dealing with such an upheaval against everyday life and everyday ideas as this, the question of what folk think is too small a matter. You must put it on a far higher platform, same as the martyrs. To make the world better was never yet a pleasant task; to take on the solemn duty of mothership be of all tasks that which rises highest above the opinion of other people. And you females have got to come to us for that great gift, for it is men, under God, decide what women shall be mothers and which shan't."

She left him then, and walked along the hills by herself. She ascended beneath Blackslade, passed the home of Mr. Sweetland, and, roaming onward, circled half the cup of the Vale, and found herself presently near the house of the Smerdons. It was here that one met her known to Araminta; she came across the girl, Margery Reep, sitting in a sheltered spot amid the Bone Hill Rocks. And in her lap was her baby.

Margery proved very proud to exhibit her achievement, and the other woman marvelled at her cheerful indifference to fate and opinion.

" They tried their bestest to make Jack's father look at it different; but there 'tis, Jack can't do nothing; 'tis the ' evil eye,' no doubt; and while his father won't let him wed, we can't. Nought hath power to strengthen up Jack to throw over his father; and nought can weaken his father to go back on his oath against me. So now we be pretty well reconciled to it, and my mother, too. We've called it Daniel, after my father, though it ain't christened, because of the hitch, and parson ban't disposed to christen it till we'm married. They say he's playing with a soul, but he don't care. Look at un— ban't he a dinky dear? "

The baby was pale and feeble. His little weak eyes stared fixedly upon his mother. Presently a fatuous smile lighted them, and he showed his toothless gums. In an ecstasy of joy Margery cuddled her child to her.

" Ban't he a darling? And can laugh, you see, though, Lord knows, he can cry, too. He ban't very strong, the doctor says; but he'll grow to strength."

She rubbed her ugly face against the child, then took off his little hat to show Araminta his hair.

" I suppose Jack thinks a lot of him? "

" Who wouldn't? Yes, he's a good father. 'Tis a wonderful thing, us three. I was feared first what people would say, and all that; but now, seeing how 'tis and no fault of ours, I don't care a cuss for anybody, so long as I've got Jack and the babby."

" You don't feel to care what people think? "

" Good Lord, no! What are the people to me? They

seemed somebody before; but since—why, they'm nothing at all—dust and shadows! This here lovely, tibby lamb be the only one that matters in the world."

" A fine thing to be a mother, then? "

" I didn't know such a poor creature as me ever could *be* so fine," answered Margery. " A woman don't know she's born herself—not till she bears."

" I thought that was all cant and humbug—spoke by mothers to hide their own miseries and troubles."

" I don't know about nobody else," answered the other. " I only know what comes over me every time I wake in the night and hear his little pipe."

" And he looks a beautiful thing to you, no doubt? "

" ' Looks '? " cried Margery. " ' Looks a beautiful thing '! Why, good Lord, Araminta, he *is* a beautiful thing! Who could think or say otherwise? And who knows better than me? Haven't I counted his very eyelashes? "

" And nothing else matters? "

" There is nothing else to matter. He's the great master-piece of the world to me."

The other considered curiously.

" You've got all the earth in your arms, then, when he's in 'em?"

" All earth—and all heaven," said Margery.

CHAPTER XXIV

Miss Nelly Gurney of Dunstone Mill was narrow-shouldered, thin, and plain. She belonged to the careful and troubled order of beings. Long before her invalid mother died, she had mothered her father; and afterwards she devoted all her energies to the widower's welfare. Being as serious-minded and stable as he was volatile and frivolous, she promised to prove the stand-by and anchor of her family; but Abel married again, after her mother had been dead eight months. To the race of the Hawkes did Mr. Gurney go for his second wife, and found Sarah, a laughter-loving, lazy, and unambitious woman of thirty-five—a year his daughter's junior. Nelly took the matter to heart and protested to her father that she had proposed to dedicate her life to him and felt his action to be a bitter outrage. But her alarm was ill-founded, and none challenged Nelly's place in the house. The stepmother made her attitude exceedingly clear.

" You needn't take on about having to sing second," she said. " If it hadn't been for you, and the sure knowledge that there was somebody here eager and willing to do everything, I shouldn't have took your father. In the past I've refused half-a-dozen, just for that reason and no other; that marrying 'em looked a bit too much like work and too much like a family. I hate work, and be always too thankful and willing to give anybody all the credit if they'll take it off my shoulders. And you're a towser for work, and never so happy as when dog-tired and worn to the bone with doing other people's. And that'll suit me down to the ground, I do assure you. You shall reign, and I shall be mighty pleased to let you. I'm the easiest woman to get on with in Widecombe. For why? Because I ask for nothing but to be let entirely alone."

Nelly was comforted, after a fashion, at this explanation, and time proved that the second Mrs. Gurney had spoken the truth. Her elderly husband doted on her, and since her rule of life had always been his own, as far as possible, he fell now into exceedingly lazy ways, considered pleasure before business, and was well content to let his eldest daughter control the mill and its finances.

Nelly need not have feared that her work in life was ended; instead she found it doubled; yet such was the genial nature of the stepmother, her ceaseless good temper and kindness of heart, that to quarrel with her or establish permanent grievances proved impossible. Sarah loved jollity. She took her husband to every revel and fair within the district; she made him spend the money that Nelly had helped him to save; she reposed absolute confidence in her elder stepdaughter, and declared the most genuine admiration for Nelly. Her ceaseless fear was that the woman would marry and leave Dunstone. If she ever prayed, it was that this might not happen; yet now came the threat of it, and Mrs. Gurney found a cloud on the blue of her horizon.

Nelly's father endeavoured to dispel her fears. He declared himself positive that no such thing would happen.

" Nelly's one of them fine, busy creatures, like ants," he said. " She loveth to toil and use her wits and good sense for the nest. But she's not a man-lover—you can't even say she likes 'em. Mark the scornful way she treats them. Never a smile, or a side-look, or a little kindly word for 'em."

" But some men fancy that kind. 'Tis the hard sort of

woman draws 'em by instinct, because they feel that such a female will stand between them and the rough edge of the world."

" She's a deal board with a conscience—to say it kindly. And what sort of male wants to wed a deal board? " asked Abel.

" Plenty of 'em. When a man gets up over sixty, same as Samuel Sweetland, he don't take a woman, like a china vase, for the outside. Anyway he's after her, and I feel terrible anxious about it. We know he's desperate. He's been offering himself at sale prices to anybody and everybody, so Mary Hearn declares. In fact, he went to Mary, too, and, knowing her, I should have thought she'd have jumped; but she didn't, and so he's on the market again, and ready for anything in a petticoat."

" We can do nothing but advise her against him; and, perhaps, to do that would be just to set her on," declared Mr. Gurney. " She thinks so terrible poorly of my judgment that if I warned her——"

Sarah laughed.

" Yes, the dear, anxious creature! I believe she feels like a mother to me and you; and that's where my hope lies. She'll reckon 'twould be a case of desertion to let us face life without her. You must put it like that. You must say that you and me feel Dunstone wouldn't be Dunstone without her."

Abel Gurney beamed at this idea.

" When you do take the trouble to think, there's none so quick and witty as you," he said. " You're right, Sally. It won't do to run down Sweetland; we'll just sing small ourselves, and make her feel that we should be a pair o' babes lost in the wood without her."

" And it's perfectly true," declared Sarah. " We should be; and so would your children, Bassett and Philip and Madge. I hope that the boys will marry soon, for they be more than wife-old, and you'd be freer if they was wedded. Of course Bassett will bring his wife here, because the mill be his when you fall out. But Nelly—you talk to her; we're in time for once, though it ban't like you and me to be punctual. But don't waste a minute. And if you think 'twould be a clever thing to make Nelly a present——"

" I will after, not before," said Abel. " I'll choke her off this if I can."

He spoke to Nelly on the subject, and said that his wife, with woman's wit, had felt others envied Dunstone Mill in the possession of such a treasure.

" But I ask you, my dear, how do you think me and mother could get on without you? You very well know that my

Sarah married you as well as me. 'Twould be half the bargain broken if you was to leave us. But don't think that we put ourselves first—not at all, Nelly. If it was another, I should have said nothing, and suffered in silence; but with a person like Sweetland——"

" Well, what? " asked Nelly. " What about the man? "

" Man—so to call him," answered her father. " And since the murder's out, I suppose I may speak? "

" No, you needn't," she answered bleakly. " You'm a day behind the fair—as usual. You can sleep in peace, and so can stepmother. I've got my work in life, and it lies only too bitter clear afore me. My work is to my hand and happens inside the mill. And even if 'twasn't so, I've got no use for a husband. The likes of me have our virtues if they ain't showy. And one of 'em is to know exactly our own worth, and what we be good for and bad for. If there's one thing I see clear, 'tis myself; and if there's one thing I know, 'tis that the real men ain't got no use for me. And so when Mr. Sweetland came to me——"

" Came—d'you mean he's come! " cried Abel.

" Come and gone. And if you and stepmother ever looked farther than one another's faces, I dare say you'd have marked the shadow of a flutter about me in the evening of Friday last, when I came in. But you never do, and so you didn't see it. He met me in the lane by ' Rugglestone Inn.' He was riding home, and appeared to be down on his luck. He had a grievance. He spoke against the female sex, and let out presently that his sister was a rare handful. She'd been bringing gossip from the village, and he hadn't liked it, and he'd told her if she was a decent, self-respecting woman, she wouldn't lend a ear to such nasty fables. He didn't tell me the details and I didn't want to know 'em; but I've heard 'em since. I knew in my bones what he was after by his voice. It sounded like as if it was bursting out of soap bubbles. He said he respected me and had long felt what a helpmate I should make for him, and that, what with my tact and patience and all the rest of it, he was sure that I should be so clever with his sister Harriet as I'd proved myself with my fool of a stepmother. ' Fool ' was his word, not mine. Not that your wife ever denied that she was a fool. And so I told Samuel Sweetland. In fact I stood up for Sarah against him; and so he left that subject and returned to me, and said that he'd take me and lift me up to be his wife."

" To think of that! And you never let on by so much as a wink."

" I was pleased at first—I own to it," admitted Nelly; " but very soon I smelt a rat. He was in a proper tremble all the time, and took lozenges to clear his speaking-tubes and keep his voice down, for it ran up into his nose. But only for a moment did I fancy myself a bit, and then I guessed that he'd never have come to an up and down, hard-featured, small-eyed woman like me, afore he'd tried in a good many places else. I called home a few stories I'd heard about him, and felt 'twasn't love, nor nothing like that, but just the smart of failure that brought him."

"You told him so! I know you," cried Abel.

"No, I didn't. That wouldn't have been like a proper woman. I'm not proud. I didn't want him; but I didn't see no reason to be rude to him, just because others had filled his eye first. If I'd known what was coming, I might have been saucy and took the whip hand; but I didn't. I saw he was a good bit put about and meant business, and so I thanked him and declined the offer. And I explained that my work in life was you and your wife, and that I should feel a traitor to my own dead mother if I left you and the mill to the mercy of the world."

"Well spoken, and I bless you for it!" said Abel, "and your reward will make angels wonder without a doubt some day. What did he say, and how did he look when you refused him?"

"'Twas dark, and I can't tell you how he looked," answered Nelly. "He said something to himself first which I ban't goin' to repeat. In fact, he cussed fearful, and I shouldn't have thought he'd ever heard such language in his life, for he never goes among men much. And then he turned to me and asked me if I had took leave of my senses."

"Couldn't believe his own, I reckon. He's a vain, knock-kneed old item, and if, as you say, he called my wife a fool, I'll have it out with him next time we meet."

"You'll do no such thing, father," answered Nelly. "I'm telling you secrets, since you had to be told, but I dare you to tell 'em again, or take any notice. Let the man alone. He had the edge of my tongue before he left me, so there's no occasion for you to interfere. I didn't mean to say nothing sharp or harsh; but he began it, and when he asked me if I was mad, I said I wasn't. I said, 'I quite appreciate the compliment, Mr. Sweetland, and shall always remember it in your favour.' Then he forgot himself altogether, and, from offering marriage, went to the other extreme, and insulted me shameful 'You needn't give yourself airs about it, however,' he says, 'and you needn't think you was the first I offered for by a dozen, because you wasn't.' The silly mumphead gave himself away like that to anger me! But after that I reckoned my nice feelings were properly thrown away on the man, so I let him have it. ' No! ' I answered back, like a flap of lightning. ' No, I wasn't the first to have no use for a stuck-up old ninny, with a face and a voice like a ewe, and I shan't be the last—*I shan't be the last*! ' 'Twas a sudden rage made me say such a poisonous thing."

" He deserved it," declared Mr. Gurney. " He properly deserved it; in fact, never a man deserved it more. 'Twas a raking shot, and it leaves him in a fair quandary so far as I can see, for if he dares to seek another woman, he'll go afore her with all the pluck and hope crushed out of him and haunted by a cruel fear that your words will come true."

" 'Twas nasty to tell me he'd offered for a barrel load of others first."

" And if you had took him, 'twould never have gone well, after that. T'other women—how many be known to himself and his Maker alone—would all have come forward sooner or later to congratulate you and whisper a thing or two. There'd have been no dignity."

CHAPTER XXV

THE despondent Sweetland felt little consoled by an invitation to Sibley Shillingford's wedding. Indeed, the circumstance, reminding too acutely of his own disastrous fortunes, served rather to cast him down. He was bewildered and demoralised. The psychological effect of these reverses could not be exaggerated, and Samuel's sister began to be much troubled for him. She only guessed that fate was treating him ill, for he had ceased to confide in her, and, since his suppression of the truth on the memorable night of his dual defeats at Kingshead and " Genoa Villa," she could only learn what was happening from other sources than himself. His secret enterprises furnished exceedingly painful experiences for Harriet, because Miss Hearn's was not a reticent nature, and she allowed herself to speak very freely when next Samuel's sister visited the post-office. As for himself, Mr. Sweetland declared that he would never go near it again. A little later, too, when Harriet was beginning to recover from Mary Hearn's egregious narrative, there came Nelly Gurney with her stark indifference to the nicer shades of feeling. From no unkindness did she speak, however, for she soon forgave Samuel's display; but Nelly saw no reason why the incident should be hid in so far as Miss Sweetland was concerned, and, indeed, doubted not that Harriet knew all about it.

Upon the strength of these shattering surprises the farmer's sister acted. She approached him in tears, revealed her grief and implored him to come to her with his troubles.

"These dreadful things ought not to be exploded in my face by third persons," said Miss Sweetland; "it isn't decent and it isn't fair. I'm all in a maze and feel quite useless. I can see terrible changes coming over you. I know that you have a great sorrow. In fact, you appear to have a dozen; and it's driving me frantic to know that you leave me out of everything, and deny me your confidence, and feel that I am not strong enough to be of any use. A bottle of whisky lasts three days now, and it used to last a week. That shows. And your usually gentle temper—— Oh, Samuel, can I do nothing? Is it impossible for me to help? There's nothing else for me to live for if I'm never to be any good to you."

This appeal was more than sufficient to break down Mr. Sweetland. He had been exceedingly miserable since starting on his path of concealment, for his nature was ill suited to the bearing of any burden single-handed. He was thankful beyond words to hear his sister's proposal, and he responded instantly. In half an hour, Samuel had laid the entire series of his misadventures before Harriet. He even told the approximate truth about them; and he did not hesitate to admit that only a foolish but manly pride had prevented him from confessing his various failures at the time of their commission.

They wept together.

Then Miss Sweetland struck a note of resolution, and heartened Samuel's fainting soul.

"There are as good fish in the sea as ever came out of it," she said. "I am proud—very proud—to think that I am privileged to help in this matter. The most acute observers may be mistaken in character—especially feminine character. Because all these women are rubbish—don't contradict me—I say 'rubbish.' Because your eyes were obscured to their real natures—— However, we shall see."

"You're a keener student of character than what I am, seemingly," admitted Samuel. "I was a fool not to remember that. You weren't my dear Tibby's right hand for twenty years for nothing. I want to find a woman worthy of you and me; and it don't seem as if I was equal to it. I lose my temper with the wretches, and then I feel disgraced."

" Not at all; not at all. 'Tis the women that are disgraced," declared Harriet. " Let 'em be swept away, like a dead man out of mind, and look round again."

She added that he might count upon her loyal aid, and even promised to be busy herself on his behalf—an undertaking that immensely cheered and fortified Samuel. Indeed, he declared that better times were in store, and began to regain his self-respect. He could even bear to consider the approaching wedding.

Gabriel Shillingford, who always spoke of the " nuptials," was a little bewildered by the composition of the wedding party; but the Smerdons desired to invite their friends and relations, and they had intermarried with almost every family in the Vale.

For his own part, the master of Blackslade would have preferred a small, select company; but finding this impossible, he contented himself with inviting a few old friends, and leaving the rest to Sibley and her sweetheart. As a result, the farmer's resources were heavily strained, and the people in secret doubted the wisdom of so lavish an entertainment. Near fifty folk sat down to the breakfast, and three times as many were at church. The hosts of the Smerdons were present, but Whitelock chose his friend, Pancras Widecombe, for best man, while Gabriel gave away his daughter. The bride was clad in white, the bridegroom in grey.

Of bridesmaids there were no less than six, and since the bridegroom was not equal to presenting each with a gift of value, his father, Peter Smerdon, had done so. Each wore a little brooch, and all were dressed in pink dresses and yellow straw hats trimmed with pink roses. They were Petronell Shillingford, Tryphena Harvey, her chosen friend; Susie, Katie, and Jessie Smerdon, sisters of the bridegroom; and Sally Turtle, daughter of Mr. Timothy Turtle of the " Rugglestone," and parlourmaid to Mrs. Windeatt. For at such times as a wedding in the country, employer and employed will often ignore their accidental relations and meet in friendship and equality. There is no gulf fixed between mistress and maid, for they may be related by ties of blood or marriage.

There came also of the bridegroom's party Peter and Jane Smerdon, his parents; his maternal grandmother—the precious link with Bishop Jewel—and all his younger brothers and sisters. His married sister, Emma, was present, together with her husband, Young Harry Hawke; Old Harry Hawke; and Baby Harry Hawke in his mother's arms. There was a doubt as to the baby's coming, but Emma pleaded that he might be present at so historic a ceremony. Other Smerdons arrived from afar; while of neighbours, Arthur Pierce and his wife were invited from the " Old Inn "; William and Grace Coaker came from Southcombe; and their son, Elias, also came. Mrs. Louisa Windeatt of Kingshead, Mr. Samuel Sweetland, Miss Harriet Sweetland, and Mr. Birkett Johnson, all of Tunhill, were there; while the pleasure-loving Gurneys of Dunstone, Abel and Sarah, were naturally invited, with Nelly and her eldest brother, Bassett. Of this party all came save Nelly. From Chittleford arrived the Dunnybrigs and their niece, Araminta Dench; while Timothy Turtle of " Rugglestone Inn " supplied the liquor, and organised the service of the meal.

There came from Venton, Uncle Tom Cobleigh; his widowed daughter, Milly Gray; and his son, Christian; while the Coplestons of Southway and the Langdons of Northway were also represented. Miss Thirza Tapper accepted an invitation, and the new doctor—one Hugh Grenville, a young man of handsome exterior and empty pocket—was delighted to be present and meet so many prospective patients. Doctor Grenville had taken rooms at Woodhayes, and hoped to make a practice in the Vale. He attended Gabriel for a wounded foot, and his name was enough to assure him reverent acceptance at Blackslade.

So many desired to witness the register that the vicar, who was no friend of Gabriel Shillingford, protested; but not before the flamboyant Pancras, who wrote an enormous hand, had rendered himself and his signature immortal. With many a flourish, sprung from superabundant vitality, he wrote:

> *Pancras Widecombe, his hand and pen,*
> *Good luck to them both, so be it. Amen.*

And the vicar, an artless and arid man, was much annoyed.

A crowd emptied from the church and lined the pathway to the lichgate. Pancras hurried forward with some bags of rice, which he distributed to men and women beside the carriages.

" Scatter it over the bride and bridegroom," he said, " but don't fling it at anybody else."

Then came the procession of guests, two by two, young and old. It was an inspiration of Sibley's that the venerable grandmother of the bridegroom should leave the church with herself and Whitelock. Each took an arm, and the people shouted welcome and greeting as they emerged into the air together. But some held it for an unlucky omen that this aged creature should thus come between the newly-wed man and woman.

" They didn't ought to have dragged out that old death's
head to the feast," declared Samuel Sweetland.

Then a flourish burst from Nicky's accordion, where he and
Nanny overlooked the procession, and with his most pathetic
expression of trust and hope he lifted up his voice and shouted :

> " I love Jeee—sus!
> Jeeeee—sus loves me! "

From the tower thundered out the bells, and Mr. Shillingford, now quite dazed and mentally obscured, began giving
the date and history of each to Doctor Grenville, who walked
beside him.

" The bells! Have you heard about them? A pretty good
lot, and some ancient. The two trebles were cast from a fine
tenor which was unfortunately crazed. One, dated 1632, was
made by subscription of fifteen men and maids. It is all
recorded on the bell itself."

But the doctor did not listen. He was admiring the pink
bridesmaids.

Mrs. Smerdon, who emerged tearfully on her husband's arm,
stopped a moment to listen to Nicky's hymn.

" Would it do to ax 'em? " she inquired. " I'd like to think
that poor little wretch of a woman had got a full belly for once.
There'll be such a lot that two more won't matter—put in a
corner somewhere."

" We might ask," answered Peter Smerdon; " Shillingford
can't but say ' no,' and 'tis the last word he ever does say."

" I'll invite 'em, then, and take the risk," declared his wife.
" If Nicky will only keep quiet. 'Tis a red-letter day for us,
and we ought to let as many as can share it; and the poor
soul, with all his faults, is blind."

She turned to Mrs. Glubb.

" You and your husband be bidden to the feast, Nanny,"
she said. " I'll take the risk; but I do pray that you'll bear
yourself seemingly, Mr. Glubb, for if you don't Mr. Shillingford
will blame me."

" Glory be! " cried Nicky. " Where's that beast, Mogridge? Shout out to the swine that we be going up, Nanny!
'Twill turn his gizzard green! "

The rice was flung, the bells rippled and thundered overhead; the bride and bridegroom drove off together, while others
also drove; but many of the guests went up on foot to Blackslade, and admired the decorations that fluttered over " Rugglestone Inn " and the floral garlands and banners hung out at

Venton and at Chittleford. Sibley's home had never been so gay. Its austere aspect was hidden in flowers and bunting. A triumphal arch ascended above the entrance, and the date, stripped for once of the sulky ivy, shone out with a face of genial eld from a chaplet of roses and ribbons.

Mr. Shillingford and his daughters moved amid the company, who came and went to the master's study, where the wedding presents were displayed. There sat grandmother Smerdon, already much exhausted, and she kept repeating the same words in a parrot voice:

" The presents be spread out here; and both the fathers have given money; and the tea-caddy's my gift."

All exclaimed with admiration, and were surprised to find such abundance of offerings.

Gabriel met Nicky and Nanny. Mrs. Glubb had led her husband to a seat under a laurel, and they were arguing as to whether he should or should not play his accordion. She carried the instrument and he wanted it.

" Dammy, I tell you a flourish will whet their appetites," he said; but she advised that he waited till afterwards.

" I'm all in a twitter as 'tis," she declared, " for 'twas only mother Smerdon invited us—not any of the Shillingford lot; and he may give us the boot at the last minute. Here he cometh—rise up, Nicky, and bless the man! "

" Good luck and long life to your honour! " cried the musician. " And may you live to have brave grandchilder on your back. And we be come—me and my wife—because the bridegroom's mother bade us. And there's witnesses to prove it. And I hope to God you'll let us bide, for such things seldom happen to us."

" You're very welcome, both of you. Everybody's welcome," said Gabriel. " I wish you could see the flowers and banners, Nicky Glubb, for they would delight you. But your wife will tell you how brave they are."

" 'Tis like a heavenly paradise," declared Nanny, " and all Miss Shillingford's work. The wonder of it! Not a cartload of proper shop-people could have done it better. And a noble pair they are, sir, and may God send them blessings."

" And the gifts so rich and rare, I hear," declared Mr. Glubb. " And God on His Throne knows that I shouldn't have been behindhand at such a time, but we live on the smell of an oiled rag—me and my wife—owing to our cruel poverty, and no fault of ours, though the will was there."

" I hope you will do well, and play a tune afterwards," said Mr. Shillingford. Then he moved away.

CHAPTER XXVI

THE river was in flood—turbid and turbulent. Its voice shouted hoarsely through the Vale, and the water-meadows were submerged. Webburn for once had attained to significant proportions, and swept along with the strength of a giant. The time was late August, and the day was Sunday.

A man stood by stream-side, and watched the brown water leap and batter the bridge. It was Pancras Widecombe, and he smiled to see the river dash herself, unavailing, against the buttress that he had built, and foam and shout and fling the yellow spume of her mane aloft in morsels for the wind to carry. A thunderstorm had followed a month of fine weather, and to-day the face of the valley was changed.

Sally Turtle happened to be at home for Sunday, and now, as Pancras expected, she appeared from the direction of " Rugglestone Inn." The bells had stopped when a flash of red broke the hedge, and a tall girl in her Sunday finery leapt out into the road and sped towards church.

" I'm late as it is, and can't stop a minute," she declared.

" Chuck church, then, and come for a walk. The choir can holloa very well without you for once."

But Sally would not be tempted.

" Father's gone twenty minutes ago, and he'll be vexed for me to miss. He likes me to be there, and he'd like you better if you went."

" I do go—off and on. I was at the wedding, wasn't I? "

They walked to the church porch together, and when Sally had entered, to take her place with the women singers, Pancras lighted his pipe and prepared to leave the churchyard, that he might seek company in the village.

A man stood among the graves, beside an open one. His attitude was listless; his hands were in his pockets and his head dropped forward. It was Jack Mogridge, and Pancras approached him.

" Morning, Jack. A stormy night. How did you fare up to Bone Hill? "

" Us was awake all night, but not along of the storm," answered the other.

" And this pit be for poor old Grandmother Smerdon? "

" Yes, 'tis."

" All along of that wedding—so they tell me. The great

excitement, and the fuss they made over her, and the feast, and one thing and another, was too much for her strength."

" 'Tis true, my Margery's mother was called in to help nurse her at the end, for 'twas more than Mrs. Smerdon could well do single-handed. The old soul's mind was quite gone long afore she died. She thought she'd just had a babby! Her last word to be understood was to my Margery's mother. ' Be it a boy or a cheel?' she said. And my Margery's mother thinks that her mind was working backwards, as the human mind will afore death."

" A very good thing that she's gone, however. And to lie pretty near Daniel Reep, I see. The old be dropping out; and for that matter we forget 'em before they're dead a'most, for once anybody's got well over eighty year old, you hear no more of 'em. The burden of the world's on middle-aged shoulders—not that I'd have it so; I'm all for youth. 'Tis us young men have the nerve and pluck to dash at things and carry 'em through willy-nilly. After you'm up home forty you know too much, and look all round a subject and grow cautious. Because the more you know, the bigger coward you be."

But Jack paid no attention to these sentiments. He appeared more dreary and helpless than usual, and could not take his eyes off the grave.

" The water has settled in it, I see," said Pancras. " You'll have to bail it afore the funeral to-morrow. Why, such a light weight as Granny Smerdon would float there! "

" A lighter than her be gone, however. My babby died last night."

" Good Lord, Jack! you don't mean that."

" Last night—in the midst of the thunder. And his mother screamed out that 'twas a cruel, heartless thing for his little soul to set forth on such a savage night. Off her head she went, and tore a lot of her hair out. A gashly thing to see such a sight as that, Pancras Widecombe. Poor nipper—never would fatten. And as for the next world—there 'tis. There's no doubt thrown upon it by my father. A chrisomer he was—not baptised nor nothing, owing to me not being married to Margery, because father wouldn't let me do it."

" You're a weak worm, Jack. I'm terrible sorry for your trouble, but if you had the pluck of a mouse, let alone a man, you'd brace yourself up to throw over your hateful father and take Margery and marry her."

" I won't deny that this have shook me," declared Mogridge. " 'Tis very hard in my opinion that the child may not even lie in the churchyard. And me the sexton's own son, and chief grave-digger, under father. But he won't hear of it. 'Tis to be put under the hedge, where the ground be doubtfully holy. You know—over there, where they buried that suicide from Leusden."

" You do make me frantic, Jack! " cried Pancras. " Damn it all, if you're a father yourself, why can't you act like one? To let your own flesh and blood, and your girl's pride and joy, be put away like a pet cat! It passes belief! Don't you do it. If your old man be such a cruel devil that he'd deny the infant Christian burial—why—in a Christian country and all! What stuff are you made of? And at such a time, with Margery's heart broke, no doubt! For the Lord's sake, Jack, show yourself a grown man and act like one. Defy your father once for all! You be first grave-digger, as you say, and who shall forbid a grave-digger to make a grave for his own child? Don't you stand it, for if you do, every man in the Vale will spit at you as you pass by."

" 'Tis very much what Margery said to me this morning," answered the other. " She's terrible wishful for the little chap to be thrust in along with his Grandfather Reep. I was considering of it when you came. But in my rash way I half wondered if we could——"

He broke off.

" Of course you could, and I'd be very pleased to help you," said Pancras. " I'd put the mother's wish in such a matter higher than the command of the Queen of England; and if she wants her child to lie beside her father, there he should lie. I'd fight the world to let it be done."

" You'm in a daring spirit, and I wish I was the same," answered Jack. " But I'm very easy to crush, even in my most upsome moments, and at a time like this, with my Margery all over the shop, I be gone weaker than usual. She sucks comfort from the thought of the child lying down beside old Daniel. She said queer things this morning—just when 'twas getting light. ' My dear father hated like hell to go in all alone with the moles,' she said; ' and now, if my blessed boy can creep to him, 'twill comfort him. Two's company! ' she said, and 'twas all her mother could do to quiet her down. Michael Arnell, the carpenter, be going to knock up a little coffin for nothing—he's at it now—a live Christian, that man— and Margery and I half thought to—— You won't tell, so help you, God, Pancras Widecombe? "

" Me tell! I'll lend you a hand, whatever 'tis! "

" The doctor will give his certificate to-morrow. 'Twas a sort of a sinking he died of. And then—to-morrow or the next night—well into the small hours with a lantern—me and Margery half thought—and if I make all suent, father'll never see it. Because, to tell you the secret truth, I'm growing that hard-hearted now that I sometimes feel that I wouldn't care what I done against father."

" I'll be up over the churchyard wall at two o'clock to-morrow night; and don't you put it off; and tell Margery that I be going to help, and proud to do it. ' Down with all tyrants' —that's what me and Birkett Johnson say. You put the child there, and I'll help with a bit of money for a brave stone presently."

" Not a stone—no, no; that's going too far," declared Jack. " I wouldn't venture on a bold deed like that for such a young child as mine. I shall be very well content and so will his mother, if we can rush him in by night and nothing said. Poor wretch—she's yowling round like a cat as have lost her kittens, this morning."

" You'll get another child," advised Pancras. " That's the manly thing to do, and 'twill give Margery something to think about and distract her mind."

" She don't want no more. She never could bide another."

" You marry her, and get your father off your chest. So long as you knuckle under to him, you'll be miserable, and never count for a man like other men."

" 'Tis almost beyond belief that I can do it," answered Jack; " but if I can lift myself to it, and get over the fear of what will come after, then you may say my child won't have died for nought."

" To-morrow night let it be, Jack, and you tell Margery that Pancras Widecombe is on your side. 'Twill prove a tower of strength to her. And I'll go further, because I hate a tyrant like Alfred Mogridge. I'll be your best man afore the people when you come to be married, to show that I think nought of what you've done. I'll be your best man, just the same as I stood for Whitelock Smerdon! I'll be your friend, Jack."

" 'Tis amazing kind, and will lighten Margery's sufferings a lot, and I'm sure me and her will be cruel obliged to you," answered the other. "You'm a fiery hero and a man of courage, and very well thought upon; but I shouldn't like for you to get cold-shouldered for it, I'm sure. In a word, I ban't one of the lucky ones, and never was."

They talked a while longer; then the congregation emerged, Pancras joined his friends, and Jack Mogridge, already full of fear, hurried away from the grave of Margery's father before his own father came out of church.

CHAPTER XXVII

MR. ALFRED MOGRIDGE had been called upon to suffer in several directions for his obstinacy, and both men and women strove to bend him from the unreasonable attitude he chose to assume; yet he hardened his heart under tribulation and still contrived to exercise absolute control over his weak-minded son.

But under certain stimulus, even a coward may exhibit the equivalent of courage and rise above himself. What no rational advice, no raillery, no sarcasm could do for Jack Mogridge, death and his lover's agony was able to effect. The extinction of his son and Margery's grief thereat powerfully affected him, found a wavering manhood deep hidden within him, proved strong enough to upset life-long traditions of surrender and obedience.

Under that conviction he spoke with Margery presently, and she lent a willing ear to him. It was night, and they sat with Mrs. Reep. In a corner of the kitchen on a chair lay the coffin of the child.

" I can do it now," said Jack; " there's such a raging wrath in my inwards, that I'd front the Dowl to-night and give as good as I got. 'Twill last for a bit, and then 'twill wear off, and I shall most likely shrink up again, and my old man will get uppermost. But, for a bit, I care not a pin about him. Evil eye or no evil eye, no worse evil could have happened than this, and if you help me, I'll defy him now—this instant moment—while I'm strong enough to do it. He saw something flash in my eye and went to bed, doubtful like, afore I come in here. But I didn't start till the man was asleep and snoring. And now I've fixed up with that fear-nought chap, Pancras Widecombe. He'll be in the churchyard a good bit afore daylight. And so I be going to dash at it! I'm that desperate to-night that you'd think I was drunk, but I ban't."

" 'Tis the father in you fighting to the top," said Mrs. Reep; " and I hope to God 'twill stay there, Jack. You once break the wicked spell he has cast over you, and the rest will be easy; and if you can only act while this here courage is boiling in you, all will come natural, and you'll find yourself married to Margery, and look back in years to come and wonder however 'twas you could have lifted your father above God Almighty."

The girl came and put her hand in Jack's, and sat by him. He stroked her shoulder sadly.

" I don't know as to that," he said. " My rage might last so long as to put up the banns. And then, please God, knowing they was up, He'd give me courage to go on."

" Your father would forbid 'em," said Margery.

" Not he," declared Mrs. Reep. " He wouldn't dare do that. 'Tis the powers of darkness make him strong. He'd never lift his voice in church, for fear of the Lord's hand."

" I hope my great courage will last up to the banns," repeated Jack; " for if they be once axed out, everybody would be o' my side and help me to go through with it, and even offer me work after. But that's to come. What be now afore us is to bury our dead one in old Daniel's grave; and that I'm going to do this instant moment."

" And I be going to hold the lantern," said Margery. " And you'd better grease the wheelbarrow afore we go, because it shrieks, and might easy wake your father."

A little later they crept silently away through the night. Mogridge pushed the wheelbarrow with the coffin in it, and Margery walked beside him and carried the lantern, which was to show him his work. They went through a moonless night. There was no wind, but a gentle moisture fell out of the dark sky.

The girl resented their secret task.

" 'Tis a blasted shame us have got to do it like this," she said. " Our babby have as much right to a proper funeral as any other, and they be a lot of cussed, cowardly wretches to deny it to him—a dear, li'l good boy as never——"

She ceased, and wept as she trudged forward.

" Don't take on," he answered. " What's the use? We've done 'em all right. He'll be there—where we all shall be, sooner or late. And if he rises along with his family on the Last Day, then he'll take his chance with the rest. 'Tis all very clear to me, and you needn't think our precious babby be going to get into trouble in the next world just because that fiddle-faced fool down to church wouldn't baptize him till we married."

They came to the burying-ground, lighted the lantern, and found Daniel Reep's unmarked grave. Then Jack went to a shed where the sexton's tools were kept, unlocked it, and fetched a pick and spade.

" Four feet deep be enough," he said. " Four feet deep and three feet long be ample. Hold the lantern while I cut the turfs extry thick. If us takes 'em off deep enough they'll go in again without flagging, and father'll never notice. And we'll spread that barras apron I brought, so as not a pinch of soil will be left on the grass after."

They began their work, and Jack's shadow danced enormous on the church wall while he dug, and Margery held the lantern.

He laboured for half an hour, then Pancras joined them. The stonemason applauded their courage mightily, and took the spade from Jack.

"You have a rest and a pull at your pipe," he said. "And here's a drop of sloe gin. I fetched it along specially for your missis. 'Twill warm her."

But his words were far more cheering than the cordial. To be called Jack's "missis" brought a ray of comfort to the bedraggled woman.

"And if his courage holds out, he's going to have the banns up Sunday, and chance it," she said.

"Well done him! And of course his courage must hold. Why the devil not? What's the sense of going in leading strings to a darned old terror like Mogridge? 'Tis bad luck enough to be son to the man without being slave to him."

"Keep the earth on the apron, Mr. Widecombe," said Margery. "Us wants to make a clean job and leave all suent, so as Mr. Mogridge shan't find out."

"And I say 'let him find out,' and the sooner the better," declared Pancras. "Why, good powers! he can't dig the child up again."

They dug the grave and lowered the little coffin into it.

"Mr. Arnell made the box for friendship," said Jack. "And a lot of trouble he took, as you can see. And me and Margery won't forget it."

They buried the dead, and Pancras began to fill in the grave.

"He lies now but two feet from his grandfather, and you must tramp on the earth a bit when you've got in a little more," explained Jack. "But I'm afraid that, do what we will, the thing won't be hid. 'Tis so dark we can't tell what a jakes of a mess we be making."

Then Margery spoke.

"Hark!" she said, "there's somebody coming!"

A footstep sounded on the gravel path, and then ceased. A man emerged from behind the church tower and came stumbling over the graves towards them.

"Be that you, policeman Chave?" asked Pancras. "Because, if so, I'm glad to tell you as I am here, and all is right and proper."

But it was not policeman Chave.

"What May games be these, then?" shouted the furious voice of the sexton as he approached.

"Be brave, Jack—for God's sake be brave!" said Margery.

" And if you can't be, you slope off while your legs will carry you, and leave him to me and Mr. Widecombe."

" I *am* brave," said Alfred's son. " I'm sweating with bravery—I don't care a damn for the man. I——"

Then Mogridge burst upon them.

" Explain this—explain it ! " he said. " You tell me how you dare, and then I'll tell you what I be going to do. Come here, Jack Mogridge. You come over here to me, you cunning snake ! A'creeping out of the house when I slept; and if it hadn't been as I was woke by your letting in the blasted cat, as climbed on my bed, I should never have knowed."

Pancras Widecombe prepared to bear the brunt of the sexton's attack, but it seemed that Jack had told the truth, and no longer feared his father, even in the actual presence of the old man.

" 'Tis done, and you can't undo it," he said. " My child lies under the ground beside Margery's father, and he's got to bide there. His small bones will soon enough be dust, and who's hurt? "

" God's hurt," answered Mr. Mogridge. " God's hurt, and I'm hurt likewise, and the law and order and religion be all hurt; and, what's more, don't you talk to me in that tone of voice, Jack, because well you know I won't have it."

" No doubt you be terrible surprised," answered his son. " I'm surprised myself; nobody more so. You've done it now; you've gone too far and egged me into such a proper savage state that I don't care what I do, no more than a mad dog. My child be buried in holy ground, and he'll stop there; and I'll marry the mother of it afore the corn do kern. Yes, I will —I swear it."

" We'll talk about that after," answered the sexton. " You're drunk, no doubt, else you wouldn't ope your rabbit mouth so wide. Well may the night cover you, you godless rip ! and you'll call on the hills to cover you also afore I've done with you. But that's for us, not for this shameless female, nor yet this noisy, mischievous fool, as was born in the gutter, and ought to have been left there. The likes of all you trash to go digging graves in holy ground by night ! My God ! what'll happen next in the world? And all for a wretched, misbegotten, unbaptized thing with no more soul than a dog——"

Here the man was silenced, because Margery Reep, without a second's warning or previous hint of her purpose, flew at him. Straight and strong as a swooping kestrel she flung herself on the man. Her big hands met on his throat and the impetus of her sudden charge threw him backwards. His head caught the curb of a grave and was wounded.

" There—there! " screamed the frenzied woman, scrambling off him. " That'll teach you, you anointed devil! My fingers have itched to tear your eyes out this many a day, and if it hadn't been for Jack, I'd have done it. And you lie there, you coarse, cowardly, blackguard beast. You lie there till my child's grave be made all decent and proper. And 'tis you killed it, you murderer, for if us had been married afore all men, everything would have falled different. You move, and I'll scratch your toad's eyes out! "

Mr. Mogridge groaned and spoke.

" You shall all go to clink for this," he said. " I'll not rest till the three of you be put away, and when you'm behind bars on bread and water, you mind this : I shall be here to heave up that coffin! I'll fight the parish and parson and the whole world afore I let your bastard brat bide here; and I'd fling out his godless scoundrel of a grandfather, too, if I could."

Margery was going to attack again upon this speech, but Pancras caught her and held her back, while Jack stood in doubt.

" Fill up the grave—fill up the grave! " cried Widecombe. " Your old man's all right, else he wouldn't be so lively with his tongue. Finish and put home the turf and get out of this, you and Margery there. 'Tis no use kicking, Margery, I ban't going to let you go. We can't kill the wretch, though he deserves it."

Then Alfred Mogridge rose from the earth and himself departed.

" Wait for the daylight! " he said. " Hell you shall have to-morrow."

He staggered off, and Pancras spoke again.

" 'Tis done, and you needn't fear, Jack, for I'll watch over it till morning, and the old man won't come here; he'll go to parson and the churchwardens and have the whole thing thrashed out from top to bottom. And you'll come off all right and be married. And don't you be savage and violent, Margery, else you'll turn the people from you and spoil all; but if you keep meek and mild, but firm, like Jack here, then everybody will be your friend."

" 'Tis the dew of the morning," said young Mogridge, " and cock-light over the hills. Us will go home, Margery dear, and Pancras will be so good as his word and keep watch that nothing be done against the grave. You'm a brave wonder, Margery, and I be all your side, God, He knows. But now I'd best be away back—for to fetch brown paper to father's head."

" You be yielding after all I've done! " she said; but he swore it was not so.

"Don't you think it. I'll never yield no more—not after to-night—not after what he said against our little chap. That settled it. And 'tis only his opinion, whether or no, and he's an ignorant old man, and he be wrong oftener than right. And don't you fret as to that, because, later on, when we can breathe again, I'll put that question afore some scholar who be equal to it."

"I wish I'd killed him," said the bereaved mother. "Then they'd hang me and I'd go to my baby."

They smoothed the green turf, and built up the mound of the grave where they had broken it.

CHAPTER XXVIII

TOM GURNEY, the blacksmith, had much to think about, for into his bustling and somewhat brutal existence had come another necessity for collision with his fellow-men. To his own mind, he did not put it so, because, in his judgment, Arthur Pierce was not a man, but a mere futile organism, useless to the world, useless to himself, and a source of dire tribulation to his wife. The situation became intolerable, and Gurney was now divided between Mabel Pierce and his own business interests. He could not advance both, for the attitude of Widecombe, albeit tolerant enough in most directions and indifferent enough to the conduct of the individual, proved not indifferent upon this subject. Gurney had succeeded too well, and become too prosperous and important a person in the community to escape envy, jealousy, and their consequences. Many were willing enough to criticise him unkindly, and make his private conduct the excuse, though in truth it was his public success that awakened enmity. Tom's doubtful attitude to the Pierces enabled certain men, who really cared not a button about it, to protest, to censure him, to harass him. Their private reasons were concerned with his local power; his morals were the stalking horse beneath which the attack was made. For reasons of pure jealousy not a few had joined the Johnson faction, and were looking forward with pleasure to the approaching ceremony of the mock funeral.

The details were kept as secret as possible, and the conspirators had one and all taken oath to reveal no word of their purpose; yet now, two days before the event, there came the man, Christian Cobleigh, son of Uncle Tom Cobleigh, to the blacksmith by night; and seldom did that silent creature talk so much. Speech was painful to this sly, taciturn spirit, and only provocation and natural cupidity now tempted him to so many words. He was tall, thin, and dark, with black hair, shorn close to his head, and a black moustache and beard also kept very close. His brown eyes never held another pair; his hands were never still.

Gurney, his work done, sat alone in his kitchen, with tobacco and troublesome reflections. He still clung to the prosperity that he had built up on twenty years of hard work at Widecombe; he regretted the increasing need to desert it; he cudgelled his brains whether there might not yet lie some middle road whereon his dual ambitions could proceed successfully together.

Then came Christian, and asked for speech.

" And welcome," said Tom. " 'Tis the last thing you're used to want. Must be some matter a bit out of the common if you seek to hear your own voice. Has the Slate Club gone scat, or what is it? "

" You earn more out of listening than talking, most times; but just now I'm hopeful to earn a bit out of talking, too. And the Slate Club's all right, and will be—so long as I'm secretary of it."

" Well, have a drop of drink. I can give 'ee beer, but nought else. I never drink no spirits."

" No more don't I. But you'd better list afore you drink; because, if I can't interest you, I won't bide. In a word, there's a plot out against her—Mrs. Pierce, I mean; and I know about it."

Gurney nodded. He was not greatly astonished.

" I've smelled this in the air a good while. I've seen it in the jackal sort of way a good few men sneak past me."

" 'Tis like this : I didn't want to go in it—I'm not that sort; too fond of minding my own business; but my father drew me in; and he's a power among 'em, because, along of his great age, he knows——"

Christian broke off.

" But that's telling. The thing be this : I've heard what's in hand—all about it—and I think 'tis a cruel, wicked shame, and my blood boils against 'em; and so I come to you."

" You're going to give 'em away? "

" No, I ban't. Beggars can't be choosers. I never give nothing away. I've been unlucky lately, betting."

" You'll gamble the boots off your feet afore you've done with it."

" Very like. 'Tis a great craving—worse than drink. 'Tis a voice always crying in me to get something for nothing. I'm made so, and it's a pity; still, us have all got our failings. But in this case I don't want anything for nothing. I want money for a bit of news, and that news is exactly what be going to be done against Arthur Pierce's wife, and where, and when."

Gurney nodded.

" I see—just a question of what it be worth to me."

" As to the worth, since you be known far and wide to set such store on the woman, it ought to be worth all you've got and a bit over to know what these rogues have planned against her. And this I'll say for nothing : that such be the deadly thoughts they've hatched out of their minds, that the female never can hold up her head here in public again after. So there 'tis, and in my opinion five pounds wouldn't be a penny piece too much to pay for what I know."

They haggled as to the price for half an hour, and Christian Cobleigh was stubborn. He would only bate this high demand by half a sovereign, and he insisted upon ready money.

But, the cash in his pocket, his revelations were complete. He withheld no detail of the forthcoming rite; he explained that it was to be held in the field above the " Rugglestone Inn " at a famous mass of granite known as the " Rugglestone." There would the grave be dug, the hanging take place, and the great doll, intended to represent Mrs. Arthur Pierce, be buried with all ceremony.

" They've got it to be the very living daps of her," declared Christian; " 'tis Mabel Pierce to the colour of her stockings. That imp, Pancras Widecombe, have come out with great gifts and astonished everybody. They've gone through it all half-a-dozen times, like a lot of play actors, and 'twill be a cruel, solemn, far-reaching thing, without a doubt."

The blacksmith spat on his hands in anticipation.

" 'Twill be far-reaching enough," he admitted.   " 'Twill reach so far that some of these hookem snivey cowards will wish they'd never been born in the morning after. Saturday week, at five o'clock, the fun begins? "

" It do—to give the people from round about a chance to be there. I dare say there'll be two hundred come from up over for it, and a lot from Newton and Bovey."

He gave all details, drank a glass of beer, and then went

off home to Venton. It was understood that Gurney should promise never to mention his informer, or explain how he had discovered the plot. He considered deeply when Christian was gone, and then walked over to the " Old Inn," that he might speak with the unconscious victim.

Fortune favoured him, for Mr. Pierce had gone to bed with a face-ache, and Mabel was in the bar alone.

" Thank God! " she said. " I was just going to shut up and slip round and hear the sound of your voice for two minutes. He's gone to bed, poor wretch, with a swollen jaw."

" Shut up shop," he said, " and come out in the field for five minutes. No, it can't go on, and there be them in Wide-combe as mean to take damned good care it shan't go on. And I know their names and their plans. 'Tis not because of our friendship, but for my fame and strength and success, that they be doing it. If I was Bell in the almshouse, or that blind adder, Glubb, they'd never think twice about it; but when a man once gets his head and shoulders above the crowd same as what I've done, then the rest be like a pack of coward wolves at his throat, keeping up each other's courage and leap-ing to pull him down."

" Be they going to strike at you, then? " she asked.

" Yes, but not fair and square—not to my face. Too cowardly for that. 'Tis their plot to hit me through you. They be going to blast your good name and make the place ring with it."

Mabel laughed.

" That's more than they can do—so long as you be by my side. You know that. What do I care for the whole rally of 'em, or their bark or their bite, while you be here? Now go, and I'll put up the shutters and look at Arthur, and then I'll come out to you."

" No custom to-night? "

" Nothing to name. Old Harry and Young Harry came in, and young Coaker, and a stranger or two, and your second hand at the forge. That was all."

He left her, to meet again a little later at a familiar tryst, where was a hazel hedge that flung a heavy shadow to hide them under the white moonlight.

Then he described the entertainment planned, and Mabel gasped and gurgled with horror as she heard the details. But when he explained his own intentions she demurred. They talked a very long time, and the spectacle was presented of a strong man being slowly worn down from his resolves by the equal resolution and quicker wit of a strong woman. Tom Gurney was not wholly convinced when they parted; but she knew him well enough to be sure that her advice would be followed.

CHAPTER XXIX

ARAMINTA DENCH, though a woman of no sure and steadfast character, took but little time to decide against Valiant's proposal. She dreaded only one thing on earth, and that was poverty; she trusted Mr. Dunnybrig to be honest and just; but the disabilities of the situation were complete from every point of view save her uncle's, and when Araminta thought upon her aunt, she felt quite safe. It was not enough that Araminta should comply; the wife had to be considered also, and Jane Dunnybrig could not be called an Old Testament disciple. She held very definite opinions, regarded herself as a working Christian, and subscribed to the ordinary values of married women.

Therefore, Araminta temporised, and waited until Valiant should break his archaic purposes to Jane. She had little doubt of the result, and wished the decision and refusal to come from her aunt, so that the man should not be angered with her.

Dunnybrig spoke no more to her on the subject for the present, though from a chance word she perceived that he had assumed she was willing. She did not deny it, though she had done nothing to justify him in this belief. She guessed that the farmer was negotiating on the subject with his wife; and she was right. Many biblical hints were daily dropped by Mr. Dunnybrig, and when he considered that the hour was come, he approached the matter and laid his enterprise starkly before Jane. He spoke to her by night after they had gone to bed, and, as a preliminary, he read the history of Abraham.

" 'Tis a strange fact," he said, when the light was out, " that the people say I walk arm-in-arm with God."

" Many a true word be spoke in jest," answered Mrs. Dunnybrig quietly. She knew quite well what was coming. A hundred signs had contributed to it. His continued talk of offspring and the Lord's will had wakened dormant suspicions. Therefore, Jane was ready, and she was fearless.

She lay alert now, all senses stung to battle, intuition at highest pitch, monogamic instincts marshalled to protect her, and religion also upon her side.

" Yes, they say I walk arm-in-arm with God, and they mean it for an offence. But 'tis they, not me, who look foolish. We hear on every hand how Jehovah's ways be past finding out. Yet, for my part, I never will grant it. Time and again I've catched myself seeing eye to eye with Him and thinking alike on nearly every subject under the sky. Often I've said to myself, for experiment like, what I'd do about a thing if I was God, and how I'd tackle it, and where I'd punish if need be, and where I'd reward. And 'tis a most amazing fact how life generally falls out just so, and the Almighty takes the very line I'd have took myself."

" Not amazing at all. Why do you say that? If you keep close to heaven in your prayers and in your ways, and live the life of a Christian man, and never let Jesus out of your sight or mind—well, how can you go wrong or make mistakes? "

" Take that Jack Mogridge and the girl he's to marry presently," continued Valiant. " I said a long bit ago, after dressing down his father, that the thing to happen would be for the unblessed child to die, and then the eyes of the nation would look upon the scandal and see that right was done. And the child did die, and Jack, they tell me, is stung to the courage of doing right and wedding the girl, though his father may rage and gnash his teeth till he's tired."

" For that matter you did talk to poor Jack, and so you may take a bit of the credit to yourself."

" I want no credit. I'm only mentioning it. There's greater matters forward than that. There's a voice sounding night and day to me, and now 'tis time to tell you what the voice is saying. Some men mightn't think there was any need to tell you; some men might obey the call as a matter of course and raise up seed at the command of their Maker, and expect you to bring up the children at your knees and take full joy of 'em, because they were mine. But I'm not like that. I respect you, same as I always have done and always shall do, and your handmaid won't cast any shadow between us. She's only called to do her duty, you understand. What us have got to do is this : to put the matter outside any paltry human opinions and prejudices. We let small things seem large and suffer them to bulk big and hide the things that truly are large. But I've always strove to keep all questions in their proper place, and 'tis only since I heard the Lord's angel telling me by night that I must make a man or two in my own image afore 'tis too late—'tis only since that came upon me as a duty to face—that I've weighed the matter, or troubled about it. Where God's finger points, man must go."

" This don't surprise me as much as you might think, Valiant."

" So much the better. I hate concealment, and have been at good pains to show which way my thoughts were leading. You see, in a manner of speaking, I be Abraham over again."

" Yes, my dear; but I ban't Sarah, and Araminta Dench ain't going to be Hagar—if that's what you're aiming at. There's nothing like plain speaking, as you say, so we'll be plain as the sun, if you please. This thing be got in your brain, and angels have put it there—so you say. Well, there's all sorts of angels—good and bad—and all sorts of dreams— good and bad likewise. Now you say every word what you want to say; and then you can listen to your wife."

" I don't like your tone of voice, Jane," he answered. " There's heat in it. This subject must be approached by you same as it has been by me. 'Tis a religious matter—far, far above any silly, small feelings—for or against. I say that God have told me that I must add to the human wealth of the nation and fetch a few children into it, because it is not His will that my pattern should be lost. In a word, I am to have five children before I die."

" Are you? Well, you shan't have 'em before I die, anyway," declared the woman quietly.

" Can you be so small and selfish about it? " he asked. " Now I never should have expected that! I must try and make you see with the Lord's eyes, Jane, and then all will take its proper place."

" I do see with the Lord's eyes," she replied. " And my Lord and Master is Jesus Christ."

" He came to fulfil the law, however, not to break it. He had no quarrel with Father Abraham. You can argue upon details later, if you think 'tis seemly so to do. For the minute what matters is this. I want your handmaid, Araminta, to be the mother of my children, and she's pretty nearly agreed; but naturally she be terrible anxious to do nothing to hurt you. So far as I can see, 'tis all so straight and simple as the stem of a fir-tree. And as to having five by her—three boys and two girls—that was shown me in broad daylight, when I went up over across Hameldon a bit ago on my pony. ' I will lift up mine eyes unto the hills, from whence cometh my help,' I said to myself. And there, upon a rocky place in the wilderness, where the old men buried their dead, I saw five stones lifted up; and three were tall and two were short. So there 'tis. And when you say there are more sorts of angels than one, Jane, meaning thereby that 'twas a devil troubled my dreams, I must tell you that you are wrong. You know my character and my record; and the devil as dared to come afore me, waking or sleeping, would be a mighty bold piece of goods. So now let's hear how it strikes you. And if it have given you the flutters at the heart, I'll up and fetch you a drop of brandy."

"It haven't given me the flutters," said Mrs. Dunnybrig. "I'm long past flutters when you are the matter, Valiant, and well you know it. But I should reckon as you'd give Araminta the flutters—unless she be harder brass than even I think her."

"If you could talk without being personal like that, us should get on better," he declared; but she held it a matter purely personal, and tried to show him the significance of the reality apart from his dreams.

"'Tis a personal matter," she said, "and never was one more so, and your trying to mix yourself up with Abraham and Isaac and Jacob won't make it different. What be the people planning to do this instant moment? Why, they be going to hang a effigy of a woman who be cruel to her husband : and how much fearfuller a thing is a man cruel to his wife! The Old Testament days be over, and you know it; and I didn't marry you under the Old Testament; I married you under the Prayer-Book. 'Tis perfectly well understood and accepted that a barren wife do stand for ever between an honest man and a family; and if he goes into matrimony, a man has got to do it open-eyed and take the rough with the smooth."

"And so has a woman," he said. "But the rough you've never suffered, and never shall while I can stand between. I want you to have joy of my little ones afore you be too old to do so; and what more reasonable and suent and fitting altogether than that your own niece should be the chosen instrument of the Lord?"

"Don't you begin again," she answered; "'tis my turn now, and you promised to listen. And I say this : I've been a good wife to you, and a loving and a patient."

"You'll have the first place of honour at my right hand."

"What's that, if another woman has the place of honour everywhere else? Can't you see? This ban't the Holy Land : 'tis Widecombe. One man, one wife—that's where we've got to now, and it ban't for you to go back, all on your own, to the old manners and customs."

"There's no such thing as ' old ' with God Almighty, Jane."

"You're deceived—bitterly and cruelly deceived; and if you

think such an outrage could happen in any Christian country anywhere nowadays and not set all decent people buzzing at your ears, you make a very great mistake."

"Leave that side," he answered. "Leave that side. My conscience is perfectly clear and perfectly settled about it. If I thought 'twas wrong, then I'd cut my hand off rather than do it; but 'tis right and proper, and the Lord have put it into my heart to offer, and have put it into Araminta's heart to consider the matter."

"Have He?" she replied. "And what will He put into my heart about it, do you think? I know very well."

"It have got a sentimental side," said Valiant. He was restless and had risen out of bed, and now sat upon the edge of it drumming on the floor with his toes.

"Yes," she admitted, "it have got a sentimental side. The very bare idea be enough to make a wife weep tears of blood, in my opinion."

"Not at all—I don't mean any such thing. I mean—well, I should have imagined that a child-loving woman like you would have doated to see my children on your knees."

"Yours—and another woman's? Why, good God in heaven! where's your common sense and knowledge and wit, Valiant? Be you daft? What do you think that women be made of?"

"I know what they *was* made of," he retorted, "and you can find out for yourself in the Five Books; but what they be made of now—— They be sunk into a sort of feeble and selfish pride. A woman—one woman—what is she in the wilderness of women?"

"She's herself, and she's got her pride, and 'tis neither selfish nor feeble pride. And she's got her sense; and she's not going to be one in a crowd, along with a heap of brazen-faced columbines and all the rest of it. And one word's as good as a thousand: I won't have it, and if you dare to touch another woman I go."

"You'd better recall that and consider the situation in a prayerful spirit, Jane," he said. "'Tis not for nothing that God speaks to a man in dreams. I've pleasured you for forty years; but you never came between me and my Master."

"'Tis one of two things, Valiant, and a choice of evils at best now. Either you are humbugging yourself something shocking, or else you're going mad; and 'tis more like the last than the first, in my opinion; for you can see life clear enough when you please; and I've always said and believed, for all your strangeness, that you walked closer to God than most men—till now. But never again will I say it."

"That's your narrowness," he answered. "While everything I did or said suited you, of course you put it down to the Almighty; and now, just because He has pointed out certain things that I should never have hit on single-handed; and just because these things lower your fancied dignity and importance —then you get up in arms and pretend that 'tisn't the Lord at all that's calling to me. For a woman as have dwelt forty years under my roof, to grudge God five immortal souls of my getting! Why—how can you sink to it? I wish you could see yourself as your Maker and me see you, Jane, for then——"

" Have done! " she cried. " I tell you that I've been patient with you always. My patience was butter to the bread of our married life, and if you knew how thick it had to be spread over all they forty years, you'd give me some credit. But this —I'll never, never, never suffer it, and more wouldn't any self-respecting English woman, let alone a Ford of Tavistock. We hold our heads high, and it have been quite punishment enough to me to bear no children, which you very well know. And, at the time of hope and disappointment, you supported me through it and behaved like a man, and said 'twas the Lord's will."

" So it was," answered her husband. " So it was, Jane. But that's neither here nor there. The question is this : ' Be Valiant Dunnybrig to have a hand in the next generation, because the Lord have looked upon him and seen him a man well fitted so to do? ' That's what we've got to answer. 'Tis a feeble race nowadays, and we be frightened of putting far-reaching questions to one another, and still more frightened of answering them. Us shan't sleep to-night, for I can hear by your panting how 'tis with you. I'll fetch ' Horrors and Terrors,' and give 'ee a few chapters."

He rose off the bed, lighted a candle, and went down for the book; while she sat up, shivering with doubt, burning with anger.

While he read, she speculated on the future, and planned her own course of action. She had helped him before, when his dealings with his fellow-men reached difficult crises, and she would help him now to escape from this abominable hallucination. Her anger departed as he read on, and she mourned for him. She itched to be up and doing. For an hour the thunder of " Horrors and Terrors " rolled harmlessly upon her ears; then it faltered and ceased. Valiant, who had returned to bed with the book, at length dropped asleep over it; whereupon Mrs. Dunnybrig shut the volume, extinguished the candle, and slipped from her bed. Morning had touched the sky, and a cock was crowing out of the darkness.

CHAPTER XXX

THE theatre chosen in which to pillory Mabel Pierce lay above
" Rugglestone Inn " and beneath the Moor. Here stood the
famous " Rugglestone," an enormous mass of granite alleged
to weigh a hundred and ten tons. It was a logan, but no
hand could rock it, and Mr. Turtle, who held a sort of pro-
prietary interest in the boulder, stuck stoutly to an ancient
Widecombe saying : that only with the help of the church-
door key might the mass be made to move. Two enormous
blocks of granite were here supported by a third. They lay
on rough ground watered by a stream and littered with stones.
The larger logan, whose weathered sides and mossy top faced
south, sustained a rowan sapling that sprang up from its
midst and sucked life out of the stone. A light of golden-
green moss and silvery lichen shone over the mighty boulder;
ferns and pennyworts embroidered its face and sides; a tonsure
of grass—green in summer, in winter, grey—ascended upon its
crown. Beside this master rock stood another, wreathed in a
great ivy tod; and now there came an evening when both the
" Rugglestone " and its neighbour were covered with close-
packed humanity, for the event of the mock execution was to
take place at their feet.

Fifty people scattered the field, and around an old shippon at
the upper end there swarmed a cluster of men, who came and
went, ran hither and thither, and gave directions to each other.
Upon the " Rugglestone " itself, overlooking the grave that
opened beneath it, stood Gabriel Shillingford, for to him, as
an antiquary, the rite promised exceeding interest, and he was
at present concerned more with the archæological aspect of the
revival than its immediate significance. But although not a
few, including his daughter Petronell, Mrs. Louisa Windeatt,
and Samuel Sweetland and his sister from Tunhill, stood
beside t' farmer and listened to his discourse, others were not
so indifferent, and approached the event with personal emotion.
There were factions in the field, and those who resented the
matter congregated together and held a firm front. Here
stood Old Harry Hawke, his son Young Harry and two
labourers from Woodhayes. With them appeared Elias Coaker;
though it was not conviction that brought him, but a natural
inclination to take the weaker side. A Smerdon or two—
younger brothers of Whitelock—also assisted Mabel Pierce's

supporters, and certain men were drawn to them—from no interest in the heroine of the event, but because their private enemies happened to be on the other side. This evening promised good opportunity to pay off old scores. Thus, Mr. Bell, of the almshouse, had gone over to the enemy, because he hoped, after dusk, to get in a hearty thump or two on the jaw of blind Nicky Glubb.

With t e minority was also gathered Alfred Mogridge, who meant to pluck a crow with Pancras Widecombe, while a cousin of Tom Gurney's, who was in the blacksmith's secrets, had driven over from Pondsworthy to take his place in the fighting rank. Tom Gurney himself had not yet come, but his supporters expected him to take the field at any moment.

When Elias Coaker taxed Adam Sanders with supporting the forces of disorder, the constable explained.

" Don't know nothing about that," he said. " I've got my orders, and so have Ernest Chave yonder, and they be to do nought so long as these people go about their fun in a quiet and decent way. And I hope you men won't interfere with them, because then they won't interfere with you. 'Tis an old custom; and when 'tis all over you can have your say, and not sooner."

But Elias scorned such counsel.

" 'Tis another old custom to knock your enemies on the head, and we've just so good a right to play at old customs as them," he said. " There's a difference of opinion going to be decided afore very long, and we've got every reason to defy these chaps, as be set on dragging a woman's credit in the dust."

They had come where a pole and transverse beam ascended.

" 'Tis here," said Alfred Mogridge, " that the creatures be going to hang up their mommet.* They'll string it up aloft, and then pull it down and bury it, with all the beastly insults they can think upon."

" And we'll let 'em go so far as the hanging," declared Old Harry. " You list to me. I can't fight, but I can give advice. You suffer 'em to go through with their foolery, and then, when 'tis done, and they be going to bury the doll, you young men will dash in altogether and properly surprise 'em, and tear the effigy of Mrs. Pierce to pieces afore their eyes."

" Policeman Sanders be gone to speak to Policeman Chave at the gate," said Young Harry. " They'll take the side of the weakest, according to their custom, so if we're winning, we'll have 'em against us at the finish."

" I'll go over and talk to them," declared his father.

* *Mommet*, scarecrow.

" The time is at hand, for there's Mr. Shillingford and a good few women and non-fighters perched up 'pon the ' Rugglestone.' "

" I wanted for Mrs. Pierce to come herself and face it out," said Mr. Gurney's cousin. " And Tom axed her also, I believe; because, as he very truly said, our side would fight a lot better if she was there to see; but she wouldn't come. And t'other side wanted for Arthur Pierce to go and stand up on the rock out of harm's way; but he's taking the affair ill, and says that 'tis the last straw that will break his back."

A man approached, hatless and excited.

" 'Tis Christian Cobleigh," said Harry Hawke the younger. " He's against us, as we all know, and we can't have no truck with him to-night."

" No, no," declared Christian. " You'm out there, I'm your side. I've throwed 'em over long ago. I'm on Mabel Pierce's side, I do assure 'ee."

A crowd of men and boys, and a few women, wandered about the field. Their numbers increased. They crowded round the grave and the gallows; then they sought to penetrate the old barn, but were prevented. Presently the church clock struck six, and the ceremony began. Hardly had the bell ceased when another sound—harsh and hideous—a burlesque of a bell, rolled out from the shippon, and to its painful reiteration a procession emerged from the building.

Nicky Glubb, led by his wife, came first. They were both clad in black; indeed, a significant feature of the procession was its funereal aspect, for only one flash of white broke the monotony of darkness. Nicky played his accordion and Nanny shrilled a hymn. She was supported by the voices of six boys who followed, walking two by two. Next came Birkett Johnson, who played " undertaker." He wore a top hat with a mourning band, an old frock coat of his master's and a huge black tie. He carried a black staff and marshalled the procession. To Pancras Widecombe had fallen the important part of " clergyman." He marched along in a nightshirt that Sally Turtle had converted into a surplice; and over it he wore a gigantic black stole, half a foot wide. A book he carried, while upon each side of him there marched a surpliced boy. One bore a candle and one a bell. Next came a grotesque figure, the " hangman." He also wore black, and his eyes were hidden behind a black mask. Horns sprouted from his head; he carried a pitchfork, and presented some confusion of ideas, since he was half an executioner, half a demon. No less a man than Jack Mogridge played this part. He had begged for it to testify his emancipation, and also because he would be disguised and beyond reach of recognition. After

Jack walked the " bearers "—six stout men, led by the small figure of Uncle Tom Cobleigh in venerable attire. Three young farmers went in this company, and it included Bassett Gurney from Dunstone Mill, and one Willes Langdon from Northway.

In their midst they bore a chair, wherein sat the effigy of Mabel Pierce. Her peculiarities had been much accentuated, and the figure, with its enormous bosom, massive legs, and scarlet face, was greeted with shouts of laughter and groans of scorn. It wore a cotton gown, and a straw hat trimmed with paper flowers. Its black hair spread over its shoulders, and in its hand was a whip—the mythical weapon with which Mabel was said to have struck her husband on more than one occasion. The figure brandished this scourge, and a man, who walked behind the chair, pulled a string and worked the doll's arm up and down. On the back of the chair was a square placard bearing this legend : " *Behold the Widecombe husband-beater* ! " The dummy bulked larger far. than life.

Mr. Timothy Turtle and half a dozen other men brought up the rear. They bore marrow-bones and cleavers—to be used later; while a boy, left in the shed from which the procession had started, beat regularly upon a great metal pan and imitated the passing bell.

Then to the gallows marched the procession, and drew up in a ring there, while the crowd pressed round them. All was done in order and, without any haste or disturbance, for the supporters of Mabel Pierce felt a little awed by the solemnity of the scene. The rival faction outnumbered them considerably, and Tom Gurney still tarried.

Then Pancras spoke :

" My friends," he said, " we will now sing the hymn of the husband-beater, before we give this woman to her doom ! "

The effigy was brought under the gallows, and while Jack Mogridge tied a rope about its neck, Nicky played a new tune; the boys sang to a slow measure the song that Uncle Cobleigh had taught them; and the men thundered in time on their marrow-bones and cleavers.

Thus ran the dirge :

> " There is a wife lives in this place
> Who beats her husband to sad disgrace.
> She beats him black, and she beats him blue,
> She beats him till the blood runs through !
> And if this woman don't mend her manners,
> We'll have her skin and send to the tanners;
> And when the tanners have tanned it well,
> Her hide shall be hung on the nail of hell ! "

Twice the song was shouted slowly, and then came the ceremony of the execution. The cumbrous effigy was dragged aloft with a dozen men at the rope. It was then allowed to spin awhile by the neck before the face of all beholders.

And still the woman's friends looked for their leader; but he did not come, and Elias Coaker prepared to take his place.

"Hold on a little longer yet," he said to the others, who meant to join battle with Johnson and his party. "Let 'em get a bit further with their foolery; then we'll go for 'em."

Presently, the execution over, Pancras Widecombe cried out in a loud voice :

"We have seen this female well and truly hanged, and now we will bury her! "

Whereupon Nicky gave a flourish on his accordion, and Jack Mogridge lowered the figure down. It was placed on a bier, with its whip and placard uoon its breast, and then marched to the grave.

Many had watched the ceremony thus far with profound interest, and from his perch on the " Rugglestone " Gabriel Shillingford descanted at length to Mrs. Windeatt, Samuel Sweetland, and others, concerning these old-time rites. None as yet perceived that a faction resented the business very bitterly; but at the graveside the Hawkes, Coaker, Christian Cobleigh, and a dozen others were massed solidly together and, after the hanging, certain independent spirits from afar found their chivalry wakened, so that they protested against this assault upon a woman, and joined Mrs. Pierce's supporters.

Nicky's hopes of a real battle promised to be amply justified. Indeed, his wife told him as much, and while the funeral procession approached the grave, she spoke to her husband, when he rested a moment from his labours.

"They Hawkes and a lot of chaps be getting shoulder to shoulder under the rock," she said. "There'll be a proper tantara in a minute."

"Be Tom Gurney there? " he asked; but Nanny could not see the blacksmith. "The dusk do come down," she replied, " and I can't swear to 'em; but there's Elias Coaker and some of these young Smerdons and the men from Woodhayes. And that old devil, Bell from the almshouse, be crept behind 'em."

"He's come for me," declared Nicky. "You bring me to the man and let me get my hand in his neckerchief—I ax no more."

The moment the bier was deposited Pancras began, but his sermon was punctuated by the first growling of the storm.

"Stand further off, you men! Don't you be so damned pushing, Young Harry Hawke! "

" Keep back, Coaker! Where's they police got to? "

Thus spake Johnson, Turtle, and others; but Elias proved a good general. He still sought for Tom Gurney, and expected the blacksmith would spring out of the increasing crowd at any moment. The men and women on the rock craned to see the effigy, and grey evening stole over the scene.

" We are met," began Pancras hurriedly—" we are met, my brothers and sisters, to commit to the earth the dust of a woman that beat her husband. 'Tis proved beyond a doubt by the mouths of witnesses that this Mabel Pierce——"

" Shut your silly mouth, you ginger-headed fool! " shouted a man behind the crowd, and it seemed that the sense of the meeting went with him.

" Hold on," whispered Coaker to his friends; " they'll all be our way of thinking in a minute. Let him talk a bit more and they'll roll him into the pit himself."

Pancras was staggered by the interruption and laughter that greeted it; but he made another effort, while Johnson and Turtle and Mogridge busied themselves with ropes, and Uncle Cobleigh uttered directions.

" Oh, my dear friends, let it be a lesson to one and all," continued the stonemason; but he got no further. Somebody outside the crowd flung a clod of wet earth, and so excellent was the aim that it hit the preacher on the back of the head, burst like a shell, and splattered his surplice. Magnetically this unexpected signal precipitated the conflict.

" Come on! " yelled Elias. " Tear up that scarecrow, boys, and if anybody stops you, break their necks! "

" Police! Police! " shouted Mr. Turtle. " 'Tis all being done decently and in order, and if there's trouble it ban't of our making."

But the police could not reach the centre of disturbance for some time, and meanwhile the forces closed.

From their rock, uplifted above the strife, Mr. Shillingford, Mr. Sweetland, and their company perceived the full clash of arms, and Mrs. Windeatt was more than once disposed to descend into the fray when Mabel's champions seemed like to be worsted.

Petronell watched her old lover do deeds of daring, and marked the collision between him and the bewildered Pancras; for before the preacher could get out of his muddy gown it was torn off him, and he was wrestling in the grip of young Coaker. The struggle revolved about the dummy figure, and no Greeks of old time fought fiercer for their fallen dead than Hawke, Elias, and their party on one side, against Birkett Johnson, Pancras Widecombe, and the promoters of the procession on the other. The old men were either knocked down or pushed out of the way; but some wisely ran off, and the first to wriggle out of the throng and escape was Uncle Tom Cobleigh. He cried to Gabriel Shillingford, and the farmer, leaning down from the " Rugglestone," dragged the little man up into safety.

The din increased : rough hands were thrust out upon the doll and as quickly beaten off; from wrestling the men's tempers rose to fighting; blows began to fall, and the local police, with three others to help them, were thrusting in, shoulder to shoulder.

Nanny had tried to drag her husband out of the battle, but there sneaked up Mr. Bell and kicked the blind man on the stern; whereupon Nanny was translated to Bellona's incarnate self, and, not content with leading her husband upon the venerable coward of the almshouse, attacked him, too. Buffeted and bedraggled, Mr. Bell screamed for help, and when a policeman ran to his rescue, the frenzied Nicky, now beside himself, struck out wildly, fastened with both hands upon the officer's throat, dragged him into the dust, and bit his ear. The accordion, breaking from its strap, flew off his back, and Mr. Bell, perceiving the accident, revived a little of his self-respect by trampling the instrument to pieces under Nanny's eyes. It squeaked and screamed in dying agonies beneath his heavy feet.

Now was the struggle at full tide, and a rolling battle of men foamed this way and that like a fierce sea round the " Rugglestone." Nicky had chosen his antagonist ill, for the police were soon weary of suffering blows from both sides and returning none; when, therefore, this assault was made upon one of their own limited company, they awoke to personal interest, and concentrated their forces upon Mr. Glubb. Indeed, the concentration was necessary, for he fought with lion-like fury, and Nanny, having failed to catch Mr. Bell, returned and did her best to assist him. Her a policeman picked up bodily, and bore shrieking and scratching from the fray; but it needed four others to control Nicky and make him a prisoner. The battle raged a little longer, and then the smaller side and the weaker sex most gloriously triumphed. Pancras went down before the heavier fist of Elias. Mr. Johnson and Mr. Turtle were similarly discomfited, and fragments of their fancy dresses strewed the field. Jack Mogridge, the executioner, suffered more than most, for he was captured by a sudden sally of four, headed by his own father, and bundled, hoofs, horns, and tail, into the grave dug for the dummy. Christian Cobleigh, on the other side, also received specially rough treatment as a traitor and one probably responsible for this organised opposition. Somebody seizing the whip which accompanied Mabel Pierce's image, had dealt Christian ugly blows across the face, and he sat now, half-stunned, in the hedge, not far from Pancras Widecombe, who was also out of action and bleeding freely.

Then descended darkness upon the scene, and the people gradually thinned away. For the fight was over; the spectators departed; a dozen men were soon tending minor hurts in the bar of the " Rugglestone Inn "; while not less than half a dozen, including Christian Cobleigh, Elias Coaker, and Pancras Widecombe, trailed off to the quarters of Doctor Grenville at Woodhayes, that their gashes and bruises and broken crowns might be attended to.

The doctor mourned very heartily that he had not been present at such an event, and while he plastered Pancras Widecombe and put a couple of stitches in the eyebrow of Christian Cobleigh, he heard all particulars. Young Grenville had just returned from Newton Abbot and was able to solve one great problem.

" And seeing 'twas all for Tom Gurney and Mrs. Pierce," said Elias, " I shall never understand why for the blacksmith didn't come and lend a hand. If alive, you'd have reckoned the man would have been there to lead our side at such a time."

" I saw him and Mrs. Pierce at Newton," declared the doctor. " No doubt they thought this was just the evening to mind their own business."

" By Gor! Bolted! And while we were fighting tooth and nail for 'em, they——"

A messenger came running for Doctor Grenville. It was a boy from the " Old Inn."

" A telegram have just arrived for master," said the lad, " and he's rolling on the floor, and the potman says that without doubt he's in a cruel fine fit."

CHAPTER XXXI

Widecombe was mightily shaken, and the waves of this great storm swept here and there until scarcely a homestead but felt the beat of them. Public opinion had seldom been so stirred, and there was, in addition to the actual whirlwind of debate awakened, a self-conscious undercurrent of conviction that the hanging of Mrs. Pierce's effigy must have resounded to the far corners of the earth.

In truth, half a dozen paragraphs in half a dozen local papers represented the extent of the world's attention. After forty-eight hours had passed, the event was forgotten beyond the Vale; but there it reigned paramount for some time longer, and from it there sprang minor incidents that served to keep the battle in men's minds.

Two days later a party at the " Rugglestone Inn " retraced each feature of the conflict, and Birkett Johnson, in whom had suddenly awakened an instinct for strategy, explained to Mr. Turtle and Christian Cobleigh how certain flank movements must have changed the course of the fight. Then came the familiar, slow stump of heavy boots.

" Aw jimmery! 'tis Nicky Glubb! They've let him out," cried Pancras.

The squat, toad-like figure entered, and Nanny, flushed with triumph, led him amongst them.

" Three cheers for Nicky! " cried Mr. Turtle, and then they hastened to learn the news.

" We all thought you was going to have a month, Glubb," said Johnson.

" No doubt," answered the blind man. " A pack of filthy cowards that you be! And I dare say you'd have liked for it to be six—some of you. Give me a pint, Tim Turtle, I'm very near busting for beer. But there 'tis, the justices be men, thank God, and though they've done wrong in my case time and again, for once they've done right, and the Honourable Masterman be so good as his name, and the Honourable Kitson is a true Justice of the Peace and a Christian gentleman."

" He came afore 'em——" began Nanny, as Nicky dipped to his beer; but he gulped and then silenced her.

" You shut up. I be going to tell this story. Afore 'em I came, with half a score of peelers round me, and told 'em how it had took a regiment of police to carry me off the field. ' I'd have fought with my fists, your honours,' I said, ' but I be stone blind, and a man as can't see be at a great disadvantage in a bit of work like that. But where I grips I hangs, your honours,' I said, ' and it didn't ought to count against me that I use my teeth and boots, so well as my claws, for what's a poor, defenceless blind man to do? I done what I believed to be my rightful duty,' I said, ' and I ban't going to deny to your honours that I enjoyed it, because I did; and I done my bestest as I always do; but you mustn't think as 'twas all one way with me, because I catched some proper clouts from the police, both fore and aft, your honours, and if they'd had the wit to hit me in the guts instead of on the head, they'd have settled me sooner; for my head's iron. But I be a proper nest of bruises, your honours, and black and blue from head to heel, and I lost a bucket of valuable blood, and I had my accordion smashed to matchwood—and I know who done it. But that's for another time and place. And I ask your honours to deal gently by an afflicted creature.' Like that I talked to 'em; and then the Honourable Kitson up and axed where was all the other prisoners. The bench had heard about the adventure, for it shook the country by all accounts, and, of course, they expected a rally of culprits. But, instead of that, it come out that the police had only got hold of me!

"The Honourable Masterman laughed at that. 'Good Powers!' he said. 'Do you tell me, Inspector, that all your chaps put together was only able to catch one of these brawlers, and him a blind man?' And the Inspector said I was the only one who fell foul of the police. 'He was like a mad dog,' said Inspector, 'and P.C. Chave and others will testify to it. They hit him on the head, but he wouldn't drop, and then he deliberately tried to bite off P.C. Caunter's ear, so they had to take him in charge.'

"'You're a liar, Mister Inspector,' I told him. 'I only gived the constable a gentle nip, because he was screwing my arms out of the armholes; and so would anybody.'

"Well, in a word, they dismissed the case, and the Honourable Kitson, the Chairman, said 'twas a poor bag for the police on such a great occasion, and he reckoned I'd had enough, whether or no. Then I blessed the man to his face, and told him I'd not forget it; and then, striking while the iron was hot, I reminded them that my means of livelihood had been scat to atoms by that blasted dog, old Bell, and ventured to say that if another musical instrument weren't forthcoming I'd be on the parish, willy nilly. They took the hint, and I've got two pound, but 'twill call for another yet, and I expect a proper subscription to be made by our side."

"Us shall be ready and willing," promised Mr. Turtle. "You suffered for right—leastways, I think so, though there's a good deal of different opinions."

"Of course," declared Nicky. "There always is afterwards. But the money must be got together afore Monday, for then I go to Newton to buy a instrument. 'Tis a chance of the people to show what they think of me, and I ought to rake in pounds and pounds."

"You will," foretold Christian Cobleigh. "You should get a subscription book—'twill cost but a penny—and carry it round, and see everybody in Widecombe with twopence to spare and tell 'em of all your cruel trouble."

"Teach your grandmother!" responded Mr. Glubb. "D'you think me and my wife don't know how to raise the wind?"

"You did ought to go to Bell first," said a labourer, desiring to anger the blind man; and he succeeded instantly.

"Him! The scum, the dirt! You wait! I'll be up-sides with him, if it ban't till we meet in a Better Land! And when the day comes, if I find him up there, I'll break his damned harp over his head, so sure as my name be Glubb!"

"Take care what you do, Nicky," warned Mr. Turtle. "You've made a great escape; but you'll be wise to let Bell alone in future. If you was called up afore the Bench again, it might go different."

"Liberty ban't everything," answered Glubb. "I'll have justice on that man if there's justice left amongst us. I hear that as soon as they told him I was free, he called on the hills to cover him and took to his upper room, and hardly dares to put his foot out. But I shall have the crack o' doom into the small of his back afore long. Or else I'll tear his throat out; 'tis a question which—maybe both."

He grew quieter, and listened to the situation.

"'Twas all wasted, in a manner of speaking," said Pancras Widecombe, "for in fairness we must grant we got worsted. Elias here was one too many for me, though I'm very wishful to have a try against him again."

"When you like," answered young Coaker.

"I shall go lame for evermore," declared Johnson.

"Then that poor Mogridge—they pushed him in the grave and sprained his thigh; and my fine image—masterpiece though it was—they tore it all to ribbons. And the baggering thing about the whole business be that neither Tom Gurney nor yet Mabel Pierce was within ten mile of the place all night! And Tom have left his business to be put up for sale; so, of course, they'll never come back no more, and all our trouble vain."

"I won't allow that," declared Johnson. "'Twas us that brought matters to a climax and cleared the air. Now they be gone, we honest men can breathe again."

"And how's Arthur Pierce?" asked Nicky. "Seeing what I've done and suffered for that shadow of a man, he ought to fork out five bob to his own cheek, if not more."

"He will," promised Widecombe. "He gladly will. At first, when the blow fell, he yelped about the place like a cat that have had her kittens drowned; but Doctor Grenville have given him a physic strong enough to make the dead come up out of their graves, and, what with the peace and quiet at home, and the stuff tightening up his inner works, Arthur tells me that already he's plucking up a trifle of his courage."

" And in my opinion 'tis a very nice question now what his friends ought to do about it," said a man, regarding Mr. Turtle doubtfully. " However, I'm a poor drinker at best; but some of you soakers—you'll have to think twice whether you bide here, now the woman have gone, or whether you go back to Pierce."

The point had already occurred to one or two of the company, and all felt it very delicate.

" 'Tis each for himself, of course," declared Pancras. " But for my part I shall bide along with Mr. Turtle, though that's not to say but I'll have a drink at the ' Old Inn,' now and again, as chance happens."

" 'Twill have to be thought upon," admitted Birkett Johnson. " But we mustn't say nothing afore Mr. Turtle in his own bar. It wouldn't be civil."

" What shall you do about it, Nick?" whispered Nanny, and he answered aloud :

" My way be clear enough. Us'll see whether Tim Turtle here, or Arthur Pierce, will take the properest view about the new accordion. So far as we can, me and my wife do unto others just exactly the same as they do unto us."

CHAPTER XXXII

THERE came a letter from Mr. Blatchford, the lawyer's clerk, to William Coaker, and, while Elias shared the chatter at ' Rugglestone Inn," his mother and father spoke of him. One fondly wished that certain things might happen; the other bade her be more sensible. It was not, however, of Elias that Mr. Blatchford wrote; his letter concerned Tryphena.

" You are to understand that her worldly position is very greatly improved," explained the lawyer. " Her father had invested in land, and owned some house property at Sydney,

New South Wales. This property has appreciated in a very startling manner, and we are advised from Australia that the estate is already worth several thousand pounds more than was the case three years ago. Nor has high-water mark yet been reached. Miss Harvey may fairly be accounted an heiress in a small way. Her uncles, with whom we have consulted, are of opinion that she should be informed in general terms that she will some day enjoy good means. Should she display any desire for further education, or wish to acquire accomplishments, such as foreign languages, or drawing, or painting, or playing on the pianoforte, we are of opinion that steps ought to be taken to gratify her ambitions.

" Further, we urge upon you the importance of not allowing these facts to become too generally known. Miss Harvey might otherwise fall the prey of fortune-hunters, or other dishonest persons. We feel confident that you will exercise all discretion, and should any problems present themselves concerning her future, you will inform us."

Mr. Blatchford expressed a further personal regard for Mr. and Mrs. Coaker, recollected their hospitality, and hoped that all Southcombe were well and prosperous. Thereupon Grace called her niece, and the girl's uncle informed her of these facts. Tryphena was very interested.

" How lovely 'twill be! " she said. " I'm sure I ought to be very much obliged to somebody."

" You can thank your dead father, my dear," answered Uncle William. " I reckon he understood the ways of it, and knowed this here land was worth snapping for the sake of the future. You may be worth thousands in a year or two and you be growed a very important person, and I'm sure Aunt Grace and me will be feared of our lives about 'ee now. You must be ever so sensible, Tryphena; and you mustn't go talking about it to Dick, Tom, and Harry."

" Why not? " she asked. " Surely everybody who cares for me will be glad? "

" And hungry for a bite as well. You'll have all the boys running after you for one thing."

" Don't you talk that nonsense, father," said Mrs. Coaker. " Tryphena is a very clever girl—quite clever enough to keep a secret, I'm sure. And she's got to think about some higher branches of schooling if she wants to—not about lovers nor no nonsense like that. There'll be an allowance made for your wishes and money to satisfy them."

" But I shan't have time, Aunt Grace."

" Yes, you will. You mustn't be so busy about the farm. It ban't for you to feed the chickens and all that no more."

" What am I here for, then? "

" Because you be your mother's daughter, my dear. That's the reason. And much we love you to be here, I'm sure, and very cruel we should miss you. But you must rise to it."

" I look to Shillingford and his daughter to be a lot of use in this matter," declared Mr. Coaker. " There's blood in Shillingford, and to be haughty and only neighbour with the bettermost is natural and proper to him. You must tell him, because he can be trusted. And don't you be frightened. You must come to it gradual, and master the great idea of cash. For instance, you'd hardly believe it, but suppose you was to say to me, ' I want a proper piano and a music-stool all complete, Uncle William ! ' Well, I shouldn't laugh at you. I should just say, ' Very well, Tryphena, my dear, you shall have it ! ' "

" How wonderful ! But—but—there's no hurry for that. Only, if such a thing will be within reach, how much easier it would be to get Nicky Glubb a new accordion ! When he comes out of prison presently, it would make things better and brighter for him, wouldn't it, if he found Nanny had a lovely new accordion, only waiting for him to play it."

" For that matter he is out," answered William Coaker. " I heard but an hour agone in Widecombe. They've let him free, and he's very busy already getting up a subscription for another instrument. I'm sorry for it, for a beastlier noise than he was wont to make I never heard—I'd sooner listen to pigs; but the man must live. You can subscribe towards the new machine if you mind to do so; but there's no call for you to buy him a new one. You mustn't go chucking your money away to the right and left afore you know the value of it, Tryphena. That won't do at all."

" I want you and Aunt Grace to have a lot," she said. " 'Twill never be known how good you've been to me, and money can't pay what I owe you; but it can put a new tin roof on the thatched byre, and it can turn out Uncle's old worn-out pony to rest for evermore, and buy him a fine new one. I shall be twice as useful now, because a good giver's a useful sort of person. And I can learn new lessons and pay clever people to teach me to be clever, too."

Uncle William laughed.

" We must keep a sharp eye and a tight hand on you, young woman; and if I have any word in it, I'll take very good care you don't play about with no money till you've learned the worth of it. New accordions for Nicky, and roofs on my byre and ponies for me, and a gold crown stuck wi' diamonds for Aunt Grace, and a few more things—and all afore you've heard your luck ten minutes! Now you go to bed, and thank the Giver and ax Him to help you with the future. And bless the clever father as did so wisely, and then was swept away afore he had time to reap what he'd sowed. He was a saving man, remember."

"Yes, he was. His pleasure was to work, and if you work hard in Australia, there's always something to it. So he prospered. And don't you think I'll forget him, Uncle. 'Tis the last thing I'll do."

She bade them good-night and departed; then they talked concerning her, and Mrs. Coaker was anxious.

"I think for my part 'tis a pity she knows."

"She had to, however," answered the man; "because it's not fair for her to live like a country girl any more, and mind our poultry. She had to know her power, that she might help herself and enlarge her mind, and learn and travel if she's minded to. Widecombe ban't no place for a young, lovely thing like that with thousands of pounds in her pocket."

"She's all heart, the dinky dear. Her eyes be just lamps of goodness and loving kindness. She trusts everybody and fears nought. All her thoughts get out through her heart; but us must teach her to be different, and let the head be door-keeper. I wish—I wish——"

"What do you wish, then?" he asked.

"Why, a mother's wish, I suppose. Knowing our Elias like I do, I wish—— And yet no doubt 'twould be taken in a wrong spirit. But when you think how strong and resolute he is, and how tight his head's screwed on, and how he hates humbug and nonsense, and scorns wrong-doing and anything dishonest —when you think of all that, you can't help feeling that such a man as Elias——"

"But that couldn't happen—never. Even if he loved her with all his heart, this would very soon choke him off. He's proud as Lucifer. I know what he'd say."

"But Tryphena thinks the world of him."

"You must see the world afore you can think the world of anybody. Plenty of time. But don't you look that way, missis, for 'tis very unlikely."

"She'll have to marry somebody, however."

"Ah, you mothers!" he said. "A bit ago you chode me and told me not to talk that nonsense when I warned Tryphena against the boys. Now 'tis *your* boy, and, of course, no maiden in her right senses—rich or poor, or homely or fine—could resist him. But he's too fine himself, my old dear, and when he hears tell about this, any feeling he may have had for her —though I don't think he had any—will vanish away."

Elias himself returned home at this moment, and told them of the scene at " Rugglestone Inn." He was much interested in their news, and expressed clear opinions regarding the future.

" Before all else, bid her keep her luck quiet. She's wife-old, and a little, simple-hearted thing who would believe whatever was told her. There'll be all sorts after her and her money now—a proper hare hunt for certain. And 'tis our duty to protect her against the time she comes of age and goes into the world."

" She's fonder of you than any young man, come to think of it," answered his mother, and Elias laughed.

" Long may she keep so—then there'll be no danger. We're responsible for her, and if I'd loved her heart and soul before this happened, which I never did, I'd mighty soon be off her now. I've felt like an elder brother to her from the first, and shall go on doing it. And I won't have no love-making here."

" She's planning to spend already."

" Yes—on other people, I'll warrant."

" And when I said like you did just now, as she must keep quiet about it, what does she answer? Why, that everybody who cares for her will be only too delighted to hear about it ! "

" You must explain to the lawyers, and ax 'em to keep her as short as they can."

" A new roof to the shippon, if you please," said Mr. Coaker. " That was pretty near her first idea. And the sense of the child, too ! She's thinking of lessons; but she don't know what she'll larn yet. The wisdom of the earth lies in her reach, and she's clever enough to want to have a dip at it."

Elias approved of this.

" A very witty thought, without a doubt. Lessons will keep her out of mischief, if 'tis a woman that teaches 'em."

Mrs. Coaker stared at her son.

" Good Lord, Elias ! You talk as if you was an old woman yourself," she said.

" I'm sorry for Try in a way. Because a rich girl always sees men at their worst. The fortune-hunters be at her like wasps at a honey-pot, and the decent chaps, who might feel they like her for herself, be hedged off by pride, owing to her cash."

" More fools them," answered Grace Coaker. " 'Tis weak-minded in my opinion for a man to hold back where he knoweth he'd be welcome, just because the woman's better off than him. 'Tis very hard on the woman, because she can't drop the handkerchief if she's self-respecting."

" Money, in fact, lifts a man or woman up to be on the

same level with the gentlefolk," explained Mr. Coaker. "These be the sort of troubles that come to them when they want to go courting. 'Tisn't often that such things fall out among us. Life goes more natural-like with us, because the bettermost have built up a lot of silly nonsense round them—a whole wilderness of manners and customs, and odd and funny tricks of behaviour that we get along mighty well without. The higher you go, the more be reality hidden from you, and there never yet was a royal king as knew so much about the bedrock truth of things as a working tinker. For why? Nobody tries to hide the truth from the tinker. He can smell it and break his shins on it so soon as he pleases. But there's always a busy bustle going on between truth and the upper people; there's always an army of somebodies and nobodies to keep the truth from reaching their fine noses."

"But we be altering all that double quick," declared his son. "The truth's knocking at the rich man's door at last, same as it have knocked at the poor man's from the beginning. Truth be running like a fire through the veins of the people."

"There's a levelling going on, slow and sure," admitted William Coaker. "And the wise men begin to see that the poor depend on the rich and the rich depend on the poor. Do away with one and you'll do away with t'other. I was hearing Birkett Johnson on that very subject. A man full of peculiar knowledge is Johnson. ' 'Tis like this,' says he, ' everybody's himself and none other, and according to the gifts so the man. Here's a chap be a glutton for work, and here's his brother be born tired and never got over it. Well, we mustn't praise the one nor blame the other, and the worker's labours must go to help the loafer. 'Tis no credit to the worker to make more than his share, and no discredit to the loafer to make less. Each man be born so. And so him that steers a kingdom and him that steers a plough, and him that sits under the hedge eating begged meat, should be all equal, and their reward should be equal. That's Socialism, so Birkett says, and he thinks that the world would go on better than ever if us ran it like that."

"They ought to put the fool in a mad-house, then," declared Elias. "There's too many eating without working as it is, and if us had a world run that way, there wouldn't be enough work done to keep it sweet, or enough corn saved to go round. 'Tis death to the strong to talk so. You fling the strong, bound hand and foot, to the weak, and make a world like an emmets' nest—all equal."

"I told Johnson something like that," replied Mr. Coaker, "but he answered me most steadfast that the days of kings

and tyrants was doomed. ' Every man be worth just exactly as
much as every other in the eye of the state,' says he, ' and
some will be more useful, and some will be less, and some may
make against progress and may even have to be put behind
bars; but it will come to be known that everybody must be
himself, and all will be treated alike and have his proper share
of the world's good things and *no more.*' There's one lot of
thinkers, however, as would make this difference between
useful and useless, and Johnson actually says 'tis doubtful in
another hundred years whether the right-down wasters and
sick folk and wicked folk will be allowed a hand in the next
generation. But 'tis only the very cleverest people
think about breeding the unborn at present, and their
childer don't interest most men and women half as much as
breeding cattle, or dogs, or potatoes. Birkett says that if we
can put down the lunatic asylum by studying the poultry-yard,
then it might be worth while to do so for the sake of the
unborn."

" There won't be so much breeding done in future," foretold
Mrs. Coaker. " Wrong or right, 'tis amazing how hard-
hearted the girls be getting about babies. The command to
increase and multiply be only attempted in a man's income,
not his family. God knows where the soldiers and sailors will
come from presently, when England be crying out for 'em."

CHAPTER XXXIII

SEEN over against the flank of Hameldon, the main road
dropped zigzag into Widecombe like a stroke of white lightning. The Vale was brightened with increase once again; the
Moor shone under its brief bravery of roseal heather and
autumn gorse.

Like bosses on a concave shield, the elms and sycamores
darkened the valley hedges and studded the village; whilst
amidst them on the lower hills, the patterns of the fields were
bright with grain or verdant under turnips and swedes. All
honey-coloured was the ripened wheat, and the wind wove
pale light through it and bent the waving stalks to show
the poppy and cornflower and gipsy rose; while the roots in

their lush sprawl of prosperous foliage, shone apple green and glaucous green and jade. Corn, indeed, had already begun to fall, and the fields that yielded harvest were here ruled and straked with light and darkness; here spotted with little mows, where the wheat-sheafs were thrown together to support each other on the stubble. Among the high-climbing fields—dividing them and stretching in strips of wilderness between them— sank the heath, like a huge hide flung upon the hills in barren leagues of gold and grey; and here and there, as it had been holes torn in it, stood isolated crofts on the savage integument of the Moor.

The hedges were gay with knapweed and hawkweed, the village gardens were bright with dahlias and canterbury bells. Lofty rows of scarlet-runner beans towered round about in the cabbage patches, and a famous purple clematis, that festooned the porch of the " Old Inn," was flowering once again. In the bottoms by the river, men were cutting rushes, and red kine grazed at streamside, or stood knee-deep in the pools; while aloft the heaths were scattered with sheep and cattle.

A party of women, who climbed Hameldon, now sat down to rest above Kingshead Farm, and beheld this scene out-spread before them. They were all natives of Widecombe, and lived within a mile of the spot where now they sat; yet this vision was rare in their experience, and presented the charm of novelty. Then Miss Tapper, who led this company, bade them rise and proceed upon their way.

" Now, Mrs. Gurney, and you, Mrs. Hawke," said she, " I'm sure you're rested, and we'd better get on. It's two good miles to Grimspound yet."

Mrs. Gurney and Mrs. Hawke, evidently the most lethargic of the company, roused themselves, and the women, five and twenty in number, climbed onward.

They represented one of Thirza Tapper's most cherished enterprises. She wasted little of her time, and was always full of business. Rebuffs and scorn seldom discouraged her; she hesitated not to beg for her schemes and even make enemies by her importunity if the object justified such self-sacrifice. Her Drug Fund, for the Christian natives of Equatorial Africa, flourished; she was an officer in the Society for Prevention of Cruelty to Animals; the Girls' Friendly Society also knew her; but " The Mothers of Widecombe " was her own creation, and the mother who once entered that notable company rarely escaped from it again. None exactly knew the significance of the Mothers of Widecombe, or what they did, or stood for. When asked by sympathetic friends, Miss Tapper declared that they represented the vital principle of combination and mutual support; but as to why they combined and what they supported, she did not choose to be explicit. She insisted that it was a Bond, or League of maternal souls rather than maternal bodies; but the Mothers of Widecombe were none the less expected to meet in the flesh at least twice a year; and she who evaded the summer picnic or the winter social tea had need of a very excellent excuse for the defection. Mothers once under the dominion of Miss Tapper lacked heart or courage to break their bonds. Yet middle-aged matrons had been known to whisper in the ear of young mothers that they would do well to think twice before joining the League. Miss Tapper demanded sacrifice of time—a commodity most precious. When she came into a cottage to talk, it meant half an hour, and her counsels were those of perfection. But she spent twenty-five pounds a year on her cherished scheme, and membership demanded no subscription.

The annual summer holiday was afoot, and the mothers, carrying baskets, marched forward over Hameldon with Miss Tapper in their midst. A maiden or two had been permitted within the maternal ranks, for Tryphena Harvey was with them, and Sally Turtle came forth from Kingshead to join her old mistress. She brought a contribution of two cold roast chickens from Mrs. Windeatt, and Thirza felt no little gratitude.

Margery Mogridge, now the lawful wife of Jack, walked timidly but very proudly by another young mother. One or two of the elder matrons still refused to know her; but Miss Tapper's attitude gave them pause. She called Margery to her side presently.

" We shall have a brief rest when we reach Hameldon Beacon," she said. " You are not tired, Margery? "

" Oh, no, miss. I be going along very clever, thank you. The baby won't be born for months yet."

" I hope it may prove healthier than the last, Margery, and as your mind is at ease now, and you can feel happier about yourself and your husband, I've no doubt that it will be."

" Please God, 'tis a girl," said Margery, " for I shouldn't have the heart to face another boy. 'Twould be like treason, miss, coming so quick after my darling little dead un. Us shan't never, never have such another dinky thing as him."

Two mothers in the rear, and beyond earshot, were grumbling to see the whortleberries.

" 'Tis a cruel waste of time," said one, " and all this here money under our feet. To trapse over to they roundy-poundies, just to eat and drink, when us might be picking hurts and selling 'em. They be fetching fivepence a quart to Newton Market, and now's the accepted time."

" You and me will come up over again," answered the other. " And I'll bring my Minnie and Jacky and Bobby and the babby; and you can fetch up your childer. They'm old enough to pick. One day last year, me and my eldest girl and my grandfather made five shilling. 'Twas all us could do to carry the berries home."

Elsewhere Young Harry Hawke's wife and Mrs. Sarah Gurney from Dunstone Mill, who was not a mother, but had joined the throng simply for their annual festivities, discussed another member fifty yards ahead of them.

" She's one of they ' though I say it as shouldn't ' sort of women," explained Mrs. Hawke. " Pretends to be modest as a violet in the hedge, and yet she's as proud as a jay, really— though Lord knows what for. Only a woodman's wife, and just as common a creature as anybody else save for a longer tongue and more cheek. That's all the difference."

" And her childer, what she makes such a fuss about, be all rickety, and her husband's not honest; and yet she bears herself as if she'd drawn a prize," added Sarah Gurney.

Emma Hawke looked spitefully at a tall woman ahead of them. She wore a pink blouse, a blue skirt, and a showy hat, and she marched in the van of the company and carried a heavy basket.

" Her pride'll come a cropper yet," declared Young Harry's wife.

At Hameldon Beacon a halt was made, and thirsty mothers mopped their faces and looked longingly at the bottles of ginger-beer and lemonade. But Miss Tapper disregarded the hint.

" We can quench our thirst with a few whortleberries," she said. " Wash your fingers in that pool, Tryphena, and gather me six large ones. Six will be enough."

" Don't you do that, miss, till I've had a drink out of the water," said Emma Hawke.

The Beacon on Hameldon is not the summit of that great hill, for north of it the Moor still climbs where the boundary-stones of " Two Barrows " and " Single Barrow " lead to " Broad Barrow," a rush-clad cairn that crowns all. Upon this day of light and shadow the plateau already showed signs of summer heat. For the waste was scorched a little and the ling thirsted. Immense free horizons stretched upon every hand, and the world rolled out vast and dim beyond encircling hills. The air danced over the planes of the desert

places, and there was no sound at this height but the drone
and buzz of insects on the wing and bees in the heather.

Hameldon seemed endless to the Mothers of Widecombe, but
Miss Tapper cheered them on, and the tall girl, despised
of Young Harry Hawke's wife and her kinswoman, set a
good pace and strode steadily forward to the north. Anon
they reached the venerable fragment of a cross nigh the
northern slope, and soon stood where the hill fell again under
Hameldon Tor. Beneath them now, sunk into a ragged ring,
grey Grimspound spread to welcome the party. In the midst
thereof stood ruins of Neolithic homes—hut-circles—many so
perfect in structure that it needed little imagination to set up
again the leathern tent cones that crowned them, and see the
smoke curling above the lodge from many a hidden hearth.
Due south lay the great main entrance of this fortified village,
and due south opened the doorway of each prehistoric home.
With cobweb grey they scattered the green enclosure, and the
whole venerable village spread at Hameldon's foot in a dimple
of the hills.

But the mothers were more concerned with bread than stones.
They saw grateful patches of shadow beneath, welcomed the
goal, and descending, soon stood within the shattered walls of
Grimspound. The younger and more energetic visitors opened
the baskets, spread the tablecloths, and prepared the meal; the
elder and exhausted matrons reclined motionless in patches of
shadow, and panted like sheep after such unwonted exercise.

Miss Tapper directed that a bottle of ginger-beer should be
served out to each way-worn mother, and soon was heard
popping, gurgling, and the sigh of contentment.

Tryphena sucked her bottle with the rest, and appeared
to win instant relief therefrom.

" There's nothing like ginger-beer for putting life into you,"
she declared.

" Long may you think so, my dear," answered the giver of
the feast. " Only the pure in heart care for it—at least, that
is my experience."

By chance it happened that on this identical day another and
a much smaller party had also chosen Grimspound for a revel.
Not a quarter of a mile distant sat Gabriel Shillingford, and
his daughter, Petronell, with young Hugh Grenville and Louisa
Windeatt. The doctor, who was now established at Blackslade as a friend of the family, had planned this entertainment,
and persuaded Petronell to prevail upon her father to make
holiday. And more they planned : since Grenville desired on
this occasion to enjoy a closer understanding of Miss Shillingford, he had suggested a fourth in the company, and it was

Petronell who advised that the mistress of Kingshead should be asked to come. Quite innocently had Gabriel fallen in with this plot, and though Louisa saw through it swiftly enough, she made no demur.

Hugh it was who provided the entertainment, and his guests rebuked him when he produced a bottle of sparkling wine and other luxuries. But the repast proved exceedingly successful from Grenville's point of view. All were in good spirits, and Mr. Shillingford responded to an influence that the widow usually exercised upon him. She, however, felt not as unconscious of asserting the charm as Gabriel was when answering to it. But answer he did; his difficult letters were forgotten for a while; his financial entanglement was suffered to slip from his mind during these agreeable hours. And when the meal was ended, and Mr. Shillingford accepted a good cigar, and puffed it with enjoyment, while he dwelt at length on the past honours and glories of Hugh Grenville's family, both Petronell and Mrs. Windeatt knew that the man was happy for a season.

While the giver of the entertainment planned how to set forth for a stroll with Petronell alone, accident solved the problem, for there came a petition from the larger party.

Miss Tapper's quick eyes had marked the little company not far distant, and the presence of Gabriel at Grimspound inspired her with an idea. When lunch was done she addressed her guests.

" By good chance, Mr. Shillingford of Blackslade is here to-day. I see him yonder with his daughter and others. He is a most learned man in everything to do with the Moor, and will, I know, be only too pleased to come and give us a little lecture on Grimspound, and what it means, and all about the savages who used to live here, and their wonderful ways, and so on. Then we shall take back with us some useful knowledge, and combine amusement and instruction in a very happy manner."

But the Mothers of Widecombe barely concealed their consternation. They had fed well; they felt happy and comfortable; they were enjoying their own conversation, and setting the world right in their own way. The significance of Grimspound was a matter of grand indifference to them; to improve that shining hour was the last thing any of them desired or deserved.

" There are lessons to be drawn from this place," declared Miss Tapper firmly, " and Mr. Shillingford, I hope, will draw them. There are sermons in stones, as the poets say, and Mr. Shillingford may show us how to get something practical as well as interesting here. You shall be spokesman, Tryphena, because you are acquainted with Mr. Shillingford. Go to him and say that the Mothers of Widecombe are taking their annual outing here, and that they would feel it a great honour and condescension in him to come among them, when he has finished smoking, and tell them a little about the ruins. Of course, you will explain that you come from me."

Tryphena departed, and the unhappy mothers cast blank looks upon each other A few of the more fortunate were so placed that they could creep away unobserved; and one or two of high courage and quick invention declared they had promised to gather whortleberries for their husbands and must set about it, under pain of trouble at home; but the more spacious and elderly were powerless. They sighed, and composed themselves to the ordeal; while some, feeling the hand of sleep heavy upon them, gradually turned their backs to Miss Tapper that their somnolence might be concealed from her.

Meanwhile Tryphena delivered her message, and Gabriel Shillingford declared himself well pleased to oblige the inquiring visitors.

" I'm glad to hear they are interested," he said, and Petronell and Louisa Windeatt smiled behind his back.

Then Grenville spoke.

" But we've heard it all as we came along, so Miss Shillingford and I will take a walk while you pour light into the maternal mind. I want to go down to Headland Warren below there and see about tea."

" The mothers will drink tea there; they won't want us," declared Mrs. Windeatt; but he would not be denied, and since Petronell supported him, they soon departed together.

Then, accompanied by the mistress of Kingshead, Gabriel Shillingford set out.

" Don't talk very long to them," she urged. " They're all sure to be lazy and drowsy after their luncheon."

" Just a sketch," he replied. " I shall strive to make them take an interest in the place; explain it as far as I can, and help them to see what it looked like in Neolithic days."

" Be merciful, that's all. Remember you are in the position of the man in the pulpit. They can't run away."

" 'Run away,' Louisa! Why should they want to run away? Surely nothing so interesting as Grimspound——"

But Miss Tapper now welcomed her friends.

" This is more than kind—more than kind—most generous, I'm sure. Of course, one wouldn't have asked for oneself; but you know, where my League is concerned, I put everybody under contribution. I thought if you were to stand on this rock——"

Mr. Shillingford was soon discoursing upon the primeval village.

"As the circumference of the wall is fifteen hundred feet, you will easily perceive an enormous body of warriors would have been needed to defend it," he began, "and a very learned man, who has devoted much thought to the problem, has decided that Grimspound was not a fortified village or cattle-pound, but rather an *oppidum*—a Latin word meaning a place of refuge. There are only twelve hut-circles within it; therefore in times of peace but twelve householders dwelt there. They were the *oppidani*. This was the system in later centuries among the Gauls, who, no doubt, adopted it from the Stone Men.

"Grimspound is exceedingly ancient, and dates from an early period in Neolithic or New Stone times. The evidence it furnishes is negative rather than positive, yet the learned gentlemen who have wrestled with the difficulties that it offers, have arrived at much the same conclusion, and believe that the remains are of profound antiquity. I shall now tell you how the place looked perhaps ten thousand years ago, and then I shall interest you very much with the details of the life of Neolithic man and woman."

He continued steadily, and mother after mother succumbed to his solemn voice. Many slept; one even snored. A soporific sabbatic atmosphere crept through the company. It hung heavy in the air, as though an anæsthetic had been liberated. Perhaps only Tryphena and Gabriel himself were thoroughly awake and alert as he proceeded. As for Mrs. Windeatt, she dozed in the very presence and at the right hand of the lecturer; while Miss Tapper, from an attitude of enthusiastic and keen attention, set as a standard for the Mothers, had now sunk to a bleary benignancy. Nature struggled with her, and it was only by ascending to the very highest plane of her being that she triumphed, arrested her eyelids, strangled her yawns with abdominal convulsions, and kept awake.

Elsewhere, young Hugh Grenville walked with Petronell, and advanced their intimacy by a bold stroke or two. He knew that he interested her, and since love-making was among his principal amusements, he practised it now. He wanted a wife, and Gabriel's daughter attracted him very strongly. He had a gift of sympathy, which seemed more genuine than it really was. He charmed confidences; it was a habit with him to do so. Petronell now found herself under the spell.

"Of course, between a sane man and woman there need never be any humbug," he said. "A woman naturally finds men the most interesting things in the world, and a man naturally finds women the most interesting. The instinct of every human being is to feel about for a kindred spirit. Some people soon tire of the search; some never tire of it, and pursue it to the end despite all disappointments; a few have the luck to be successful; while some *think* they have found the kindred soul, and discover, perhaps too late, that they have not."

"I was like that," she confessed. "I thought I'd found my kindred spirit. But I hadn't."

"You've been engaged, then?"

"Yes."

He sighed very deeply.

"Somehow I'm sorry," he said, "though I dare say you'll tell me it is very impertinent of me to express any opinion upon a sacred thing like that."

"It wasn't sacred in the least. I broke it off. Do you care for sport?"

"What's your view?"

"I hate sport and everything to do with it."

"My very words to a man only yesterday! That's a great bond between us. And there are others. You love culture and you are tremendously clever. I'm rather doubtful if you are in your proper environment. It doesn't seem the perfect one for you."

Experience had told him that every girl in the world is flattered by being told she is not in her proper environment. The reason, he had never attempted to examine; the fact, he knew.

Petronell admitted that he was right.

"Though how you were so clever as to find it out, I don't know," she answered. "The truth is the people who love me don't understand me. They know too much about me, I suppose. I'm discontented; I admit that."

"You're ambitious, not discontented; and, as to understanding you, to understand you is to love you, I should think, and you mustn't be angry with me for saying so."

He skated on the edge of romance, but felt not quite sure of facts, and did not commit himself. He was handsome, poor, and of Dionysian instincts, but a coward. He had always told himself that a wealthy wife would be necessary some day, and Petronell fascinated him against his worldly wisdom.

They proceeded to the rabbit-warren below Grimspound. A farm stood there, and a wild-haired woman and her daughter were labouring with preparations for Miss Tapper's tea.

"I doan't know as I can promise," said the mistress. "They Widecombe Mothers will be down here like a flock of hungry crows come presently; but if you doan't mind going in along with them——"

The doctor willingly agreed, and Petronell raised no objection.

At Grimspound the lecture had reached a massive and monumental conclusion.

" The Megalithic remains of Europe," said Mr. Shillingford, " are due to the Ugric rather than the Celtic races; we must once for all decide that those vain myths relative to the Druids and Phœnicians shall be blown to the winds, because real and positive knowledge concerning the prehistoric remains of Dartmoor is yet in its infancy, and our wisest guides are the first to admit it. Therefore, I urge my hearers to remember what I have told them; and I earnestly beg them not to indulge in hasty theories about these venerable stones, but suspend their judgment until accurate observation and detailed description have rendered it possible to arrive at more definite scientific results."

Gabriel beamed upon the recumbent and dispirited Mothers, and descended from his perch; whereupon Miss Tapper expressed the thanks of the League, and hoped heartily that on some future occasion he might again meet them when making holiday. Herein, however, she paltered with truth, as a subsequent conversation testified.

" I am the first to admit a mistake," declared the lady to her flock as they trailed homeward in the dusk of that glad day. " It was an error on my part. Mr. Shillingford, though he is kindness made alive, and we must never cease to be grateful, has the wrong touch for that sort of thing. And I don't blame one of you for going to sleep. I was actually drowsy myself—entirely owing to the way he handled the subject. I hoped that he was going to be amusing and tell us some funny stories, and make us all laugh; for, of course, many funny things must have happened in those days. But I suppose he never heard of them."

CHAPTER XXXIV

THE inevitable collision between Araminta Dench and Valiant Dunnybrig's wife was delayed, because Jane waited for her niece to take the only possible step and depart from Chittleford.

Araminta, however, remained in deep uncertainty, and presently Valiant Dunnybrig declared it was time she made up her mind.

" I won't deceive you," he said. " The missis can't see this thing with my eyes. She lowers the whole tone of the argument, and takes a human, not to say worldly, view of the situation that makes me very uneasy. I'm disappointed, too. I rather hoped that so many years of married life with me— however, they haven't. She's like a good many others, and can be wonderful easy and generous and large-minded in the matter of other people; but when any difficulty touches her, she tightens up and becomes as greedy as the grave and as jealous as death. However, I'm still perfectly clear; and, if you are also, there's nothing to be done but go ahead full steam in the name of the Lord, and hope, in His own good time, that He will open my wife's eyes."

Her answer to this was to seek Mr. Dunnybrig's wife, and on a day when the master was from home, Araminta came before Mrs. Dunnybrig. The latter, on hearing that she wanted some private conversation, was glad to know it.

" I expected you. I've wondered why you delayed. It's hurt me that you hung fire, for you're a decent, clean woman, and have a good conceit of yourself, and don't want to make yourself or me a laughing-stock, let alone your poor uncle," said Jane.

" I see you know what I'm here about. 'Tis much like this. You're a plain speaker, and so will I be. Look at it. I've got nothing in the world but this place and you and him. If I'm cast out——"

" Where's your self-respect, woman? " cried the other furiously. " It have took me all my time to be patient with him, but I ban't going to be patient with you—not if you talk like that. What's poverty against wickedness? D'you mean you've sunk so low and trust God so little that you'd sell yourself for a home? "

" Yes, I do," answered Araminta. " And I'm not the first and won't be the last. 'Tis very fine for you, all fixed up and secure, to talk so grand about selling yourself; but how many pauper women wouldn't sell themselves for a home? Of course, I don't love him—any more than he loves me—'tis absurd to think so, or pretend so. But he's a good man with a pretty fair pinch of the prophet in him, and—and—if you be going to be nasty about it, Aunt Jane, so will I ! "

They measured each other, and Mrs. Dunnybrig restrained her temper.

" I don't want to be nasty, God knows; and I don't want

you to be nasty, neither. You can't quite see how this looks to a forty-year-old wife. And belike that don't matter to you. But I beg you to consider another side. God A'mighty don't speak in visions and dreams nowadays, whatever He may have done in the past, and this dreadful vagary of my husband's be no more from God than your temptation to accept it be from God. In a word, I think his mind's softening and if that's so, no doubt you'll see 'tis no time for him to be—— There, I'm cool again, and pray you to be, Araminta."

" His wits ain't weak," returned the other; " whatever be his faults, his wits are clear enough. I want you to understand that I have not committed myself, Aunt Jane : but I'm in a strong position over this job, and I don't see why, just because you tell me to do so, I should throw up the chance of a lifetime and walk out of Chittleford a pauper."

Mrs. Dunnybrig broke loose again.

" You shameless trollop ! Can you talk like that and ax me to make a bargain about it ! "

" Of course I can. Ban't all life a bargain—a bargain with your fellow-creatures? Ban't every day a bargain? 'Tis all a bargain, I tell you, and I want to make a bargain now, this minute, while he's out of the way. I know it's all nonsense; but my future ban't all nonsense—not to me, anyway; to be cut off with a shilling by Uncle Valiant ban't nonsense. I hate being poor—like hell I hate it; and I won't be poor ! "

" You want me to pay you to go? Well, since you put it on a business footing and not a religious——"

" You'd best to leave religion out ! " retorted her niece. " Whatever else your husband is, he's a burning light of religion, and a long sight greater at that than you or I be. So, if 'tis to be a matter of religion, he's very likely quite right, and you be quite wrong. But I'll leave religion out and put it down in cash."

" You cunning wretch ! You'd screw my hard-earned savings out of me ! "

Araminta was amazed.

" You ban't playing fair," she said. " You want it all one way. You didn't treat *him* like that. You was clever with him, and patient—else very well you knew he'd have asserted himself; but with me you don't care what cruel things you say, or how coarse you speak. 'Twould be fairer if you tried to put yourself in my place. God knows I don't want to do such an outrageous thing; but 'tis more outrageous still to find myself bound for the workhouse. I'm dangerous, and you'll do well to help me instead of hindering me. It have got to be a bargain, so 'tis no use kicking at the word. If I go, I must have means to live upon, or else proper work and a clear future. And if those things ban't found, I shall go through with it and do what he wants, and call it religion and laugh at you! "

" You loathsome woman! You hateful thing! You snake, that have turned and bit the hand that fed it! This is the reward for all I've done—the payment for taking you out of the gutter. And now my savings—my poor savings, earned through many a long year's self-denial—my savings, to buy you off—to pay you not to take my husband away from me! Little did I think where your cunning and slyness would land us. Little did I dream a low thief to lure a man on——"

" I'm going," said Araminta. " I won't hear no lies of that sort. You're beside yourself, else you wouldn't sink to 'em. Who am I—a plain, homely, everyday, hardworking thing, with no wit nor good looks nor nothing—who am I to tempt men, or make 'em think twice about me? Shouldn't I have had a husband ten year ago if I'd been the tempting sort? I'm good and clever and a very useful and a warm-hearted creature, and I'm wilⁱling to work and ready to love and worship any man—any man who thinks I be worth picking up. I'm a good wife wasted, though I say it as shouldn't; but the men never see farther than the points of their own stupid noses where we be concerned. They'm warned off by the outside—silly zanies. And since you've insulted me, you can hear me. I'll live my life, and if I once give myself to your husband, I'll be better than gold or diamonds to him; and where will you be then? You've done it now, and you'll live to cuss your short sight to the end of your days. I know you couldn't stand it; I never meant to ax you to stand it. I only wanted you to show me a way out. But I'm not going on the streets for you or anybody."

" Get out of my sight, you withering wretch! " cried Mrs. Dunnybrig. " Not another word will I speak or hear, and if my husband can list to you and lust for you—such a worthless, hateful, foul-mouthed, wanton terror—then 'tis time, and more than time, I tore up roots and left him. You'll soon have your eyes opened, for every sane Christian in Widecombe shall know it, and shriek out against you. And if you ban't hounded from the place and your name a byword——"

" It won't happen," said the other coolly. " Widecombe have just had a pretty good dose of minding other people's business. And it ended in broken heads and no use to none. We'll talk of this again, Aunt Jane, when you can see it a bit more from my point of view without losing your temper about it. I didn't seek your husband, or trap him, or anything like that. He came to me—and if there's a bee in his bonnet, the Lord put it there—and—I'm not going to quarrel with the only friend I've got in the world for nothing.''

She spoke confidently, but she was far from confident. She, too, suspected that her uncle might be losing his reason, for that is the common assumption of the human mind before any proposition outside the rule of the herd. Never before, despite her brave words, had the prospect appeared so ugly and unattractive. Her aunt's attitude was not expected; she imagined that Mrs. Dunnybrig would have approached the problem in a more businesslike spirit, and did not know that the older woman, shaken to the core by this event, was for the moment unhinged and in no case to argue with a rival.

Now Araminta walked out to commune with herself. She designed to climb into the Moor, and consider the situation anew in the light of her aunt's indignation. But then it seemed that the angel of the Lord met her—so at least, in a sudden rare accession of prayerfulness, she put it to herself after the event.

As she took her sunbonnet and wandered listlessly forth through the deep, overshadowed gateway of Chittleford, Miss Sweetland was also setting out from the farm on the hillside above. Harriet stood a moment at the wicket and spoke to Mr. Johnson, who happened to be passing by. She had received a sort of roving commission from her brother to find him a wife, and while, in the first enthusiasm of their renewed and perfect understanding, the lady entered with a light heart and large hope upon her task, yet, now that it had come to the actual work, a thousand difficulties presented themselves, and her spirit flagged. She had sounded nobody as yet, for the field was restricted and she had no mind to make a mistake. But Samuel was impatient; he questioned her sharply every evening; yet on the occasions when she had hinted at a name, he had uttered a snappy negative and declared some wonder that she could have considered any woman so obviously impossible. So far he was neither helpful nor grateful. Mr. Birkett Johnson stood to some extent in Miss Sweetland's confidence. He knew that his master desired a wife and that his master's sister was anxious to find him one.

'' This here love,'' he said to her now, '' be a very doubtful gift, and I thank my Maker that it never came my way, for a more discomfortable thing you can't name. Love delights in indecencies. You get old men after young women, and young women taking old men. A fearful state, and ruinous to the self-respect. Here's master yowling out for a wife, and Widecombe laughing at him, because he can't get one. I hate to meet the people, for I know what they think."

Miss Sweetland sighed. "We must trust that the Lord will provide," she said.

Then she went her way; and as she descended from Tunhill she met Araminta Dench climbing the road to the Moor. Sight of the woman quickened inspiration. She took swift survey of her, perceived that she was downcast, and noted that she had a good figure and a straight back.

"Now, of all strange things!" she said; "if I wasn't coming to you this instant moment! Yes, to Chittleford I was coming, in hopes to catch you alone. Are you busy, Miss Dench? May I walk along with you a little way?"

"Yes, if you mind to," answered Araminta. "I ban't busy—only bothered. Life can be a very bothersome thing, miss."

"So it can, then, and often darkest just before the clouds break away. Now, Araminta, if I may call you so, I want you to listen to me. In Bible phrase——"

"Don't!" said the other passionately. "For God's sake don't begin on me with the Bible no more. I've had enough Bible of late days to last me all my life."

But Miss Harriet was not baffled.

"I understand—Mr. Dunnybrig. I dare say it gets on the nerves. We in the Establishment don't use it so lightly. And I was not going to use it lightly, I assure you; but we will leave that. Now I want to ask you a very curious thing, Araminta; a very unusual question from a sister, perhaps. But tell me, what do you think of my brother, Mr. Sweetland? Of course, he moves out of your sphere. Indeed, he is a lonely man, and his great intellects don't find people here to respond to them."

Araminta, occupied with her own difficulties and ignorant of Samuel's affairs, did not see the drift of this speech.

"He's a good, kind man, and no doubt clever if you say so, Miss Sweetland."

"But what is your opinion?"

"I haven't got none. I've only spoke half a dozen words to him in my life."

"But your feeling is respectful and friendly?"

"Why not? Of course, like everybody else."

"Well, it may astonish you to know, Araminta, that Mr. Sweetland has thought more of you than you have of him," declared Harriet. The lie was difficult to her, but once told she found it quite easy to elaborate.

Araminta stared, and the other proceeded.

"You must know that my brother and I are much more

than an ordinary brother and sister. We understand one another in a most extraordinary manner. We think, alike and we judge alike. He is a proud man and very sensitive; he is also a terrible subtle student of human nature. Though you little knew it, he and I have—sit down on this stone, Araminta, before I tell you. In a word, Mr. Samuel wants a wife. Be composed. It is sudden and tremendous; but these things always are sudden and tremendous. You might think he ought to have approached you in person; but there is a reason for that. He has highly-strung nerves, and it is my business to prevent these nerves from being tortured too much. Such is the fineness of his feeling that a refusal from you would upset him for many weeks. But if you refuse him to me, I can temper the stroke and help him to bear it. If, on the contrary, you feel that you could love him as much as you respect him, then I can bring him the glad tidings, and, when he approaches you in person, all painful preliminaries will be over, and you will meet, not a stranger, but your betrothed husband. It may seem strange to you, Araminta, in your lowly sphere of life; but the higher people often arrange things in this way. No doubt photographs pass, but in your case you know already what Mr. Samuel is like. His thoughtful brow and blue eyes and so on."

The younger was quite silent, and Harriet's hope waned.

"Don't—don't put away this matter without deep thought," she urged. "Affairs of this kind never happen by chance, and, at the risk of annoying you, Araminta, I must mention holy things, and beg you to make it a matter of prayer, as I have. My common sense is seldom at fault; I am positive you are the woman for Mr. Samuel, and I know what a husband is waiting for you in my brother. It will be a glorious thing for you to find yourself his wife. And you will have me, too. I know my brother absolutely, and my experience will always be at your service in moments of difficulty or doubt. I shall be a tower of strength and an ever-present shield, Araminta. Not that you will want a shield, far from it, for the woman who loves my brother and becomes Mrs. Samuel Sweetland, will find him her light and her joy and abiding hope. He is a marvellous and many-sided man. There is a light, boyish side to his nature you would never guess as a stranger. I have even known him to imitate the sound of farmyard animals ! "

Silence fell between them, and still Araminta answered nothing.

"Speak—speak—say you will consider it. At least you owe such a man that," pleaded the other.

Then it was Miss Dench who in her turn invoked higher powers.

" 'Twas like my wickedness to tell you not to mention the Bible," she answered. " But God knows I've had a terrible time of late, and ban't quite mistress of myself. I beg forgiveness for that. And you be the messenger of the Lord without a doubt, Miss Sweetland. Perhaps you'll know better some day how this finds me. And—and I'm quite willing to take Mr. Samuel if you honestly think I'm good enough for the man. I'm homely, but I'm cruel nice in my person, and thrifty, and know the value of money only too well. I'll hoard his pence for him and make sixpence do a shilling's work, and I'll devote my life to him, and to you; and, God helping, I'll larn the deeps of his character, and plot and plan to brighten his days. And I'm sure nothing will be too hard."

Harriet panted with triumph. A mist rose before her eyes. She succumbed beside Araminta, took the younger's hand and kissed it fervently.

" You'll marry him—oh, my dear woman ! "

" Yes, I will—if he can do with me after we've had a tell about it."

" This is a great and solemn day," said Miss Sweetland. " There will be rejoicing in heaven. And that I should have been chosen ! I'm quite as happy as you are, Araminta—perhaps more so. I gather that I came to you at rather a lucky moment. That lifts the whole affair, of course. It only wanted that, because that means Providence at once. Be religious when you go before Samuel. But not too religious. You understand. No doubt you'll be wishful to come up this evening and see him. But you'd better wait for twenty-four hours—until I've told him the great news and worked him up and got his nerves tuned to the meeting. Meantime, say nothing at all."

" I certainly shan't," answered Miss Dench. " And there's a lot of very good reasons why I shouldn't. Of course I can't regard it as settled till I've seen Mr. Samuel. And if it goes through, I'd be exceeding thankful for Mr. Samuel to let the wedding, and all that, be very quiet and secret. I don't ask without a good reason. But, of course, he may want a flare-up, though it ban't the rule with widow men."

" Better and better ! " cried Miss Harriet, radiantly. "Who shall say after this that marriages are not made in heaven? I see—oh, yes, I see a happy dawn. I see a most beautiful union complete in every way ! No, Araminta, Mr. Samuel won't want a flare-up. He hates anything in the nature of a flare-up. He is not a young man. He has buried a noble character in the shape of his first wife. He is a most dignified person in his ideas about these things. In fact, I believe a secret marriage, quite out of reach of all prying eyes, would suit him best. I feel quite giddy to have, as it were, brought it off at the first—however, we have said enough. We are both moved. It is a very emotional affair, and I must get over my excitement before I return to my brother."

" If I was to come up to-morrow night, would that be time enough ? "

" That would do very well. It will give him a few hours to collect himself and get over the first shock of joyful surprise; while at the same time it will not give him long enough to get nervous and worried before the meeting. I may have to be present at it. You must not mind that if he wishes it."

" I should very much like you to be there," declared Araminta. " I feel as if I knowed you a lot better than him."

" Kiss me—kiss me ! It will be the first of many kisses, I hope. And now I'm going straight home to Mr. Samuel. Let me look at you and the colour of your eyes. You are rather pale."

" I've had enough to make me lately."

" You understand the dairy? "

" Ess, I do."

" Say no more—God bless you, Araminta."

They parted, and while Araminta Dench climbed aloft, Harriet pattered home as fast as her legs could take her.

She was enormously elated at her achievement. Only one shadow dimmed the rosy light in her soul; she could not be absolutely certain how her brother would view her efforts to bring him happiness, and she had not heard him mention Araminta Dench, save in the earliest days of his campaign, when he dismissed her from the competition as being too young.

CHAPTER XXXV

LIFE at Blackslade, now that Sibley and her husband, White-lock Smerdon, had returned to it, was much changed. For, speaking generally, there were now developed two interests at

Blackslade, and the four persons vitally interested were established in two camps. Sibley and her husband represented all that was practical and businesslike; while Petronell and her father stood for an order old, and were destined soon, at the present rate of progress, to follow that old order, and vanish from the forefront of affairs at Blackslade. Neither side saw the inevitable, and all parties entered upon the new régime with hope and trust. Whitelock counted on his common sense to stay the downward drift, and believed that he would succeed in building up his father-in-law's position by hard work and system. He deplored the unmethodical ways at Blackslade, regretted countless minor extravagances, old-time rules of the house, and the large support of venerable and superannuated pensioners that Gabriel considered seemly. Doles and gratuities ate up an appreciable part of Mr. Shillingford's income, and here, as well as elsewhere, Whitelock Smerdon resolved to make a change. Sibley was on his side, heart and soul, and her knowledge of the situation promised to save time. Petronell, too, welcomed her sister home again, and believed that all would be well.

For a time life went smoothly enough, though in the privacy of their own company Sibley and her husband deplored the situation. Indeed, the man grumbled not a little.

"There's a terrible deal of hard work afore me, and that's clear," he said. "I didn't know for a minute that your father was in such a properly tight place, and 'tis a question whether, with all the will in the world, I've got the power to see him through."

"I didn't know neither," she declared, "and shouldn't now, but for being your wife. He never let us into his money secrets, and Petronell never wanted to be in 'em, and trusted him to keep all floating. 'Tis a pretty pinch he's got in; but you and me working together ought to get him out."

"We must, of course. I shall have to begin on him afore long. After six months I shall tighten up a bit. But ' tricky ' ban't the word; because he's so terrible lofty-minded and so full of high ideas. It's all play-acting and moonshine and silliness, having a lot of old men and women and old horses and old dogs all eating their heads off at every corner; and meantime the tradespeople be writing and threatening untold things if he don't pay their bills."

"His ' difficult letters '—why, I mind when it was no more than one or two a week; but now they gain upon him, and he's at them half his time," said Sibley.

"And well he may be," declared Whitelock; "and they'll

drown him if nothing's done. I don't say that I can save the situation—that all depends on him."

Sibley cheered her husband, assured him of her support, and suspected that not her father but Petronell would prove the difficulty.

" She's a dear girl, but she's prouder even than father, and you can't argue with her, because she doesn't know the value of money, and doesn't want to. A great power of dreaming and a cheerful conceit—not of herself exactly, but of the family. She believes all the stuff father talks about they dead and gone Shillingfords, and seems to think it don't much matter what you eat, or whether you can pay for it, so long as you have gentlefolk's blood in your veins."

" And he's so easily hurt," grumbled Whitelock. " I never met a grown man so tender. Time and again I tread on his corns without meaning to, or knowing, till the mischief's done. Never was a kinder man. We'll win him round But I do wish he wasn't in such a mess. 'Tis hard on us beginning life with a load of debt round our necks."

" Not yours, however. You've never owed a farthing," said his wife.

" And never shall do," he promised her. " You know my family. ' Where there's no money, you can't afford to owe money '—that's what my father says. And, though poor as a nest of rats, we was never in debt. There was another very wise saying of my father's : ' I'd beg sooner than borrow any day,' he often told us."

" Father's different," answered Sibley. " According to him, borrowing be honourable, and begging shameful. But please God there'll be no need for him to do one or t'other if he listens to you."

In the paternal camp Petronell and Gabriel would talk of the change; and she—romance again in her life—could afford to be cheerful and sanguine; while he, with every disposition to trust Whitelock, and a lively faith in the young man's energy and cleverness, was doubtful here and there.

" I never can forget his bringing-up," said Mr. Shillingford. " It was of a very quenching character, and his early years must have passed under conditions of such penury that, of course, they have left a mark. He will be niggling. I don't say it in an unkindly spirit; but life has made him a niggler. My position at this moment is confessedly involved. Circumstances have combined to cloud the horizon in a way I cannot parallel. My difficult letters take quite a moiety of my working day. But that is no reason why Whitelock should count

halfpennies and cheapen straws. Demand and supply appear
to be a sealed book to him. There is a mean inclination to
live from hand to mouth, like the fowls of the air. He does
not, in fact, understand what it is to be a man of affairs. Real
property is, of course, an idea hidden from Whitelock; but
we must enlarge his horizons. There is also a coarse strain,
for which his early days were responsible. He ventured to
hint last week that my old riding horse ought to be shot."

" What did you say, father? "

" I said nothing. I looked at him and left him. I think
he may have been ashamed. I hope so. I am growing fond
of Whitelock. I should miss him. He has great qualities—
the Jewel inheritance. And Sibley is happy."

" I wish she was more like us, all the same," said Petronell.
" It's all right to be full of common sense, and practical, and
so on. But she's pretty, and does things and thinks things
a Shillingford ought not to do or think. I know she's talked
it all out with the Smerdons at Bone Hill; and Miss Tapper
knows n.ore than there's any reason for her to know; and
that hateful Mary Hearn at the post-office said to me last time
I went in, that she was sorry about the corn-dealers at Newton.
They are relations of hers, it seems."

" Yes, I must talk to Sibley. She doesn't mean it, but
so often a wife's mind is coloured by the husband's view.
Sibley mustn't be sordid. And, in any case, to take our cares
to others is to go begging—a very dreadful course. For why
do we tell our neighbours that we have troubles? To win
their sympathy—nothing else. We are simply getting something for nothing—sympathy for nothing. A most undignified
thing, and almost indecent to a right-minded man or woman."

Thus stood the forces that were in reality opposed, albeit
they believed themselves united. Friction was bound to come,
and it began actively, but not between the men. Sibley's
patience gave out first, and she quarrelled with her sister. The
situation thereupon defined itself quickly, for Whitelock, of
course, took his wife's view, since it was inspired by him,
while Gabriel Shillingford, after impartial inquiry, summed
up for Petronell.

The sisters fell out upon the subject last mentioned, and on
hearing how Sibley hesitated not to announce the family difficulties, Petronell taxed her with that offence and scorned her
for such conduct. Whereupon Sibley grew hot and answered
from an angry heart.

" My dear woman, don't be such a fool," she said. " D'ye
think 'tis any news to Widecombe that we're hard up? Don't
everybody know it, and don't everybody feel it, for that matter?

Be there a shop, or mill, or smithy round the Vale that haven't a right to dun us for their money? And 'tis a good bit more sensible to admit humbly and contritely that we're in a hateful mess, and hope presently to pay every penny, than to sail along with our noses in the air, as if we was the mainstay of Widecombe, and full of money and prosperity. Everybody knows that we're cornered and haven't got twopence to jingle on a tombstone, so 'tis about time we let the people see that we know it too, and not go gaily on, like a butterfly flying into a thunderstorm."

"How mean you are!" flared back Petronell. "Why, it's an everyday thing with old families to be at the end of their resources. Do you think that Widecombe is going to be unpleasant to father for a few paltry pounds, shillings, and pence? Everybody knows their money is safe; everybody worth considering is proud of father and the high stand he takes. You oughtn't to be always snapping about money; it's not worthy of you. You bring life down to a petty, vulgar business."

"Do I? Well, no doubt I'm petty and vulgar, and my husband too. But Whitelock's got a natural sort of objection to starting life as a bankrupt. He can't live on air and fine opinions, anyway; and more can't I; and if you and father ban't satisfied with his struggles to stiffen up and cut losses and stop our silly senseless expenses, then 'tis better that him and me should clear out afore bad blood's made."

"Only rats leave a sinking ship," retorted Petronell calmly, and her sister showed exasperation.

"There you are! That's just you and father all over! One minute you say that father's way is best, and then, the moment I grumble and think that me and my husband be better away, you say we're rats. Oh, Lord! if you only had one spark of common fairness in you, Petronell!"

"And if you only had a little more of father in you. Can't you see what a delicate thing it is? Money is the tenderest subject in the world to a proud man. One ought hardly to whisper it."

"Better Whitelock whispers it to-day than the creditors bawl it to-morrow. Surely to God 'tis wiser to be frank among ourselves, and admit we're in Queer Street, than let Tom, Dick, and Harry county court us before next Lady Day? There's a lot of men about quite as honest as father, if not so grand, and they be awaiting the price of their stuff that we've eaten and drunk, or put on our backs, as the case may be. And if we ride the high horse much longer, there'll come a proper crash, and 'twill be good-bye to Blackslade altogether."

"You're so fidgety," answered Petronell. "Such things

don't happen to men like our father. He moves in a big slow way, like a great cloud in the sky; but you and Whitelock are so busy and frightened. You can't set things right by shooting father's faithful old horse, or cutting down the few old trees for timber. It is ideas like that that make father despair of Whitelock."

"The despair be t'other side," retorted Sibley, "and you'll live to see who was right to despair. Father seems to think he's a gentleman farmer, and behaves as such, and goes on as if he was only working Blackslade for fun."

"I never will criticise my father," answered Petronell. "I trust him, and I'm positive that a man with his mind and ideas, and universal goodness and patience with people, will be all right in the long run. Whitelock ought to remember that it was never known that a righteous man had to beg his bread."

"It so happens that Whitelock knows different," said her sister. "Many and many a righteous man have begged his bread, and, what's worse, begged it in vain. You say we meet troubles half-way, and surely, surely that's the proper manner to meet 'em. They be real, not fancied. We don't dream— me and Whitelock. We can add up figures and subtract 'em, and we know that you can't pay a bill for ten shillings with half-a-crown. Blood and long descent and all that stuff be no mortal good nowadays, and when the brokers knock at the door, it won't be no use you and father telling them we're Shillingfords."

So they wrangled, while elsewhere, on the same day, White-lock, visiting his parents, grumbled to the same tune. He was a little more sensitive than Sibley in some directions, and his position as a new arrival in the house increased this delicacy.

"My father-in-law properly mazes me," he declared to his mother. "I hurt the man every day of the week. I see him flinch, as if I'd trod on his foot or run a pin into him; and then I go dumb and wonder what the deuce I've said. There are some things I can't tell my own wife, though I can tell you. Not but what Sib's my side, through and through. Lord knows where she came from, for a woman with less nonsense in her doesn't live. She's always chipping with Petronell now, and more'n once I've had to use my authority and bid 'em shut their mouths."

"Petronell Shillingford will be out of the way afore a year's gone," prophesied Mrs. Smerdon; "ess—I know it. Father was up over, helping Stone to cut a faggot of furze, a bit back along, and he seed Miss Petronell and young Doctor Grenville so thick as thieves up under Chinkwell Tor. Sitting very near in each other's laps, if you please! They'm tokened, I doubt. And when I turned it over, I said to your father, ' That's good news,' I said. ' For why? Because if she's away, Whitelock and Sibley will be able to set about Gabriel Shillingford to the truth of music, and give the man no rest till you've woke him up and shook him to the innards! ' "

But Whitelock's thoughts followed Petronell.

" No doubt Shillingford will be very pleased. All the same, 'tis only more trouble in the long run. Doctor Grenville's a penniless creature, and worthless at that. I know a thing or two about him, and I know his relations haven't any use for him. But of course her father—Petronell's—will be only too glad and proud for her to wed a Grenville. Shillingford do seem to think that it's much better for your great-great-grand-father to have been a famous man, than for yourself to be a decent neighbour, and self-respecting and able to pay your way. Lord knows where us all will get to. I ban't very happy about it, for if ever a man was doomed to the workhouse jacket, that man's my father-in-law."

Martha Smerdon revived a rusty legend.

" Wasn't there talk about a miser in the family, and a buried treasure to Blackslade? "

" Talk, yes. They've got a lot of silly old tales like that; but they be all knocked on the head years ago. Gabriel Shillingford's father went along much like he do, only he married a rich wife, who kept the wolf from the door for half a century or so. But he turned the farm inside out and upside down fifty years ago, on the chance of finding a bit of cash. They be like that, the Shillingfords. They'd sooner dig over a field, on the chance of finding a box of money, than plough in muck on the chance of raising a bit of corn. 'Twas rainbow gold, and only wasted his father's time. As for Gabriel, he's not interested in the money, only in the miser's ghost, as was said to walk. He'd sooner see that ghost than be left a legacy. A hopeless fashion of man."

His mother cheered him.

" Look forward," she said. " You and Sibley will get a lot of childer presently, and they'll keep Gabriel Shillingford out of mischief. He'll soon grow old and harmless, and so long as he's content to walk about and spread his tail, like any other well-meaning, useless peacock, he'll do no harm. He's fond of children, and he'll tell your little ones brave stories and leave you a free hand. I see how 'twill fall out. 'Twas the same here with your grandmother. First she minded my children; then my children minded her. He'll vex you less and less."

" I've got Palk away," said Whitelock, alluding to a time-foundered labourer. " Eighty year old I believe he was, and still drawing man's pay. I put it very strong, and said that I bore no grudge against Palk, nor nothing like that; but the old man did nought but poke about and quarrel with the workers and waste their time."

The man drank tea with his mother and then returned to Blackslade, the better and more cheerful for having grumbled. On the way he met a happy spirit and chanced upon Jack Mogridge, who now dwelt with his wife and Mrs. Reep.

" 'Tis much the same with us," said Jack, " allowing of course that you be an important man and I be nobody. Still, I'm my own man now, and that's something. You've took a wife and live along with her and her family, and I've took Mrs. Mogridge and live along with her and her mother. 'Tis a very fine state for me to be married and talk about ' Mrs. Mogridge ' every day of my life, just as if 'twas nothing at all."

" You don't find the novelty wear off? "

" Devil a bit! We wake up fresh to it every day, and the first thing ever I say is ' Good morning, Mrs. Mogridge '— like that, just for the pleasure of hearing the word."

" I'm very glad 'tis well with you, though little you deserved it."

" I did not. I was a slave to father, and he's not forgiven me for breaking loose, and never will. He don't know me no more now I've left him, and 'tis a thought awkward sometimes, living next door as we do. He's growed terrible silent of late, and goeth like a man asleep. I'm sure I've forgiven him and wouldn't do him no harm. And Mrs. Mogridge be going to have another child come presently, so perhaps that will soften his heart."

" You'm like my mother," answered Whitelock. " You put a power of hope in the unborn."

" Couldn't be like a cleverer woman," answered Jack. "And I do hope a good bit from the coming child. And between you and me, I'm thankful that t'other be dead. There'd always have been a bit o' a cloud over it, and human nature is such that the poor child was bound to be bitter when he seed his lawful and religious brothers and sisters—and him an outcast and not recognised by the Church and the Law. Yes, he was better in his grave, though Mrs. Mogridge weeps on and off for him to this day."

They changed the subject.

" What's this be whispered in Widecombe about Mr. Shillingford owing very near forty pounds to Tom Gurney? " asked Jack. " You see, Tom be off with Mrs. Pierce, and he wants to sell his business, lock, stock, and barrel; but he can't; and meantime everything have been gone into—his book-debts and suchlike—to see what his business be worth in open market. And they say that there's a pretty brave item against your father-in-law, and against Willes Copleston, of Southway, also."

" I know all about it, Jack. But don't you waste your time with other people's business. You mind your own and save money."

" And so I do," declared the other. " I got five gardens now. I got Miss Tapper's and the little bit to Woodhayes for old Harry Hawke. And 'tis very sad that my father will sometimes stand by the hedge and look at me working, and say things out loud—not to me, but so as I shall hear 'em. He do scoff cruel at my work, and ax anybody passing to come and look at a fool spoiling a garden. 'Tis very painful for me; but I've never said a harsh word to my father, nor thought an unkind thought against him. And I never will. I've often fairly startled Mrs. Mogridge with my great patience; but there 'tis; he's my father, and I'm hoping any day that 'twill come right, and that a smooth answer will turn aside his great wrath against me."

" Be sure it will," answered Whitelock. " He can't go on sulking for ever. And 'tis very silly in him to scoff at your gardening, for what you know you learned from him, and none other."

Jack was delighted at a revelation.

" The cleverness! " he exclaimed. " Why, 'tis the living truth, and I'm very much obliged to you, Whitelock Smerdon, for mentioning it. And next time father stands by the hedge when I'm to work and calls a passer-by to watch, be damned if I won't remind him of that! "

CHAPTER XXXVI

TRYPHENA and Petronell made holiday together at the latter's suggestion, and to Ponsworthy they went, a hamlet of little cots straggling down the sides of hills that met where a bridge of one austere span carried the road across West Webburn.

The rosy wash of its cob walls, its ancient thatches and primeval peace made Ponsworthy distinguished. The place was buried in the profound seclusion of water-meadows and great woods. Only a feather of violet smoke thinning on the morning wind told of homes in this green combe. The girls drove out in a market-cart from Blackslade. Then they stalled their pony and took their luncheon-basket into the winter glades of Lizwell. Unknown to themselves they followed the road that Sibley and Whitelock had trodden on a vanished day of Spring; but now the leaf was down, and the Webburn sisters, their meeting visible to all eyes, foamed into each other's bosoms stormily amid the tangle of tree-trunks, and between banks all russet and tawny with fallen leaves.

Tryphena was now full of ingenious schemes for the spending of money, both upon herself and other people. She wanted Petronell's advice ere embarking on various enterprises; while Gabriel Shillingford's daughter, to whom Tryphena was now grown her most precious woman friend, had a great item of news. They surprised each other.

" You're so clever at doing beautiful things, Petronell, that it's for you to say what I might try to do. Of course I shall never play the piano, or sing songs or make pictures like you can, nor yet do such sewing as yours; but I might learn a little. Then there was an idea that if I worked at it, and went twice a week to the lady nuns at the nunnery near Newton, they might teach me to talk French. But, somehow, I'm not very wishful for that. 'Tis possible, they say, that I might have to go to Australia for a while, about my father's money; because things have taken a great turn, and I'll be richer even than I am yet; but they don't speak French there. Wouldn't it be a very great and fine thing for me to learn the piano? "

" You might do everything," answered Petronell. " You'll be an heiress, Try, and it's your duty to yourself to grow as clever and accomplished as you can. You might start a governess for yourself! "

" Funny you should say that. My cousin, Elias, thought the very same. But I'm afraid his idea is that I ought not to stop here at all, but go to a town. I wouldn't do that for anything. I'm always for the country, and I love Widecombe, and when my two uncles at Exeter asked me if I'd like to go there to live, I said I'd enjoy to pay them visits, but I wouldn't leave Aunt Grace for anything."

" What do you think of Elias? " asked Petronell, and a flush of colour touched Tryphena's cheek.

" I think he's a very fine man," she answered. " He's got

beautiful, proud ideas, and makes the other men seem rather small."

" I believe you love him a little bit, Try."

" I do, then! 'Tis funny telling you—of all girls; but you're the greatest and best friend I've got in the world, Petronell, and I don't keep any secrets from you. Somehow I couldn't tell you, because of what you'd been to Elias. And yet who could better understand? "

" Never mind me; what about you? "

" Well, there it is. I'm sure I love him, and if he only could love me, I'd do great things for him and build him up. But he's a steadfast man, and has taught me a lot. You can only love once, in his opinion, and if anything goes wrong with it, you're done for, and have to turn your attention to other matters. He told me frankly that he should never love again, and no more he will."

" Nonsense! He must love you down at the bottom of his heart. He's proud as Lucifer. It's only your money chokes him off."

" Oh, no, it isn't, Petronell. He told me how he felt long before my money came."

" You'd make a heavenly little wife for him, Try."

" No, I shouldn't at all. He's far grander than me in his ideas; he's as grand as you are—quite. He hates anything petty. And he's miserable about you still, for all he says not. D'you know, he can't bear to hear a fox named to this day? We were riding on Hameldon a week ago, and he was bright as a bee, and telling me the names of the places, and full of fun, too; and then the hounds went by, half a mile away, and they quenched him. ' Damn the foxes! ' he said. ' 'Twas a fox ruined my life, Tryphena.' He's just as fond of you as ever, though he pretends he is not, Petronell."

"Good Heavens! my dear thing, what are you saying? Why, to-day, this very minute, I'm going to tell you a mighty piece of news! I planned to come here just for that. I've got to tell somebody, and of course 'tis you. I'm engaged to be married, Try! "

The other's grey eyes grew round and her lips opened.

" Petronell! Then it wasn't all over with you when you stopped loving Elias? "

" You little goose! Mayn't a girl love twice? "

" She can't—she really can't, Petronell! Elias says that a man can't, and if a man can't, then of course a girl can't either."

" Oh, dear, what a green little bud you are—and your cousin

no better. Where a tree fell and died, may not a new tree grow? "

Tryphena gasped and stared before her in genuine dismay. " This upsets all that Elias has told me; and I'm sure he believed every word of it. And if this is true—oh, if it's true, you and him can never come together again! "

" And did you really think we ever could have come together again, Tryphena? There's nothing so dead as dead love."

" But his didn't die, Petronell. 'Twas all talk about it dying. And if it had died, really and truly, and if people can really and truly love twice—then—then—oh, dear—I'm all in a muddle. I didn't know such things could happen."

" Listen, you dear Try, and don't be a baby. It's like this. I did love Elias with all my heart, and when I stopped loving him, because he didn't love me well enough to please me in such a stupid, trifling affair as the life of a fox, then my love died—died—died. It really and truly died, and while it was very ill, if Elias had done just the right thing, it *might* perhaps have got well again. But he didn't. His pride kept him from it, and so my poor sick love got worse and worse, and died and was buried."

" But his——"

" Well, if his has been lingering on ever since, which I very much doubt, then the sooner it's properly knocked on the head the better. Why, what on earth is love worth that won't kneel and cringe and say it's sorry, if it has been wickedly wrong? "

" He did—he did say it, Petronell."

" Did he? I forget. I don't think he did—not often enough, anyway. Now I love somebody else, and it is the real thing just as much as the other. And it is better and finer than the other, because the man is better and finer than your cousin."

" I don't believe that, Petronell."

" You will, then, when I tell you his name. It's Doctor Grenville! "

Again Tryphena was stricken into amazement.

" Good gracious! D'you mean it? "

" I do mean it. They're a noble family, Try, and date back far enough to satisfy even father. A very renowned and glorious race; and you know him yourself, so I needn't tell you what he's like."

The younger was too honest to say a word against Hugh Grenville, because she felt nothing but admiration for him.

" He's very handsome—far the handsomest man I've ever seen—or you either, Tryphena; and he's very clever, and he has a magical touch. It was love at first sight with him. And he's never loved anybody before. He lives for me. There's a most extraordinary understanding between us. It's almost uncanny—utterly different from what I felt for Elias."

" How wonderful ! "

" Yes—so I felt it—wonderful and beautiful, Try. Everything seems small beside it—all our bothers and everything."

There was a long pause. Tryphena ate no more. This startling news had spoiled her appetite. It meant so much. She had exalted the faithful and patient Elias into a hero of romance. She had indeed fallen in love with him, because she could not help it, but well she knew that he still cared for Petronell under his assumption of indifference; and she had guessed and hoped that they would come together again some day.

" And what will Elias do then, poor man? " she said blankly.

Petronell laughed.

" You waste your pity, Try."

The woods and waters interested them no more, for to minds so pre-occupied, Nature's theatre was empty. The evening closed early, and it had grown dusk before they started homeward. Their talk ran into sad channels then—at least, they rang sadly on Tryphena's sympathetic spirit, for Petronell spoke of long waiting and many anxieties before she and her lover could wed.

" We're all hard up together," she said, " and we must wait and hope for better times. It is wonderful how love makes poverty shrink into its true shape. Nothing from outside can hurt a man and a girl, Try, if they love each other with their whole hearts and souls. People say that love distorts everything and makes us see crooked; but I say love puts everything into its proper place, and makes all else small by comparison. It's the grandest thing in the world, and there are pretty real compensations, too; because a man can only love such a poor girl as I am for herself. Even beauty is a sort of riches, though. And that's why poor, ugly girls, if they do get a husband at all, get a proper good one. The love they win must be pure to the bottom."

" Of course, Dr. Grenville is too good-looking to like anything ugly about him," admitted Tryphena, " and now he's got the loveliest thing in the world, and well may he be proud, Petronell."

Tryphena spent the evening at Blackslade, and the most desirable accomplishments for her were again considered. The family differed upon this question, and Sibley and her husband advocated a course of study having figures for its basis.

" You try to learn what money means," said Whitelock.
" You'll have tons of it, by all accounts, and 'twill be a tower
of strength to you and a great saving of trouble, if you grasp
its meaning and go into the higher branches of arithmetic
right away."

But Mr. Shillingford thought otherwise.

" Leave that to men," he said. " Your revenues and estates
will all be administered by hirelings. You can't help that, and
nothing ruins the finer feelings and senses more than an eternal
struggle with accounts. Difficult letters entirely blunt high
opinions; they come between the mind and all the best things
in the world. I shall always regret that I did not employ a
factor, or bailiff, instead of looking after my affairs myself;
though Blackslade would hardly have justified such a step."

Sibley sniffed, but said nothing, and Petronell, appreciating
the sniff, looked unkindly at her sister. After supper, Tryphena, full of secret purpose, asked Mr. Shillingford for a new
book, and Gabriel, lighting a candle, went to his library with
her. Whereupon she assured him that she had a most important and private matter to discuss, and begged that he would
spare her a little of his time.

" I'm Petronell's greatest girl friend," began Tryphena.
" Her very greatest, Mr. Shillingford, and I want—oh, it's so
difficult, because she and you are so proud. But I'm not going
to be frightened of you, for all that."

" Good powers! I should hope not. Frightened of me or
my daughter! "

" Perfect love casteth out fear," said little Tryphena positively. " And I love you and Petronell, and I want you to be
nice to me and make me very happy indeed."

" You've only got to ask. You're the sort I like—old-
fashioned, serious-minded, wishful to understand the things
that matter, and kind-hearted with it all. You're a very rare
girl in your way, Tryphena, and I think a great deal of you;
and if you were a young woman easy to spoil, I should not
pay you these compliments to your face; but you are not. You
can't spoil a girl who is fond of literature, and Sir Walter
Scott's romances, and other fine things."

" Money's the very thing I want to talk about."

" Then don't. Talk of something more beautiful. There
are few subjects that interest me less."

Tryphena hesitated, then plunged.

" It's like this," she said. " Petronell and I have got no
secrets, and I know that you are horridly poor just for the
minute, dear Mr. Shillingford, and I am extraordinarily rich.
And the kindest, sweetest thing that you could do to me

would be to take as much money of mine as ever you wanted, for Whitelock to use in his clever way—so as to free you of a lot of little stupid bothers, and give you more time for important things. Please, please do, because I love Petronell so much. And you've often said that to give harmless joy to a fellow-creature is the best we can do in the world. So please, dear Mr. Shillingford, do give me some harmless joy—you must—you must—and if you won't for your own sake, then you might for Petronell's.''

Gabriel smiled at the eager girl.

" What a friend! This is the most beautiful thing that you have done, Tryphena. It is twice blessed; it blesses you and it blesses me—you for offering and me for hearing your offer. Such a circumstance greatly softens the edges of life and elevates the mind. Your father, or else your mother, must have been of very distinguished stock to hand on such high principles to you. And as it is well known that the child most often partakes of its mother's disposition, then, no doubt, you have got to thank her for your nature. She was a cruel loss, for certain. Better such a priceless gift than even your father's riches. For riches are a doubtful touchstone, Tryphena. You can buy power, but not content and not happiness or health.''

He preached on and held her hand the while. He wandered exceedingly from the starting-point, and it was a considerable time before Tryphena could bring him back to it.

Then, when she thought that all was well, he horrified her by refusing most definitely to accept gift or loan.

" Such a thing looks small beside the thought of the thing,'' he said. " You have given me a far greater treasure than a thousand pounds, or what not. You have shown me how much my Petronell and her welfare is to you; you have exhibited a regard for the house of Shillingford that is exceedingly affecting to me. Money shrinks to a mere glorified mould before these spiritual signs. You have pleased me; and to show you how much, I am going to give you a present.''

" Oh, but dear Mr. Shillingford, I want to give *you* one! ''

" Enough! Enough! The thought is the real gift. The rest is, of course, out of the question and quite impossible. And you shall have my big ' Haydn's Dictionary of Biography,' Tryphena—the copy with the pictures of eminent men that I have interleaved during the last thirty years. For your very own you shall have it, and I can think of nobody who will value it more.''

" Oh, Mr Shillingford! ''

" Yes; and remember that it is really a thing above money, owing to its interleaved portraits."

" I couldn't, Mr. Shillingford. Just think of all the time and trouble you have taken."

" Time and trouble are a poor man's money, and they will often produce what no money can purchase—as in this case."

" I'll take it, then, and proudly I'll take it; and can't you do what can do so easy, and accept a little gift from me? Money's of no worth on your own showing, and from me to you and Petronell——"

He shook his head again.

" Your importunity is excellent—like everything else about you; but you don't understand the peculiar odour that sticks to the precious metals," he said. " A time will come when you will acquire that subtle perception for which there is no word; but you are too young as yet. The young hesitate not to accept money cheerfully, for they have the fine imagination to look through it to the desirable things it represents; but after a certain age, it cannot be offered with propriety to people of proper feeling. You may give them almost anything else; but not money. To better a proud man's financial position and lighten his load in respect of worldly welfare is the most difficult thing in the world. Perhaps it is impossible. He is as suspicious and wary as a lapwing over her nest. To hood-wink such a man and put money into his pocket, in spite of himself, requires extraordinary gifts of diplomacy. In my case the feat would be quite beyond human artifice. But of grati-tude I have the most generous store, and am not only quick but proud to acknowledge obligations. I am in reality a rich man, with this advantage over the worldly rich—that I can give of my riches of understanding and experience with both hands, and nobody need mind accepting my gifts, since they leave me none the poorer. Hoard those riches, my little maid, and never fret because people won't take your money. Money, too, has its uses, but they are on a lower plane."

Tryphena went home presently, and consoled herself with the thought that Petronell would soon be married.

" And a wedding present she shall have," thought the girl, " and they can't say nothing against that, whether or no." Her mind soon occupied itself pleasantly with the " Dictionary of Biography," and that led to other possibilities.

" I'll buy him a fine book or two next time I go to Exeter," she told Elias.

CHAPTER XXXVII

THERE was a little school at Widecombe—a survival of the old hedge-schools—and a dozen small children studied there. Hither came Miss Tapper on her way to the village, that she might speak with the old woman who kept it.

Patience Leyman was a bearded and ancient wight of forbidding aspect and narrow principles—a withered, wiry creature, thin as a threadpaper, and with a head so much too large for her frail body that its weight appeared to have bent her into a permanent arch. Miss Leyman's centre of gravity was often endangered : she tottered in her going, and carried a man's stick to support her. She suggested the bird of wisdom in her brown shawl, horn-rimmed spectacles, and black bonnet of ancient pattern; or she might have been compared to some great moth that fluttered in the dimpsy light; for she was seldom seen abroad before evening. Then she walked through the lanes alone, for she was unsociable and unfriendly to grown-up people.

But the children liked her well, and were happy with her. She reserved her smiles for them, and her rule was light. On three little benches they sat, in the parlour of the cottage, and Patience occupied a dog-eared armchair, with her books beside it on the table. Adults puzzled why the young folk liked her; but mothers made no question, and thankfully paid the trifling fees that the schoolmistress demanded. She reigned absolutely, however, and was capricious—a fact exemplified upon the occasion of Thirza Tapper's visit.

Chance had been playing some pranks with Miss Tapper, and she was a "little under the weather," as she described her situation to intimates. The Drug Fund languished; a part of her own small fortune also dwindled, and certain investments had fallen many points and withheld a dividend. Again, she had just received a hint from the pastor of Widecombe that she was taking too much upon herself in the affairs of the parish; and, lastly, Mr. Samuel Sweetland, for whom she continued to entertain a tender regard, based on certain experiences of the past, had cut her openly and pitilessly in the public thoroughfare before the eyes of Old Harry Hawke and Pancras Widecombe. Samuel, mounted upon his horse, had certainly ridden past her without drawing rein or lifting hat, and when she caught his eye and smiled upon him, he had looked through her without one shadow of acknowledgment. But these untoward events seemed only to sting Miss Tapper to duty. It was her fine principle to work doubly hard under the light of misfortune.

She called now upon the schoolmistress, and, leaving her children nodding their small brown and flaxen heads over their slates, Patience came to her door.

" What do you want? " she asked without ceremony or conventional greeting. " 'Tis school hours."

" Good afternoon, Miss Leyman. You mustn't stand here. It is far too cold to keep you at your door. May I come in? I won't detain you long."

" 'Tis school hours, I tell you, and I hate for unthinking people to call in the midst of 'em. Come in, and be short, if you please. Sit down if you mind to."

" I'll keep you no time. It is about the little Nosworthy girl—Sally Nosworthy. It seems you have sent her away, and the child's broken-hearted that you won't take her back, and so's her mother. I look after the mothers, Miss Leyman, and you look after the children, so we ought to work together. You teach——"

" Common sense—that's all. I don't pretend to teach nought else. 'Tis my wish and will to bring up the childer with a pinch of that, so as they'll better the fool pattern of men and women folk here, when they grow up. Just common sense, ard the way to understand and remember. Books ban't no use to 'em. 'Tis the experience of an old woman that have seen through and through life that be the use to 'em. Patience alive I am, and need to be, for of all things hardest to teach humans, common sense be the hardest. So hard, that once they be grown up without it, God's self can't get it into 'em."

" All most true and exceedingly interesting, I'm sure; though perhaps common sense isn't so rare as you think. If you went about more—— However, I mustn't keep you. In a word, little Sally Nosworthy. You've dismissed her—expelled her, so to say. But do think better of it. Do take her back, for her mother's sake."

" You waste your wind, Miss Thirza Tapper. I didn't send her away without a reason, and she don't come back. There's little I don't forgive in a young child—boy or girl. But she lied to me once and again. And then thrice she lied. 'Tis in her blood—look at her mother's eyes—there's a lie in the pupil of each of 'em. For her father's sake I'd forgive Sally; but there's the other children."

" You can't forgive her just once more? "

" Would you? "

" She has had her lesson. I think I would give her one more chance."

" More fool you, then. If you be so weak with the mothers as you'd have me be with the childer, 'tis little enough good you're doing 'em."

" I came to give advice, not take it," answered Miss Tapper rather warmly. " You forget to whom you are speaking, Patience. Surely my influence and our friendship of such long standing——"

" There's no friendship between us—none at all, and never was. I'm twenty-five year older than you, and my head's hard as a nut still, thank God. 'Twill outlast my body. You mind your own business and let other people mind theirs—then you won't bark your shins quite so often as they tell me you do."

Miss Tapper considered. This was sharp physic, but she kept her temper.

" Well, good-bye, Patience. I'm sorry that you don't feel that it is a case for mercy and forgiveness. You understand children so wonderfully well that——"

" No soft soap, miss! and now I must go back to school. I can't listen to you no more," interrupted Miss Leyman. She left her visitor abruptly without another word, and Thirza, reduced to silence, felt her face grow hot and her ringlets flutter as she left the house. The school-children's voices rose in a little murmur behind her, like bees on a bed of thyme. She went her way wounded. Life continued to frown. Was her power slipping from her? Was she to pass out of life and strife and be a thing forgotten before she had reached the age of sixty? She repelled the cowardly fear; she felt the east wind upon her hot cheek, and braced herself to re-establish her position and regain the public esteem in those particulars where it seemed to wander.

To the post-office she came, and was cool and self-contained outwardly as she stood before the portly figure of Mary Hearn. But her temper had not quite recovered its balance, and the sight of the postmistress, in her most arrogant mood, failed to complete the good work of the winter wind. Mary proved egotistical. Indeed, she began quite graciously.

" A bite to the wind, but you ain't one to fear the weather, Miss Tapper—no more than I be. Have you heard as Widow Hext have fallen—her as had the dole under Sampson Jerman's will? Yes, she's dead, and there'll be a Parish Meeting next Thursday to decide which old woman is to take the money. And I hope you'll throw in your voice with Vicar Brown and ax him to vote for old Milly Aptor. She did ought to have had it afore the Widow Hext, for that matter."

" My interest is promised, Mary."

" Which old woman be you supporting, if I may ask? "

" I would rather not say. Privacy—not secrecy—but privacy —is very desirable in a place like this."

Miss Hearn smiled.

" Well, well—I'm not one of the talking sort—and, anyway, it don't matter much, because Milly Aptor is safe to get it, whether you want for her to or not."

" I'll ask for a packet of stamped envelopes for my official letters, and twenty-four halfpenny stamps for circulars."

" Certainly," answered Miss Hearn, and Thirza took out her purse. But the other made no haste to serve her.

" Did I ever tell you about them Dexters I stopped with when I went to Exeter for change of air? "

" No, you didn't, Mary."

Mary considered, then laughed.

" 'Tis always interesting to see human nature working between a husband and wife. A tanner he was by trade and a gentlemanly man. But she had the money—Mrs. Dexter had. A very clever woman, but too hard on him. Would have good value for her cash. I heard from her yesterday. She says that she's sent her husband away on half-pay for a bit, and reckons he'll think a good bit more of her when he comes home. Curious how things happen. Now, if you'd asked me, I should have said that she was in a declinement; but, by the look of it, she's as well as ever, and he's sick. He's gone to the sea for his health, and she'll keep him cruel short, if I know her If that man had a few hundred a year of his own he'd never go back. No love lost, because he's got a large heart that she can't fill—yes, a very large heart Adolphus had. However, as he truly said to me—for he confided in me a good bit—' a large heart,' he said, ' be only a torture if you've got an empty pocket.' "

" Ah," answered Miss Tapper, without sympathy, " there's one man kept in his place, at any rate. If women could only get the world's money in their keeping the power would be theirs—every rich wife knows that."

" So it would, then," admitted Mary, " but the dratted men take very good care that we shan't. Look at our wages—look at mine. Shameful tyranny 'tis, for if I can do a man's work and have got a man's headpiece, why the mischief shouldn't I have a man's money? No, it isn't us that earns money worth naming—'tis the hussies get men's money—not women like you and me. 'Tis the hateful, doubtful sort that get big money out of men. They be nasty wretches—I mean men in the lump."

" There are good and bad men. I have had the privilege to know a great many who respected women and blessed their mothers—dead or alive—and took a high tone. A packet of stamped envelopes and twenty-four halfpenny stamps, Mary."

Miss Hearn hesitated. It had always been a gall to the postmistress that the other addressed her as " Mary," while she was expected to say "Miss Tapper." The note in the customer's voice also angered her.

" Oh, yes, there are good and bad, of course. I know that —better than you, perhaps—for I might have been the wife of a good man, if I had liked. So I speak quite without bitterness, because my maiden state is my own choice. Of course, a good many can't understand that. To be asked in marriage is a wonderful experience, and I'm almost sorry for all the hosts that have missed it. 'Tis an interesting and tragical affair to see a proper man on his knees asking for you to share his life."

" This is a subject that women of nice feeling do not discuss, Mary."

The tone stung the other to insolence.

" Oh, my! Grapes are sour, perhaps. Who's discussing it? I ain't. I only say you don't know how interesting it is— that's all—Thirza! "

Miss Tapper started, like a pony stung by a gadfly.

" You forget yourself, Miss Hearn, and you forget your customer. Serve me, please, and try not to be so exceedingly offensive. Some day you'll be reported."

" Shall I? Some day you'll—— Bah, you're a puss—that's what you are—an old puss, forgotten and passed over—and I snap my fingers at you! And no man ever wanted you, or could want you. Hateful they may be, but they're not born idiots."

Miss Tapper drew herself up, she fought to keep her temper, and failed.

" You vulgar-minded creature! " she said. " It is a scandal —a downright scandal—that any department of the public service should employ such a coarse and nasty woman. And know this, Mary Hearn, since you force me to speak—out of honour to my father's memory—I, too, might have been a wife, and I have known what it was to have an honourable gentleman——"

" Names, names, please! " cried the other. " Easy to talk, but not so easy to believe. You'd like us to think the Lord of the Manor wanted you, perhaps, or the Bishop of Exeter. A cunning old vixen—that's what you are! Thirza Trapper you ought to be called. But you ain't trapped one of 'em yet,

for all your cunning. If you was open and straight, you'd
tell the man's name, same as I will. I ban't shamed to say
'twas Samuel Sweetland offered for me, and I refused the man,
and he went raving out of my sight. He denies it, I believe,
but he won't deny it on the last day—the coward. And now,
since you say they've offered for you, let's hear what fashion
of man had the pluck to try for ' Genoa Villa.' "

She set her arms akimbo, and looked down with a wry
mouth at the smaller woman.

" You drag your sex in the dust, you shameless wretch!
Not only do you dare to claim privileges that were never offered
to you, but you lie and besmirch a pure name."

Miss Hearn uttered her well-known, horselike neigh—a
signal of mental excitation soon to escape control.

" A lie—is it? And who's the biggest liar? Names—names,
you pinnicking grey tabby! I'm a liar, am I? You shall hear
more about that. For twopence I'd pull your silly old wig off."

She swayed and shook and threatened to subside.

" I go," answered Miss Tapper, " and I report you to the
higher authority. You are a foul-mouthed woman, and you
pry into the letters and mis-conduct the post-office. Your vulgarity I overlook, since it is beneath notice; but as a public
official——"

" Mother," shrieked Mary, " mother, come here! "

She began shouting, rolling her eyes, and striking her hands
on the counter.

" I don't care in the least if you have hysterics or not,"
continued Thirza Tapper steadily. " You deserve everything
to happen that's shocking and bad; and if you were an honest
and clean-minded woman, your nerves would never get into
such a state. It serves you very well right! "

Mary's mother hastened in to see the postmistress collapse
behind the counter. She dragged a pile of official documents
to earth in her fall.

" Cut your daughter's staylace—she's brought it on herself
—I intend to report her," said Thirza. Then she went out and
set her face homeward, while Mary's mournful clamour faded
behind her.

But this brave attitude was only assumed, for as she tottered
down the lane, tears filled Miss Tapper's eyes and she restrained
a sob. She felt herself tortured, wronged, and sorely smitten.
The world had suddenly become an impossible place. She
stood at a lonely gate into a turnip-field, and clasped her
hands and lifted them over the top bar. Then she spoke aloud
and invoked the deity.

" O, Lord God! don't let Thirza Tapper despair! " she said,

and a blackbird, startled by the petition, fled chinking away down the hedge. The gloaming had fallen out of a green and golden sky. It was beginning to freeze.

Thirza found herself better and braver for the prayer. She believed her duty to be quite clear and returned home to do it. Many had threatened to report Miss Hearn, but none had as yet risen to the act.

In her garden appeared two figures, and Miss Tapper marked Jack Mogridge at work and Margery watching him. The young pair were now under her patronage, and flourished accordingly.

" I shall want you to go to Ilsington with a letter to-morrow, Jack. It must be posted there, and not in Wide-combe."

" Yes, miss; and I've planted they forget-me-nots, and left room for a rimlet of boughten tulips, if you please; and us shall want twenty of 'em to the least."

" My order will be for two dozen, Jack; and how's your father? I heard a bad account of him."

Jack straightened himself.

" Mrs. Mogridge here seed him but yester-eve. But he don't speak to her, as you know. In fact, since I withstood him and went my way, he's falled into a very rash and furious silence, miss. He never neighboured with the people kindly; but he's worse than he was. And, God knows, I be wishful to be friends, now that he's took the evil eye off me."

" He didn't take it off," said Margery. " 'Twas you broke loose from it."

" Anyway, I'm free, and I want to be a son to the man, because he's growing old and haven't what you may call a friend in the world. I offered for to bide an hour and dig through a shillet in a grave as was too hard for him, but he just looked up and said I might go to hell for any use he'd gotten for me more; and I offered to call Mrs. Mogridge's new babe after him likewise, but he said that he'd brain it if I did."

" We must hope his heart will be touched in God's time," said Miss Tapper. " I think he's mad myself."

" And since Mrs. Mogridge went to it with a light heart and a wedding-ring, the new babby has proved a very fine creature, as you know, miss. With any man but my father, such an infant would fetch him round."

" We must hope," repeated Miss Tapper; " and you can come for my letter the first thing after breakfast."

CHAPTER XXXVIII

THERE fell the solemn meeting of Mr. Samuel Sweetland and Araminta Dench, and it followed one of equal significance between the farmer and his sister.

" There was a time," confessed Harriet, " when I should not have gone out of my way to be an angel of good news to Araminta. But these things often happen differently from what we expect. There is no doubt that I was led to her, Samuel, like—like Abraham was led to the ram in the thicket. And I found her panting, as it were, for the friendship of a good man and a good woman. I have often thought her lot at Chittleford might be difficult, and—though she was all caution and charity—I still believe it is. She is shy and womanly—not sly, as I used to think. She has very fine qualities; she——"

" Yes, yes, yes," he said, interrupting her. " You naturally think a lot of her, and I dare say you are right. Only don't say any more, for 'tis a very curious thing about my character that if I hear a person praised up to the skies, I always begin to pick holes in 'em. 'Tis a sort of fearless rebellion against taking anything second-hand. I like to form my own opinion."

" We think alike most times, however," answered his sister, a little crestfallen.

" We do; and for that reason I feel a great hope rising in me. But leave the rest to me. You've been a masterpiece of cleverness, and done a very skilful thing, Harriet; but now —the male creature being what he is—you'll do well to drop right out of it and leave the rest to me entirely. Nothing must come between me and the woman and the romance of the situation. Everything else must be forgot—all they horrors with the other women and everything. I must come upon her in a bold, conquering fashion. I've had some nasty facers for my self-respect lately, and I shall be very glad to get it back and forget the past. I'll meet her and offer myself boldly and bravely, and put out of my mind that any other body have been on afore to make the paths straight and the way smooth. You understand the male nature that far, don't you? "

" You're so subtle and baffling," she said; " but I do understand, Samuel—so far as a woman of moderate cleverness can understand a man like you."

" That's all right, and goes without saying. And what I ax now is for everything else to go without saying—for my self-respect. If things be thrust to the back of the mind resolutely, and we take a bit of trouble to forget 'em, then forgotten they will be. When do she come up? "

Harriet took the hint, saw the force of this make-believe, and succeeded in speaking with Araminta once again before the great meeting. Of course, Miss Dench also proved quick to see the point, and so it happened when the future wife and husband met that she made no allusion whatever to the preliminaries, and neither did he. Araminta suffered his advances delicately, helped him when emotion strangled his highest falsetto, and treated him with a mixture of reverence and regard that very perfectly fulfilled the requirements of the moment.

" Be seated," he said, when his sister introduced Araminta and fled away. " Be seated, Miss Dench, and don't feel nervous before me. This is rather a peculiar meeting, and you may have been puzzled to know why I did not come——"

" Please," she said, " don't talk about that. You were busy; you had the weight of the farm on your shoulders, and it is a busy season. I have often wondered, as you rode down past Chittleford, how you found time for your work, and even sometimes whether you would ever find time to court another wife. And yet I knew—such a man as you—would be sure to wed again. But little I thought——"

" Naturally, naturally. But my eyes are pretty good, Araminta. They've often rested on you. We men hide our feelings carefully, for it is dangerous to be too friendly with the sex. There's a sort of woman—however—now, without false modesty, let us look at one another. ' Taste and try before you buy ' is a very good motto. I will get a lozenge from the mantelpiece, for the damp in the air of late has rather tickled my tubes."

He rose and assumed the youngest, jauntiest mien of which he was capable. He took a lozenge, flung it lightly into his mouth, and turned to regard her. She sat with her hands folded in her lap, and looked at him quietly and respectfully.

" It seems almost too wonderful to be true," she said.

He beamed, and permitted himself to consider her figure.

" A womanly woman I would have, and you are all that," he declared. " Not that the soul and spirit don't come first, but you are rich in both, I hope. Little by little I have come to feel great admiration for you, Araminta. I have watched you, and weighed your character and found it wasn't wanting. Then, you see, like a hawk I swoop! And I'll no more take ' no ' for an answer than the hawk takes ' no ' from the hedge-sparrow. I have you in my toils; I——"

But he felt these sporting similes were cheapening the situation, and abandoned them.

"Those that God hath joined, let no man put asunder, Araminta; and I do honestly believe that He has joined us—or is about to do so. I love you. When a man of my age tells a woman that he loves her, it is no light thing, and she must not take the word in a light spirit. You must regard yourself as enveloped and embraced in a stronger nature than your own, Araminta. A masterful man—one accustomed to his own way in all things, who says to his servant, Go, and he goeth—has found you and marked you for his own. You are his chosen, his ewe-lamb henceforth. I want you to be my wife! Don't start—don't shrink from me. It's sudden—to you; but I have been preparing for this supreme event for a considerable time. In me you will find—but words are vain things—I see in your eyes that your answer is to be ' yes '! "

"Oh, Samuel! You're like a whirlwind! " she said, with her arms round his neck.

He wiped the moisture from his brow.

"My God! It's terrific—it's terrific! " he murmured. Then, as he fell back in his easy-chair, her intuition inspired her to further feats. An instinct to sit in his lap was discarded, for she weighed eleven stone; but she knelt by him and kissed his hand. She simulated the profoundest emotion, and he really felt it. Then, to escape the strain, he began to talk of business and the future.

"I thank God Who has smiled upon my suit," he began, "and on my knees I shall thank Him, and I hope you'll do the same, Araminta. But now let us steady ourselves by looking at the practical side. If you'll get a chair and stick it here, I can put my arm round you. Ah! you mustn't mind that, for it have a right there evermore. That's the arm that be going to come between you and trouble; and when it ban't at work for you, your fine waist will be its favourite place, no doubt."

Mr. Sweetland's poetry astounded himself only less than Araminta. She sat beside him, and cried a little.

"I like to see them tears," he declared. " 'Tis fit and seemly that you weep afore this shattering change in your life. If I wasn't a man of character, and fierce in my nature, as becomes the male, I should weep, too, I dare say. But I'd sooner laugh. You see, we reckless dare-devils don't know our luck so often as not. We want, and to want is the same as to get, with a fighting nature. So there it is—we'll wed and we won't waste no time about it."

"That's as you please, Samuel. I shall live for you, and only for you from this night."

"And me the same. Well, I've a fancy to let this thing burst upon Widecombe as a bit of a surprise. I'll bow to you, of course; but still, that's my wish in the matter. You may feel different, however."

"A woman's hour be her wedding-day," she answered, "and yet, though 'tis natural that I should want the wide world to know my good fortune, let alone the Vale, I'm with you there. I don't want no show and fuss and flare-up."

"Good!" he said. "Bursting with sense, I see—as well I knew you would be."

"Yes—I'd like our marriage to be right away from here. I would like to slip away from Chittleford unbeknownst, and meet you far ways off—to Exeter even, or Plymouth. And we'll be wed so quiet as mice, and then either come home again, husband and wife, or else go off for a few days' holiday-making if you felt the need. But I shouldn't. And I've got nothing to bring you but a good head and loving heart, and pluck and courage. 'Tis all one way, Samuel."

"I won't hear you say that, Araminta. I'm very well pleased to do my share. And your opinions echo mine—a very hopeful sign To Exeter we'll go, and get married afore the registrar. I've got a sort of feeling that I'd like it so. But if you feel, like some, that 'tis an unfinished thing without religion——"

"Not at all. I'm properly sick to death of—I mean I'd like it best. I want the secret to be kept till we come home and surprise everybody. And touching money and my future and all that, Samuel, I know that I can trust you to do everything that is right and proper."

"You can," he assured her. "Have no fear for figures. You're a luckier woman than you have any idea of in that matter."

"You'll never regret wedding me, Samuel. And now I'd best be off—else Aunt Jane will wonder where I'm to."

"I'd like to tell Valiant Dunnybrig; but it will seem all the more tremendous if I burst it on him after."

"On no account tell him," she said. "I beg you'll respect my wishes there. Afterwards you shall tell him, and 'twill sound like thunder on his ear, to find what a man of iron you are. But it will seem even more wonderful to him and everybody if you keep dumb about it till afterwards."

He admitted this. He saw himself amazing the people. She saw in his eyes what he was reflecting.

"They little know the man that's among them," she said.

Then Samuel bade Harriet enter, and she did so. She kissed them both, and her brother acquainted her with the situation, as though this was the first she had ever heard or dreamed of it. She played her part admirably, and was overcome.

" Money you'll want," said Mr. Sweetland to Araminta. " There must be secrets and a bit of a plot. You go by night as you say, and Johnson—no lesser man—shall meet you at the head of the road above Upper Dunstone and drive you into Newton. Then, by the earliest train, you go off to Exeter, and there am I, in flame new clothes, upon the platform. Harriet and Birkett Johnson will be the witnesses. I see it all."

Further details were left for future discussion, and Araminta, the richer for a purse with ten sovereigns in it, returned to Chittleford. Then, when Samuel had watched her walk from the outer gate, he returned and embraced his sister.

" Don't think," he said, " because I have gone out into the world and won a fine woman, that I shall ever feel one spark less of love for you, Harriet. I think we shall be happy. Everything seems to promise that way. I feel as if I'd known her a long time already, and that's a good sign."

" That's her cleverness," said Harriet. It was Miss Sweetland's first mistake.

" No, not at all," he said; " it's my pushing nature. I went over her like a regiment of soldiers. I had her gasping at my feet in two minutes after she came in this room. There's a lot more nature in me than I thought, and I'm very pleased with myself, Harriet."

" And very good reason so to be," she answered.

CHAPTER XXXIX

THE sequel of Samuel Sweetland's final love-affair was not long delayed, and the first who felt the shock of it proved to be Valiant Dunnybrig himself. For he had come to believe that Araminta Dench would be led to do her Maker's will, and gloriously exhibit the ordinances of the Old Testament before a world that had sunk away from them.

But the case was altered, and Araminta, from the safe standpoint of Samuel's affianced bride, found herelf horrified and insulted beyond all measure when she reconsidered the patriarchal Valiant's plans. She asked herself how any self-respecting married man could dare. She was quite furious for a little while; but at heart she hated her aunt far worse than her uncle, and in any case now, her previous attitude to the problem made any assumption of insulted virtue and injured innocence a little difficult. In time to come, as Mr. Sweet-land's wife, she guessed it might be possible to get in a shrewd thrust or two; but for the present, instinct bade her vanish from Chittleford as swiftly and as suddenly as possible.

In collusion with her future husband she put this purpose into practice, and on a certain Sunday, when he returned from morning worship, Mr. Dunnybrig asked for his niece and learned that she was gone.

"I had a bit of a sermon-sleep to-day," confessed the farmer. "Our man says well, but his tone of voice—for all the world like a guinea-hen that harps on two harsh notes —his tone of voice is such that it often huddles my eyelids over my eyes against my will. To-day I only lifted 'em when the people rose."

His wife was agitated, and now he perceived the fact.

"What's the matter, Jane? You be wisht and pale as the moon."

"And reason for it. She's gone—she's bolted! Her bed wasn't pressed last night. Tis too painful a thing to talk upon any more. God knows that I've said enough—to her and to you—yet what wife wouldn't? And I suppose it has come over her at last that it weren't vitty for her to bide under this roof no more."

Valiant fell back in dismay.

"Gone!" he said. "Gone without a word or sign! No letter nor nothing?"

"Nothing. She's took her things, such as they were, and her good books—Bible and hymns. She's left a few worn-out clothes, and be just gone—vanished, like the dew upon the fleece."

He was silent a moment; then he turned on his wife. His voice rolled out loud and deep and slow. He assumed a tragical attitude and lifted one hand. He showed more grief than anger, and his manner was minatory but not scolding. He preached at her and prophesied.

"This is your work, Jane Dunnybrig. Only a woman knows the weapons to use against another, and a woman's weapons be poisoned as often as not. You have drove her forth, then; you have fought and fretted that poor wretch till her womanhood went down and her trust in God tottered, and her duty was hidden from her. Your work—to let your own narrow and hateful pride rise up between this handmaid of the Lord and her duty—your work to come between God's chosen, and keep precious human souls out of the world; your awful work to think to put a spoke in the wheel of Providence! May God forgive you, as I do; and let the punishment of your sin be this, Jane—that you have sinned in vain. Know that this doubtful thing shall be most surely accomplished now, because I go to find Araminta to-morrow morning, and the Lord will lead me to her. Yes, I shall take my stick in my hand, and put my hat on my head, and go forth into the world to find her; and God do so to me and more also if I tarry till I have found her and brought her back—never to leave Chittleford again! "

But Mrs. Dunnybrig was far too thankful to succumb under this terrific indictment. It seemed clear that Araminta had gone, and Jane knew perfectly well that not her own insults or powers of persuasion had brought about this result. She did not flatter herself that her niece had listened to her; indeed, latterly, Araminta had exhibited a good deal of quiet insolence in the presence of her aunt—the insolence of a small nature in sudden possession of power. But now she was gone, and Jane prayed that for ever she was gone. She heeded not her husband's thunder, therefore, but felt pretty sure he would not find Araminta. Valiant forced Jane on to her knees presently. Then he prayed long for Araminta, and made his wife say "Amen." She obeyed, offered no opposition, and did not attempt to deter him when he set out to seek for his niece on the following morning.

For Monday brought no news of her; therefore Mr. Dunnybrig, communicating his plans to none, took money, packed a carpet bag, and set out to find her.

The direction of his search he made a matter of prayer, and was led presently to Plymouth. Here for a week he sought in vain; and then he went to Exeter, being impelled thither by a dream.

CHAPTER XL

TRYPHENA HARVEY loved the great pictures of tl e sky above
Hameldon. She lifted her eyes there many times in the day,
and delighted at the manifo'd wonders that the clouds wove
above the hill. Sometimes unshadowed blue filled the air, and
a firmament of lustrous purity reigned to the zenith, while
Hameldon swept in many mingled hues against it. More often
a pageant of vapours offered, now high, now low; now in the
upper air, now lapping the earth, enfolding it in mystery and
concealing it from the tame valleys spread beneath.

Tryphena sat now on a November day above the highest
cultivated land, and looked down with doubt and uncertainty
upon Widecombe. The world was sad-coloured round about
her, and the wind made a dry mournful tinkling in the legions
of the dead heather-bells.

Life puzzled Tryphena; she could not understand why Mr.
Shillingford declined to let her help him, and why Uncle
William Coaker also refused the new roof to the farm-buildings
that she had asked to erect. Everybody seemed to think that
she ought either to keep her money, or spend it upon herself;
and yet Tryphena knew this was not the right and proper way;
for neither Gabriel Shillingford nor Uncle William practised
what they preached. Then she was moved to make further
experiments, and being out of tune with Hameldon—the friend
who gave so much, but could receive nothing back—she turned
her eyes to the valley and considered the little dwelling-houses
and the people who lived in them.

There were matters of moment afoot, and Tryphena had
heard that Mr. Tom Gurney, being unable to sell his business
to his satisfaction, was returning to it. Mrs. Pierce would
not accompany him until her husband had taken the needful
steps. It was then understood that she intended to become
Mrs. Tom Gurney, and join her new husband.

Her eyes turned to the post-office, then to the forbidding den
of Nicky and Nanny Glubb. The sight reminded her of a
former determination. She had heard from Nanny that sub-
scriptions for Nicky's new accordion hung fire; while, against
this statement, other people assured Tryphena that the Glubbs
had already collected enough for ten accordions, and continued
to beg and thrive on false pretences. This Tryphena hesitated
to believe. She smiled now, reflected that here at least an
offer of practical friendship would not be refused, and set out

for Southcombe. From her new money-box she took a five-pound note, in guilty thankfulness that neither her aunt nor uncle were by to see the deed; then she went down into Widecombe and called upon the Glubbs. Nanny saw her approaching.

" There's that rich maiden from the Coakers coming ! " she cried, looking out of the window. " She's been chucking her money about like grass on a hayfork, and I'll lay she wants for us to have a bit for the subscription ! "

Nicky was smoking after a dinner of Irish stew; but he knocked his pipe out and thrust it into his pocket.

" Dust a chair for her, you little devil, and be quick about it; and get me my blind man's Bible—and dust that, too—and put it open beside me. If she's got any more money to chuck away——" He ceased, for Tryphena's knock fell on the door.

When she entered, Nicky's black nails and stubby fingers were pawing the Word, and his ferocious countenance was tuned to his occupation.

" Good-morning, Mrs. Glubb; good-morning, Mr. Glubb—what a nice smell of dinner ! " said Tryphena.

" Is there? That's funny ! " said Nicky; " for God's my judge me and my poor wife haven't had nothing to call dinner for three days. We live on the smell of other people's dinners most of our time. I feel Nanny over now and again, and my tears fall, for she's getting so thin as a winter hedge, poor wretch. There's few in Widecombe to lend a thought to the bellies of the deserving poor."

Tryphena abandoned this subject, and took a chair that Nanny thrust forward.

" 'Tis the only one, save master's, that we can trust," she said. " But 'twill bear a beautiful, long-legged fairy like you, no doubt. And that's my dear husband's Bible you be looking at. He's very near wore out the New Testament fingering over it by day and night; for day or night's alike to him; but, as he says, it don't much matter now, cause he've got most of it by heart—ain't you, Nicky? "

" Ess, fay—years and years ago," declared Mr. Glubb. " I've won to the light that don't come from sun or moon or stars, young lady; and as for my poor eyes, God have got 'em in His holy keeping, and will put 'em in my head again when I get to the New Jerusalem."

Tryphena was touched by this thought.

" Not but what I know you're as pretty as a picture," continued Nicky; " and so good as you're beautiful, by general reckoning. And to think as you be sitting under my humble roof be a proud thought for me, and my wife, also. We be flung aside, you see, along of my fearful misfortune, for my musicker was tored to shreds by that bad old man, Bell, to the Church-house. So there 'tis—my power of earning have been took from me. However, no doubt at the appointed time I shall be allowed to scrape together enough pence to buy a new accordion."

" I heard you had got together more than enough, Nicky."

" Ah! That's just like Widecombe! " he said. " Even the harmless blind ain't sacred from lying tongues. Let the hard-hearted sinners give instead of talk. Each mean creature thinks t'others will subscribe, so there ain't any cause for him to do it; and as Widecombe be full of mean creatures and few others—what's the result? "

" It's a curious thing about money," said Tryphena, " that nobody seems to want mine; only the clergyman, Mr. Brown, is inclined to take any."

" Then they're no Christians," declared Nicky. " A good Christian did ought to be as ready to receive as to give—though less blessed. That's what I say, and 'tis a good and comforting thing to fall in with a young, prosperous Christian maiden girl that feels the same."

" It's so selfish to think of nobody but yourself," continued Tryphena. " I'm improving myself a great deal, you know. I'm learning the piano at Newton, and French at the Convent; and I feel as you say, Nicky, that I ought to be doing good to others beside myself."

" Of course you do, and so should I if I was young and rolling in money. And I wish you'd thought to try the accordion instead of the pianer, for 'tis a far handier instrument and not quite so difficult, with rich results when once mastered, and cheaper to buy; and gladly would I have given you lessons—as many as ever you wanted—just for love and good friendship. That's what I feel—to give of my best and ax nothing back. But few—few there be like that now. They be all underground and gone to their reward, but me and my poor wife. Yet I've known a few of 'em. There was that old Daniel Reep. He called himself a naturalist—God forgive him —but he was a fierce and rash poacher of fish and birds. 'Twas in his blood to be slaying. And yet many and many's the pattridge and pheasant as found its way into our cooking-pot when he flourished. 'Tis a very selfish, grasping world, and sometimes in my weak moments, when life be darker than a blind man's night, I cry out and doubt whether God cares for the sparrows so sharp as He did used to do."

"You mustn't think that, Nicky," said Tryphena. " You and brave Nanny have got a great many friends, and I'm one of them, and if you will accept it I should very much like to help with the accordion; and now I must go, because I'm keeping you from your reading and your wife from her work."

She rose, felt in her pocket, and found the note.

" Good-bye—good-bye—and I hope we shall soon hear a new accordion under the yew-tree," she said. Then she put the note in Nanny's hand and hastened away. They lifted up their voices, and shouted and screamed benedictions after her; but she was barely out of earshot when Nicky's tone changed.

" You say five, but be sure it ban't ten, you artful wretch? "

" 'Tis like your beastly nature to doubt," she answered.

" Call in a neighbour—ax Mary Hearn to tell you what it is."

" Then let me feel it—let me hold it," he cried. " And don't you breathe a word about it. Mary Hearn! Likely! That terror would bleat it from one end of Widecombe to t'other. None must know—else there won't be another penny come in."

" I hope to God she won't tell nobody what she've done," said Nanny.

" Not her—not her. She's not that sort—she's one of them simple saints, she is. She won't let her right hand know what her left hand doeth."

" They'll milk her to Southcombe, mark me," prophesied Nanny. " There'll be a proper lot of people clawing after her money."

" And us with the rest, I should hope," he said. " You must take a bit of watercress up over for her now and again. 'Tis wonderful how watercress, and a pair of wet boots with the soles out, do soften the heart."

Meanwhile, Tryphena, hastening away to escape the blind man's blessing, met one of whom she had already thought that day. Mabel Pierce approached, and the girl stared a greeting of doubtful surprise, for she did not know that Arthur's runaway wife had yet returned. The woman nodded and was passing to a hired carriage that waited for her; then the younger smiled, and her not unfriendly greeting made Mrs. Pierce stop.

" Just off to Bovey, I am," she said, " but I shall be back again to stop along with Mr. Gurney afore the spring. I hope your aunt and uncle ban't enemies to him or me, Miss Harvey? "

" No, they're not," said Tryphena. " Only they didn't think you were coming back till—till you had married Mr. Gurney."

" And I shouldn't—not to stop. I've just been along with Arthur—my late husband, so to call him. A talk be better than writing letters. He was a good bit astonished to see me walk in; but, much to my surprise, he's twice the chap he was. He's going to have a bill of divorcement all in order at once; and I be very much interested to see that 'tis with him as with me; he's taken a new lease of life, seemingly. He'd look the sun in the face now. And if us can be good friends again when I come back to Widecombe, then I hope the people will mind their own business, and let all go suent and easy. You may mention what I tell you, Miss Harvey. I'd hoped to have fallen in with one or two older women than you— them as were once my friends; but the few I catched sight of appeared to be took sudden with the palsy or St. Vitus' dance when they saw me."

Then, entering her cab, Mrs. Pierce drove away; while Tryphena told of her adventure on returning to Southcombe, and Mr. Coaker commented upon it.

" It shows what good may come of cutting a loss," he said. " Few have the pluck to do it—specially in matrimony; and often enough a suffering creature haven't got power, though the will may be there. But in this case that blusterous female took the bit in her teeth; and so she be saved alive, and her husband likewise. For the change in Arthur be far more than all the doctors in England, and all the cod-liver oil in the sea, could have brought about. I heard him dressing down his ostler last week, for all the world like I'd talk to Webber if he did wrong! His nerve be coming back with a bound. Why, he's had his sign painted again in flaming red and gold, and he's got a brave new suit of clothes with a pattern of chequers that you can see all across the green ! "

CHAPTER XLI

VALIANT DUNNYBRIG's search for Araminta Dench was not protracted. Miss Dench indeed he did not find, but Mrs. Sweetland confronted him after he had been at Exeter three days.

He dwelt in a small lodgment nigh the cathedral; and in

the close he came face to face with his niece on her husband's arm.

Samuel had striven hard to accommodate himself to Araminta; he had paid her the compliment of affecting a more youthful mind and body than he possessed. He was very proud of her and of himself. For a time he struggled gamely to keep up the fiction of youth and jollity. Then, perceiving the truth was otherwise, Araminta begged him to desist, and he relapsed thankfully into advanced middle age. Her consideration soon made him love her in earnest. At her suggestion he cut short the honeymoon, and husband and wife were returning to Tunhill on the day after they fell in with Valiant Dunnybrig.

At Widecombe the great event was already known, and her brother's marriage had been generally announced by Samuel's sister; but Mr. Dunnybrig still knew it not, because his wife was unaware of his address, and could not inform him. She indeed suffered severely, though the discovery of Araminta's achievement allayed her distress in vital particulars.

Now Valiant stood before the wedded pair, tall, grey, patriarchal. A long coat, which he had purchased in Plymouth, floated round about him; his beard swept his breast; it seemed to Araminta that some venerable figure of stone had received the breath of life and alighted from its niche in the western wall of the cathedral to speak with her. But she felt glad that this had happened, and greeted Mr. Dunnybrig cheerfully.

"Here's Uncle Valiant! What could be better! and he'll tell those who don't know already!" she said.

"Yes, here am I," said Mr. Dunnybrig, "and here are you, and here is Farmer Sweetland, seemingly. But why? Why did you leave Chittleford, like a thief in the night, Araminta Dench; and why are you on this man's arm in gay apparel? The first question I can answer myself; the second is for Samuel Sweetland to answer. You ran away, being a weak vessel that feared persecution, and thought it better to continue at peace with your fellow-men than at peace with your God. So much for that. I vowed to find you, and I have found you. But how? Why are you holding the arm of neighbour Sweetland, Araminta Dench?"

"Because she's not Araminta Dench," piped the new-made husband. "Because we are one, my dear Dunnybrig! Araminta is my wife! You are doubtless staggered, if this is the first you have heard of it, and I'm very sorry to think that you have wasted your valuable time hunting for her.

Your wife must have heard a long while ago—last Monday week, in fact."

The master of Chittleford stared from one to the other. Then he spoke to Araminta.

"You did this thing to escape from——"

"Not at all," she interrupted hastily. "I accepted my dear husband's offer of marriage the moment he made it, and proud I was to do so; and since he wished our wedding to be private, without any fuss, I just slipped away with him quietly. And I wrote to Aunt Jane the very Sunday after, and told her what a proud and happy woman I was. And if you had been home, Uncle, you would have understood."

"But it's all right now, and if you will come in here along with us and have a bit of cold meat and a glass of lemonade, Dunnybrig, I shall be proud to stand treat," said Samuel. "We're bound for home to-morrow. Araminta wants to get to work, and feel her way round Tunhill. And don't you think the worse of us for keeping our little plot dark till 'twas hatched. I'm a modest man, and hate all show and display."

Still Valiant Dunnybrig was silent. His mind seemed incapable of accepting the news of Araminta's marriage. He perceived, however, that Samuel knew nothing of the past, and considered whether he should be told of it. But he relinquished the idea.

"I thank you for your offer of food, but would rather pray than eat at present," he said.

"Come back along with us to-morrow," suggested Samuel. "'Twill be a regular triumphal procession if us all go back in one chaise! Mine's to meet us at Bovey in the afternoon, and I'll pay for all."

But Valiant declined.

"My work is done, and I shall go back to-night," he said. Then he shook hands with them, left them, and turned into the cathedral.

CHAPTER XLII

"THEY'LL be saying the old words that Elias told me," declared Tryphena Harvey. She walked on a day in December beside Gabriel Shillingford's horse and looked up into a sky dark with snow. They had met by chance and went along together, for Mr. Shillingford was on his way to Kingshead, while Tryphena had promised to drink tea with Miss Tapper and a few friends at " Genoa Villa."

" And what words were those? " he asked. " Your cousin Elias is growing more thoughtful as he gets older."

" The words are supposed to be spoke by people in the ' in country ' when they look up to the Moor on a snowy day such as this : ' Widecombe folk are picking their geese— faster, faster, and faster ! ' But it should be ' Widdicote '— —an old word meaning the sky, so my cousin thinks."

" I have drawn up a list of ancient sayings. Observation breeds the homely ideas you hear. ' The wisdom of many and the wit of one,' as we say. If you come to me on Wednesday afternoon, Tryphena, I will read you a list of hundreds of wise sayings culled from all languages, though of course done into English by scholars."

" I'll come gladly, Mr. Shillingford."

" And you shall hear some very fine things out of that book you bought me. It is a most amazing book. I had always thought of it as a work of fiction, beneath the notice of serious men; but it is fiction only in the same way that Shakespeare is. There are gleams of wisdom and noble thoughts on every page. ' The History of Don Quixote,' I mean. It is a most important, wise, and beautiful work; and there are good jokes, too, and also poems. For people who understand jokes, which I do not, the book no doubt has special charm."

" I'm sorry you're going to Mrs. Windeatt's," said Tryphena, " because that means she isn't coming to Miss Tapper's tea-party. And I much hoped she was."

" I cannot tell how that may be," said Gabriel. " At any rate, I go to drink tea with Louisa Windeatt."

" Please to give her my love, Mr. Shillingford. She's always been simply heavenly to me."

" I'm glad you like her so much, Tryphena. I have a great admiration for her beautiful character. Well, here we part. I hope you will enjoy your tea-party. And keep your eye on the weather. To-morrow the Vale will be white. Nature has made her preparations thoroughly."

They parted, and Mr. Shillingford climbed the hill, reached Kingshead, and gave his horse to a hind. Then, shaking himself free of snow and doffing his outer coat, he appeared before the widow.

They spoke of the weather first, and next of Tryphena Harvey.

"She's a precious thing," declared Shillingford, "and makes you feel sorry that the old-fashioned sort of girls have disappeared. She belongs to a past age, in my opinion—no doubt owing to having been born and bred in Australia. Her parents evidently brought her up in the old way, to be unselfish and think of something beside her own pleasures and amusements. And their teaching has stuck to her."

"Yes, she's a bit of the old world, I believe."

"She came to me to take her money! "

"You told me about it."

"My heart was much touched, Louisa."

"It was very pretty of her. Now tell me how you get on. Does young Arnell, the carpenter's brother, work for you, after all? "

"He does not. He discovered that he would prefer to be a carpenter, too. It is rather a good thing that we are not commanded to take apprentices by law, as in the old days; for you need to look mighty far now to find young men who want to go on the land."

"The rich desire the poor to remain idiots always, and don't understand that they are fast being educated out of idiotcy. But that is changed now. The poor are tired of it; they're tired of ploughing other men's land and gathering other men s corn."

"You might as well say a banker's clerk is tired of handling other men's money. A thing is only worth what it will fetch. Your radical ideas make me very uneasy now and again, Louisa."

"And your conservative ideas make me feel the same," she said. "Go nearer the fire and warm your feet. As to rich and poor, it is like the whale and the thresher. You've heard of the battles they fight, and the lean, wiry thresher, with his scourge of a tail, always beats the fat monster in the end Well, the poor are the thresher, Gabriel."

"I suppose it is so. We live in sight of immense and shattering changes. I was thinking of the irony of fate just before I met Tryphena Harvey. It is most vexatious and disagreeable. The Fitz-Ralphs, who took the name of Shillingford, owned the Manor of Widecombe once. My creditors never seem fully to appreciate what that must mean to a sensitive man. Have I ever told you about——"

"Yes, yes—a thousand times! "

"It will bear repetition. One need not go back beyond the days when Baldwin de Shillingford was lord of the manor and rector of the church."

" ' And he had a son named John, to whom he left his lands, tenements and rents.' "

Mrs. Windeatt quoted the familiar phrases, but Gabriel was not amused.

" True," he said; " then followed William, who sold all to Sir William Huddersfield. But this deplorable William, who alienated the property, had a very different sort of a brother. I mean, of course——"

" The famous John, Mayor of Exeter."

" Yes—from 1447 to 1450. It is very pleasant to me to see you know our history so well, Louisa."

" I know; but now do talk of something nearer."

" Don't think it wearies me," he answered. " Far from it. I am always delighted to refresh my memory with that hero. A learned, shrewd, brave man was John Shillingford."

" ' He would ride backward and forward between Exeter and London as if the distance was nothing.' "

Mrs. Windeatt quoted again.

" Well done! That is just what he did—and laughed at all the highway dangers of those days. Justly enough he acquired great fame, and John Hooker said many notable things about him."

" ' That he was learned in the laws of the realm, and so on.' "

" I'm afraid I must be repeating myself," said the farmer. " Well, just a note on Blackslade and then, if you would rather, we'll change the subject. Blackslade was written ' Blacheslach ' by the Normans. It occurs in Domesday— one of the real consolations in my complicated life, Louisa. Yes, it is in Domesday."

" Stop! Stop, Gabriel! "

" Black means ' bleak,' of course; and ' slade ' a little dene or valley, or a green plain in a wood."

" You don't want me to ask you to go away, do you? But I shall in a minute."

He stared out of his solemn eyes.

" I'm sorry. I get so self-absorbed. It is blameworthy. But these things are my only interest and pleasure. They are harmless, and cost nothing, Louisa."

" Nonsense, Gabriel! You shan't be pathetic and senti- mental with me, because I won't have it. These things *oughtn't* to be your only interest and pleasure, and they cost a great deal. Look at the books you buy. There are plenty of other things in life a thousand times more interesting and pleasing than all this nonsense over old history—things more exciting and alive and close."

" For instance? "

" Well, which is better, to get old history by heart, or make new history yourself? "

" That I shall do, willy nilly," he answered. " It is even within the reach of imagination to see myself called to leave Blackslade."

" You never shall! "

" Thank you for being so positive, Louisa. It is like your brave heart and plucky view of things. But really, in my darker moments, I have considered the chance of it. Hope fools one so curiously. I find my life, which ought to be highly dignified, is not dignified in the least. Instead it has become just a sort of passing from one unpleasant event to another. A voyage without a harbour, you might say. Perhaps the harbour is death."

" Why, you're not sixty yet."

" There are times when I feel as much, if not actually more. You see, I am engaged eternally in making bricks without straw, Louisa; and when I'm not doing that, I'm writing difficult letters. I am called to put up with a great deal of rudeness. And yet there is no excuse for bad manners. Men have owed me money, but I have not lost my temper or treated them discourteously."

" That I am very sure. But——" she hesitated. " I don't think life ever can be making bricks without straw—if you're a Christian. Can it? Doesn't religion find the straw? "

" Well said! You are right. It was a lapse—I didn't look all round the subject. That is a very beautiful remark, Louisa —that religion finds the straw. I have lost my faith in religion, just as my creditors appear to have lost faith in me. This must be looked into. You have a very fine nature, Louisa. I told Tryphena so not an hour ago. We joined in praising you. She loves you. And so do I—yes—in the highest possible sense."

" You've said it now! "

" In the highest possible sense. Between us these great words may be used, and leave no loophole of misunderstanding. You have helped me very often, and I am not dead to gratitude. If circumstances—but things are as they are."

" ' If circumstances '—go on there, Gabriel. That sounded as if it might have been interesting."

" The paths of life that we may not explore always look the most interesting."

" Yet those who have explored them will be sure to tell us they are not. And what was the path you would have liked to explore, Gabriel—' if circumstances '——? "

" Had not made it impossible."

" Yes? "

" You."

" Man alive ! "

" Don't think I'm speaking off book. I'm not as quick as many men to discover a thing; but once discovered—I said, climbing the hill just now—I said to myself : ' How often I come up here ! ' And then I reflected, and ran over past days and months, until I was quite disconcerted to think how often. I very nearly turned back for shame."

" ' Shame,' Gabriel? Oh, don't say that. You know very well the welcome that's waiting."

" I do indeed know it—and how undeserved; for ten to one but I come to prate of my own affairs and weary you to death, as I have to-day."

" No—no."

" My road is a thought doubtful, Louisa. But I rest in hope it will grow clearer as I advance—and then—if—if you——"

He rose suddenly and went to the window.

" You are to be snowed up by the look of it. I must get going."

She came over to him.

" Thank you for what you've said. It has made me feel a very happy woman, Gabriel."

" I'd make you happier yet—if the power was in me. There's none like you in the world, Louisa. But there it is. One has to face it—winter and so on."

" Go away now," she answered. " I've heard enough. I want to think and think. Oh, if you were sensible instead of sensitive, my dear man ! If you'd let me do what you won't let that grey-eyed girl do. For pity's sake, Gabriel, if you care for me a pinch, let me have the chance to show I care for you ! "

He laughed at that.

" You're a wonderful woman—one of the old, fine sort. We shall meet again before long, I dare say, and maybe I shall be better company. There's to be no marrying in a hurry—my Petronell and Hugh Grenville. Of course the match isn't made public yet. 'Tis to be in the paper. ' A marriage has been arranged.' But his people are not well pleased, and want it delayed."

Her lips tightened.

" The longer they wait the better."

" You don't like him ! "

" No, I do not. Such a man is not good enough for Petronell."

" Louisa! He's in the direct line of the great Sir Richard Grenville! "

" He's sly and mean and crafty. I've quarrelled with Petronell already; but I'm not going to quarrel with you."

" We must have this out. You amaze me. The young fellow has struck me as manly and ingenuous and simple-minded."

" Go home," she said. " Get down the hill before the drifts come. Don't think me uncharitable and unkind. I care more for Petronell than any girl in the world but Sibley—you know that."

She put his hat and riding-stock into his hands.

" I should like to stop," he answered; " but you are wise, as usual. I had better be gone. This is the way the snow would fall when I was a boy—the winter's to come."

He left her, and on the way home met Valiant Dunnybrig. The elder man was also on horseback.

" Winter and trouble be roving the earth, seeking what they may destroy," said the master of Chittleford.

" We all have our difficulties."

" And puzzles. I thought my puzzle-time was ended, Shillingford, for I felt my hand in my Father's hand so firm, that I hardly needed to look where I set my foot. But let them that think they stand take heed lest they fall. This runaway marriage between my niece and Samuel Sweetland have been the surprise of my life."

" No doubt, no doubt—a mystery in its way. But we never can fathom the vagaries of the human mind, Dunnybrig."

" There's more to it than you know. I misunderstood God in that matter, and I'm punished pretty severely. Doubt got in me—like a plague of sickness. I have passed through stickle places, neighbour."

" You miss her, no doubt."

" Yes, I miss her."

" And Mrs. Dunnybrig must, even more than you do. But happily Araminta has not gone far off."

" Yes, Mrs. Dunnybrig misses her. We have Faith Arnell, the carpenter's sister, come to live with us to take her place. She's related to my wife."

" A woman—well, a sad woman, who takes a gloomy view of life—so her brother tells me."

" She is not a woman. Merely a female—no more than that. As busy as a bee, I grant. But her hum is dreary and bitter. She passes through the chambers like a dead leaf blown by the east wind."

" A chastening woman."

" She has been sent for a purpose, and I know it.   I described her to my wife as ' a horror of great darkness,' and Jane couldn't deny it."

" You'll make a change presently. 'Tis idle to live with the wrong people if we can help it."

" I don't say she's the wrong person, Shillingford—any more than I say that this is the wrong weather. She may be the messenger of the Lord's will; she may be the bleak and biting arrow of truth, shot into my home by my Maker for His own good reasons."

" God sometimes speaks doubtfully to try our wits," said Gabriel.

" Without a question He does, and 'tis a very wise thing in you to mark it."

They had reached Chittleford's great gate, and a man, passing on foot, stopped to open it for Valiant.

" Thank you, Christian Cobleigh," he said.   " See to it, Christian, that your father lies close at Venton while this weather holds. It might pinch him off, like a withered apple, if he were to go afield until the cold breaks."

CHAPTER XLIII

THREE days before the Christmas festival, Widecombe was shocked by another sudden disappearance; for hardly had the course of life run smooth again after Samuel Sweetland's sensational and secret marriage; hardly were tongues tired of discussing the departure of Araminta, or necks weary of craning to see her enter church upon her husband's arm, when Christian Cobleigh of Venton set a crown upon his doubtful career, vanished from his native village without warning, and struck not less than five-and-thirty homes with consternation. Concerning his departure there existed no mystery at all. On Monday he was known to be about his usual business; on Tuesday the taciturn spirit could be nowhere found; and with him dissolved away the accumulated funds of the " Rugglestone " Slate Club. Upon the very morning of the annual distribution did Christian convey himself into the void, and when the club met at " Rugglestone Inn," the treasurer failed to keep his appointment. Messengers to Venton met with tidings that the younger Mr. Cobleigh had not been seen for twenty-four hours, nor could search discover the archives of the club left in his care. Uncle Tom Cobleigh and his widowed daughter, Susie Grey, were in the extremity of grief, and Doctor Grenville had been called to visit the ancient man, for he was harshly stricken by the blow. None, indeed, censured him, but the club evinced an unruly and recalcitrant attitude under its tribulation. A painful evening was spent at " Rugglestone Inn," and since the sinner had taken himself out of reach, every member blamed another, and each found in his neighbour some contributory cause of the universal blow. All now agreed that Christian Cobleigh ought never to have been appointed treasurer ; everybody indicated to everybody else that a man famed for his love of sport, was of all men the least likely to resist temptation at a pinch; everybody protested that power had been given Christian to draw the funds out of the bank previous to distribution. It was calculated that he must have taken at least five-and-fifty pounds; but whether to pay old debts, or to convey himself out of his native country, mattered little to his victims.

Venton was swallowed in darkness, and the disgrace of this tragedy reflected heavily on all therein. No news reached Uncle Cobleigh, and he believed that his son must have gone abroad. But grudging spirits suspected that he was not entirely outside Christian's secrets, and knew at least where the man was hidden. That Christian should have ruined his career for fifty pounds surprised the more reflective; but the fact remained, and Christmas was thereby clouded and shorn of small joys in many a small home.

There came a night, about a month after this disaster, when Susie Grey helped her father into his coat and wrapped his muffler about his bald neck, that he might set forth to " Rugglestone Inn " and take his part at a very important meeting of the defrauded slate club.

A large company had assembled, and it was patient and orderly. The shock and loss were digested; the disappointment was dulled; the folk approached their problems in a spirit of good-fellowship and good-will.

Nearly thirty men crammed the taproom of the " Rugglestone Inn," and through a tobacco cloud, gilded by lamplight, one might have marked familiar visages amid the throng—now clear, now dim, in the fog of the smoke. At the top of the table a white smudge, seen fitfully among moving heads, indicated the beard of Valiant Dunnybrig, who sat in the chair; elsewhere a bald head or two caught the light and made a focus for it among the hairy crowns of the club members.

There were present in the company Birkett Johnson, Nicky Glubb, Pancras Widecombe, and many others from the farms and village. Arthur Pierce, who understood the principles of the famous slate club, of which he had once been secretary, consented to come, that he might assist the reconstruction; and William Coaker; Elias Coaker; the Hawkes, father and son; Peter Smerdon, from Bone Hill; and Tom Gurney, the blacksmith, were others of the more notable people present.

It is to be remarked that all old differences and ancient feuds had sunk away in this assembly. Time forgets not even the most sequestered heart, and in the light of this grave disaster to the slate club, ancient enmities had their quietus; the defrauded lamb and swindled lion lay down together. Nicky Glubb might never have differed from Birkett Johnson; Elias Coaker might never have struggled in battle with the flamboyant Pancras Widecombe; Tom Gurney himself might never have outraged the sensibilities of the Vale. In the light of this upheaval, men made common cause. They were, in fact, assembled to form another slate club on the ruins of the old; and they proposed that the new institution, in virtue of its complete equipment, perfect system, and efficient control, should banish painful memories of that destroyed by the robber act of Uncle Cobleigh's son. Into this company crept the little figure of Uncle himself, and it was remarked that the ancient man had physically shrunk under his grief, for when Pancras and Mr. Turtle liberated Uncle from his hat, his coat, and his scarf a mere bent and earth-coloured shred of a man remained.

Valiant Dunnybrig made a kindly allusion to the master of Venton at the beginning of the proceedings.

" Before we bury the past, neighbours, I'll say one word and ask you, for the peace of an aged soul, to let Uncle Tom here understand that none among us bear him a grudge in this matter. 'Tis true that he got Christian Cobleigh; Christian was the fruit of Uncle's loins; but we are not allowed to know beforehand what sort of figure our offspring be going to cut in the land of the living. And if we did, no doubt a thoughtful member here and there might choose to be childless, for the sake of the unborn. I have it from Uncle hisself that Christian was a very hopeful fashion of young youth, and quite up to his name, until he went to Totnes Races in his nineteenth year. And there the devil came along, in the shape of a betting man, and Christian fell under the curse of gambling.

So, afore we get to business, I'll thank you to express to Uncle that not one amongst us think the worse of him for what part he had in his son. I put up a vote of confidence in Uncle, for his mind be a good bit shattered by this dreadful affair, and it will be a great relief to him and his widowed daughter to hear that the Vale don't hold him guilty."

" I beg to second that," said Birkett Johnson, and the company agreed without dissension.

" And now us'll get to business," cried Nicky Glubb. " Us don't want no more bleating and snivelling. Somebody will call for a vote of forgiveness for Christian Cobleigh next, or perhaps a stained-glass winder to him in the church."

They silenced the blind man, and Mr. Dunnybrig addressed Arthur Pierce.

" We wish to know all about the club you was interested in, Pierce—its rules and regulations, and suchlike."

" You shall hear what I can tell, and I'll stand by the door, because there's more air moving there," said Arthur.

A personal wonder struck not a few that the shattered husband had arisen from his own ashes, and, again, could face his fellows thus boldly.

" Time was when the sound of his own voice frighted that man, and hark to the dog now! " said Glubb audibly to a neighbour.

" 'Tis this way," began Mr. Pierce. " I've looked at your rules, and I see you was a bit foggy in a good few particulars. Your club went on very poor lines, and, so far as I can see, 'twas more of a goose club than a proper slate club. To provide against illness be the proper reason. The members give their weekly sixpence, and a penny a week extra for the doctor, and one and all strictly keep the rules and regulations. The man amongst you who has the ill luck to fall sick should be allowed ten shillings a week for ten weeks of the year; but you make no time limit, and, what's worse, you don't have no regular paid members to visit the sick cases and report on 'em."

He continued in this strain, and elaborated the principles and practice of the slate club he had known.

" And when all's done," concluded Arthur, " then, three days before Christmas, the members come together for the ' Share-out,' and they take equally what funds be left over after all expenses are paid. It happens this year that your share was going to be extra good."

" 'Tis no good crying over spilt milk. We'll forget that part," declared Mr. Dunnybrig. " The thing is to begin the new year on better lines, and with surer foundations and a larger understanding of the advantages we can get from such a club. And I'll join for one, and my men shall join; and I hope every man here will join, and when he goeth home, he will blaze the ' Rugglestone ' Slate Club abroad and get his neighbour to join.''

" And don't let it be run so as any damn rogue can steal our money no more," said Nicky.

" You wasn't in it, anyway," answered Johnson.

" No more I was, but can't a man feel for his robbed neighbour? " retorted Nicky. " And I be going to be in the next—if a honest secretary is chose."

" As to that, the treasurer didn't ought to have temptation thrust in his way," explained Mr. Pierce. " He should only be allowed to hold sufficient money in hand to meet everyday expenses and pay the sick members their money."

" Then our business is to enrol members, build up the new club, and appoint officers," declared Mr. Dunnybrig.

They proceeded to elect officers, and Mr. Dunnybrig himself accepted the post of chairman.

" I thank you," he said, " and that being so, I ought to have a voice in appointing the vice-chair. And I submit that it would be a great salve to Uncle Cobleigh's feelings if we put him in the vice-chair. I propose Uncle for that purpose."

There was silence, however, and it grew painful. None seconded, and Uncle Cobleigh spoke.

" No, no—not for a moment. The sins of the children be visited on the fathers often and often. I quite understand. I wish the club well, and shall be a member to my dying day—which can't be far off. But it ban't right that I should be lifted up to any high place in the matter—owing to my age and the sad facts of the case. And if I could do so, I'd give every man back what my son stole from 'em, and perhaps, if the lambing season be all I hope, I may do so; and me and my darter—and—and—God's my judge, but this—awful blow——"

Here sorrow choked Uncle Cobleigh. He bent lower and lower and tears fell from his eyes.

" Don't take on—don't take on, Uncle," said Birkett Johnson. " We know how 'tis with you. I propose Mr. Sweetland for vice-chair. My master has the matter much at heart and will be a good friend to the new club. And he would have been here to-night but for his wife. He's took a cold in his head, and she wouldn't let him face the night air."

" I vote Mr. William Coaker for ' vice,' " said Pancras

Widecombe; and Nicky Glubb, with his thoughts on Tryphena Harvey, seconded the proposition. Another labourer suggested Mr. Turtle, and Arthur Pierce seconded.

Mr. Coaker won the greater number of votes for the position of vice-chairman, and then Valiant Dunnybrig suggested that it might be well to appoint joint treasurers.

" It makes more work, but 'tis safer—what do you say, Pierce? "

" 'Tis a very wise thought without a doubt. And one can't so much as smell the money without t'other, so there's no fear of any painful accidents," declared Arthur.

To this delicate and important task came Birkett Johnson and Whitelock Smerdon. It was decided that no better men could be chosen; while Pancras Widecombe, to his immense gratification, was nominated as secretary.

" 'Tis a great lift up for a workhouse boy," declared Nicky Glubb, " and he ought to stand drinks on the strength of it, if he's made of the proper stuff."

" Five members must now be appointed for the committee," explained Arthur Pierce; " and two members must be appointed for stewards to visit the sick. That's an important thing, because they get paid."

" And they have a delicate task, because to decide whether a member be really sick or only pretending calls for a great cleverness, and may make enemies," added Dunnybrig. " Not that among a lot of honourable Christian men, anyone would sink to get sick-money under false pretences, I should hope."

" Don't you hope nothing like that, Valiant Dunnybrig, because 'tis vain," declared Mr. Glubb. " Where big money be the matter, 'tis stark madness and flying in the face of human nature to trust man, woman, or child."

" No doubt you know, Nicky," answered the master of Chittleford.

" Then there's the doctor," continued Arthur Pierce. " When you've elected your committee, you must seek young Dr. Grenville and see if he'll accept the appointment for a year."

The committee was then considered, and both Turtle and Pierce were invited to sit upon it.

" I can't and I won't, and 'twould be indecent to ax me," declared Timothy. " Surely to God you see that? The first thing the people will have to do must be to decide if the club be coming here any more. So I'm prejudiced."

" And the same here," said Mr. Pierce. " You can't ask me and Turtle."

A committee was therefore elected without them, though the matter took some time, because Nicky proposed himself and argued long with Mr. Dunnybrig as to the propriety, or even possibility, of so doing. It was finally decided that Nicky might propose himself, but since none seconded him, his services to the club were lost.

" You be our honary accordion-player," said Pancras, " and that's something."

" Honary be blasted ! " answered the blind man, who was much annoyed that none desired him in office. " All you blades will rake a bit out of this, and why for should I be denied, just because I'm blind? "

" It isn't because you're blind; it's because you are not required, Nicky Glubb," explained the chairman. " We need but five men, and the sense of the meeting is that you're not one of them."

Nicky growled.

" The sense of this meeting wouldn't load a louse," he said. " However, if I ban't in it myself, I'll have my knife in it every day we meet, and if I'm ill, as I generally be in the month of February, I shall look to the club to see me through it."

" That's what we be here for," said Birkett Johnson.

" Subscription cards will be printed and a book of rules given to each member in due course," announced Valiant Dunnybrig, " and now, as appointed secretary, Mr. Widecombe will read out the rules of Arthur Pierce's old club that worked so fine."

Pancras read the proposed rules, and none demurred until the twelfth was reached.

" *That at the death of a member of this Society, each member shall contribute one shilling, and the amount so realised be paid to the widow (on furnishing the secretary with her marriage certificate) or next of kin; and on the death of a member's wife, each member shall contribute sixpence, to be paid to the husband within one month, under penalty of a fine of threepence.*"

" That's silly bosh," declared Mr. Glubb. " Any fool would rather be fined threepence than pay sixpence. Besides, why for should us have the call for money always hanging over us? Because a member dies, that's no just reason why I should fork out a bob for his missus—marriage certificate or none."

A good few were of Nicky's opinion; but on taking a vote the law passed.

" Same for one, same for all," declared Dunnybrig.

" The next rule—No. 13—will hit you harder than the last, Nicky," said Arthur Pierce, and Pancras read the regulation.

" ' *That if any member, during club-hours, curse, swear, or give the lie, or come into the clubroom intoxicated. or call anyone by an improper name, he shall be fined one penny for every offence.*' And what do you think of that, Mr. Glubb? "

" You'll drop a lot more under that rule than the last, Nicky," declared Timothy Turtle.

" 'Tis a blasted interference with the liberty of the subject, and I call on all men to refuse to pass it," said Nicky. " Why —good Lord A'mighty!—not to cuss them that deserve to be cussed, and not to give the lie to a liar, and not to be drunk if you choose to be drunk—'tis Socialism, and I won't sign to it for any living man! "

" Besides," declared a labourer named Sandy Blake, from Blackslade, " you can't in reason order us not to come into the clubroom intoxicated. For why? There ain't no clubroom to come into."

Nicky was argued down; but he declined to be a member. The list of the fines awoke increasing indignation within him, and when his wife came for him, before the termination of the meeting, he called upon her loudly to take him home.

" Lead me out of this," he said. " 'Tis a herd of poor spiritless dogs that I be got in, and they don't care what chains they put round their necks, so long as there's bones in their plates and straw in their kennels. A cowardly crew, all wanting to keep each other warm, like bugs in a rug. No fight, no fierceness, no spirit among 'em. To tell me how I be to talk and drink! My trouser-buttons, what next? Take me out of it! I won't be a tame rabbit for all Widecombe—blind as I am! "

Some jeered, but Nicky's ribaldry far exceeded theirs.

" Rabbits! " he bawled as he withdrew. " Fat, pot-bellied rabbits! I won't neighbour with you! I don't want your dirty doles! You be a lot of mean red cockroaches! "

He was led away, and the meeting concluded with a vote of thanks to Mr. Dunnybrig.

In a fortnight the club numbered seventy-two members, and complete success promised to crown its activities.

CHAPTER XLIV

WITH Spring came the public announcement of Petronell Shillingford's betrothal, and the event provoked less interest than Gabriel had expected. He wearied the humblest ears with the Grenville family; but found an inclination on the part of Widecombe to judge his future son-in-law upon the practical, if narrow, basis of his own record. The indifferent were cautious and said nothing; the kind-hearted declared that the doctor was very good-looking; the plain-spoken expressed a hope that Hugh Grenville had sown his wild oats.

" Wild oats! wild oats! " exclaimed Mr. Shillingford. " What are you talking about, Peter Smerdon? But you probably don't understand the meaning of great traditions, or that expression of the French, *Noblesse oblige*. It means that the nobly-born go under a debt to their ancestors, and they have to discharge that debt by remembering that from the great more is demanded than from the humble. A Grenville has to deny himself much that might be a temptation for other young men. A Grenville should be like Cæsar's wife, in fact."

" And what was she like? " asked Peter.

" Above suspicion," answered Mr. Shillingford.

" Ah! so he is then," admitted the other; " by all accounts he's soared high above suspicion. 'Tis proof positive—unless that girl to Chagford's a liar. However, if he's going to be one of the family, you won't find me say a word against him."

" I have his word," answered Mr. Shillingford. " I have Doctor Grenville's word that in certain directions his prospects are exceedingly bright. He is, in fact, marking time here."

" Oh, I never heard that name for it. However, he's won your fine darter, and I hope her high nature and religion and so on will pull him up. Who have he got belonging to him? "

" His family lives in East Devon," answered Gabriel. " He has a widowed mother, three sisters, and a brother. Concerning the brother he has little to tell us. But he lives at home. His mother was a Westonhaugh. What a vista that name opens to the thoughtful mind! Two of his sisters are married, but the eldest is not. She lives with Mrs. Grenville. In the case of his sister Kate, she is wedded to a soldier, and is in India at present. His other married sister

—Winifred—is the wife of the Reverend Septimus Stephens, a scholar of Cambridge University, who has published a volume of sermons, and has five children."

Mr. Smerdon nodded.

" And what do they all think about it? " he inquired.

" I shall be able to answer that question at a later date," replied Gabriel, " because my Petronell pays the family a visit. In fact, we start on Monday next. I say ' we,' because Mrs. Grenville has expressed a wish for me to visit her along with my girl. It is natural. And I have little doubt that before I leave Honiton Piffard—that is the name of their township—I have little doubt that we shall arrange for them to come and spend a fortnight or so at Blackslade."

" Lord, to hear you! And where's the money coming from? "

" Good-bye, Peter," answered Gabriel. It was now Mr. Shillingford's practice instantly to terminate any interview with Whitelock's father when conversation threatened unpleasantness.

In due course the young doctor of Widecombe, leaving his slender duties in the hands of an Ashburton physician, went to prepare his relatives for the coming visit; and then arrived a day when Mr. Shillingford and Petronell departed for Honiton Piffard. Mrs. Windeatt, on her way to a meet of hounds, dropped in at Blackslade to witness the start. In a covered carriage, hired from the " Dolphin " at Bovey, did father and daughter set out; and Mr. Shillingford wore his silk hat and a new overcoat, while his luggage was packed in a new portmanteau of russet leather, with the letters " G. S." stamped thereon in gold. Petronell wore a new dress and hat. She was happy, and very beautiful to see. Sibley preserved a semblance of animation until the vehicle drove off; and Whitelock also endeavoured to be cheerful; but his grin was ghastly, and perished before the carriage was out of sight. Then did Sibley break down and retreat, that Louisa Windeatt might not see her tears.

But Whitelock was not so particular.

" Poor toad! " he said; " enough to make her cry. 'Tis all a sickening sham and show, and the life's being knocked out of us, I do assure 'ee. There's my wife going to be a mother, please God, next April, and the place doomed, and a whisper of brokers if nothing be done afore Lady Day; and him going off as if Petronell was to marry a millionaire, instead of a vicious young rip that's not worth the boots on his feet."

" I know," answered Louisa. " I know all about it. The thing's all wrong, Whitelock, and in anybody but your father-in-law it would be infamous; but there's nobody quite like him in the world, and so there are no standards to judge him by."

"Yes, there are," answered Whitelock. "A bankrupt is a bankrupt, and the standards they are judged by are very well known."

"It mustn't be. It shan't be, Whitelock. I've come here this very morning to see you and Sibley about it. I only pretended I was going hunting. You can take my horse into the stable and I'll seek Sibley. And I don't mean to leave Blackslade till something is settled."

Louisa presently explained her fixed determination to play good fairy at Blackslade, while Sibley declared it a physical impossibility, and Whitelock, when he joined them, mournfully believed that his wife was right.

"Then listen to me," said Mrs. Windeatt, "and I think that I can convince both of you."

"Money's not merely tight; it don't exist. There won't be food for the cattle in a month."

"And I'm sure I'm terrible fond of father," added Sibley; "but 'tis very hard on Whitelock to spend all his wits and skill and great cleverness in trying to keep other people out of the workhouse."

"The thing to do," declared Mrs. Windeatt, "is this. We must make Mr. Shillingford believe himself much richer than he really is."

"Good Lord, Louisa!" cried Sibley. "What you want to drive into father is that he's a pauper, and ought to act according."

"You misunderstand. I mean that he must suddenly find himself richer by a considerable deal of money, and I'm going to work it. Yes, this is to be my privilege, and you needn't thank me, either of you. I may have something to gain."

"If you mean a mortgage, Blackslade's mortgaged up to the roof-tree a'ready," said Whitelock.

"I don't at all. But what must happen is this. He must suddenly discover that he is richer by a great increase."

"He is richer by a great increase, only 'tis too late," answered Sibley. "Whitelock have got a clear hundred pound more out of the place this year than ever it yielded afore; but that's no use. There's over a thousand pound of debts."

"Suppose we were to find two or three thousand pounds?"

"He'd pay a town-crier to seek the owner," declared Sibley.

"But if it appeared beyond all possibility of doubt that it was his *own* money he had found?"

"How could that be? We don't live on a tin-mine!"

" But there might be a silver-mine, or some such thing under your floor."

" You beat me, ma'am," said Whitelock bluntly. " Fairy-stories ain't no use in a fix like this."

" Well, you and Sibley are not proud and silly, are you? "

" Don't know about silly. Some might say we was a couple of zanies to bide here, for we be doing no good to ourselves, God knows, and mighty little to anybody else. But as to pride—no, we ain't got a pinch of that between us."

" Very well, then. Now, doesn't it occur to you that this is just a case for the family ghost—the far-famed miser Shillingford of old? "

" Not a doubt of it," laughed Sibley. " 'Tis just a case for him; but, like most of the ghosts ever I heard of, he don't come forward when he might be most useful."

" Don't laugh about it; that ghost has got to appear again."

" Really, Louisa! Can't you hit upon nothing more likely than that? "

" No, Sibley, I cannot; and if you had a pinch of imagina-tion, I'm sure you'd see the possibilities. The ghost first. What is he supposed to be like? "

" Father's father had a labourer who saw it. And that's the nearest we've got to him. An old man with a long white beard. That's all that we can say."

" Capital! We could easily imitate an old man with a long white beard. Whitelock could be the ghost himself, and you could see him! "

Sibley stared; then her eyes flashed understanding.

" He could see himself for that matter," she said, rising quickly to woman's natural heritage. " Yes, he could see the ghost himself ; but he needn't tell father that 'twas in a look-ing-glass he'd done so! But—no, no—Louisa. A ghost's too ridiculous to be true, nowadays."

" Not at all; a ghost is too ridiculous not to be true now-adays. Hundreds of people believe in ghosts, and jump at any chance to hear a real ghost story; and this will be real, because the proof of the pudding's in the eating. Your family ghost knows that the heir is fearfully hard up and so he appears at the critical time, and shows the secret of his buried treasure."

" Won't do," declared Smerdon, " and I'll tell you for why. Granted that in your sporting spirit, and for kindness to the Shillingfords, you're game to plank down a good dollop of cash to clear the air and put my father-in-law on his legs again with a few hundred to the good—granted that. But what shape be it going to take? He's quick as lightning about detail when any old, ancient thing's the matter, and the money would have to be a hundred year old at the least, whatever shape it took."

" I've thought of that. Indeed, I felt so positive that you sensible things would think just as I do about the matter, that I have taken the first steps. Now let's go out and see how the land lies. We've got to decide where the ghost has to appear and where the treasure is to turn up."

" And somebody else must find the treasure," declared Sibley. " The oldest part of the place will be best, because the ghost couldn't have hid anything in the byres built fifty years ago. The old stable, with cobblestone floor, that stands by itself below the well—that's the place."

They went out, and Mrs. Windeatt examined the stable. It stood apart—a time-foundered edifice, that cried either for restoration or destruction.

" The very thing," she declared, " and for more reasons than one. What's it used for now? "

" For nought," answered Whitelock. " We keep the fowls in it—they roost there. 'Twould cost two pounds to away with it."

" And how much to make it ship-shape again? "

" Ten or twelve, at the least. But we don't want it."

" I think you will, though. And I'm sure Mr. Shillingford won't mind if you say you want to rebuild it."

" He'd be delighted. He likes the wretched thing, because it is old," answered Sibley.

" The floor's the point—the vital point for us. Old cobble. Now, would it be possible to bore underneath and make holes in such a way as not to destroy the stones? "

Whitelock considered.

" It could be done," he said. " We could run under and lift the stones in patches and drop 'em again. But that's making work. 'Twould be easier just to break 'em out and put 'em back."

" The point is this," declared Louisa Windeatt. " We hide away valuables worth two thousand pounds and more; but two things must be thought of—in fact, three. First, the treasures have got to be old; second, when they come to light, they have got to look as if they'd been there a hundred years; and, third, nothing must suggest to the finder that they have not been there a hundred years or more."

" You talk as if it only remained to bury a lot of treasures," said Sibley. " The first puzzle's surely the biggest; to get old things that are ever so valuable and yet will go into a pretty small space."

" That was my part," answered her friend quietly, " and that I've done."

" Done, Louisa ! "

" Yes, Sibley—done. I didn't go to London for nothing—hateful place ! I've bought what cost me—no matter the figure —and what, no doubt, when sold again will bring in not so very much less. Just a lot of rubbish, in my eyes ! But means to an end. It's all stored away at Kingshead, and if you both come up to-morrow, we'll plan the next stage of the plot. I have snuff-boxes and Sheffield plate and shoebuckles and miniatures and old jewellery. I went to shops above suspicion and no doubt got my money's worth. And the next thing is to pack these treasures—in crumbly wood boxes, or something—and insert them under the cobblestones. We three, working together, can do that easily enough. Let your two men and Joan go to Ashburton Revel next week, and we shall have Blackslade to ourselves."

" But—but—Louisa—don't you see—we can't—we really can't ! " began Sibley. " Thousands of pounds—good heavens !—it's a fortune. And what on earth d'you get out of it ? "

" We've passed that point," answered Mrs. Windeatt firmly. " That aspect of the matter is quite understood. I'm not doing this for fun—perhaps not all for friendship, either. Don't you worry about what I get out of it, Sibley. That's my affair. Drive up in the market-cart to supper to-morrow, and then you can bring back the box with you, after it's dark."

The enterprising lady left Blackslade an hour later, and when she had gone Sibley Smerdon and her husband discussed this great event. Whitelock was in magnificent spirits.

" 'Tis out and away the best luck that have happened to us since we married," he said. "And the fine thing about it 'pears to be that there's no call to fret, or feel at all uncomfortable. You mark my words, Sib, that widow have got her own ideas about the future. She sees the interest on her money all right —and she ain't going to wait for it till the next world, neither."

" She's very fond of father," admitted Sibley; " and, what's more to the point, he's exceedingly fond of her; but I don't really believe he knows he's fond of her."

" You can't say. Besides, if Louisa Windeatt understands anything, it is how to get her own way. And just think of the joy and glory of it."

" I be thinking of the ghost," she answered. " You was going to have that blind, white hoss put out of his misery, now father's away? ' Jupiter ' has to die, and father sadly sanctioned it afore he went. And if you was to use a good bit of his tail, 'twill make a very fine beard for the ghost, and cost nought," said Sibley.

Her husband applauded.

" A proper idea. And I've got another. If it could be done safely, I did ought to show myself to one or two of the men. Us will have to tell a few good-sized fibs one way and another, I'm thinking."

She admitted it.

" Who don't? " she asked. " Blackslade be run on fibs, so far as I can see, and one more or less won't do no harm."

CHAPTER XLV

MRS. WINDEATT had, indeed, laid her plans very carefully from the moment that she heard Gabriel Shillingford designed to be absent from home. She did not once allow herself to think of the preposterous nature of her schemes, and, by postponing problems that must have proved fatal to a less impulsive spirit, had escaped many of these problems altogether. So far, chance had aided her. She had bought many precious things capable of being put up in small parcels, and something approaching genius in Louisa was quickened by her secret emotions. The purchases were such that none could question them. She had considered the sort of articles a miser might be supposed to collect a hundred years ago, and had invented a miser of some imagination.

She suffered no pang of doubt at this season, but hastened events and allowed herself little time to think. The Smerdons came at the appointed hour, and were amazed at the gems and trinkets, the snuff-boxes, miniatures, cameos, and Sheffield plate, that Mrs. Windeatt had collected.

" I did one really clever thing, and only one," she said. " Anybody could have wandered about and bought these toys.

But I thought of how and where they would be discovered, and I went into an old bookshop, and then another, and then a third, and finally was able to buy quite a pile of newspapers dating back more than a hundred years. Some were from the West Country. And I got a book published at Plymouth in 1794; and if that is torn up, it will do to wrap round some of the little trinkets."

"My stars!" said Whitelock, "you be thrown away in a place like this. Such cleverness never was heard of in Widecombe."

"And us haven't been idle," declared Sibley. "We've looked out some rotten wood and suchlike to bury along with the treasures. For everything must be dead right, else father will find out. And if he does——"

Mrs. Windeatt shivered.

"Once get him well off the scent," she answered, "and he won't get on it again. A good deal depends on the way the discovery is made. First there's the ghost. That's mentioned to him when he comes home, and allowed to pass. Then, when the excitement has waned, the ghost's treasures come to light. But who is to find them?"

"We'd thought of that," replied Sibley. "And my idea is that, presently, Whitelock says the barn must be done up and made ship-shape. Then Whitelock will get Pancras Widecombe, or somebody else quite to be trusted, and explain the work. And the work will be such that Pancras can't do it without finding the treasure."

"Of course, he'll want to believe in the ghost," added Whitelock. "'Tis his natural bent of mind to believe firmly in everything doubtful; and when the stuff comes to light, he'll read it all as clear as sunshine. And to-morrow night I be going to dress up and appear to Sandy Blake and Joan. The thing is just to let 'em get a sight of me in the dimpsy light, and then be off."

"They'll talk and compare notes of what they have seen, and that's all that need be done," added Mrs. Smerdon.

They discussed the matter for an hour, weighed details, and added touches to the plot. It was understood that the staff at Blackslade would all take holiday on the occasion of the Ashburton Revel; and when the men and women departed, Louisa intended to arrive, that she might assist Whitelock in his labours.

Then the Smerdons drove home again with a simple wooden crate which contained the treasure that was destined to modify the future of so many lives. They conveyed the case to their bedroom and locked it up there. The value of it was even more than Mrs. Windeatt had indicated, for the lady had made no mistake on that score.

"It do all go so straightforward that I be almost afeared," declared the man; "but 'tis my turn now, and the ghost have got to be seen. I won't trust myself in broad day, but just at twilight I'll creep out with the leather-birds.* I be more afeared o' the dogs than the men!"

His wife promised to look after the dogs, and since his disguise was exceedingly simple, Whitelock felt that he might easily slip out of it if danger threatened. On the following evening at dusk he walked down to the neglected barn, entered it, and, behind a farm-cart that stood within, rapidly slipped on a long brown coat that came below his knees, a grey beaver provided by Mrs. Windeatt, and a beard of white horsehair, collected at the death of the old horse, and arranged upon a wire by Sibley. Thus attired, he stepped boldly forth, and presently passed the kitchen window. Again he walked slowly by, and the serving maiden, Joan, at sight of an ancient stranger, came out to the back door. By that time Whitelock had moved away into the back yard.

"Who be you?" she shouted; but he made no answer, and went beyond her sight. Returning to the barn he lurked there until the slow footsteps of Sandy Blake fell on his ear. Then he emerged again, and gave the labourer an excellent view of him. Once more Mr. Smerdon was challenged, and once more made no answer. He had done all that was necessary, and now hastened into the wood above Blackslade, doffed his disguise, and returned home as quickly as possible.

"I seed a queer, old, shambling man round the house a bit ago," declared Whitelock, when he sat after supper smoking in the kitchen. "For a minute you might have thought 'twas Valiant Dunnybrig, for he had a flowing beard; but he was shorter and not so straight in the back, and he wore a terrible queer old beaver hat and a long coat. He was standing beside the old barn afore dusk. But when I went to ax him his business, he'd gone."

"And I seed him, too," said Sandy Blake. "He comed out of the barn just afore I passed it."

Joan exclaimed.

"Why, he went past the kitchen winder! Twice he went by and I ran to the door to see who 'twas. 'Who be you?' I said to the old man, but he didn't take no notice."

Sibley, who sat beside the fire, put down her work and exhibited considerable astonishment.

"Good powers, you people!" she exclaimed. "D'you know

* *Leather-birds*—bats.

what you're saying? Was he rather stout, and did he have a silver-grey beaver on his head, and a long brown coat, and a white beard to his middle, and did he go with a long stick?"

" The very daps of him! " declared Whitelock. " Did you see him, too? "

" I did—by the barn," confessed Sibley. " And I seed him yesterday also; but I didn't like to whisper it for fear of terrifying Sandy and Joan."

" Terrifying of us? " asked Joan. " Why for should an old man with one foot in the grave terrify us? "

" Just because he's not a man at all, and hasn't been for a hundred years! " declared Sibley. " Why, you talk of one foot in the grave, Joan; that creature has had both feet in the grave for ages and ages."

" What the devil are you talking about, Sib? " asked Whitelock. " And you've gone shivery! What the mischief's the matter? "

He rose and went over to his wife, who put her arms round him.

" Pull down the kitchen blind, for God's sake! " she said, " else we'll have the thing looking in the window. 'Twas a ghost! The famous ghost of Miser Shillingford! 'Tis a well-known story how he died a hundred and more years agone and left great treasure. No doubt something be going to happen. Oh, dear! "

They were silent, and Sibley shivered.

" Don't you go out of my sight, Whitelock," she commanded. " I won't be left alone a moment."

But her husband counselled courage.

" The creature may mean no harm," he said. " Have a drink of brandy, and say your prayers twice over to-night."

Sandy Blake had been slowly accepting this startling circumstance. Now he spoke and stared round-eyed.

" My imers! I've seed a spectrum! " he whispered. " If what you tell be true, there ain't a doubt but I've faced a ghost from the grave! "

" And so have I—and never guessed it," declared Joan.

" Thank the merciful God as the truth was hid from me," continued Sandy. " To my dying day, morning and evening, I'll thank Him that the truth was hid; for if I'd known about it, I'd have most certainly gone out of my seven senses and never got in 'em again. To think 'twas given to me—the son of Martin Blake—to see a wishtness! "

" 'Tis a very solemn thing, and I hope it won't happen to none of us again, for I don't like it no more than you, Sandy," answered Smerdon. " But such things don't fall out by chance; there must have been a reason—and I wish I knowed it."

"They do act without reason so often as not," said Joan. "My mother seed one down to Pondsworthy a bit afore I was born; but nothing came of it, except a mark on the small of my back, like a black butterfly."

"To think that the son of Martin Blake have looked on a ghost!" repeated Sandy. "'Tis the strangest thing that have ever fallen out to any member of my family. And if anybody had told father as he would have a son as would see a ghost, he'd have laughed the man to scorn!"

"Let's go out and see if 'twill show again in the dark," suggested Whitelock; but this Sandy declined to do.

"Enough be so good as a feast of them May games," he said. "I don't want no more. I shall lie in a muck o' sweat all night as 'tis, and think every owl that hollers in the wood be old long-beard on the move!"

This all led safely and comfortably to the day of the Easter Revel, upon which Sandy and his fellow-labourer departed after breakfast, and Joan joined her friends in Widecombe at an early hour. Before nine o'clock the farmhouse was deserted, save for Smerdon and his wife. He had already been working hard for an hour when Louisa Windeatt arrived from Kingshead.

The women stood over Whitelock, encouraged his great efforts, and inspired him as best they might. Utmost ingenuity characterised the widow's suggestions; for she was playing a game that involved her own future. The find would need to prove genuine beyond all suspicion, and the exact disposal of the treasure demanded anxious thought. In the first place it must appear that there had been no tampering with the cobble floor of the barn; and, in the second, when the treasures were brought to light, evidences of lengthy sojourn underground would be expected to accompany them.

Whitelock drove tunnels from various points and sank a miniature shaft. A drain-pipe, long stuffed up, fell in the midst of the barn, and this he examined, with the result that by working from the aperture to right and left it was possible to make chambers of a size to conceal much of the treasure. These holes opened but a few inches under the cobble-stones. While he worked, Sibley and Louisa wrapped up the Sheffield plate and other articles in the old newspapers and the sheets of the ancient book.

"In a week or two they'll be all mildewed and rotten," prophesied Louisa, "and then nobody can possibly say how long they have been down there."

Nothing was done carelessly or left to chance, and not until dusk had fallen did young Smerdon cease from his task. Then all was finished; the accumulated rubbish drawn from the old drain was rammed back into it; every evidence of meddling with the ruin was most carefully obliterated, and a litter of fresh fern thrown over the cobbles.

" I'm going to stable my pony here for a fortnight now," explained Whitelock. " I'm going to clean his stall and mess about there, and whitewash the place, and so on; so he can bide here, and 'twill all help to make things fall suent and natural."

So the mine was laid and the conspirators took tea together and rested from their labours.

" The next thing is to let three or four weeks or even more pass before the discovery," explained Louisa.

" And meantime we must rub in the ghost," added Sibley. " I burned the horsehair beard and the old hat yesterday, and I've got the long cloak tied up in a parcel for you to take home to-day, Louisa."

" What time do Petronell and your father come home? "

" Soon after noon Monday next. No doubt he'll ride up over to have a tell with you about the Grenville people afore long. I'm sure I hope they'll use him well and please him."

" They cannot fail to do that," answered Mrs. Windeatt.

Yet her hope in the event proved not wholly fulfilled.

The farmer and his daughter duly returned to Blackslade; but while Petronell was happy enough and held the expedition entirely successful, it appeared that Mr. Shillingford went in some shadow of doubt, if not of actual disappointment.

CHAPTER XLVI

An institution was threatened at Widecombe, and Nanny Glubb fell ill. Steering her husband home in the rain, and shedding her own pitiful cloak that it might protect the new accordion, she returned wet to the skin on a chill winter day, and presently developed congestion of the lungs.

The possibilities of life were thus rudely thrust upon Nicky and awoke first in him a riotous truculence. He snapped his stubby fingers in the face of Heaven and defied fate; then the parish nurse—a woman of iron, named Rebecca Cann—went over the blind man remorselessly and left him cowed.

He sneaked in to Nanny on a day before the crisis and sat with her, while the nurse walked forth for half an hour. At first the excitement of the illness and the attention it occasioned was agreeable and lucrative to Mrs. Glubb and her husband; but now the turning-point of the battle approached. Nicky had endured three days of indescribable misery, and Nanny was grown too weak to cheer him.

Finding herself alone with him for a little while, however, the courageous creature, despite her own tribulations, strove to minister with whispered words, while Nicky banned human life in general, and more particularly his present torment, the parish nurse.

" Oh, my God! " he said, " that bitch, Rebecca Cann! Moor-stone be soft compared to her. I talk and I cuss and I stamp, and she goes on her way like the angel of doom. And if you perish, 'tis a blasted dog and a tin pot for me. And everybody hates me, so the people will be sure to steal my money."

" I ban't going to perish," whispered Nanny. " 'Tis outside right and justice that I should be took. Whoever heard of the Lord snatching away the blind man's prop? And no dog would bide with you, for they can't stand the music; and even the stranger dogs passing down the road will stop and yowl, as though somebody had trod on them, when they hear you playing and me singing."

" Gospel truth," he said. " And through the night watches I weary the Lord's ear for you, Nanny. And if I had the money for it, I'd get ten doctors to you instead of that Grenville and this parish beast. She be more like a steam-roller than a human woman."

" She's very clever and saves me a lot, and soothes me when I dream. The dreams be properly awful, Nick."

" The money's coming in, and so's the jelly and the chicken-broth. 'Tis all right it should, but nobody thinks of my belly, and when I was fumbling round for food and drinking down the fust thing I could find yesterday, I chanced to come across some stuff that terror was keeping for you; and she gave me hell; and then in my fury I let loose on her."

" Don't you quarrel with her. She's all right. You must bear it."

He held her hand and inquired after her symptoms. A

measure of sentiment awoke in him at the touch of her fiery fingers.

" Good God! " he said; " to think of a creature like you, so thin as a herring and cold as a frog, rising up to such fierce heat. 'Tis like as if you was burning away! "

" I tell you I shall get well," vowed the little woman. " If I was going to croak, I'd very soon know it; but I ban't."

" See me out," he begged. " I don't ax much of you, Nanny, and I've never wanted you to do what was beyond your power; but I command you to see me out, for this dose have showed me very clear what I be without 'ee."

Then came callers, and for a moment Nicky felt his way into the kitchen.

It was Margery, Jack Mogridge's wife, and she brought a little grey cross of lichens decorated with the scarlet cups of peziza. But this was not for Nicky. To him she carried a pudding basin from Miss Thirza Tapper.

" She won't come again herself till you be ready and willing to apologise for what you said when she was here last; but I'm to explain, please, that she don't want your language to stand between Mrs. Glubb and this basin of stock."

" 'Tis Margery Mogridge I hear. Well, you can tell Miss Tapper that I'm a changed man. The hand of the Lord be heavy on me, and you'll be pleased to say that I wept tears of blood out of my old blind eyes all night after I'd called her a —no matter. Tell everybody that be worth powder and shot how I've got a broken and a contrite heart. Let 'em know I'm always here, lying at the door of my dear wife's sick-chamber, and always ready and thankful to hear a friendly voice. There —you try to remember that, and tell everybody as will list to 'ee."

Margery promised to obey.

" I be going now to put a cross of they little red toadstools on my first child's grave," she said.

" Don't talk of graves—'tis far too doubtful a subject with my wife gasping like a fish behind that door," he answered. " You be off, and mind what I say."

He returned to Nanny, but she did not speak, and his quick ears, trained to the least sound, judged by her breathing that she slept. He sat beside her, and then went to the fire and put a little coal upon it.

Through his eternal night the old man's mind moved busily, and he perceived that much good might come of this disaster, if only Nanny were spared. Did she die the workhouse stared him in the face, and he rebelled with frantic loathing from the thought.

Another caller arrived, and Mr. Samuel Sweetland and Rebecca Cann entered the cottage together.

" She be sleeping very peaceful just now, Miss Cann," said Nicky. " And I mended the fire a bit ago, for, by the shivering sound of un, I thought he was dropping a bit low."

" I made the fire up afore I went out," answered the nurse, " and 'tis a pity you couldn't have done what I said, and left it alone."

The door of the sickroom closed behind her, and Nicky shook his fist at it.

" If anybody had told me I could suffer that babbling beast, and not strangle her——" he began; then he turned to the visitor who had already spoken.

" 'Tis the gracious goodness of Farmer Sweetland I hear ! "

" The prayers of the people will be asked for her next Sunday in church," announced Mr. Sweetland. " I was passing, and thought that you and Nanny would be glad to know that. Mr. Brown has no objection."

Nicky's jaw hardened.

" ' No objection '—little hop-o'-my-thumb ! ' No objection ' —I should hope not."

" You mustn't talk like that. I hope all goes well. And I have brought you a bottle of elderberry wine."

" You good soul—you large-hearted Christian ! " cried Nicky; and then, when Mr. Sweetland had billowed away, feeling faint at the atmosphere of the cottage, Nicky put his head into the sickroom.

" That old bleater from Tunhill have brought a pint of some filth made out of wild berries," he said. " You'd best look at the bottle, nurse, and see if 'tis worth keeping afore you pour the mess down the sink. And they be going to pray for her in church o' Sunday. If they'd take up a collection, there might be more sense in it."

Miss Cann condescended to taste the elderberry wine.

" 'Tis harmless, and that's all you can say for it," she declared. " No doubt his new wife raked it out of some hole and wanted to be rid of it."

There came also Valiant Dunnybrig to the house of sickness, and cornered Mr. Glubb for an hour. At another time Nicky would have held his own; but the spirit of him continued to be largely crushed by fear of a dreadful change in his fortunes, and he endured Valiant's solemn adjurations with scarcely a retort.

" I have come to comfort you, and in the spirit that lets the past bury the past, Nicky Glubb At such times, whether we be smitten ourselves, or have to stand and see our friends and neighbours smitten, we are led to cast back a bit and look forward also, and see how we stand, and what we be gaining in life and what we be losing; and also the worth of what we seek or shun."

" Gospel truth ! " admitted the blind man. " Gospel truth, Valiant Dunnybrig. I've had the very same feeling of late days, though of course not in such fine language."

" You're chastened," answered the farmer, somewhat surprised to see bulldog Nicky in this sober mind. " You're chastened, and I'm glad of it; because if you ope the door of the soul in a humble and God-fearing spirit, there's always a passing angel very ready to walk in. Life—what is it, Glubb? The answer depends on the creature. To some—like those poor noodles, Abel Gurney and his wife, at Dunstone Mill, 'tis a make-believe thing, and all kiss-in-the-ring and other such vain fooleries; to a man here and there 'tis fine sport, and no more; to Shillingford 'tis a dream and a looking backward. But you've got to go forward, whichever way you may *look;* and since his eyes be always cast behind him, his foot slips—as Shillingford's have done. To me, Nicky Glubb, and I hope to you, life is a game of skill invented for us by Almighty God. But we must play fair and keep His rules."

" The very thing I've always done," declared Nicky. " 'Tis hard, but not beyond human power."

" Quite beyond human power, though well within the Almighty's. We all misunderstand the Lord sometimes, but we haven't all got the pluck to admit it. Instead of that we go snivelling round and pretend the Lord's misunderstood us."

" Wonderful ! " declared Nicky. " Never did I hear a truer touch."

" And as for life, or this passing buffet of the flesh, we call life, you'll find that though you back heaven, or trust in earth; that though you look ahead, or live for the day; that though you take it lying down, or fight every inch of the road; that though you watch and pray, or sleep and swear—yet when the end's in sight, we shall see the truth unfolding, and count up where we've hit and where we've missed. Life's half panic and running away; and it's half fun and joy, and comfort and warmth, and tickling of the five senses. And life's half dross and trash and half good grain, pressed down and running over. 'Tis fallow land, and every day we sow in it, whether we will or not. The thing is to choose the grain. And when the game's up and the candle have to be douted in this world, afore it can be lit in the next, then we shall see that life be all experience, Glubb—life's all a learning; and, however it may have treated us, 'tis better to have lived it

than not, for without the race there's no victory, and without
life there's no death, and without death there's no life ever-
lasting."

"I should like to give you a good lump of money for them
beautiful words," declared Nicky; "but there 'tis—I've got
nothing for anybody but the prayer of an afflicted man."

"It is enough," declared Dunnybrig. "I hope that it
may please God to spare your wife. But if one goes, remember that sackcloth and ashes in this world be a very good
preparation for purple and fine linen in the next."

The master of Chittleford went his way, and Nicky, according to his wont, criticised the visitor after he had gone. "All
powder and no jam," he said. But other people were more
to the blind man's taste. Mrs. Sweetland brought invalid-
food; Sibley despatched good things from Blackslade, and
Petronell carried them. Grace Coaker sent chickens; the
vicar presented coals and two bottles of parish port. There
were rumours of an entertainment to defray Mr. Glubb's
expenses, and this great matter was brought to Nicky's ears
by Tryphena Harvey. She came to see him, and heard the
joyful tidings that his wife was through the worst phases of
her illness, and might recover.

"She be going to live!" declared Mr. Glubb, "and no
doubt afore very long that graven image, the parish nurse,
will be able to go about her business. Us must pour strength-
ening food into Nanny, so as to get her on her pins again so
quick as possible. I've told Cann in plain words that, if ever I
be took ill, I won't have her let loose at my bedside, and she
says in her cold-blooded, devilish way, that if 'tis her duty to
come, she'll be there, whether I like it or not."

"We are going to do a great thing," said Tryphena.
"There's to be a concert in the big room in the Church House.
A proper concert, and money charged for coming to hear. All
the money will go to you and Nanny."

Mr. Glubb at moments of excitement always felt the need
of motion.

"Take me out, my dear; let me stump along for a mile or
two, while you tell me about it," he said.

Tryphena had led Nicky for an airing on one or two occasions, and now he got his hat from its peg and walked beside
her. She held his hand, and they went along the Vale together,
while she explained the enterprise.

"It is intended to be after Easter, and everybody who can
do anything in public is going to perform. I'm sure you and
Nanny would be very proud to hear how many are anxious to
appear."

" Most of 'em want to show themselves off, no doubt. I be the only professional musicker in the Vale."

" You'll play a tune, of course. But you can't do the whole concert."

" Oh, yes, I could," declared Nicky. " But t'others wouldn't like that. Who be going to lend a hand? "

" Ever so many. First there's Doctor Grenville. He plays on his banjo for you. And he's saved Nanny's life, too, so you ought to be very much obliged to him."

" I see through that easy enough," declared the blind man. " If they scrape up a bit of useful money for us, he'll get his bill paid; and if they don't, he won't. That's how he stands, and nobody knows it better than him."

Tryphena was shocked.

" You really oughtn't to be so mean-minded, Nicky," she said. " I shan't tell you any more if you're going to say things like that. And they want me to play a little tune on the piano."

" Be you game for it? You haven't larned very long. 'Tis like this : if the people were coming in without paying, then you —or any beginner—might play, because they've no right to grumble, and they be there at their own peril; but when folk have put down money—if 'tis only threepence for a back seat or a penny for standing room—then they be lifted into a paying public, and have the right to demand good value for their cash. They stand on their rights most steadfast then, and won't be put off with trash. 'Tis getting money under false pretences to lure 'em in and give 'em rubbish what ban't worth listening to. Like that shameful Primrose League feed, you mind, a bit ago. Sixpence a head was asked, and then the tea didn't go round, nor yet the buttered buns! A proper hell of a row I made about it, for one, and voted liberal the next election."

Tryphena was much discouraged.

" Then I certainly won't play," she said. " I quite see what you mean."

" Who else be going to venture? " asked Nicky.

" I hardly like to tell you. But of course it's for you and Nanny. Charity covers a multitude of sins, Nicky. And the people will quite understand that we are not professionals."

" They'll grasp hold of that, no doubt," admitted Nicky. " Still, if the state of the case gets known, I dare say a good few real clever people from round about would help you. It might be a witty thought if you was to trot me round the country."

" No," answered Tryphena firmly. " I won't do that. Perhaps I oughtn't to have told you anything about it yet. We shall arrange a very interesting programme. And there will be some surprises for the Vale. People you'd never expect have offered to do things."

"We'll hope for the best," he said, "and trust the folk will come, if 'tis only for the sake of the cause."

Then Tryphena touched another matter, reminded thereof by the apparition of a withered man, who approached upon two sticks from the opposite direction.

"Here's Mr. Bell coming back from having his bad leg dressed by Dr. Grenville. Oh, Nicky, I do wish you would forgive him and make friends. It's so wicked to harbour malice!"

"Never!" cried Mr. Glubb. "I'll forgive him when he's paid for his sins, and not sooner. If you'll lead me to him and let me have but thirty seconds with him, then I'll forgive him —but not afore. To think that old stinging-nettle be fed up with food and coals, and doctoring wasted on his worthless bones, and my wife threatened with death! It makes me shiver for God A'mighty!"

"Come home!" said Tryphena. "I can see you're going to be wicked again now Nanny is out of danger. I'm ashamed of you!"

"Turn round, then, and keep that lame dog to leeward," answered Nicky. "And take care nobody pays for him to come to the concert, for, if I smell him out there, I'll jump down off the platform afore all the people and rub his nose on the planching!"

CHAPTER XLVII

GABRIEL SHILLINGFORD found no difficulty in believing that his daughter and son-in-law had seen a ghost. They fondly sought to evade lying in this matter, and neither stated more than the literal truth. They declared that they had seen an apparently aged figure with flowing white hair hanging from his chin, a brown coat and hat of ancient pattern; and their implicit falsehood much pleased the master of Blackslade. It scarcely needed the further evidence of Sandy Blake and Joan to make him welcome this authentic spectre with good-will.

" I hope I may be permitted to see him," said Mr. Shillingford.

" I believe there's a great deal more in it than meets the eye," declared his daughter. " I don't think he walked for nothing. He may have known all about the pinch we're in. He may have wanted to talk to somebody."

" In that case I have a right to hope that he will appear to me," said her father. " I am thankful now that we did not pull down the old barn, for there are well-known connections between ghosts and places, but it is, of course, a very obscure subject."

" Of co rse," answered his daughter. " 'Tis well understood that ghosts be so fond of places as cats. All the same, if the barn ban't pulled down, 'twill fall down. Whitelock was mentioning it but two days before you came home. It ought to be repaired. The ghost couldn't mind that."

" It might be restored," admitted Mr. Shillingford. " Restoration is an unhappy necessity for all old buildings made with hands."

He dismissed the subject, but when he went to see Mrs. Windeatt soon afterwards, he detailed at extreme length all that he had gleaned from Sibley, from Whitelock, and from Sandy Blake, concerning the spirit's appearance.

" Their accounts agree in every particular," he said. " It is perfectly clear that they all saw the same thing, and that it moves about my old barn. Needless to say this has been a source of satisfaction to me. It lifts Blackslade in my eyes not a little."

" Nobody was in the least frightened? "

" Nobody. I ought to say, however, that my ploughman, Blake, declares that he would have been frightened had he known of the supernatural character of the visitor. No doubt that is true. I believe people, gifted in a certain mental way, may often see ghosts in their daily life—perhaps every day of their lives, in the open street, or church, or lonely road—and never know they were ghosts at all."

But Louisa felt no interest in this disquieting theory. Her conscience pricked her before his ingenuous spirit. She felt that she had been deceiving a child.

She changed the subject, and begged to hear how he had fared with the Grenvilles at Honiton Piffard. Whereupon his face fell somewhat.

" Of course I speak to you freely," he said, " and anything I may say is sacred. I have no fault whatever to find with the family themselves; but they don't know anything about their race, and, what is even stranger, they don't seem to care. Of course, in common people of no descent, this would not prejudice a man like me; but in Grenvilles——! No doubt it is a cadet branch of the race—one knew that. But the baffling thing is that Mrs. Grenville only remembers back to her husband's grandfather; and he was—a furniture dealer. Not a manufacturer—not, as one might say, a knight of industry—but a retail purveyor of suites, as they call them. She is an exceedingly nice woman in herself—of the race of the Weston-haughs—a fine old family—but—again, she has a weak-witted son who lives at home. An exceedingly nice young fellow in himself, but mentally deficient. I think Doctor Grenville ought to have mentioned him, but he did not."

" What is the unmarried sister like? "

" She is engaged to a solicitor at Bristol, who may become the town clerk of that city; a man named Blower. Mary Grenville is gifted, though not handsome. She models flowers in wax, and is very intelligent. I fired her to take some interest in her family."

" Is Hugh nice to his mother? "

" His manners to her," said Mr. Shillingford, " are not such as to challenge attention either way. He is not so serious-minded as I was led to think. If you see him in the bosom of his family you see a different man. His mother has spoiled him, and his sister also. In some ways he falls short of what a Grenville might be expected to reach. His taste is—I won't say low—but it is not cultivated. He allows himself too much latitude of speech in the presence of ladies. The things he says are not spoken seriously, but you may often judge of a man's mind by what he thinks funny. Tell me what a man laughs at, and I know if I should like that man. He said once that he would rather keep a good corner public-house than be a member of any learned profession whatever; because there was more money in it and more fun. Everybody laughed but myself."

" I'm sure Petronell has found no spots in the sun? "

" Not one. And, after all, that is the vital thing. Mrs. Grenville likes her, and she likes Mrs. Grenville. At least, that is the idea they convey to me. I think that his family wanted Hugh to marry somebody possessed of ample wealth. But, as his mother remarked to me, young people take these things into their own hands."

" Wasn't she very much impressed with Petronell's beauty?"

" She never mentioned it. She gives me the idea of a woman

who is a little bored with everything. Polite always, but never enthusiastic about anything—except the time to go to bed. She retired early, and would always be quite vivacious when she said ' good-night.' Some people have a cowardly love of sleep, Louisa."

" True," she said. " But where are the women who can do with six hours like men can? I want eight."

Mr. Shillingford, having inquired sympathetically concerning the things that were interesting to Louisa, discussed his own affairs.

" It is idle to deny," he said, " that my temporal outlook causes me grave anxiety; but only anxiety on the plane of worldly affairs. And against it one may set this appearance of a spirit from the grave. I have derived quiet consolation from it in the midst of my difficulties."

" I'm glad," she said. " I only hope the poor ghost isn't fluttering about for nothing, or because he has no better occupation. He might have even talked, if anybody had been sensible enough to attend to him."

" He might," admitted Gabriel. " On the other hand, it is possible that he sought somebody else, and was not prepared to make any statement to Whitelock or Sibley, or the servants. I have a sort of idea that he was looking for the present head of the family—for me, in fact."

Before he left her, Mr. Shillingford became personal, and spoke openly of his regard and admiration. He drank three cups of tea, planned a future meeting, approved very heartily of Sibley's wish—that Mrs. Windeatt should be gossip to her coming child—and then went forth in good spirits.

But an event still lay before Gabriel ere the day was done; it was destined that he should play his part in tragedy.

One of the lesser Smerdons met him as he descended to the bottom of the steep road from Kingshead. The child was hastening to Woodhayes. He stood a moment and uttered his great news between gasps.

" Mr. Mogridge—be hanging—from a rope—in his house— and all the people be there—and I be running for the doctor ! "

The child fled on, and Gabriel considered. His inclination was to go upon his way, but he conceived that his duty might lead in the other direction. He rode up to Bone Hill, there-fore, and found a small company standing in the dusk about the cottage of Alfred Mogridge.

Peter Smerdon approached.

" He's gone ! Mogridge be gone ! " he declared. " There's not a doubt of it, for I was at the cutting down. He's been cruel wisht of late, and odd in his intellects. 'Tis a very strange thing how children find out if a man's mind be shaky. But a week agone I was coming home from the village, and they imps from Patience Leyman's school was just let out, and half a dozen of 'em were dancing round poor old Alfred, like flies round a hoss's ears; poking their tongues at him, the little devils, and making game. I thought perhaps he was bosky-eyed and unsteady in the legs, and drove the rascals away—girls, too, some of 'em—but 'twas worse than being drunky ; and Jack Mogridge here tells me that he's seed it coming on this longful time, and often ran to his father's rescue."

Jack appeared at this moment, and saluted Gabriel. He was very excited, and his words tripped one another up.

" 'Twas my wife found un," he said. " She went in to look after his tea, for he's been ailing with a tissick in the chest for a day or two, and he's been too weak to fight against her cooking his food, though he said he knew she meant to poison him. And there 'twas—she put on the kettle, and lit his paraffin lamp, and toasted a bit of bread for him; and then she called high and low and got no answer; and then she sought, and there he hung—only separated from her by a deal board all the time ! For he'd gone in the scullery and rigged a rope to one of they hitches for the runner-towel. And his feet weren't three inches off the ground; but an inch is so good as a mile to a hanging man. And Margery said he looked all the world like one of they great turkeys outside the shops at Christmas—only larger, of course."

" She showed sense, by all accounts," declared Young Harry Hawke, " for she didn't waste no time. Another woman, and many men, would have run off to give the news; but she got on a chair, and took the bread knife, and cut him down the instant moment she found him."

" She did, and 'tis a great credit to her," declared Jack. " She cut the rope and he fell lumpus in a heap. And then she rushed to me with the fatal news."

" He's had one foot in the grave for a good while, in my opinion," continued Young Harry Hawke; " and he hated his fellow-creatures to the end."

" 'Tis unsound mind, without a doubt," said Peter Smerdon, " and we mustn't say hard things. He's put by a bit of money against his latter end, they say."

" And me and Mrs. Mogridge be a good bit interested to know how he's handled it," declared Jack. " She wanted to rummage over his things the minute after; but I said, ' No,' I said, ' us must wait for policeman and doctor, and do all things in order.' "

Miss Tapper hurried up at this moment.

" Does Margery need any support? " she asked.   " This is no place for women, and I only came on behalf of my fellow-woman."

" No, miss, thank you kindly," answered Jack.   " She's just looking over father's secret places and cupboards for the minute, and Policeman Adam Sanders be in there along with the corpse, and my mother-in-law's there, too.   And the doctor will be here come presently."

" Are you sure he has gone?   Was nothing done to bring him back to life? "

" 'Twas too late, miss; I felt his heart and loosed his collar, but the old gentleman was plum colour, and dead as pork.   I hope he didn't suffer nothing to name, but I'm very much afraid by the looks of him that he did.   I hope you will come in and have a good look at him, miss.   I'm sure he'd have wished it."

But Thirza Tapper declined.

" Certainly not," she answered; " and you had better tell your wife that, in my opinion, it would be much more decent if she went home, instead of rummaging about among a dead man's things before he is cold."

" I have told her, miss.   I said that very thing; but Mrs. Mogridge is a good bit excited at this turn of events, and she've took the law in her own hands."

" She feels a bit of a heroine, I reckon," explained Peter. " 'Tis a great thing, no doubt, for a woman to cut down a hanged man—and him her father-in-law."

Doctor Grenville rode up at this moment, dismounted, and gave the rein to Jack.   A few men entered the house with him, and there came a swift declaration that the sexton was dead. Then Miss Tapper went her way, and Gabriel Shillingford walked his horse beside her.   Through the gathering night they passed a dozen men and one or two women hurrying up to Bone Hill.

CHAPTER XLVIII

TRYPHENA HARVEY went happily along to an appointment at Woodhayes. She felt herself the busiest young woman in the world, for besides her lessons in piano-playing and French, her letters to her uncles, her varied interests in the affairs of her present neighbours and many friends, and the rumour that she might presently be called to visit Australia, there had come into her life the astonishment of a gift. So, at least, the new thing appeared to Tryphena. Moved by the accidental but startling discovery that " trees " rhymed with " breeze," and " bowers " with " showers," that " home " chimed harmoniously with " roam," and that " snow " and " flow " made music to her ears, Tryphena embarked on the perilous path of prosody, and wrote a poem in three verses. On this day in late February she was full of the joy of the creator. Twice she stopped, pulled the rhymes out of her pocket, and read them through. The last verse pleased her best—

" And now I see the darling Spring,
　She really is awakening;
　And very soon will rise and dress
　In all her starry loveliness.
　Forget-me-nots are in her hair,
　Her eyes are blue, I do declare;
　Primrosen make her petticoat,
　And all around her pretty throat
　Bright buttercups and daisies go—
　The only chains that she shall know.
　The little children weave them for her
　Because they all do much adore her."

" It's poetry ! " whispered Tryphena to herself, " or, if it isn't, it sounds like it. Oh, who can I read it to? "

The desire of the artist was upon her, the first longing to impart the thing she had made. She took her treasure trustingly, and thought that it must surely give some of her own delight to another.

" Suppose I stop the first person I meet and read it to them ! " she thought.

But the first person she met was old Uncle Tom Cobleigh, and Tryphena perceived that her rhyme of Spring could not be expected to add to his happiness. Indeed, he gave her no opportunity to approach it.

"No news from Christian yet," he declared. It had become a sort of catch-word with him. He employed the phrase at all chance meetings, as another would say " good-morning " or " good-night "; nor did Uncle confine the remark to his acquaintance. It was enough that he passed anybody to provoke the assertion. Callous folk laughed nowadays when they saw him coming, and said to each other, " No news from Christian."

" But sure you must soon hear," prophesied Tryphena, and Uncle echoed her.

" Without doubt I must soon hear," he admitted. For a moment he stopped and took a pinch of snuff from his waistcoat pocket. The stimulant cheered him.

" Spring's coming," he said.

" Yes, yes—quickly. I've felt it very much the last two days."

" And maybe he'll come with it. 'Twas a season he liked. It may draw him back home."

" I hope it will; I very much hope it will," answered Tryphena. " I am going to see Dr. Grenville now, about the concert we are getting up for Nanny Glubb. It will be a splendid affair, and I hope you'll come."

He nodded, but spoke no more, and the girl, bidding him " good-bye," went on her way to Woodhayes.

Where the Vale narrows at the feet of Hameldon stood the grey eyrie of the Hawkes. It was surrounded by trees, and faced east. Byres and barns stood round about, the great hill towered behind, and it was still streaked with snow in the shadowy gullies, where no sun could come. Winter woods, all ash-coloured, rolled up the hill in the thin veil of many boughs; from a cleft behind the farm gushed a rivulet, to join Webburn beneath; while round about the homestead there ranged little fields that crept aloft until the Moor thwarted their advance. The walls of Woodhayes were slated against the weather, and the slate was discoloured harmoniously with orange-tawny lichens. Before the portals spread a flower-knot or two, and the grass plat, from which sprang some firs and elms, was surrounded by hedges of holly and box. A single apple-tree also lifted wide boughs before the entrance, and in the grass beneath, many a galaxy of chill snowdrops danced to the buffet of the wind. A little house of glass extended over the portal, and within it was Emma Hawke, carrying a new baby on her left arm. With her right she worked among the plants in pots, and strove to strip away the dead leaves, and make them tidier.

"Nobody don't care a rush about these things but me," explained Emma, "and if 'twasn't for my trouble they'd all have gone home long ago. Half my flowers be dead as 'tis. That's thanks to this blessed babby."

"He's a flower himself," declared Tryphena.

"A brave li'l bud, sure enough, and my first be deadly jealous of him a'ready."

Doctor Grenville had heard Tryphena's voice, and now appeared to welcome her.

"Come in, come in," he said. "Petronell is not here yet, but we can begin without her."

"You told her ten o'clock?"

"I said ten; but she's a lazy girl. She'll turn up presently."

"Petronell's not lazy," declared Tryphena. "You know very well she isn't."

None knew that better than the blonde Hugh Grenville. He had not asked his betrothed to this meeting.

"She may have misunderstood me. Well, we'll begin. Have you hurt your finger?"

"It's nothing—only a whitlow."

"Nothing! A whitlow may be very serious. Let me see it."

He made a great business of the finger, and informed Tryphena that the ailment was not a whitlow, but would certainly need dressing for a day or two. He then bound it up with immense care, cut a glove and made a finger-stall, and inserted the wounded finger.

Tryphena laughed at him.

"You couldn't make more fuss over a proper patient," she said.

"I would do more than that for you," he answered, "a great deal more."

"Because I am Petronell's friend?"

"No, because you are mine. At least, I hope you are. I want you to be."

He was gallant, and still Petronell did not come.

"Now for the concert! Well, we must plan it on the basis of twelve items. That will be enough. There are certain to be some encores. You will be encored—I shall be encored."

"Petronell will, I shan't. In fact, I've changed my mind. Nicky Glubb talked to me quite openly. Just think if they hissed me, or told me to stop, or anything like that!"

"Well, sing then, instead of playing."

"I can't sing."

" You can sing like a bird. Petronell has often told me what a jolly voice you have." His ardent eyes made Tryphena cast down her own. She was impressed with Hugh Grenville, and found his admiration agreeable. But she attributed it to her friendship for Petronell. For a moment, in the genial atmosphere of his praise, she thought of reading her poem to him. Meantime he spoke again.

" If you don't do anything, I shan't. I shan't sing or play a note if you don't perform."

Tryphena laughed at this threat.

" How would it be if I recited a poem? "

" A recitation? Good! You must recite it to me first, some time or other. I might be able to give you a few hints, because I'm an old hand at that sort of thing. In fact, it was a toss-up with me whether I'd be an actor or a doctor."

" How interesting! " she said.

" I can act, though I say it," declared the versatile physician; and he continued to do so for the benefit of the unconscious visitor.

"Well, there are three items fixed up, at any rate : your recitation; Petronell's pianoforte solo, Beethoven's ' Farewell to the Piano '; and my banjo song—I have not decided which, yet. That leaves eight or nine items."

" Nicky will play his accordion."

" Yes, I suppose he must—wretched old man; though we hear enough and too much of that every day of the week. It would be much better if neither he nor his wife came to the concert at all, but of course they will."

" Nanny wouldn't miss it for the world."

" I wish we were doing it for a nobler cause—the church or something."

" But think of being blind. You can't forgive a person too much if they are blind."

" You would be an angel from heaven, blind or seeing," he said lightly, and, before she had recovered from such a compliment, Doctor Grenville returned to the subject.

" That's four items, then; and I have others. The bell-ringers are going to give their show. Old Harry and Young Harry are great bell ringers, as I know to my cost, for they jangle away in the kitchen five nights out of six; and the troupe consists of them and two other men, Arnell the carpenter, and one of the Smerdon boys—Patrick, I think."

" And Elias, my cousin—Elias Coaker. You forget him. He's a great ringer."

" I didn't know he belonged. I should have thought he

had something better to do at Southcombe than make that row," said the doctor.

" That's five items all told; and now I'll astonish you. Who do you think is going to sing? "

" Pancras Widecombe for one."

" Yes, he is, and—now laugh, Miss Harvey—Arthur Pierce for another! Would you believe it? He offered when I was last in there, getting some cherry brandy to fill my flask."

" It's most extraordinary," declared Tryphena. " I remember him the very first day I came to Widecombe—years ago. And he almost trembled if you looked at him, and broke a vase, and seemed as if his legs would hardly hold him up."

" It's a very remarkable psychological study," answered the other. " As a medical man, of course, I understand these things. It was a clash of opposite natures. They were poison to each other—he and his wife. And, as she had the stronger will, in time she would have poisoned him altogether, and he would have died. And sometimes I feel, when I think of dear Petronell and look ahead, that—that——"

He broke off, and Tryphena's grey eyes grew round and full of questions.

" That—what? " she asked.

" That I am not worthy of her," he sighed.

" Nobody's worthy of Petronell—nobody. But she loves you with all her beautiful heart."

" Leave it," he said. " I hope I am wrong; but sometimes a cloud of doubt comes over me that I—that she—that both of us, in fact, may be—however, I didn't ask you here to bother you with my private affairs. They are a nuisance for the minute, and you've complicated them infernally. A shame, isn't it, to accuse an innocent young person of such crimes? Well may you look puzzled; but I don't think you're a bit more puzzled than I am."

He rattled on ambiguously, and left Tryphena no opportunity to ask the questions in her mind.

" That's half the programme settled," he said, " and I've got a pal in Exeter, an amateur conjurer, who's going to do some tricks. But we must beat up more local talent, Miss Harvey. The people like to see their friends in the glare of the footlights. They don't care a button whether they succeed or fail. The fun consists in watching them, and the more ridiculous they appear the more the audience appreciates it."

He discussed the possibility of a play, and tried to tempt Tryphena to perform a duologue with him. This, however, she declined to consider.

" I could no more act than fly over the moon," she said. " Besides, if anybody does such a thing with you, it ought to be Petronell."

He laughed at that, but soon grew grave again and sighed.

" I find myself confidential with you—goodness knows why. Because you are Petronell's friend, I suppose. I'm in trouble in a way. I can trust you—you are so clever and quick. But if I have seemed rather distracted this morning, there's a reason for it. That experiment—I mean, the visit of the Shillingfords to my people—was not quite a success, Miss Harvey."

" Yes, it was," answered Tryphena. " Petronell liked your mother very much, and thought she was a very sweet and kind lady."

" The point is that my dear mother didn't—I won't say didn't *like* Petronell—but——"

" Not like Petronell! " gasped the girl. " Nobody in the world could not like Petronell."

" She saw her good points; but my mother is a very keen student of human nature, and she felt quite convinced, after studying Petronell very carefully and sympathetically, that her temperament and mine are not exactly suited to each other. It's a great bore."

Tryphena took some moments to measure this tremendous statement.

" Do you think so, too? " she asked presently. " Because if you do——"

" I? Good gracious, no! I'm not a man to change. I have plighted my troth to Petronell, and she has plighted her troth to me. I'm only vexed that my mother, who never errs in her understanding of character, should for once have made such a frightful mistake."

" Yes, it's a pity—her own daughter-in-law to be. But no doubt you'll soon be able to show her how wrong she is."

" I trust you, of course, not to whisper a word of this, Miss Harvey. It is a most difficult and delicate matter."

" It's not my business," answered the other, " and I wish you hadn't told me. It's an uncomfortable, silly sort of thing, and if your mother is as sweet and sympathetic as Petronell thinks, then it seems queer that she should feel like that to Petronell, and say nasty things about her behind her back."

" Not nasty things. My mother is a wonderful woman, and above any mean act. She admires Petronell's character, and her pride, and so on; but she doesn't think she's the wife for a poor man."

" I don't want to hear any more of this," declared Tryphena. " It oughtn't to be said or thought."

She was concerned, and felt angry both with the doctor and his family.

" Anybody who thinks to find a more wonderful girl than Petronell wants better bread than is made of wheat," she declared.

" Exactly what I said to my mother. I'm glad you feel like this, because you echo my own sentiments. You are splendid ! You see through a thing so quickly and easily. You've cheered me—you really have. And you mustn't misjudge me, Miss Harvey. I should feel that acutely, for I am a very sensitive man. When I grow anxious and troubled about my engagement, it is quite as much on account of your friend as on my own. I care too much for Petronell to—well—a poor husband may be quite as unfair to her as a poor wife would be to me. You understand—you look all round it? I believe that there can be no poverty, in the real sense of the word, where there is perfect love. But I love my mother, too, in an almost sacred sort of way, so you see I cannot help feeling distressed that she does not think as I do in this matter."

" I'm going now," answered the other, " and I shan't say a word to Petronell about this; but I hope you will. If your mother—there it is. Either you agree with her, or else you don't."

He detained her and meandered on a little longer. His purpose was to interest Tryphena in himself, and it is certain that he succeeded. His good looks and noble sentiments alike impressed her. He suggested a young man of the loftiest principles. Incidentally he paid Tryphena a number of little compliments. She was surprised on reconsidering the conversation to note how intimate Doctor Grenville had become. Once he laid his arm on her shoulder to impress a point, and left it there a long time.

Tryphena found herself quite unable to understand his difficulties; but she was also a little flattered at his confidence. She begged him, finally, to be frank with Petronell and explain everything to her.

She departed with the doctor's voice in her ears, and the brilliance of his eyes still flashing in her thoughts. She was rendered unhappy by this encounter, yet trusted that a man of such high moral ideas and pure devotion to Petronell would soon find his problems solved and his sky clear again. She hated Mrs. Grenville very heartily, the more so that she felt Hugh Grenville's mother must have deceived her future daughter-in-law and left her under very false impressions. That the man himself was creating imaginary difficulties as an excuse for future action, Tryphena did not dream.

She went homeward; found the first celandine shining like a star in a sheltered hedge; sought, without success, for a white violet where they were said to grow; listened to the lark music, which now rippled over Hameldon ceaselessly; and then, her young heart seeking the thing that for the moment gladdened it most, she peeped about her guiltily and brought forth her poem again.

Still, she longed to show it to another, and hesitated between Elias and Petronell.

CHAPTER XLIX

A VERY magic moment animated the high elms in the valley beneath Blackslade. They were yet innocent of leaves, and the rain had drenched every branch and twig. Indeed, it still poured down heartily, though the west was at last swept clear of cloud. The evening light now shone upon the rain, and, beating into the elms, flashed a thread of pure gold along every branch and bough and twig. They glowed like molten trees against the purple darkness behind them, while easterly a faint outer rainbow and a dazzling inner one, its colours reversed, arched enormous over against the low sun. The feet of the rainbows burned into the hills; their arcs made a portal for oncoming night.

At cease of rain Gabriel Shillingford and Petronell set forth to Widecombe. She called his attention to the sky and the trees, but the master of Blackslade was indifferent to natural phenomena. The stone that had not been scratched or lifted up by man did not interest him; and since humanity could set no signet on the sky, his eyes seldom scanned it, save to learn the signs of the weather.

The time approached when Gabriel's affairs were to form matter for inquiry, and yet it was his wish to postpone the meeting until Sibley's child should be born. But an unsentimental generation deprecated any further postponement and the matter of a meeting of creditors loomed large, though the date was not yet fixed.

Father and daughter walked together, and Petronell expressed a doubt.

"I know how your mind moves," she said; "it is always stately; you can't look at things in a small or sordid fashion; but this meeting—somehow you are preparing for the hateful thing as if it was—something quite different. All these preparations—Louisa says it is more like a hunt breakfast than a meeting of creditors."

"-She told me so, too," he said. "But perhaps a woman can't quite understand. There is nothing—not even the humblest thing—that need be done in an undignified way, Petronell. It runs through creation—dignity, I mean. It is a gift. There are dignified birds and undignified birds, dignified beasts and undignified beasts. You get this feeling of birth and long descent even in wild nature. A hawk, or raven, is a dignified bird. We may not admire their manners or customs, but we can never accuse them of being undignified. A starling is an undignified bird. He pokes along, like a boy weeding, and his feet are large, and he is always snapping and quarrelling with his neighbour. Among animals you see it also. A rabbit has no dignity, but a fox has. And this meeting of creditors, since it must be—I intend to approach it in no mean, penurious spirit. We shall entreat them courteously, patiently, and kindly. Some will come from afar, and the laws of hospitality must not be forgotten."

"You are always right," declared Petronell. "And I think as you do, now you make it clear; but Hugh does not, I'm sorry to say "

"He ought to, then," declared Gabriel. "One would expect him to do so. But of late—well, I would not pain you, Petronell—still, the fact remains that of late I have noticed in Hugh rather a change of opinions."

But she would not permit this.

"No, no, father; not in big things, only in little ones. He has great sympathy with us."

At the smithy they parted, and Miss Shillingford proceeded to the post-office, while her father sought Tom Gurney. He was not in the forge, however, and Gabriel visited Mr. Gurney's home hard by.

Mabel Gurney answered the knock, and invited Mr. Shillingford to enter.

"Tom's to Newton Abbot," she said; "but I'll do as well, because he ain't got no secrets from me."

'He has some from me, however," answered Gabriel.

" You are doubtless aware, Mrs. Gurney, of what is going to happen in a few weeks' time. I have written two letters on that subject to Mr. Gurney, and he hasn't answered either."

" Sorry," she said. " 'Twas very bad manners in him; but this great business of his marriage with me has thrown him out of his regular stride, you see, and 'twill take him some time to settle down again. Besides, his cousin messed up things a lot when he was away. But, all the same, we thank God that nobody bought the business, for it would have been a terrible loss to Tom."

" Why did he think of selling it? "

" Just a bit of cowardice on his part. He feared that all the custom would leave him after he runned away with me. But I pulled him together. He didn't know that a woman can be ten times more plucky than a man in some matters. ' Sin,' I said to Tom Gurney. ' Drat sin! ' I said. ' 'Tis often only a bogey that silly men and women let come between 'em and the truth. Why,' I said, ' should you and me keep apart and be respectable and miserable for evermore, just in order that Widecombe may sleep in peace and no old maid's frosty heart be flustered? Sin's a scourge so often as not,' I said, ' and people curl up under it and suffer, like driven sheep, and deny themselves the few little good things this fleeting life can offer, for fear somebody else won't be pleased.' That's how I spoke to Tom Gurney, and first he doubted, and then he saw that I was right. Why, man alive! if you be always thinking what other people will think, you might as well be a weathercock on a church steeple and turn with every wind that blows. There be fools in the world that ban't happy unless they be eating and drinking, and sleeping and praying, and dressing and thinking just exactly like everybody else. And even Arthur, my late one, since the crash came, he sees I'm right. And we're the best of friends, and I'll drop in and have a thimbleful with him, and talk over old times in the new spirit without a pang."

Mr. Shillingford nodded.

" It is very remarkable. You exercised a bad influence upon each other. None can deny that it was well when you separated."

" Nobody with more brains than a nit do deny it," she said. " 'Tis only the church folk that won't yield. And what's the result of that? They've lost us, and though the Reverend Brown pretends 'tis a good riddance, he knows my husband's one pound a year to the charities ban't a good riddance, nor yet his tremendous bass voice in the choir. The singing be gone so thin as the twitter of birds without Tom. Another

strange thing, too. My late one have burst into song since we
parted. Yes, Pierce will sing out loud in company, I'm told.
' I didn't know there was a note in you,' I said to him last
time I was in the ' Old Inn ' ' I sang once to you when we
was courting,' he reminded me, ' and you said—well no matter
—but I never troubled you again, having my feelings like
another.' "

" That reminds me, I have business with him, too,"
answered the farmer. " In the matter of Mr. Gurney, I want
figures."

" He sent 'em."

" He did; but I let him know some time ago that his docu-
ment had been lost."

" I'll stir him up to send it again," promised Mabel. "And
I'm sure nobody in the country be sorrier for you than me and
him."

He regarded her kindly.

" What you say about the herd and the people all thinking
alike is very true," he answered, " yet there is a sort of general
level of kindly feeling and sympathy in the herd which we,
who are not of the herd, ought to try and appreciate. Pity is
a very helpful and comforting thing for some small natures;
and most people have small natures. But for others, pity is
quite the reverse."

" That's true," she admitted, " and I'm sorry I spoke. If
anybody had pitied me over Arthur, I'd have slapped their
faces."

" To feel sorry for anyone, and to tell them so, are two
quite different things," declared Mr. Shillingford. " But these
matters belong to the instinct. They are in the blood. I am
very glad I have made this clear to you."

He went his way, pleased with Mabel Gurney, and the
experience of the hour was rounded and completed for Gabriel
when anon he talked with the master of the " Old Inn."

The very pattern of Mr. Pierce's coat revealed a changed
man. He was alert and brisk. He also expressed regret at
Mr. Shillingford's embarrassments and trusted that an easy
way out of the difficulties would be found.

" For my part" he said, " I do assure you there's no hurry."

" There is, however," declared Gabriel. " I am not a man
who moves at a breathless gait, or asks anybody else to do
so; but I am a reasonable man. I was struck rather sharply
not long ago by a reflection concerning your particular account,
Pierce. I discovered, among various documents and data, the
disconcerting fact that the wine drunk on the occasion of my
daughter's wedding is not yet paid for. And this even though

the wedding of my other daughter, Petronell, must soon be the question of the hour."

Arthur nodded.

" 'Tis well to be off with the old bill afore you are on with the new," he admitted.

" The discovery cast me down," confessed Gabriel. " It was unseemly. I felt a suggestion of impropriety. Indeed, such was the strength of this discomfort that I can no longer endure it. You must be paid, Pierce, and I have come to pay you."

The publican could not quite conceal his gratification. There were already dark rumours of a composition between the master of Blackslade and his creditors, and to see his six pounds ten shillings intact was not a pleasure that Mr. Pierce had anticipated.

He took the cheque, receipted the account, and expressed lively hopes that Petronell's wedding would be an event of the autumn.

" A beautiful creature, and walks the earth like a lily of the field," declared Mr. Pierce. " He's a lucky man, and I hope your high opinion of him will be justified."

" I hope so," answered the farmer, but without his old conviction. " Talking of my younger daughter," he continued, " I have a message from her. You know that she accompanies the vocalists at the Glubb concert, and as you have kindly consented to sing, she thought perhaps you would come up some night soon, and try over your song, and bring the music for her to practise."

" I will certainly come," replied Arthur. " The song takes a bit of doing, and, so far, I've only sung it without the music —just from memory. But I may have gone astray. 'Tis called ' The Keys of Heaven.' I be a lover, and be offering a woman to go walking and talking with me, and I offer her the keys of heaven. 'Tis rather a bold song in a way, and you might think 'twas quite out of my beat; but I find 'tis a very good-natured song to my voice."

" Pancras Widecombe is going to sing ' The Heart Bowed Down,' and, should he get an encore, he will give them ' Sucking Cider through a Straw,' to show he can be comic as well as serious. Now, to sing a song in public is a feat that I could never attempt," concluded Gabriel. " I can speak in public; but to sing—no."

" Time was—and not so long ago, neither—when I should have said the same," answered Mr. Pierce; " but since Mabel was taken off my neck, to say it without gall, I have risen to heights of bravery that I never dreamed about. She wanted for her comfort another man of a different pattern from me.

Not a word against Tom Gurney, mind you. I owe black smith more than I can ever pay back."

" Shall you marry again, Pierce? "

" Marry again! Yes, when the cows begin to fly, not afore. However, if you think I'm weak in my head, of course, you've a right to your own opinion."

Gabriel hastened to declare that he entertained no such thought.

" For my own part," he said, " I esteem the state very reverently and highly."

" We must judge for ourselves," replied Arthur; " it may suit some people; to others 'tis just to be living up to the neck in a heap of misery. When Mabel ran away, I had a fit and rolled on the earth, and foamed at the mouth, and yowled like a dog. The people thought 'twas sorrow, and I never undeceived them, because it wouldn't have been manly to do so; but in truth 'twas joy! I very near went mad with joy! The only chastening thought that kept me sane was the great fear that she'd be cast off by Tom Gurney presently, and return to me after I was swept and garnished—like the seven devils worse than the first. If I hadn't been haunted by that dread, which acted as a safety-valve, I should doubtless have gone stark mad for ever! The rebound would have been too great. Freedom to the slave may be like food to the starving man—too much. So Providence planned the glorious truth—that Mabel had gone for good—should only be opened out to me by inches. I looked around me, like a mouse as have had the good luck to slip the cat, and I breathed again and gasped a prayer of thanksgiving to the Throne of Grace."

" Mrs. Gurney thinks very highly of you now, however," said Gabriel. " I was interested and gratified to hear her say that, had you been the man you are now a year ago, she would never have felt the need to leave you."

" Ban't that like a woman? Old Harry Hawke gave me that there cactus plant in the window a bit ago. ' It ban't no good to me,' he said, ' so you can have un.' Well, I took it, and nursed it and tended it with craft and patience. Then it burst forth into flower—great tassels of flame-red blossom, and the wonder of everybody that comes in the private bar. ' Be gormed,' says Old Harry Hawke, ' if I'd knowed the darned thing had such brave flowers hid in it, I'd never have parted with un, Arthur.' And I replied to the man : ' 'Twas your parting with it as made the flowers come, Old Harry. It never would have thrust 'em out for you. But 'twas my handling and skill, and the change into my sunny window, coaxed 'em out."

Mr. Shillingford appreciated this allegory.

"The case in a nutshell," he declared. "No two people want exactly the same treatment."

"I'll keep the breath of this here bar between them and me while I live. And I may tell you, in private, that I'm watching with a good deal of interest how Tom Gurney's digestion goes on. That's the test! I've heard no murmur of any trouble yet, and I hope I shan't; but so sure as you hear that whispered, you'll know only too well what it means. I'm very hopeful, however, that it won't happen, because Mabel herself be happy as a cow."

"You'll come and sing, then?"

"I will certainly come, and I thank Miss Petronell for her message."

The air was indeed full of rehearsals. Doctor Grenville took his banjo to Southcombe and dazzled the Coakers and Tryphena with his skill. He helped her with her recitation also, and won the hearts of her uncle and aunt. But Elias preserved a neutral attitude before Petronell's lover, and the fact that the doctor did not once mention Petronell struck him as strange. His gallantry to Tryphena was also of doubtful expedience in the eyes of Tryphena's cousin.

CHAPTER L.

THE schoolroom of the Church House was approached by a flight of steps in the rear of the building, and at the top of these, on the night of the Glubb concert, sat Birkett Johnson of Tunhill behind a little table. He sold the tickets, while within the schoolroom a couple of young women showed the people to their seats.

Nicky and his wife were the first to arrive, for she was now restored to health, and from their places near the door Nanny could mark the entrance and keep up a running account of the audience as it filtered in.

Flags were hung from the crossbeams of the roof, and a friend or two had sent green things to decorate the little stage. The lighting alone left anything to be desired. Twenty oil lamps hung from the walls, but many smoked, and threatened to make the atmosphere foul.

" Here come the Sweetlands! " said Nanny. " They be all in the reserved shilling places—Mister and Missis, and that Harriet, his sister. They be in the third row from the front."

The Glubbs wore their best clothes, and Nicky's accordion in its waterproof cover was under the seat of his chair.

" Who be they? " he asked, as feet shuffled past him and proceeded to the rear of the room.

" Four common people to the threp'my seats," said Nanny. " Sandy Blake, from Blackslade, and his wife and childer."

He grew impatient.

" Why the hell don't they come in? " he asked, so loud that Mr. Sweetland started in his chair, and looked round.

" Hush! " said Nanny, " or you'll scare the folk. There's lots of time. The doors be only just opened."

His keen ears detected the sound of wheels.

" There's a party come. I heard 'em," he said.

" They be trooping in by legions now," she answered. " Here's Timothy Turtle and Sally and Pancras Widecombe from ' Rugglestone Inn ' ; and here's they Gurneys from the Mill. I thought they'd be among the first—such pleasure-loving folk as them. And if Nelly Gurney ban't with them! Seldom enough she goes junketting. They'm coming up to us."

Abel Gurney and his wife, Sarah, stopped and shook hands with Nanny.

" Terrible glad you be saved alive, Mrs. Glubb," said the miller. " 'Twould have been a great loss to us all, and to Nicky in particular, if you'd been called."

" And looking pretty pert considering," added Sarah. " I'm sure I hope the people will cram the schoolroom afore the fun begins."

" Is there to be programmes? " asked Abel Gurney.

" Proper printed programmes there's to be," answered Nicky, " and they damned boys ought to be running about selling 'em afore now. Twopence they are to cost, and they can be kept and put by for a remembrance."

The Gurneys went to their places, and Nanny reported the arrival of four more people in the threepenny seats.

"And there's two in the sixpennies," she said. "They be Uncle Tom Cobleigh and his daughter, the widow."

"Where did Turtle get to?" asked Nicky, and when he heard that the innkeeper and Sally were at the back of the room, he swore.

"Then I chuck him," said Nicky; "never again do I darken the doors of the 'Rugglestone.' Proper decency did ought to have put the man in the bob seats. He shan't hear the last of that!"

"But you mind the nice things Mr. Turtle sent while I was sick—and, be it as 'twill, there's a plenty going in the shilling seats. Here's Mr. Gabriel Shillingford, and Miss Petronell, and Whitelock Smerdon, and Doctor Grenville—all in the bob places; and alongside them sit the Coplestone party from Southway—six of 'em! There's ten bob in a minute!"

"Be they boys nipping about with the programmes?" asked Mr. Glubb; "because if not, you run round to Johnson and tell him."

"Pancras Widecombe have just started them," answered Nanny. "And here's quality! Squire and his missis and young Squire, and two more from Bag Park! They be seated next the Shillingfords, and Mr. Shillingford have rose and bowed, and so have the doctor. There's a lot of hand-shaking going on, and every lesser eye be on 'em. The Squire's missis be slipping off a wonnerful coat of fur—white wi' black tails on it. She's got a low gown on, and you can see to the dip in her bosom! And precious stones be flashing up in her hair. 'Tis the colour of heather honey, and rises up on her head like a tower. And Squire and young Squire be in black and white, with glittering shirt-fronts and waistcoats open to the pit of their stomachs. And here come more sixpennies. If Jack Mogridge and his wife haven't gone in 'em! They're in black for that hanged man."

"Be they Smerdons from Bone Hill come?"

"Not yet. But come they will for sartain—some of 'em. Here's the Hawkes—Old and Young, and Emma, and her eldest. They be all in the sixpennies."

"'Tis enough for them," asserted Nicky, "because the men be going to ring their bells as an item in the show. Get a programme and read it out to me."

"Mrs. Bowden's come in. Her husband no doubt made her come though he can't, because of a tissick in the chest."

"So long as he paid for his seat, his chest don't matter," declared Nicky.

"Here's old Bell!" cried Nanny. "He's gone in a threp'my!"

" Has he? Well, I hope the varmint will like what I be going to say. 'Twill be out afore they can stop me."

" He's sitting beside they Webbers, from Southcombe; and here be the proper Southcombe people—Mr. Coaker and Mrs. Coaker, and Miss Harvey and Elias. They be all bob folk in the second row; and Miss Harvey have catched sight of us, and be coming to speak."

Tryphena joined Nicky and Nanny, and congratulated the latter on her appearance.

" It's going to be a perfectly splendid concert," she said. " All the shilling seats are sold, and more than half the six-penny ones."

" Here's the Vicar! " cried Nanny. " He's gived orders for the windows to be oped, and Pancras Widecombe be telling him that if that's done the lamps will smoke, so 'tis a choice of evils. And Mr. Brown's vexed about it, seemingly."

" Fussy fool! " said Nicky. " Who wants the windows opened? If us gets a bit fuggy, what's the odds? 'Twill only make it the more homelike. I'd let the men smoke as well as the lamps if I had my way."

" Here's Mrs. Reep, old Daniel's widow, along with the Smerdons—Peter and Martha, and a few small fry. To the threp'my seats they go."

Tryphena, perceiving that she was not wanted, returned to her aunt. She was going to recite a poem, and she felt very nervous. She had chosen Longfellow's " Excelsior," and now sat and tried to concentrate her thoughts upon it.

Doctor Grenville came to talk to her.

" You and Petronell must come into the greenroom before the show begins," he said. " There's room for us all in there, and I've arranged for plenty of liquid refreshment. My conjuring pal from Exeter has arrived. He's making up. He always gives his show in costume. He's got some old Indian loot he puts on—full of secret pockets and things. I expect he'll be the hit of the evening—after your recitation."

A hum of voices ascended in the schoolroom. The people arrived steadily and friends greeted each other and sat together and talked about their affairs.

" Here be Mary Hearn, stiff with pride, and her nose in the air," said Nanny. " And if she ban't seated next to the Sweet-lands in the shilling seats! And here's Arthur Pierce, dressed like a gentleman, and here's Tom Gurney and his Mabel. They've met Pierce in the doorway, and all eyes be watching 'em. Arthur have got on black, and be wearing a red tie, and carrying his music to the manner born! "

"Look in the programme and see what 'tis the man be going to sing," directed Nicky.

Nanny obeyed.

"'The Keys of Heaven,' 'tis to be," she said; "and Pancras Widecombe is going to sing 'The Heart Bowed Down.'"

"Where do I come in?" asked Nicky.

"You be item fourteen and last. 'Tis arranged you finish up, and then, after you've played and sung, you be going to make a speech and thank the people for me, and tell 'em how much the concert have fetched in. Birkett Johnson will have counted up the money by then."

"I hope to God he won't make himself scarce with it, like that rip, Christian Cobleigh, and the Slate Club cash."

"Not him. He ain't that sort."

She read the programme through:

"No. 1, Overture, piano and banjo, Miss Petronell Shillingford and Doctor Hugh Grenville. No. 2, Recitation, 'Betsy and I are out,' by Mr. Harold Harding."

"Who be that?" asked Nicky. "Never heard of the man."

"He's a friend of the doctor's. Then No. 3, Comic banjo song, 'The Three Coons,' by Doctor Hugh Grenville."

"I wish he'd done a duet with me," said Nicky. "I could have told him some words from the old times that would properly have took the people's breath away, and set every female in the room blushing like a rose. And if Pierce weren't a fool, he'd sing something funny. Who wants 'The Keys of Heaven' except of a Sunday? The keys of the beer barrel be more like it."

"Mr. Pierce comes next," answered Nanny, "he's No. 4; and after him there's an item printed in extra big letters: 'The Mysteries of the East, by Jam Jam-Jeeboy, the Nabob of Cochbangalee's own Juggler.'"

"You can lead me out for a drink when that's going on," declared Nicky. "That's no good to me."

"No. 6 is Mr. Pancras Widecombe, and a mournful song seemingly. Wıat do he want to have a heart bowed down for? No. 7 is the doctor again. This time playing a duet with Miss Shillingford. 'Medley,' 'tis called. Then comes the turn of the bellringers, and after them there's a comic recitation by that Harold Harding again: 'The Fox that Lost His Tail,' 'tis called. That's No. 9 of the programme; No. 10 comes next. 'Tis a piano piece by Miss Shillingford—all alone this time—Beet-hoven, 'tis."

"Solemn and dull, no doubt" said Nicky. "What's the matter with this programme be that 'tis too deadly heavy. However so long as the people have paid their money it don't matter; though there might be a few as would get nasty and ask for the stuff back again."

"They never would do that," declared Nanny. "'Tis for charity, and I be here for 'em to see 'tis genuine."

"I'll do what I can at the finish," promised Nicky. "They've done one clever thing, and only one, so far as I can see, and that is they've kept the best for the last."

"Miss Tryphena be No. 11," continued Nanny. "A recitation again. 'Excelsior,' 'tis to be. These here foreign words won't please the people, I'm thinking, for they won't know what the mischief half of 'em stand for."

"Whether or no, and whatever rubbish it may be, we must make a hell of a row after she's done, and lead the applause," declared Mr. Glubb. "She's been a very sporting friend to us, and one good turn deserves another."

"No. 12 be they bellringers again," concluded Mrs. Glubb, "and the Doctor is No. 13."

"Drat the man, what the mischief do we want with such a dose of him for?" asked Nicky.

"We must live and let live," answered his wife. "No doubt the young fellow thinks it be going to be a fine advertisement for his business."

"Like his cheek if he do. 'Tis us as be going to be advertised, not him."

"Well, you come next and you'll give 'em a good bit of music, and tell 'em what money's been drawed in, and thank 'em from me. The room be getting nicely full now."

Nicky did not answer, for he was full of thought. He had already conceived of a great and glorious outrage, and now he permitted the idea to mature in his brain.

The concert began, and the little company evinced its appreciation of the entertainment provided. The piano and banjo overture went well enough, save for the breaking of a banjo string, and the relations of the performers caused a sentimental sympathy with the effort.

But in the greenroom different emotions awakened, and the performers there assembled, in a scholastic atmosphere of slates, blackboards and scientific diagrams, could not fail to note that it was Tryphena Harvey, and not Petronell Shillingford, who engaged Dr. Grenville's chief attentions. He fussed over her continually, and exhibited a solicitation for her anxieties in connection with "Excelsior," that aroused curiosity and bred comment. Petronell was, of course, the first to observe it. Her pique took the form of a failure at the piano, while behind the scenes she devoted her attention to Mr. Harold Harding, a long-haired railway-clerk from Newton Abbot, with yearnings towards the stage. His first recitation fell flat. The folk endured contentedly, however, and Petronell assured the artist afterwards that never had the familiar little drama been presented with more power and feeling. As a contrast came "The Three Coons," presented by Doctor Grenville. He possessed no real sense of fun, but rolled his eyes and shouted and simulated facetiousness to the best of his power. The people laughed, and many who shared the singer's lack of humour appeared to be amused. Arthur Pierce, accompanied by Petronell Shillingford, sang "The Keys of Heaven," in a high tenor, that broke to shrill falsetto. No critical faculty was brought to bear upon the song, but genuine amazement and admiration for the unsuspected audacity of the singer marked his hearers.

The Mysteries of the East by the Nabob of Cochbangalee's own Juggler introduced the person of an old Indian judge's son, who lived with his family at Exeter. This young man's face was painted brown. He wore a yellow turban with a glittering jewel upon it, and was attired in voluminous silken robes, rich in secret pockets and receptacles of all kinds. He was not, as he confessed afterwards, in his best form. Among other enchantments he produced many yards of pink tape from his mouth, burnt himself in an endeavour to eat fire, and failed to deceive his audience as to the whereabouts of an orange under three metal cups. Himself, however, he entirely bewildered in the course of this experiment.

Pancras Widecombe's mournful song failed absolutely, for, coming upon the doubtful triumph of the young man from Exeter, it found the audience in no mood for pathos. He had enemies, moreover, and the deadly weapon of laughter was directed against Pancras. Though he sang his best and bowed down his heart to the very depths of a guttural and bass despair, only a long-drawn chirrup and cricket-like stridulation of merriment greeted him.

" 'Tis the fool's face, not what he be singing, that makes me laugh," confessed the elder Coaker, who was much amused. "When you think upon Widecombe, and his ever-green conceit of hisself, and his calm cheek at all times, to see him pretending to be sad and sat upon! He ought to have sung, ' I'm master of all I survey,' or some such stuff."

Few but Sally Turtle regarded Pancras with much more than laughter, and displayed his emotion in a red face and scowling expression as he withdrew.

"For two pins I'd have told 'em they was a lot of ill-behaved clod-poles, as didn't know a beautiful song when they heard it," he declared to Young Harry Hawke, with a panting bosom in the greenroom. But Young Harry loved him not, and only grinned in his face.

" How was they to know the song was beautiful? " he answered. " You ought to have told 'em afore you began."

Doctor Grenville and Petronell appeared again together in a duet, and since behind the scenes his betrothed was feeling angry and jealous, she did herself small justice before the footlights. Thrice she lost the time. It was a stammering and hesitating achievement, and the fault rested with Petronell. They did not speak to each other when they came off the stage, and neither appeared to bow an acknowledgment of the applause.

Mr. Harding next recited, and his performance was spoiled by the tragical collapse of a Smerdon girl. She fainted and was borne out to a bench in the passage, where Doctor Grenville protested audibly at the Smerdon girl's tight lacing, and ruined the secret joy of her young life—a pair of corsets for which she had " saved up " through many weeks. When she came to her senses, her armour spread in tatters beneath her bosom, and she wept and crept homewards harbouring thoughts of death.

Behind the scenes, presently, Petronell told Hugh Grenville that she did not wish him to turn over the pages of her Beethoven's " Farewell to the Piano "; but the doctor protested.

" What'll your father and everybody think? " he asked. " They'll say we've quarrelled."

She was firm, and Mr. Harding consented to perform the task. Petronell played well on this occasion, but was glad to be done with her part of a painful evening. She stayed only to hear Tryphena, very white and nervous, enter upon the recitation from Longfellow, and then she departed, bearing through the night a sorrow even deeper than that of the Smerdon girl. For she, poor maiden, found tears relieve her on the way home to Bone Hill ; but Petronell's eyes mirrored the nightly stars without a tremor.

Tryphena stumbled to the end of " Excelsior," forgetting every inflexion and gesture that Doctor Grenville had been at pains to teach her; but the affection of her friends took form of hand-clapping and stamping. Nicky and Nanny led the noise, and continued long after everybody else was silent.

The subsequent bell-ringing was a familiar entertainment, and excited no great attention, while upon Doctor Grenville's re-appearance it seemed the audience began to feel with Nicky Glubb that it was possible to have enough, if not too much of him. Not one encore had marked the concert—an unusual circumstance; but the entertainment, indeed, proceeded at low level, and few loopholes for enthusiasm were offered even to the most amiable. The general sense of the company seemed to indicate a stern duty meritoriously performed by all present —performers and audience alike.

Then Nicky came forward led by his wife. She carried his accordion and put it into his hand when he reached the platform. The greenroom was now deserted, and the other performers had entered the schoolroom to hear the financial result of their efforts. The sum was whispered to Mrs. Glubb by Birkett Johnson, as she ascended to the stage.

The blind man played and sang while the people rose and helped each other into coats and wraps. There was a sound of wheels through the night, and the speech of drivers without.

Nicky gave two songs and made the most of them, while the accordion volleyed and thundered an accompaniment. Then his wife led him to the footlights.

" Ladies and gentlemen," he said. " You be gathered here to-night to help a blind man and his wife, and specially her— because she's just fought a fearful battle with Death, and come out of the Valley of the Shadow a shadow herself. The sum that you've gived in among you for this evening's concert, such as it was, be six pound, eighteen shilling, and sixpence, including a bit for the programmes; and me and my wife thank you with all our hearts for your great goodness. And we thank all the kind people who have done their poor bestest to amuse the company this evening. And the money will help to keep me and Nanny out of the almshouse for many and many a day—where beastly, useless, old dogs like Bell be chained up; though such dregs did ought to be knocked on the head once for all in my opinion! And I hope the swine will soon be wriggling in a place as rhymes with his name! "

" Hush!   Hush!   Take him away!   Shame on you, Glubb! " shouted reproving voices, and Nicky, grinning his well-known horrible smile, shuffled off holding Nanny's hand. Many hissed him for this assault, but he cared not.

Then into the night streamed the people, and swiftly they vanished, some driving and some walking through the darkness. The real pleasure of that evening's work circled round fifty supper-tables, where the unconscious humours of the concert were weighed and measured to accompaniment of laughter both deep and shrill.

But at Blackslade there was no laughter, for Petronell refused to join the supper-party, or see Hugh Grenville, who accompanied her father; neither did any laugh at Southcombe.

for there Elias rated Tryphena very soundly for flirting with another girl's sweetheart.

Horrified and indignant she protested, but Elias would not be pacified.

" I've no axe to grind for Petronell Shillingford, and well you know it," he said. " But for her sins she's tokened to that man, and if there's not a proper flare-up to-morrow and a row that will very likely wreck the whole show, I don't know Petronell."

Tryphena wept, but Elias was stern, and would not forgive her.

CHAPTER LI

ON a day of early summer, one fortnight before the meeting of creditors at Blackslade, Pancras repaired to the farm that he might set about the restoration of the old barn. He fell in with Birkett Johnson, descending from Tunhill, and while they stood before the great doorway of Chittleford, there crept up Uncle Tom Cobleigh from Venton on his way to the Moor. He rode a pony, but drew up and spoke to them.

" No news of my son Christian yet, souls," he said.

" Be hopeful, Uncle; be hopeful," answered Johnson. " 'Tis sure that his Maker must act on the man's heart afore long. We'll trust the good news will soon arrive that he's well and has turned over a new leaf."

" And be going to pay back all the men he robbed," added Pancras Widecombe.

" Without a doubt," assented the old man. " I hope he's saving, and will soon send home a good lump of money."

" 'Tis offering for rain, Uncle, and you did ought to look out," declared Johnson. " At your time of life you can't afford to get wetted through no more."

Uncle lifted his dim eyes to the sky.

" There's things you never can forget," he answered, " and the weather be one. What I don't know about the ways of the weather ban't worth knowing. You'll bear me out, Birkett?"

" You'm very clever at it."

" If wind goeth round with the sun, the day'll be fair; if it goeth against the sun, then, when wind and sun meet, the weather's bound to go scat, and rain have got to fall. Now, for all the unshed rain in the elements, there ain't going to be any fall afore evening, because the wind be following the sun."

They praised his discernment and he went away comforted. Pancras walked beside the pony until he reached the entrance to Blackslade. He then left Uncle and went to his work. The hour was eight o'clock, and Whitelock Smerdon awaited him.

" We trust to you a good bit, Widecombe," he said. " I've had the place cleaned out so as you can see what to do. 'Twas in a jakes of a mess, and I'm surprised it have stood so long. But 'tis a very useful linhey, and though money be tight, as you know, we can't let the buildings fall upon our heads. You'll see if there's much to throw down afore you begin building up, and Arnell, the carpenter, will come so soon as you want him. But the first thing that Mr. Shillingford wishes to be done is the floor—this rotten cobble-stoning. A good modern floor must go down, with proper drain pipes. So get to work, and if you find yourself wanting help call to me. The men be on the land; but I'm here at your service."

To be set in authority always delighted Pancras. If it was only a boy to fetch and carry, the position of command caused him great satisfaction. That Whitelock Smerdon should thus submit to his orders pleased the mason and fired his spirit. He undertook the responsibility, assumed a magisterial manner, cast his eye over the shed, and bade Smerdon be of good cheer.

" I see what's wanted. I see at a glance how we must go to work. I warn you that there's a lot calling for doing, however. I came up on Sunday, in a friendly way, when you and the family was at church, to Buckland, and Sandy showed me the barn. But 'tis well within my powers."

" Go ahead, then," answered Whitelock, " and call me if you want help with the cobble-stones. My father-in-law thinks they may be useful again."

" I won't deceive you as to that. 'Tis very unlikely we can use 'em again. They belong to the past, and I'm all for modern ways, as you know."

Whitelock departed, and the other began his work. But though Mr. Shillingford's son-in-law hung about in readiness to appear when Widecombe should make his first discovery, the thing did not happen till the luncheon hour. It was a little after one o'clock, and Gabriel had just sat down to dinner with his family, when Joan hastened in to say that Pancras desired to speak with Mr. Shillingford. Indeed, she had scarcely given her message when the mason appeared behind her. Without ceremony he thrust upon the family and cared little for the mild rebuke that Gabriel delivered from the top of the table.

" You should not push in here, Widecombe," he said. " Because you came to rehearse your song, that is no reason——however, speak. You appear to be a good deal excited."

" You won't rebuke me when you hear tell," answered the other. " Under the cobble-stones, and my crowbar very near went in atop of it! And if that ban't a precious jewel, show me one ! "

He placed his find before Mr. Shillingford. It was a golden snuff-box with a miniature in the lid.

" Here's the paper 'twas wrapped in," he said. " And I couldn't let such a priceless thing out of my hand into any other but yours."

Sibley's heart beat hard. She and Petronell bent their heads over the treasure, while Mr. Shillingford put on his glasses and examined the fragment of yellow printed paper that had held it.

" The date is here," he said. " It is a London journal of the third of August, 1807 ! Now this without doubt is enormously interesting."

" The ghost ! " cried Sibley. " Oh, father, 'twas what the ghost wanted to tell us—and couldn't ! "

Dinner ceased to interest anybody, and Pancras led the way in triumph to the old barn, while Gabriel heard how the discovery had been made. Not a shadow of suspicion crossed his mind; but Petronell felt puzzled. She had never weighed the significance of the ghost, being too much occupied with her own affairs, when the apparition was reported, to trouble herself about it; but now, in broad daylight, this crude discovery and its relation with the alleged spectre, set her pondering. The thought of the ghost was pleasantly creepy, if not perfectly credible; but the appearance of the treasure bewildered her. It proved difficult to relate the ideas. The men and her sister, however, appeared to suffer from no such difficulty, and soon Petronell herself was swept out of scepticism. Sibley alone did not join the rest, but it became Petronell's pleasant task presently to break astounding news to her.

She hastened in again, to find her practical sister finishing her dinner.

" Don't get excited," said the younger; " try and accept it calmly and look at the worst. It may be all rubbish, and not worth the paper it is wrapped in; but most extraordinary things are coming to light in the old barn ! The floor is like a bran-tub at Christmas, and every time we dip in we find something fresh ! "

She showed her sister a pair of candlesticks of Sheffield plate, but Sibley kept her nerve, and exhibited great self-control.

" I don't feel a bit excited," she declared. " For why? I always felt, somehow, that that old man in the winter meant something, and when I heard it was decided to do up the barn, I honestly believed that something would come of it. Of course these odds and ends may be rubbish all the same."

" I only said that to keep you calm," declared Petronell. " They're not rubbish. Some of them can't possibly be rubbish. Look at this brooch I've put on ! Father says it may be worth a hundred pounds."

" Father ! Much he knows ! "

" Well, come and see for yourself, if it won't tire you I can't stop. It's frightfully exciting. And Whitelock believes that there may be things in the cob walls, too. To think that all the searching in the past never found them ! "

" They weren't meant to be found by anybody but us," declared Sibley with perfect truth. " That none but us should have come on 'em is very natural, according to Providence; and so like as not they've just been shown to us at this critical moment to save father."

" He said the same thing himself a minute ago," answered Petronell.

They went to the barn and watched the operations. Whitelock and Pancras had their coats off, and Mr. Shillingford, preserving a high self-control, stood and watched their operations. Beside him grew an increasing pile of precious things. He towered above candlesticks, salvers, a litter of trinkets, and a heap of paper. Foot by foot the floor was broken up and revealed the hidden hoard.

" This is an adventure without parallel in the history of any old family that I know," said the farmer. " It is an event that will become historical. Such an accumulation of heirlooms has surely never come to light before."

" They may not be worth much, however, father," warned Sibley. " They are fearfully shabby and tarnished, a lot of them."

" Their worth is the least interesting thing about them," he answered. " It is a fact that they are here, and have been, as it were, discovered by supernatural agencies. Our children's children will cherish these things for generations to come. They will be handed down. Legends and folklore will accumulate about them."

" I should think the creditors would accumulate about them," said Whitelock bluntly. " If they be worth more than they look to be, which we'll hope, then they may carry us into deep water again, and——"

" Of course," declared his wife. " There can't be two opinions about that. Pots and pans and little pictures in gold frames ain't no good to us now; but the money they're worth —if they're worth money at all—will be a godsend indeed."

" I had not certainly viewed it in that connection," answered Mr. Shillingford, stroking a melon teapot; " but I see your point, Whitelock. There are practical issues raised here. We must restrain our hope, however; we must possess our souls in patience. I see the position—I am not blind to it. In fact it is a very lamentable one in its way; because, if these things are precious, they are not ours any longer."

They argued and laboured until the floor was up and explored a yard deep; then Gabriel's heirlooms were gathered in baskets and brought to the house.

Widecombe, who, by virtue of this great event, had established himself as one of the inner circle of the family, drank tea with the Shillingfords presently, and his hearty satisfaction at this good fortune for his neighbours, and reiterated hopes that the treasure would prove of exceeding value, touched the farmer and Petronell.

" We shall always have to thank you, Mr. Widecombe," declared the latter. " We shall always think of you in connection with this wonderful day."

It was decided that the old barn must be watched that night, and Whitelock Smerdon undertook the task, though he knew that there was nothing left of value.

" It will be a hard matter to keep silence, Pancras Widecombe, but I am sure that I can trust you to do so," said Gabriel, when the mason, his work done for the day, prepared to return home. " In due course this remarkable event will become generally known; but for the moment it would turn all eyes to Blackslade—a thing I should very much dislike to happen."

Pancras promised, and, when he was gone, a further proposal for secrecy was uttered by Petronell. Indeed, she made a most unexpected suggestion.

" Hugh comes to supper to-night," she said. " And it would be the most natural thing in the world to tell him all about this."

" Who doubts it? " asked her father. " Our good is his good."

" And yet I don't want him to know—not for the moment."

" Surely the little shadow cast at that dreadful entertainment has passed, my child? "

" Oh, yes, father; I was silly and over-excited. It isn't that. And I've got no reasons, and if I had, I don't want to give them; but—but—I ask you all—you, Sibley, and you, Whitelock—to say nothing about this affair to him—yet."

" Your will is law in a matter of this sort," answered Gabriel; and then Whitelock spoke.

" Petronell's right. We can't keep this too quiet for the minute. The first thing is to have the stuff valued, and if I was you, father-in-law, I should send right off to London for some learned and honest man, who has no axe to grind in the matter, and pay him a proper sum to tell you where you stand."

They talked for a long while. Then all assisted to carry the treasure upstairs to Mr. Shillingford's bedroom.

" I cannot trust myself to see Grenville to-night," he declared, " for my mind is so full of this event that it would escape my tongue for certain. I shall retire; indeed, I should have done so in any case, for I'm going to examine everything under my magnifying glass, and piece together the ancient newspapers if I can."

When the doctor arrived, therefore, he found only Petronell to welcome him, for Whitelock had entered upon his masquerade of a vigil in the barn and Sibley spent an hour in conversation with him there. Overhead, Gabriel had forgotten the hoard of Miser Shillingford, and was entirely absorbed amid fragments of the old journals.

But Grenville did not stay to supper after all. Never since the concert had his understanding with his betrothed been quite as close as of yore. He had expressed regret and contrition when she declared her annoyance. Friendship was re-established between them; yet Petronell's spirit whispered ugly things. Suspicion and fear were awakened. She believed that Grenville was steadily planning a way down which he presently proposed to retreat. A vagueness had crept into his love-making. He indulged in generalities, where personalities had been the rule; thus the rupture and increasing intimacies were checked, and their place taken by more lifeless relations. He was careful, and would from time to time indulge in rhapsodies and caresses, to soften the edges of colder scenes. A less acute lover might have been reassured after her moments of doubt, but Petronell, her suspicion once aroused, read very accurately his line of thought and its objective relation. It was all of a piece, and, with sick horror, she began to suspect that he designed to jilt her. She fought the fear, and sometimes it retreated and grew dim, while oftener events confirmed the dread, and brought it dark as a storm-cloud to the zenith of her mind. Then, again, the sun would break through.

To-night she led the conversation to Tryphena Harvey, and his attitude to Tryphena pleased Petronell but little, because the things that he said rang false upon her ear, and his view of Petronell's friend was contemptuous. She had been easier had Hugh Grenville praised the other; but he did not.

" If you could only see that my attention to her at the concert was purely automatic—the same I should have paid to her grandmother," he said.

" We needn't go over that again. You convinced me about that, and I thought that I convinced you, too, that my behaviour was merely—well, hysterical."

" The child—for she's little more, though nearly of age—seems to me almost something out of a Sunday-school story. I've wondered what you saw in her, Petronell, quite as often as you appear to have wondered what I did. It was really rather absurd of you to push her forward and make her recite in public."

" I didn't push her forward—you did ! "

" Don't let her think you're jealous, or any nonsense of that sort," he continued, " for the girl puts you before everything else in the world, and would be heartbroken and frightened to death if that happened."

" I am not jealous," answered she; " only a very silly sort of woman is jealous of her lover. What's the good? It shows a weak nature; a beggar's cringing, mean, vile nature. Do you think I should want to keep any man against his will? "

" Now I've annoyed you—the last thing on God's earth I ever want to do."

They wrangled, and the doctor's heart beat cheerfully under his assumed concern. Then they made it up, and Petronell forgave him. Presently he declared that he had better not stop to supper, in order that she might beg him to do so.

But she did not. She grew cold again, and they parted without kissing.

His spirit suffered no pang, and he lifted an elated head as soon as the night hid him; while she wept unseen, for she knew the man had changed his mind and was not going to marry her. She felt powerless and helpless, yet had wit to perceive his calculated craft. He designed a rupture that should cast no reflection upon him. He meant to give her no loophole. An inevitable separation was his purpose, and he planned that it should happen, if possible, in such a way that none might censure him.

" He wants me to throw him over," thought Petronell, " and, though I hate him now, throw him over I will not."

CHAPTER LII

VALIANT DUNNYBRIG was quick, not only to mourn with those who mourned, but to rejoice with those who rejoiced. His own remarkable experience had left him more tolerant and patient. He was ashamed of his blindness in failing to read the will of his God—a power upon which he had always prided himself.

He met with Araminta Sweetland on the occasion of an early visit to Blackslade, and they spoke together for a moment before the old man pursued his way.

" Good morning, niece Araminta," he said. " I hope all is well with Samuel again, and that he's thrown off his gout? "

" He'll be about pretty soon, so Doctor Grenville says. And Aunt Jane? "

" She's pretty clever, thank you, and will be glad to have a tell next time you can come along. Age gets in the thin edge of the wedge with her. I mark a weakness here and there, but my strength knows no change, and I do more and more for her, so that she shan't feel she's losing her old powers."

Mrs. Sweetland nodded.

" 'Tis like that with me, in a way. My husband cries out for a lot of humouring at all times, and he's terrible sorry for himself when he's sick; but me and Harriet between us manage to keep the dish upright. I don't know what I should have done without his sister. Sometimes, in one mood, he calls for her, and won't have me around him; and then again, in another mood, he's horrid to her and must have me."

" A shallow and a futile thing," declared Valiant. " No disrespect I bear him; but at the same time respect would be improper. I'll respect none as ban't worthy of it. He's had a deal more good luck than he deserves, to the human eye."

"He's good at heart, though, of course, shocking narrow-minded. I've often looked back over my life uneasily. But there 'twas; he came, and Aunt Jane—you understand how she viewed it."

"Yes," he said; "she have the art of her family—to make her meaning clear; and, looking back, I can now say I'm glad that it happened so. There would have been a lot of earthly trouble, as too often there is when we be set on doing the heavenly will. And now I'm going to wish Gabriel Shillingford joy of his great discovery. Once more I find myself on all fours with the Almighty, and it have been a consolation to me to do so. For I asked myself, when I heard about the meeting of creditors, what I should do if I was Master, and I said that, in my opinion, I should give the harmless man another chance."

"They are very overjoyed about it."

"And so am I. 'Tis the case of Abraham and Isaac over again, and just as the knife be raised there cometh salvation from the cleverness of Heaven. Blackslade is saved, in fact."

"Did you believe about the ghost, Uncle Valiant?"

"Why for not? It all hangs together very suent. The Lord leads one man to save money, and that money, in fulness of time, saves another man's credit. The Lord be always plotting for the next generation."

"Mr. Shillingford appears greatly cheered up. He came in to see my husband yesterday, and he seemed to think it was more the race than himself that had been saved. He said : 'The individual is nothing, the race and the blood everything.'"

"Blood! Let him have the blood, poor man. 'Tis fire, not blood, be worth saving—the fire that runneth in my veins, the fire from heaven, Araminta! Fire from heaven be better than blood from doubtful robbers in the past."

They talked a little longer; then Mr. Dunnybrig went on his way to Blackslade, and soon shook Gabriel by the hand.

"I hope 'tis all true and more than true that they tell me," he said.

"All true, neighbour," declared the other. "'Wealth beyond the dreams of avarice,' as the poet says."

"If 'tis equal to paying your debts——"

"There seems every reason to think so. I have, of course, made no secret of my temporary difficulties. They had, in fact, reached such a pitch that I had planned a meeting of creditors. But now my family resources—accidentally over-looked owing to the eccentricities of a bygone Shillingford— the bulk of my personal estate, in fact, has come to light.

Somehow I have always felt there must be something wrong. It seemed to me that my embarrassments must be founded on an imaginary basis rather than a real one. And so it has proved. It looked, of course, to the world, as though a Shillingford were insolvent. That is how the situation must have struck all unprejudiced eyes; and yet I never thoroughly grasped it. My daughter, Petronell, to some extent shared my attitude. Sibley, on the contrary, took another view, and judged by appearances, as we are all too prone to do."

Mr. Dunnybrig laughed.

"You're a wonderful man in your way," he said. "Life's a dream to the likes of you, and reality nothing."

"What is reality?" asked Mr. Shillingford. "In my opinion, the only reality lies in noble ideas and lofty ambitions. My dreams, as you call them, are the nearest approach to reality that I can reach. Life itself is too pretty and too complicated to be the first thing."

Valiant nodded doubtfully.

"I see what you mean," he said. "How easy would it be to live, Gabriel Shillingford, if life didn't come between! How easy to live in the grand style, like saints and martyrs, if we didn't let the passing hour be for ever pricking into our souls like a thorn."

"That's just what I feel. And I've always tried to escape from the tyranny of the passing hour."

"We can't do it—not wholly, and not at all like you tried to do it," answered the master of Chittleford. "I've often prayed God for some star to light a lonely way for me—a way that took me far out of the rutted road. But it weren't to be. The rutted road is mine, and will be mine henceforth. We can't escape the yoke, though we may lead the team."

"You are what they call a pioneer," said Gabriel. "You have a great spiritual outlook. You probably have the blood of some distinguished Covenanter in your veins. To return to this remarkable discovery, if you will follow me, I can show you the things revealed."

They viewed the hoard.

"There is reason to hope that all will not need to be sacrificed," explained Gabriel. "You will easily understand what a great grief it is to me to part with anything at all. I feel myself only in trust for the race; I am, in a sense, a traitor to the family when I convert these heirlooms into money. I would not do it for myself, Dunnybrig. I would prefer to live in the utmost penury with these possessions round about me than part from the least of them; but I have no choice. But, after all is done, and the various claims upon my purse admitted and cancelled to the last farthing—after that—there seems good reason to hope that my family may be left with considerable additions and remainders. A valuer comes down from London to-morrow. His fee alone will be ten guineas and all expenses. I mention this to show the significance of this great event."

" Wealth be a very tricky addition to life," said Valiant. " As a man more than well-to-do I can testify to it. 'Tis a temptation to the strong to taste power, and a lure to the weak to seek pleasure—a trial that both sorts too often sink under. To be born to it be different. Them so situated come to it as a matter of course, and use or misuse it according to their natures; but for wealth to burst upon us like a strong man armed be a dangerous thing, and open to suspicion. It tempts to the ruling passion; and the ruling passion be generally of this world, and not of the next. The keenest earthly pleasures call for cash, and the keenest pleasures be the deadliest— just as the sweetest apple have got the maggot in it."

" True," admitted Shillingford. " You are a most sound thinker, Dunnybrig. Money is power, and as one that comes of a long line that has wielded power, money finds me quite ready—to spend it."

" Devil doubt you—' to spend it.' But I'm an older man than you, and have a right to speak; and so I say to you, take a leaf out of the book of Miser Shillingford, who gathered this heap."

" A good deal depends on the actual value of my posses- sions. Should they rise as high as my hopes, which I may tell you are quite moderate, then I shall attempt a certain line of action. I will be dignified and well adapted to my circum- stances. If, however, disappointment awaits us, and these things prove of less value than they appear, I shall be pre- pared to act differently—in a way not so agreeable, but equally dignified."

" When does your daughter take the doctor?"

Mr. Shillingford grew cloudy.

" Next year it will be, I suppose. To tell you the truth, Dunnybrig, as an old friend, and one for whom I feel very great regard and absolute trust—to tell you the truth, I have detected a shadow in that quarter—a little cloud no bigger than a man's hand, so to say."

" Nothing like the smell of money for bringing to light the cloven hoof. 'Tis the great curse of the world, Shillingford, that fallen man has lifted up this false standard and confused metal and value, so that cash be the measure of all. For what real value do money point to? Some of the powerfullest men this earth has ever known were powerless to gather money; and so the money-grubbing and money-worshipping world mistook their power for weakness, and turned its back on its best ! ''

" Most true," declared Mr. Shillingford. " I'm quite in agreement with you there. The need for money—represented by food and clothes and a roof over us—these paltry requirements have stood between the world and some of its most valuable people. Instead of escaping from such trifles, with minds free to serve the world usefully, all their energy and time is poured into a stupid task, which they are constitutionally unfitted to perform—namely, looking after themselves. I speak feelingly, for I might have been a much more useful man had I not been faced with enormous and quite unnecessary difficulties.''

To Gabriel's surprise, Mr. Dunnybrig laughed heartily at this amplification of his own views.

" Your point is good," he said, " but to apply it to yourself is funny—at least, so it strikes me. As to your greedy young doctor, be warned. And remember blood's not everything, even if it's anything. You're even worse than the people who put money first. For money, whatever you may say against it, be live stuff, and 'tis possible to turn it to good purpose and spend it in the name of the Lord; but birth and the blood of old, dead, doubtful men ! How you can cling to that, and praise a man's virtues only if he knows his great grand-father ! 'Tis not his ancestors mixed in a man that makes him; 'tis the work of the Potter we seek to find. There's only one sort comes true out of the world's kiln; and success depends on the moulding, not the mud.''

" In a measure, in a measure," admitted Gabriel; " but there's a great difference between mud and china clay. Nobody knows that better than the Potter, I'm sure. His material is adapted to His divine purpose, and He knows, if you do not, neighbour, that beauty is a higher thing than use. It is more difficult to be beautiful than useful, Dunnybrig, just as it is more difficult to make a beautiful thing than a useful one.''

" Now you're off on one of your rampages," answered Valiant, " so I'll leave you. But I say again that I'm exceeding glad of your good fortune—exceeding glad, indeed. The Lord pinches this man and eases t'other; but each getteth what is his proper due; and I'm very happy to think 'twas your turn for a crumb or two.''

CHAPTER LIII

GABRIEL SHILLINGFORD was jealous that the extent of his fortune should not become publicly known. From no desire either to exaggerate or understate the amount did he affect secrecy, but because he held the affair personal, and while punctilious about other people's business, expected his neighbours to treat him in the same way. But this they could never do. While the master avoided all that did not concern him, from instinct and principle, the majority of his acquaintance now found his good fortune the first topic in their mouths. According to their natures they approached the incident—some coarsely, some in a manner more delicate ; but approach it they all did. From Mary Hearn at the post-office, to Miss Tapper of " Genoa Villa "; from Nicky Glubb to the lord of the manor, the folk of the Vale discussed this remarkable discovery; and since the converse of that sardonic maxim, that we win something not sorrow from the troubles of our best friends, is true, it followed that something not joy haunted the minds of Widecombe when rumour credited Gabriel Shillingford with an immense access of riches. Certain people considered how to glean a little from this harvest; others, indeed, were content enough, since this accident meant their own money again; a few did honestly rejoice; and one was deeply interested to learn the results of her egregious performance.

She had not long to wait. There came a day when Mr. Shillingford arrived at Kingshead by appointment. He was on foot, and Sally Turtle opened the door to him.

" Missis have got a dreadful cold," she said, " but she'll see you, if you ban't feared of catching it."

" Not in the least," answered the visitor. Sally regarded him with a respect proper to his lifted fortunes, for she had very practical evidence of their magnitude. Then Gabriel went before the widow and found her with her head enveloped in flannel and her toes on the grate.

" 'Twas Bellaver Hunt Week," she explained. " I oughtn't to have gone, but I couldn't resist it, though I had a cold. And I got wet, and now I'm a wreck. Young Grenville saw me this morning."

" Don't talk," he answered. " I'll do the talking. If, however, you are not well enough even to listen, and don't

feel that your mind is in a state to weigh big propositions—
then I'll leave it for another time."

" I shall love to listen. And first, how is the baby? "

" Doing well. My grandson will be called Fabian Pomeroy
Fitz-Ralph. So far as one is in a position to say at his tender
age, he is a Shillingford, and not a Smerdon. But don't
misunderstand me. I respect the Smerdons profoundly, and
admire their qualities. Over this matter of the treasure they
have come out in a very dignified and self-respecting way.
You know Peter Smerdon's views, speaking generally. He is
not burdened with pride—either false or proper. He takes
with both hands all that is offered—on behalf of his large
family. Nothing that represents money is beneath him, so
that it comes honestly. Well, he has not so much as hinted
at the idea of participating in this windfall of heirlooms! I
confess the fact has much increased my regard for him. And
he will not regret his line of conduct. Naturally, everybody
within my own circle is going to participate in some small
measure. I design mementoes of the event in several quarters.
Not, of course, the heirlooms themselves, but——"

" Now *please* don't begin that! " she said. " Forgive a
friend—one to whom you and yours are very dear. There is
not the smallest necessity to do any such thing. A present to
Peter Smerdon I don't quarrel with, but don't, for goodness
sake, begin distributing gifts, as if you had found a diamond
mine in your back garden. After all, what is it? "

" To be accurate, it is almost exactly three thousand pounds.
I stand involved to the extent of rather more than a thousand,
and, after all obligations are cancelled, it appears that heirlooms worth at least fifteen hundred remain. And this brings
me to the matter uppermost in my mind. Will the maiden be
fetching in tea? "

" She will. I'll ring, and hurry her."

When the tea-things had arrived, and a dish of toast stood
upon the hearth, Gabriel continued :

" I have long been planning a very difficult letter."

" Another! " she said. " Oh, I did hope they were done
with."

" They are—they are, unquestionably—those involving temporal derangements of finance. But there are higher things.
I thought that I might reach this lofty altitude better in the
seclusion of my library and the company of my books. But—
no—something prompted me to come to you in person, and
speak as the spirit moved—so here I am. And now I must
embark upon an affair of the very greatest delicacy. I
approach it with the utmost diffidence, Louisa."

" Good heavens, Gabriel, you're not going to offer me anything? "

The question opened a short cut; but Mr. Shillingford never followed short cuts. He was never one to use a dozen words if he could spread his meaning over fifty.

" Our families have been intimate for two generations now. You knew my wife, and I knew your husband. Upon this foundation, and upon the still surer one of long descent on both sides, we have built up a very considerable friendship. During the summer of the year before last, Louisa, that friendship ripened, on my side, into love. I do not say that respect was swept away, because that would suggest something quite different from what I mean; but love arose in my mind for you, and other sensations were for the time being obliterated. I should say, perhaps, hidden, rather than obliterated. In fact, respect, and esteem, and admiration for your various unusual qualities—not unusual as scattered over womankind generally, but very unusual as all embodied in one woman. Well, these things are the foundations of my love for you. It rises upon your great and splendid qualities."

Mrs. Windeatt sneezed four times.

" Forgive me," she said. " I didn't do it on purpose. Don't stop. Your voice is very pleasant to me, and always was."

Mr. Shillingford regarded her with his solemn brown eyes.

" I'm sure nothing like what your voice is to me," he declared. " You have a most melodious voice—as a rule. To-day there is a quality in it that makes me feel shy, because it is so strange."

" It's only my hideous cold."

" Well," he continued, " when I found that I loved you, Louisa, I was naturally much perturbed. In secret I felt quite overcome about it, and I approached the prospect of paying court to you with an amount of animation and eagerness that surprised myself. Ten years rolled off me; but then I investigated the situation from a worldly point of view, and, I regret to say, the ten years rolled on to me again. In fact, such was my bitter disappointment, that another ten were added to the first. Because, while I was seized with this ambition—to place my heart at your feet and offer myself and my devotion to one I now dearly loved—there came the mortifying discovery that I was in no case to do so. I found, upon investigating my affairs, that they were in a most remarkable confusion. Things had happened that I had not anticipated, Louisa. Without going into details it is enough to assure you that I found myself quite debarred from what had become the greatest ambition of my life. Fired by this discovery, I set to work and performed mathematical prodigies—I did, indeed. But when I say ' prodigies ' you must not misunderstand me. I am a poor hand at figures, and what were prodigies to me proved child's play to my son-in-law, Whitelock Smerdon. Be that as it may, the result of our calculations was the same. All approach to the privilege of offering my life in your service, Louisa, was denied me. I had even become reconciled to the sorrow, though from the standpoint of that secret regret, all this business of debtor and creditor became very trivial and superficial. I took it lightly, because by the side of the real loss it appeared a very light matter. Then, at the eleventh hour, a hand from the grave is lifted and I come into my real patrimony! So, at least, I regard it. Under other circumstances I should have held the legacy as a sacred trust. But in my case it will prove necessary to relinquish rather more than a third of it. There remains, however, valuable property, and, even after a further sale of my private needs and requirements at Blackslade, when the creditors are paid off—even after that, you will still have exquisite works of art and personal ornaments with which the wife of the head of the house becomes endowed. In a word, to speak with a voice of heraldry, Louisa, if you would quarter the Windeatt palmer's scrip with my two urchins, or hedgehogs, I shall be a very proud person, and will do my humble best to make you a good husband and devoted friend as long as I live. The idea is, doubtless, a thunderbolt to you, and I only hope it won't complicate your chill. But I came to speak, and I have spoken."

Mrs. Windeatt sighed, and put out her hand to him.

" You dear, precious man! You've made—oh, such a happy woman of me! Don't—don't kiss me—you'll catch it! "

" I should like to catch it! " he said. " ' For better for worse.' I am proposing myself to be your helpmate, Louisa. I defy the cold! At times like these, when the mind is exalted with joy, and the heart beats high, and even the fire of youth flashes up from the embers—at times like these, when, greatly daring, one has greatly succeeded, one simply cannot catch a cold! You are a blessed creature, and if I cannot be the joy of your life—by reason of my natural gravity and a certain weight of mind, represented, I suppose, by the mantle of my ancestors—if I can't be all that you would have me, don't regard it as a fault; but remember the reason."

" You are all I would have you be, and I love you, and I wouldn't alter a hair in your dear head! " she declared.

" This is a great and beautiful moment, Louisa, and we shall neither of us forget it."

Mr. Shillingford actually had his arms round the lady, when Sally entered suddenly with another dish of toast. Mrs. Windeatt's eyes were shut, and her head in its flannels rested upon Gabriel's shoulder. He did not budge, but held her tightly and stared at Sally with majestic indifference. She deposited the toast, and was gone in a twinkling. Nor did she laugh when she returned to the kitchen. The solemnity of the thing that she had seen quite swept away any inclination to be amused.

Sally's presence passed without comment. She departed flushed and panting, for she herself was passing through emotional phases at this time, and when Gabriel Shillingford had taken his leave, Miss Turtle, deeming it a promising moment, spoke to her mistress while she cleared away the tea-things.

" 'Tis about Pancras Widecombe, the stonemason, ma'am," she said. " And if you'll be so good as to speak a word of advice to me, I shall be cruel obliged."

" What about him, Sally? Nothing but good, I'm sure. He can do everything—but sing."

Sally winced.

" We've been keeping company for a good bit," she answered, " and we've understood each other very well, I believe, along of thinking alike on most subjects. And now there's no doubt as I began to love him, and I hope you'll not think the worse of me for so doing."

" Certainly not," said Mrs. Windeatt. " I should think he was a most lovable young man."

" He is, ma'am; that lovable you'd never guess to look at him. Then come the beastly concert, and all the world was against him, and instead of thanking the man and clapping him for doing his best—poor though it might be—the people was rude and vulgar and hateful about it. And now they pretend, when the wind shouts in the chimley, or there's a pig being killed, or a cartwheel wants grease, or one thing and another, that 'tis Pan trying to sing. Well, that was my opportunity, ma'am, and I comforted the man with all my power, and consoled him against everybody, and said a lot of clever things just suited to his frame of mind at the time."

" Ah! If we women only knew it, Sally, a man who has lost his self-respect is the easiest prey. Recover that for him, and nothing's too good for us! "

" That's why he offered himself, no doubt, ma'am. Yes,

now nought will do but he marries me—death on it, he is! He haven't got the grand and solemn and gentlemanly ways of Mr. Shillingford—excuse me, ma'am, but I can't help having eyes, though I turned 'em into my head when I see what was going on—but for dash and fire there never was anything like him. And now I be feared of my life at what I've done."

"As for Mr. Shillingford, he has asked me to be his wife, Sally, and I have consented."

"Wish you joy, I'm sure, ma'am. Pan says that he comes of fine havage, and his relations, back along, owned all Widecombe Vale and round about. And the King of England couldn't have put his arm round you in a more lordly and loving way, I'm sure, ma'am. But my Pan—so to call him—though I haven't said the word——"

"Go away, Sally; I want to think," declared Mrs. Windeatt. "We're a pair of very fortunate women, and so all's said."

"And your gentleman and my chap—'tis strange, but there it is. Pan found they countless jools hid in the old barn, and such was Mr. Shillingford's great joy, that he up and gave Pan fifty pounds for his day's work! You'd never believe it—a year's wages in a day! And that's why Pan be at me like a tiger now, and won't take ' no ' for an answer."

"Marry him, then—and you shall have twenty-five to add to his fifty."

"Lor, ma'am! "

"And now mend the fire and leave me alone."

Sally, agitated to the soles of her feet, withdrew, and her mistress considered the mighty event of the day.

She was sad, and pretended to wonder why. But where a woman really loves, she cannot deceive with impunity. Her spirit must suffer for it—if she possesses any distinction of character. Louisa had won what she wanted, but the price was not represented by Sheffield plate and trinkets. She found that the bill had yet to be paid, and that she was the beggar now. In the excitement of the sport she had reckoned without her host: her own loyal and straightforward instincts.

CHAPTER LIV

CONSIDERABLE strength of purpose, but much crudity of design marked the operations of Doctor Hugh Grenville at this season. Those of his environment were not, however, able to judge of his enterprise until after the event, and he flattered himself that in the one quarter vital to success all promised hopefully. What others might think, when he had won his way, mattered nothing to him. It remained only to make Tryphena Harvey see with his eyes, and her simplicity of mind offered no apparent obstacle. He proceeded gaily, therefore, without the wit to mark that a simple mind is often the most difficult to achieve. She trusted him; she had pleaded secretly for him with Petronell; and now, though Mr. Shillingford's daughter went in doubt, Tryphena still strove to convince her that Grenville was faithful and true. No shadow remained between the girls, and Petronell knew well enough that Tryphena was incapable of deceit. But Grenville mistook Miss Harvey's frank friendship for personal interest, and her gratification at his attention for awakening love. He did not recognise that she held him for ever committed and sealed to another woman; or that her ready acquiescence would have vanished instantly at the first shadow of truth. Neither did he guess that Tryphena had pleaded for him behind his back with Petronell, and sought to calm her fears with honest, if mistaken, assurances that they were groundless. He proceeded, blinded by his own vanity, and now, judging the time to be ripe, invited Tryphena to one of the little picnics he was fond of giving. He implied that Petronell would also be there.

She consented, and, since the entertainment was for the day after the invitation and the hour an early one, he judged that no meeting between the girls need be feared. For Petronell was not in reality asked to the picnic, and had no part in it. Tryphena, however, consented, when the doctor brought his proposal in person to Southcombe.

The time was nine o'clock, and Grenville spent the following hour with the Coakers. Elias liked him little, but the other was unaware of it. He chatted now on indifferent subjects, but avoided Blackslade and all to do therewith. William Coaker strove to turn talk upon the Shillingfords and their fortune, but the visitor would not be drawn. He declared that he knew nothing of the matter, and that all particulars concerning it were hidden from him. The assertion surprised his hearers, and they continued to ask questions until Grenville, with an appearance of sadness, and in a troubled voice, begged them to desist.

"There are good reasons why I should not discuss the subject," he said. "It is a painful one."

He was apparently in low spirits, and by no means the dashing and entertaining young man to whom Tryphena had grown accustomed.

When he departed, she entered into some dispute with Elias concerning him, and supported Hugh Grenville against her cousin. She conquered, but only because the man would not bring forth private arguments known to himself alone.

Elias had met Petronell a week before, and their ways lying together, had walked beside her for a mile. They were good friends, and he had perceived that she was not a happy woman. She had spoken generally, named no names and specified no troubles; but her eyes were clouded and her mind suffered from secret irritation. She had said hard things of life in general, and congratulated Elias on remaining single. Asked of her own marriage, she had declared the date not fixed and changed the subject. She had mentioned Grenville's name, but in connection with Tryphena. He had marked a sub-acid flavour about her outlook, and it had taken him back to their own quarrel years before.

But this meeting, though it meant a good deal to Elias, he did not mention to Tryphena Harvey. He merely repeated an old opinion, that Grenville was not worthy of Petronell, and declared that if the doctor found himself troubled in mind, the fault was doubtless his own. To which his cousin replied that the doctor was a man of fine intellect and a great thinker.

"He comes down to our level because he knows that we can't rise up to his," she declared. "He laughs and chaffs with all of us; but only with Petronell is he really deep and serious, because her mind can understand him. No doubt to-night he has deep things to think about—difficult cases, and so on. It will be rest and distraction to him to take Petronell and me for a picnic. We meet at the stone on Hameldon called 'The Blue Jug,' and then we shall roam away where he and Petronell please."

In truth, Grenville had been exceedingly busy before his evening visit to Southcombe, and elsewhere, earlier on the same day, things had happened which accounted for his pretended melancholy. When Mr. Shillingford returned from Kingshead, engaged to be married, his great achievement actually escaped his memory before the shock that awaited him. It was Sibley who broke the news.

" That Grenville—that cowardly, cruel wretch! " she said. " He came here after you had gone out—watched you off, no doubt, and then—Petronell—he's jilted her! She's felt it coming a long time, and so have I; and a week ago, when she was with me alone, I begged and prayed her to take the first step and throw him over before he had time to drop her. But she said there were two reasons against that. Firstly, because she felt sure that was what he wanted her to do, and secondly— but that's private, and happened long ago. I can't tell you that, father, though a very good reason, too, from Petronell's point of view. So she waited—poor darling creature, like a sheep in the slaughter-yard, for him to choose his own time. And now he's done it and thrown her over. Talked a lot of rot about poverty, and not binding her to share a pauper's home, and so on. Tried to the last to make her say the word, so that he might pose as the wronged one; but she wouldn't do that. And now she's all to pieces, and ought to see a doctor—not him—the hateful rascal, but another."

Mr. Shillingford stared at his daughter. For a moment there was silence. Then her baby began to cry, and he looked at the child.

" I'm sorry you've let this affair work you up into such a flurry," he said, " because it will be bad for Fabian. However, who could help it? There has always been a suspicion in my mind since he made a cheap joke about his coat of arms. He must answer for this to an insulted father. Where is Petronell? "

" She begged me to tell you that she would see you presently. She will be better later on. Leave her quite alone for a time."

" Give her some brandy and water and tell her to go to bed," said Mr. Shillingford. " I will see her presently. This is a very dreadful thing, and I am suffering, Sibley. That a Shillingford should be called to lift his hand against a Grenville! And yet! I take comfort in this : the man is no true Grenville. The descendant of Sir Richard, of Sir Theobald and of Sir Bevil Grenville—the man who has the blood of Rollo, Duke of Normandy, in his veins—could never have done this thing."

Gabriel then sent for his riding-horse, donned breeches and gaiters, selected a heavy hunting-crop, and set forth to avenge himself in the old way. He did not pause to consider the difficulties or the impropriety of pitting himself against a young and active man. His duty seemed quite clear, and he rode to do it to the best of his powers. It is a fact that his personal affairs did not once intrude upon his mind during the ride to Woodhayes. Arrived, he dismounted, made fast his horse, and inquired for Hugh Grenville; but Emma Hawke, who answered the avenger's knock, reported that the doctor was not in. Neither could she give any account of his movements.

" I'll ask my husband if he knows," she said, " but I doubt if he does. The doctor comes and goes, and 'tis as much as I can do to get him hot meals when he cries out for 'em. I hope after Miss Petronell have got him in hand she'll make him more orderly."

Young Harry Hawke could throw no light on Grenville's movements, and the outraged father withdrew. He sought the doctor in various quarters, but failed to find him; then, feeling that he was hungry and thirsty, he returned home, to eat and drink, and comfort his child if it might be done.

She was composed, however, and in the course of their conversation told Mr. Shillingford a secret from the past, which was absolute news to him.

" Sibley has told you how for two reasons I would not throw over this man, as soon as I saw he wanted me to throw him over," began Petronell. " The first reason she gave you, father; the second she couldn't, because it was private. But you must know it. I *did* throw over a man once. I was engaged to him, and then he did what seemed a wrong thing; and I was younger than I am now, and I flung him over. Of course it was wicked of me to be engaged at all without letting you know; but I was paid out. It doesn't matter who it was. But having thrown over one man, I couldn't throw over another. It's very dreadful, but since it had to be, I must suffer it. Only how I can creep into the world again and go on living I don't know yet."

He consoled her, and strove to cheer her, by showing that it was far better to be free than bound to a dishonest vagabond.

" You would have been called upon to suffer sad things at his hand, and even the name of Grenville would have been too dearly bought in such a quarter. I may tell you that I visited Woodhayes on purpose to let the rogue know how I viewed his conduct and feel my anger. But he was out, and his punishment is delayed."

" I'd punish him very differently," said Sibley. " I'd have the law of the wretch and make him pay damages for breach of promise. I'd squeeze him, and his mother and everybody that belonged to him. I'd make a laughing-stock and an example of him for everybody to see and jeer at from one end of the county to the other."

" No, no," answered Gabriel. " We can't fight like that. In fact, fighting between him and us is out of the question. We fight our equals; our inferiors we can only chastise if they earn it."

They talked until a late hour, and then came an unexpected visitor in shape of Samuel Sweetland. It was past eleven o'clock when he arrived in a state of most genuine and genial excitement. He flung off his great coat and a silken muffler. He shook them all by the hand. His voice ran up into his head and broke and squeaked, as it always did in moments of supreme emotion and excitement. He steadied it with a lozenge.

" I couldn't sleep—I couldn't say my prayers and close my eyes without coming among you," he said. " For doubtless I be the first living soul among your friends to hear of this great and slashing news. A thunderbolt to me, though my wife and sister took it very cool, and weren't over and above amazed."

Mr. Shillingford stared, Petronell hastily left the room, and Sibley made a short answer.

" 'Tisn't a time for other people to intrude upon us," she said; whereupon Samuel turned pink and his drooping underlip trembled.

" ' Intrude '? That's a strange word. Can't an old friend and near neighbour wish you joy without intruding? "

Then Whitelock Smerdon spoke.

" It may be a joyful thing in disguise, and I believe it is so, but that's not your affair, anyway, and you must know surely that it's brought great pain and grief to one woman."

" 'Pain and grief ! ' " cried Samuel—" 'pain and grief,' you say? And to the woman? Then why the mischief did she take him? Be I hearing aright, or have my ' night-cap ' got in my head? My man Johnson gets from young Pancras Widecombe, who has it from Sally Turtle, who gets it from Louisa Windeatt, that she's engaged to be married; and then, in my sporting way—always ready to recognise other people's good luck—I rush in here about it and find you all sitting as glum as mutes at a funeral ! "

" What's Mrs. Windeatt's affairs got to do with us, at a sad time like this? " asked Sibley; whereupon Mr. Sweetland flushed to a very sunset colour with fiery indignation, and looked round for his coat and scarf.

" Damn ! " he said, " and damn again; and if you think to return civility with rudeness, Sibley Smerdon, I tell you you're no lady ! 'Tis all over the church-town that your father has offered for Widow Windeatt and that she's took him; and then, when I come in this house to rejoice with those that rejoice, according to my custom, you ask me, with a voice all lemon, what it's got to do with the Blackslade people. 'Tis flat impertinence, and I won't endure it.''

Sibley and her husband, now little concerned with the angry master of Tunhill, fixed inquiring eyes on Gabriel—to find him very nearly as rosy as Mr. Sweetland. For a moment he spoke not; but exhibited the very depths of embarrassment. Then he arose and arrested Samuel, who was blowing foam from his mouth, like a spirited steed, and endeavouring to struggle single-handed into his overcoat.

"Stop!" he said. "Stop where you are, my dear Sweetland. This is quite the most extraordinary thing that has happened. I can, however, explain it in a moment."

"I shan't stop unless your daughter apologises," said the other. "I'm a lot put about by such treatment—especially from her. Who sent a bunch of lilies-of-the-valley, costing eighteen pence, when your child arrived, Sibley Smerdon; and who sent to inquire if all was well with you for a week after you was brought to bed? I'm very much hurt, and my wife——"

"List to me," interrupted Mr. Shillingford. "We are at cross-purposes, Samuel, and a very few words will clear up all. To-day—about half-past four, or it might have been five —I offered marriage to Louisa Windeatt, and was accepted. It was a great event, and naturally I came home to tell my daughters all about it. And I thank you warmly for your friendly and swift congratulations, Sweetland. You are the first—the very first. Yes, before my own children, you come to wish me well. And why? Because they didn't know it."

"You didn't tell 'em when you came home, Shillingford? That beats belief!"

"You'd think so; but strange things happen, and our days are made up of cloud and sunshine. I came to Blackslade about as well content and thankful as a middle-aged man can ever hope to be; but what did I find? I found that Hugh Grenville had thrown over my Petronell. Think of the fearful shock! Needless to say it drove my own good fortune entirely out of my head."

Mr. Sweetland, much mollified, made answer.

"In that case, I can see with half an eye that I came at the wrong time. There are not many quicker witted men than me about, when it's a matter of knowing when I'm wanted. My ladies will tell you that. So now I'm off. This news must soak into your own family first. I quite see under what circumstances it was withheld from them; and as all your minds were full of such a disgraceful thing, of course Sibley fired up when I rushed upon you with my mouth full of joy. However, enough said. But this I will say : that I saw her good points —Widow Windeatt's—long afore you did, Shillingford. I read a good wife in that woman years and years agone, and wondered who the man would be."

" Will you have a drink before you go? " asked Whitelock; but Mr. Sweetland refused.

" Not to-night—another time. My good manners take me off as quick as may be. And you tell Sibley that I quite forgive her, and hope she's forgiven me. I've always mistrusted that man—Grenville, I mean. Held his nose too high, and went about among us a bit too big for his shoes."

He hastened off, cackling even to the outer gate; and when Mr. Shillingford came back to the house, it was to run into his daughters' arms and enjoy their kisses on either cheek. Petronell felt especially uplifted, for she experienced a martyr's joys and the bitter-sweet of rejoicing at another's happiness, while her own lay in ruins. The matter indeed happened opportunely for her, because this event in her father's life and all that it represented, could not fail to distract her thoughts from her own bereavement; while as for Sibley and Whitelock, they—with their babe between them—were awake in deep discussion of the future until the day had broken.

CHAPTER LV

GRENVILLE had planned his meeting with Tryphena that she might certainly come to him before the knowledge of his previous day's work could reach her. He wanted to be the first to tell her of his broken engagement, and intended that she should leave home and climb Hameldon before news of the event at Blackslade could arrive at Southcombe. This indeed happened, and fortune so far favoured the faithless doctor that he was able to give his own version of the catastrophe and seek to create a particular impression.

She started early, skirted the heights, proceeded nigh Kings-

head, and presently rested upon a stone above the woodlands
that fledge the eastern foothills of the mount.

The true mosaic of the forest patchwork, invisible at high
noon, appeared in the early morning hour. Each pine made
a tower of gloom in the lustrous groves; each budding birch
shone like a jewel of emerald set in the hanging woods. The
ridges and planes of the forest had not yet merged and swum
together. They discovered play and interplay of light thrown
horizontally; while the cloud shadows also swept their undula-
tions and exposed, under their purple passing, many a delicate
tracery and balanced harmony of the tree-tops that the glittering light concealed. Presently, as the sun ascended, the inter-
woven shadows, thrown by his earlier beams upon the crown
of the wood and the surface of the ferns and boulders, vanished
away and, under the more direct downward beat of his glory,
these magic passages were no more seen.

Tryphena marked the beauties of the morning, for she was
afoot very early, and, indeed, found herself an hour ahead of
the appointed meeting time. Nor did she await Hugh Grenville at the boundary stone of " The Blue Jug," as he had
directed. She knew the goyle whence he would climb up to
Hameldon from Woodhayes, and, taking her seat upon a stone
beside the track, waited contentedly with her eyes now bent
upon the woods beneath her, now lifted to the neighbouring
heights of Honeybag and Chinkwell upon the other border of
the Vale.

As for her thoughts, they were divided between Petronell and
her betrothed on the one side, and her own affairs upon the
other. For a great event threatened her. The solicitors were
of opinion that it would be highly desirable for Tryphena presently to visit Australia. The need and its objects were to be
explained to her at length in a month or two hence; but it
seemed, in the opinion of those responsible for her affairs, that
this course should be taken. Her uncles at Exeter were of the
same mind. She felt helpless before such an enterprise, and
wondered who would go with her. The idea of so long a
journey alone bewildered her, even alarmed her. The inevitable was happening, and life in Widecombe began to make her
parochial. This indeed had been observed by her father's
brothers at Exeter. It seemed to them, in conference with Mr.
Blatchford, the solicitor's clerk, that Tryphena must be weaned
away from the Vale at an early opportunity and before her
heart was lost. Once separated for a season from her mother's
people, the Harveys of Exeter guessed that she would begin
to take a wider outlook and win experiences and acquaintance
better suited to her future happiness than might be furnished

at Widecombe. They held it only fair to her that she should see a little of the world and the people therein. They judged that she must labour under disadvantages at Southcombe, and be debarred from that wider knowledge and enlightenment which her handsome fortune ought now to be commanding. There existed very sufficient reasons why she should visit Australia, and her father's brothers proposed to insist upon that course.

Tryphena hoped that the suggested journey might at least be postponed. Her first thought had been a companion, and to this proposal her paternal uncles raised no objection.

Grenville sighted the girl as he ascended, presently, from the valley. They surprised each other, for he had not expected to see her here, and she did not suppose he would have been alone. He welcomed her warmly, divested himself of a heavy knapsack which contained one of his famous lunches, and sat beside her a few moments to rest before they proceeded.

" Where's Petronell? " was her first question.

His face fell and he sighed.

" I'll tell you presently, Tryphena. In fact, I'm here to tell you. Wait a little while. You shall hear all about it soon enough."

" She's not ill? "

" Oh, no, she's all right—or I shouldn't be here. The patients, too, will have to whistle till we go back again. But there's nobody to trouble about. I mean, I wish that my practice here was larger and more prosperous. I do what I can; but there is so little to do. It was a mistake coming."

" You can never say that. Think of Petronell."

He sighed and changed the subject.

" This is the day of my life—a day great with my fate, Tryphena. I felt superstitious when I woke up; but the dawn seemed to be of a good omen—so bright and clear it was."

He did not tell her of Mr. Shillingford's visit on the preceding evening, or of his message that he proposed to call again at an early hour on the following day. Yet, as he spoke to her, the figure of Gabriel on his riding-horse could be marked by Grenville's quick eyes, proceeding leisurely through the valley far beneath—bound doubtless for Woodhayes.

" Let us start," he said, rising and turning his back on the Vale.

He shouldered the knapsack and set off as Tryphena spoke.

" Tell me why Petronell isn't coming. I specially wanted her to come. A great thing has happened to me. It looks as if I might have to make a voyage to Australia about my money. I don't want to go a bit; but if I've got to go, I should hate to do it all alone. And that's what I wanted to talk to Petronell about."

He was interested instantly. His sanguine and audacious soul pictured a most delightful sequel to his own affairs.

"To tell you why Petronell isn't coming is the whole business of this picnic," he said. "I knew she wasn't coming, yesterday."

"You made me think she was, Hugh."

"Did I? Not intentionally. But leave it for a moment. Just let me breathe a little of the Moor air, and think. I am in a good deal of trouble, Tryphena."

"Then Petronell must be, too."

"I don't know as to that. But—leave it for the moment. You are so swift in sympathy and understanding that I do believe everybody in Widecombe who knows you tries to come to you if they are in trouble."

He spoke on and strove to turn her mind from Petronell; but he failed. She pressed to know what was the matter, and when he said that she should hear everything after their luncheon, she proposed hastening the meal and getting it over as quickly as possible.

"As you please," he said. "God knows I have little enough appetite to-day, and I'm as anxious to tell as you are to hear. The whole of my future life depends on what this day may bring forth. We'll not tramp to 'The Blue Jug.' We'll stay here, above Nutsworthy."

He hoped that his luncheon would please Tryphena, and, indeed, it did, but she was in no mood to eat. Perceiving, therefore, that he was to trust to his wits as swiftly as possible with her, he set forth on the tale of his estrangement from Petronell, and described it with some histrionic art.

"To you, of course, it comes like a lightning flash," he said. "I can picture with what a shock it falls on you, Tryphena, because you have got into the way of thinking that Petronell and I were one in every hope and ambition. But, as a matter of fact, I grieve to say this hasn't been so for a very long time. We are both infernally proud, as you know, so we both hid our troubles from the world; we even hid them, or tried to hide them, from one another. But we couldn't hide them from ourselves, and at last, by a sort of mutual understanding, we felt that it was better and braver to have it out than let it go on smouldering and hurting, and making our hearts sore and bitter and wicked."

"Good heavens! You've quarrelled with her?"

"No, no, no—far from that, far from that. We are both dignified and could not sink to mean recriminations. We have never quarrelled, Tryphena. We couldn't quarrel. That happens to a different sort from us. But we have had to face sad facts; we have had to analyse our feelings and to cross-question each other pitilessly. We were cruel to each other—but only to be kind. We felt of late that the ground was slipping from under us, that our values and principles and even our religious opinions were not quite the same. Again and again we caught ourselves arguing. Then we looked into each other's faces in pain, and fell into silence. I can't tell you how the rift began, or what deep difference in our points of view explains it; but there it is, and for the last six months it has been going deeper. And yesterday, before I came to see you, we talked it out to the bottom, and we decided that it would be better far to part with mutual esteem while yet there was time to do so, and before all affection vanished. Love, of course, had vanished long, long ago; and though we could only confide it to our own hearts, we had secretly felt for months—each of us—that we could not marry each other. And each was a little cowardly, perhaps, and waited for the other to take the first step. But it was the man's part, of course. Yet, such was Petronell's quick understanding, that she spared me any unnecessary torture. We have parted, Tryphena. Friends we shall always be, I hope; but we have recognised that deep differences of feeling and conviction upon the most serious subjects would always come between us; and, that being so, we must agree to let our engagement be a thing of the past."

The listener was much bewildered.

" Poor Petronell ! " she said. " Poor—poor Petronell ! What on earth am I doing up here with you, when I ought to be comforting her? "

" A natural question, and I can answer it. Yesterday, when I left her, my heart brimmed over with grief for her and for myself. It was a cruel trick of fate—a terrible, shattering thing to crash into two lives. As if my future was not sad and grey enough without this climax ! But something led me straight to you, Tryphena. Somehow out of that great cloud of sorrow came light; and you stood in the light. For you had been so much to both of us. And my spirit craved and called out for you, and would not be put off until I had seen you. I came to tell you what I have told you now. I felt I could not sleep until I had your sympathy. For this is far worse for me than dear Petronell."

" How? " she asked.

" I can't tell you. You understand everything, so you'd understand that, too. But I'm nothing if not loyal. Time will show what I mean. I came, I say, to tell you last night, but you were not alone, and I could not speak."

He grew vague and rhetorical. He strove to move her, and he succeeded. He struck a sentimental note and affected much manly resignation under his great trial. He warmed up Tryphena presently, for she was by nature emotional; she had known the man and enjoyed his friendship and courtesies. She rated him highly and did not yet guess at the truth. Now her sympathy inclined him along the path he desired to take. For some time he delayed, until a decent interval of near two hours separated him from his confession, then he felt the moment had arrived, revealed the truth of himself, and made a great mistake—an error that had been impossible to any man not very vain and very foolish.

" You mesmerise me, Tryphena," he said, sighing deeply. " You exercise a curious fascination—mesmeric without a doubt. I have observed it before; and now, as I come to you a free, lonely, heart-broken man, I am more than ever conscious of it. You're not angry? "

" Why should I be? I'm only so very, very sorry for you both."

" Tryphena, listen! What I'm going to say is torn out of me by some force stronger than myself. It is, indeed. There is a terrible power in you that you exercise over me. It has grown stronger and stronger. Now, your words of sympathy, the look in your wonderful cloud-coloured eyes, the very way you hold your hands so nervously together—all these signs—I can't go on——"

" Do, dear Hugh—if I can help you. I want to help you as well as Petronell. Nobody in the world will be sorrier for you both than I am."

" Leave Petronell. She has many and powerful friends. She will soon be distracted. Life is full of happiness and rich promise for her. But I am alone—alone in the world without a friend, without one to care for me—alone with my wrecked life and only you—you, little Tryphena, to understand and drop a tear for me."

" I do understand, I think. I would rather bring you and Petronell together than anything else in the world. I would give her all my money if that would do it."

" Ah! how like you—you generous, large-hearted girl! No—all is well with her, Tryphena—have no care or sorrow for her. Think of me—think of me, if you can, as one who—who has long known that he has erred terribly in this matter of his engagement. When first I saw you, I knew it, Tryphena. It is sudden to you, but not to me. When I first saw

you—at a school treat in Lady Land Field—you know—I said :
' There, or nowhere, is my life! ' I went home in a dream.
I did not close my eyes for three nights. You must hear—
for if you cannot feel what I have felt—if what I am saying
does not waken something like a similar confession from you
—then my life is ended. Don't drag in Petronell. Don't misunderstand the situation at this vital moment. She and I
had parted in spirit long, long ago. Yesterday was only the
final statement and declaration of that parting. We had
drifted a million miles apart more than half a year ago; and,
for all I can tell, she feels as I do—that her life and her
salvation must now be given into another's keeping. She may
know the actual man."

He paused.

Tryphena had dropped her hands into her lap and sat
staring at him, as though her eyes would never shut again.

" I love you—only you, Tryphena. I worship you—without
you I cannot go on living. You are my life. Don't look at
me as if I was some far-off thing—beyond your ken. I am
near, a passionate, adoring man—humble, faithful, eager to do
good in the world, smitten with a frantic worship for the
only woman——"

" Stop—stop ! " she cried. " What do you think I'm
made of? You wicked creature! Me—me—instead of
Petronell! You—you thing! Oh, I shall hate every man in
the world for evermore after this! And I don't believe a word
of it—not a word. I don't believe that Petronell doesn't care.
Do you think I've been her friend for nothing all this time?
D'you think when she quarrelled with me about you, after the
concert, that I didn't make everything clear as light? And
didn't I stand up for your honour and decency? And didn't
I convince her that she was wrong and make her happy again?
And now—this ! You stupid, vain wretch of a man ! "

She started up.

" Don't come a yard after me, or I'll scream so loud they'll
hear all down the Vale ! " she said. Then, panting with anger,
she hastened from him as fast as her long legs could carry her.

But he made no effort to follow her. He merely watched
her depart. Then he laughed at his failure and opened the
bottle of champagne that he had dragged along with him.

" And now the sooner I clear out of Widecombe the better
for my peace of mind," he said to himself. " If she'd loved
me by good luck, I could have stopped and bluffed. Since
she's off—I'd better be."

The defeated doctor descended from Hameldon presently;
but the adventures of the day were not yet done for him.

Tryphena, gasping with haste and indignation, sped home-ward, and it fell out that the first person she met was Elias Coaker, riding behind a dozen bullocks. Thankful for the outlet to her emotion she poured her story upon him; but the man did not instantly echo her wrath. He considered what she told him without immediate heat, and asked for particulars.

He dismounted, weighed the force of the narrative, and cross-questioned Tryphena, after bidding her cool down and collect herself.

" You're in a pretty fair rage, seemingly," he said, " but I can't exactly see on the face of it why you should be. It stands thus : Petronell and Grenville have parted; and, as a free man, he comes to you. He didn't leave much time and behaved like the everyday sort of cad he is; but what are you in such a deuce of a passion about? "

" That he could dare to part from Petronell at all."

" Well, as to that—I know Petronell pretty thoroughly. How did he put it—did Petronell chuck him? "

The girl considered.

" He talked a lot, but I didn't gather that he took the first step exactly, or that she did."

" It rather depends on that. You'll have to hear the other side. So far as you tell me, it was mutual. Well, I don't believe a thing like that is ever really mutual. One party, or else the other, feels they've made a mistake, and has to say so. In my case 'twas Petronell that made the mistake, and had to say so. Of course, if it was her that chucked him, then you, as her friend, had better shut up and say no more about it."

" I don't believe it for a minute," declared Tryphena. " I'm positive in my own mind that—but—no, I'm not positive about anything—except that I hate and loathe him."

" That's rum. Because a man can't pay a woman a greater compliment than by offering to wed her. But you've got money, so you'll be handicapped all your life where the men are concerned."

" Nonsense," she answered. " Your heart tells you very quick if a man wants you or your money. And that wretch wanted my money. I knew it, inside me, the moment he began. I liked him, mind you—I always liked him quite well until to-day. I thought a lot of him, and was proud for him to take me up and be so friendly. But that was because he loved my greatest friend, Petronell. And then the moment he came tinkering up to me—ugh! He made me creep, like those black, wriggly things you find under stones! "

" He's queered his pitch, I see," answered Elias. " Well, I

must get on. And what you've got to do be this : see
Petronell, or Sibley, and find out how 'twas. And tell me
to-night."

" I'll get over to them now," she said. " I'm on fire to see
her and hear about it. I believe it was all his hateful fault,
for the last time Petronell mentioned him, she felt pretty
happy about him."

" If he's treated her bad—then; but perhaps it's the other
way round."

" I don't believe it—I don't believe it for a moment. If
she'd thrown him over, would he have been cheerful as a
lark, picnicking with a bottle of champagne and all the rest of
it? I'll see her—she'll see me, I know, however it is with
her."

They parted, and before they met again, Tryphena had
looked into the sorrowful heart of Petronell and heard the
truth. Her own adventure of the morning she concealed. Her
difficulty on returning to Southcombe, was to believe that
Hugh Grenville could be sane.

This concatenation produced a meeting between Gabriel
Shillingford and Elias Coaker. On the evening of that day
the elder overtook the younger on his road up the Vale, for
Mr. Shillingford was riding, while Elias went on foot. It
transpired that both were bound for Woodhayes.

" There is no wish in my mind to conceal the thing I am
going to do," declared Gabriel. " Had I met Chave, or
Sanders, the constables, I should have been equally open.
I intend a breach of the peace. From one who may at any
moment be created a Justice of the Peace this must sound
startling; but circumstances alter cases, Elias, and there are
cases where a father feels called upon to take the law into
his own hands."

To the farmer's surprise this dark saying made his meaning
quite clear to the listener.

" You needn't tell another word," answered young Coaker.
" Now 'tis my turn, and I'm terrible glad we've met, Mr.
Shillingford, because I can save you a lot of trouble. I know
what's happened, and I'm on my way to take forty shillings
or a month out of that damned doctor myself."

" You are! What's he done to you? "

" He's done something to everybody in the Vale. A thing
like this is everybody's business, and mine more than most—
for one reason and another."

" You put me in a very difficult position, Elias," declared
the farmer.

" Not at all—you don't know your luck," answered the

younger. "He'll be in a fighting mood, if ever he was, and he's no respecter of persons, and, if you was to try and thrash him, he'd play on you like a penny whistle. You're a lot too old. 'Tisn't as if he'd stand still, like a schoolboy, and let you whack him; he won't do that. He'll hit back, and nature's nature, and he's twenty-five years younger than you, so you'll look silly."

Mr. Shillingford drew up his horse and considered.

"Righteous indignation is a good weapon in itself," he said.

"Nought against a disappointed man in a hell of a rage. More things have happened to Grenville than you know of, so you go home, Mr. Shillingford. 'Tis a very fine thing in you to want to wallop the scamp; but if you failed, and got knocked about yourself instead, you'd lose your dignity, and have to spend a month of Sundays done up in brown paper and vinegar."

"Nothing could well be more inconvenient than that just now," admitted Gabriel. "But I do not fear him. A father's arm—I called this morning and again this afternoon. He has been out all day. To-night he must surely be in—unless he's run away altogether."

"I'll tell you what he's been doing," said the other; "then you'll see 'tis just as much my business as it is yours. And I won't call it ' business,' neither. 'Twill be a proper pleasure to me; but pain and grief to you at best."

Elias told of the entertainment on Hameldon, and Mr. Shillingford grew rosy with indignation, and made answer:

"I admit Tryphena has been insulted, and that it is your place to represent her; but you must understand that I do not recognise you are doing this so much on her account as on mine. I am condoning a legal fault, instead of committing it —that is the sole difference—if I depute you, Elias, to take my place in a certain act of retaliation, which I might not possibly be able to effect with such completeness as I would wish. I shall answer to the law for you in any case. The honour of a woman is at stake."

"I shan't forget that. 'Tis for two women you may say that I'm doing it. He's insulted my cousin as well as your daughter. But 'tis for Petronell, before all else, that I'll lay on to him, and you can tell her so."

"I confess this turn of events has made me very uneasy," declared Shillingford. "To execute justice oneself, fired to do so by a righteous anger, is one thing; but to let cold judgment intervene, and employ a—a fighting man—a myrmidon."

He stopped, for Hugh Grenville had come round the corner

of the lane along which Shillingford rode beside young Coaker. The doctor saw them approaching, hesitated, and then proceeded. It was he who challenged.

" I know you want to talk, Mr. Shillingford, and I'm quite ready to talk. But not at this moment—to-morrow I'll wait upon you."

" I don't want to talk. I have come——"

" To see fair play," interrupted Elias. Then he faced Hugh Grenville.

" Get out of your hat and coat," he said. " I'm here to give you a hiding, and you can fight or take it lying down—which you please."

" You'd better mind your own business," replied Grenville. Whereupon Elias knocked the other's hat off and kicked it into the hedge.

" Don't talk," he said. " Put 'em up and have a run for your money. You've earned a darned sight more than you'll get at worst."

But Grenville was not a fighter.

" If I must run I must," he answered coolly; and darted back the way he came. On foot he was swifter than Elias; but Gabriel's horse could gallop faster.

" Head the coward off! " cried young Coaker, and Mr. Shillingford prepared to do so. He thundered after the flying doctor and stopped his progress.

" For such as you, corporal punishment is a seemly and proper thing," he declared. " Coaker is going to put you to some personal discomfort; but well within the scope of humanity. You deserve——"

As he spoke, Elias arrived, and, since Grenville would not fight, the other took him by the collar and flogged him with the ash-sapling he carried.

The physician endured his punishment in silence, and Gabriel, who watched the operation without emotion, presently intervened.

" That will suffice, Elias. You cannot do more. I am prepared to bear witness, and, should he go to law, I can say that the punishment was temperate and reasonable."

Not a single word spoke the sinner. When released he dusted himself, fastened his collar, which had broken loose, and walked back down the road for his hat.

" Now he can doctor himself for once," said Elias. " Did you ever see a worm on a hook that hadn't more fight in it than him? 'Twas like thrashing a sack of oats."

" He will probably endeavour to have the law of you—

indeed, of us both," declared Gabriel. "And I hope he will, for then his name will resound as it deserves to do."

"He won't have the law of us," declared the other. "Not if I know him. He'll bolt—that's what he'll do. I understand his sort. They ban't built to face the music. He's a trundle-tail cur, and the wonder is that a maiden like Petronell didn't see through him and send him packing long since."

"I beg you will return with me and hear me relate what has happened," answered Gabriel. "We must have our facts in order and be under no confusion. He will tell a story to the police, and very possibly exaggerate, as is the way with beaten men."

"I tell you you can trust him to keep his mouth shut," repeated Elias. "There's lots like him about. Very brave with the women, but they curl up like a woodlouse if a man tackles 'em."

Several hours later, while he lay awake calmly rubbing his bruises with arnica, Doctor Grenville heard himself summoned, and the voice of Jack Mogridge came up the pipe which ascended from the door of Woodhayes to his bedroom.

It was after midnight, and Grenville had completed his packing. No serious case occupied his attention, and there was nothing to delay departure. He had indeed arranged with Young Harry Hawke to drive him to Bovey at dawn.

"Please sir," cried Jack, "I be come hell for leather from 'Genoa Villa.' The maiden was sent out for me, and roused me from my bed to run for you, because Miss Tapper's internals be rioting, and she's mindful how her father went, and reckons 'tis terrible likely she's plucked for death."

"Tell her to go to hell!" responded the medical man. "And go after her yourself! I'm not practising any more!"

Jack stared into the night at this dreadful speech. He had heard nothing of the day's work.

"'Tis very much against your good manners to send such a message to the sick," he said boldly; "but I'll take it, and I'll tell her. And it did ought to kill her or cure her, I'm sure."

A great thought inspired Jack on the homeward way, and he stopped at Patience Leyman's little dwelling and knocked up the schoolmistress. She looked out from her bedroom window upon him.

"You must forgive it, miss," he said, "for it have been put in my head all of a sudden. The doctor won't come to Miss Tapper, and she's expecting to die at any moment, and there's none with her but my wife and a know-nought fool of a maiden; so you may be saving   fellow-creature and covering yourself with glory if you'll come. And there'd be good money to it, if you saved her, I reckon; for she don't want to die if it can be escaped."

"I'll come," said the old woman. "You wait where you be for two minutes, and I'll be down house."

Soon they hastened together to "Genoa Villa."

CHAPTER LVI

MRS. MABEL GURNEY strolled over to the "Old Inn" that she might buy a bottle of spirits and an ounce of tobacco for her husband. Arthur was not in, however, therefore she made no long stay. Yet, leisure serving, Mabel desired speech with her fellow-creatures, so she dropped into the post-office before proceeding home. She found that Mary Hearn was primed with all the latest news. After a short struggle, in which each endeavoured to chatter the other down, Mrs. Gurney, being shorter of wind, was worsted; the post-mistress took the lead and kept it.

"'Tis properly bewildering I say to mother, how one thing follows another in this place. Surely there never was such another church-town as this be. 'Tis the march of events, Mabel Gurney; and everybody has a hand in 'em sooner or late. Everybody's catched up in the whirlpool, willy nilly, and you'll find the commonest, silly nobodies, without more brains than would cover a sixpenny-piece, playing their parts and catching the public eye in their turn."

"What's in the wind now?" asked the other. "Of course we come to you for the last and latest. No news ever misses the post-office."

Miss Hearn was gratified.

"The little birds will whisper to me," she said. "And the wind blows in my ear from all four quarters—I can't deny it. I ban't a poker, nor yet a pryer, but there 'tis—I don't miss nothing; and, what's more when I hear a thing, I know what it *means*. That's the secret! You, or another, might hear this or that, and 'twould be just news to you and no more, and you'd go your way none the wiser, in a manner of speaking; but with me, I see through the outer meaning to the inner meaning, and link up facts in a way that astonishes me myself sometimes. 'Twas I first gived out the match was off at Blackslade—not that anybody told me so, mind you. But the instant moment I heard that that Grenville was gone from Woodhayes, I put two and two together and knew that Petronell Shillingford was a left woman."

Mary beamed with triumph.

" Yes—he chucked her, and now 'tis whispered that her father flogged him afore he went off," said Mrs. Gurney.

" Wrong again. 'Twas Elias Coaker, William Coaker's son, that did it. And the very same night that vinegar cruet, Tabby Tapper, got ill—along of eating or drinking too much, I reckon —and sent for the doctor; and he told her to go and be damned. When I heard that I forgived the young man everything."

" She's very near well again—Thirza Tapper."

" I know—I know. Very likely never was ill. Just wanted Grenville to see the pink bows on her nightgown, I dare say. There's nothing she wouldn't sink to."

" She was ill all right. She's wasted to a thread-paper, and her voice be a thing of the past."

" So much the better, and long may it be so! If she was struck dumb, the Vale would be a peacefuller place than what it is. Tried to get me into trouble—the old hen-viper! And all she got for her pains was a printed answer that the matter should have attention. And, of course, the post-office didn't dare to lay a finger on me—well knowing I'd not brook a word."

But this was an ancient subject, and Mrs. Gurney changed it.

" They tell me Nicky Glubb's been drunk every night since the concert," she said.

" 'Tis true. 'Tis a great disgrace, and I be going to present it to our landlord and have him turned out of his house, and get respectable people there if I can. That rat-faced wife of his sneaks in here sometimes—all about nothing—and I don't like it. I shall be missing stamps or something some of these days. Then I've got my own troubles, too. You mind Mr. Dexter to Exeter—that great friend of mine with the beastly wife? Well, there's a proper tragedy there! "

" Be she dead at last, then? "

" Far from it. She's run away! You might have knocked me down with a feather. The artfulness! There was she, always after Adolphus, and as jealous as a hen with one chick, heading him off from everything in a petticoat ; and him champing the bit and wanting to expand and get a little sympathy; because he'd found, ever since I was there, that his wife wasn't the only pattern of woman in the world. And then, would you believe it! if *she* don't go off herself. What a world! A cabinet-maker's assistant in London 'twas—down to Exeter for his health—and Mrs. Dexter with only one lung, if the doctors know anything."

" Ah! " said Mrs. Gurney. " I set that fashion, and 'tis getting pretty common, seemingly. And I believe, in time to come, a shuffle of partners will be just as everyday a thing in life as 'tis in a dance. And, after all be said and done, what the deuce is life but a dance? Either short and merry or else plaguey long and slow."

" But Adolphus Dexter," continued Miss Hearn; " I confess to you that I'm in a proper twitter about that man, for he says 'tis very like he'll come down and see me afore he decides anything. And that means—well, who can say what it means? "

" He was always after you, wasn't he? " asked Mrs. Gurney.

" I don't know that he was *after* me," answered the other. " You can't tell what's at the back of their minds. But no doubt it was so, else what is he coming here about——? "

Another customer entered. It was Mrs. Coaker from Southcombe, and Miss Hearn fastened upon her instantly.

" What's this about your boy, Grace Coaker? 'Tis said he left the doctor for dead in the hedge, and——"

" I can't talk about it," answered the mother of Elias. " He took the law in his own hands and give Doctor Grenville a thrashing. He don't deny it, and he's ready and willing to abide by the results. He's waiting at home for Chave or Sanders to come in the name of the law at any moment; but so far they have not done so."

" And they won't," declared the postmistress. " 'Tis the doctor himself they'll be after, I should think. The last thing he done at Woodhayes, so Young Harry Hawke tells me, was to unscrew his plate off the front gate with his own hands. He's a goner—shot the moon, you might say—and, now he's gone, no doubt his patients will all get well, the few he had."

" 'Tis a cruel thing upon that young woman at Blackslade," said Mrs. Coaker; but Mary only laughed in her deep bass gurgle.

" They've got their new pots and pans to comfort 'em, though I dare say they ban't worth half they've given out. We shall see as to that when he pays his debts."

" And if the daughter can't get a husband, the father have found a wife, seemingly," added Mabel Gurney.

" And no doubt, trinkrums from under the ground or not,

Widow Windeatt will soon put him on his legs again," added Mary. " I hate the stuck-up nincompoop—Gabriel Shillingford, I mean. He comes in here in his grand way and never a friendly word or a bit of news."

" Why for did your boy scat the doctor, Grace? " asked Mrs. Gurney. " I can't see why he should have done it, though I'm very glad 'twas done."

" Somebody had to do it," explained the mother of Elias. " Mr. Shillingford set out to do it, but Elias fell in with him, and feeling that 'twasn't a vitty job for an old man, took it on himself."

Miss Hearn pursed her mouth, and looked unutterable things.

" There's more to that than you know yet, Grace. You wait and see if something don't come of that. It may be damaged goods, or it may not, but—well, I remember what happened back along, two or three years ago, perhaps. My memory be iron, thank God. It slips nothing. If I see a rat run across the road, I can call it back months after. And though you don't know it, and old calf-eyes don't know it—I mean Shillingford—and all the rest don't know it, I know it."

" You'm such a one for dark mysteries, Mary," answered Mrs. Coaker mildly. " What don't anybody know but you? "

" That your boy and somebody, as shall be nameless, was very good friends once, and perhaps they may be again I got it out of your niece long, long ago. That simple Tryphena. She little knew that I'd pumped her dry, and no doubt thought the secret was so safe with her as a bird in a bush; but I had it out! And I dare say it shows the woman I am that I never told a soul, but just kept my knowledge hid, according to my custom." '

" Good powers, Mary! D'you mean Mrs. Coaker's Elias and Petronell Shillingford——" cried Mabel Gurney.

" I do mean it. They kept company unbeknownst for a long time, and then they fell out. Tryphena knew."

" The puss! And never told me," exclaimed Mrs. Coaker.

" Why should she? She thinks the world of Elias, and if he told her his secrets and bade her not tell them again, be sure she wouldn't. 'Twas only my touch screwed it out of her. The people be clay in my hands, and 'tis a good thing for Widecombe that I ban't a disagreeable woman and a mischief-maker—else the place would get too hot to hold some of us very quick."

" Well—well—to think! " mused Mrs. Coaker.

" Think so much as you please, but say nothing," advised Mary. " I've thrown a light, as my way is, and that's enough

Your son took it out of Grenville, because the doctor had treated Petronell so shameful; but what his reasons were, and if he wants to be on the war-path again himself, I can't say— not yet. No more can I say if she'd look at him if he did. No doubt 'twill all come to my ears in fulness of time, and if I think you ought to be told anything, I shan't keep it from you. But don't you take any step, or let on as you know what it's all about. A still tongue makes a wise head."

"The wonder is that Elias don't go for his cousin," declared Mabel. "A bowerly girl she be, and pretty, and sweet as sugar, and rich as a gold-mine. Now, that would be a very clever bit of work, Grace—a clever bit of work for all of you, in my opinion."

"So it would," admitted Mrs. Coaker, "and I don't say I shouldn't have liked for it to happen, because I should. And the teasing thing about it is—I'm among friends and it won't go further—but the aggravating thing to my mother's eye is just this. Tryphena—a sweet maiden and trustful as a robin— be very fond of Elias—real properly fond of him. She can't hide nothing—she didn't hide that. But he never wanted her."

They debated the mystery until another woman entered the post-office, and before the advent of Miss Harriet Sweetland, Mary assumed her most forbidding air and Mabel Gurney departed with Mrs. Coaker.

The latter had quite forgotten that she came for six penny stamps.

CHAPTER LVII

Now did Tryphena feel the weight of the world upon her shoulders and struggle gamely with the problems that beset her. Elias was the greatest. The affection that she felt for him by no means obscured her perception at any time, and the thing that now she set herself to do involved neither self-sacrifice nor any sort of heroism. But she guessed that it would be very difficult, and puzzled through sleepless nights how best to act. She wanted to bring Elias and Petronell together again. She longed to do it; above all things she desired before leaving Widecombe to know that her cousin and Petronell understood and loved each other once more. Tryphena, also, wanted Mr. Shillingford's younger daughter to come with her to Australia, and indeed intended that she should do so; but a greater thing by far was Elias, and the question centred on this. Could the man and woman be brought together inside the six months that still separated her from her voyage?

She thought it not impossible, and began to bring her cousin into her conversation with Petronell. With Elias, too, she spoke of his old sweetheart, and was able at least to give him one piece of good news.

" I was with Petronell Shillingford," she said, on an evening at home, when Elias sat by the window of Southcombe kitchen mending a whip, " and she told me that she'd just heard about—about the thrashing you gave Hugh Grenville. Her father mentioned it. He hid it till now, because he thought the shock might be too much for her; but he believed that she had got over the grief, and he thought, at this stage, it might do her good to know. In fact, she asked. She knew her father meant to punish that bad man, and she asked suddenly one evening what happened. Then Mr. Shillingford told her everything, and how you took the task upon yourself, and how you did it."

" There was no need for her to have known anything about that."

" Yes, there was. It was quite right and proper; and she said very little about it, but thought a great deal. And to-day —this very day, Elias—she told me that she was glad you had been the man to revenge her. And she's got so pale and thin over it, you'd never believe."

" No doubt she'd take him back to-morrow—if he came back."

" How can you say such an unkind thing! Why, he—oh, no, Elias. She's passed the stage of hating him, because you can't hate after a certain time. It's too tiring. But she's reached the stage of being thankful he gave her up. Heartily thankful she is; for now her eyes are opened, and she sees what a mean-hearted, hateful sort of man he really was. And I've helped to show her. I didn't feel any call to hide what happened to me."

" Certainly not—why should you? A cur like that ought to be shown up."

" And Petronell sees the difference between him and—and other men clearly enough now."

" That's a good thing."

" I think she'd like to thank you herself if——"

" No doubt we shall meet again some time or other."

Tryphena felt that she had said enough; but nothing came of it, and she was not aware that on three successive occasions Elias contrived to find business on the other side of the valley in the neighbourhood of Blackslade.

He called on some pretext at Dunstone Mill, and saw Nelly Gurney. That wise virgin laboured under the usual grievances, and wished that Elias would speak to her father.

" Your head' screwed on the right way," she said. " And there's no pride in him. He'd just as easily stand being lectured by a young man as an old one. To see him—a greyhaired man—gadding about with my stepmother—'tis a crying shame; and instead of getting more sober-minded as she grows older, she's gayer every day of her life."

" It's your fault, Nelly," he answered. " And it's no good you crying out against it, when you do everything to make life easy for them, and take all trouble off your father's shoulders. Why, you and your brother Bassett run the mill now—and run it well ; and your second brother, Philip, is coming on vonderful, and your s'ster Madge is your right hand."

" That's all true," she admitted. " My father's children have been a tower of strength to him, without a doubt. But 'tis upsetting the proper order of things, and if you could see me and my brothers sometimes, sitting with our brows screwed up over the books, and father and mother off at a revel, or perhaps both gone to bed exhausted after some far-reaching foolery the day before—if you could see us the bread-winners, and them the bread-eaters—you'd shed tears of blood, I should think. My brothers be too old for their years, and my father's twice a child."

But Elias did not sympathise overmuch.

" Your fault," he repeated, " and everybody knows that the mill is doing jolly well. And your father and his wife—whatever their faults, they ban't grasping.'

" That's all you know," she said. " They'd eat money if I'd let 'em."

" If you pay the piper, you call the tune, of course. How's things—round about? "

Thereupon Nelly turned from her own troubles to those of other people. This naturally led to Petronell, as Elias expected it would. He heard of her and her seclusion, and the darkness in which she was wont to move.

" She hates the day, and told me so," said Nelly. " She'll wait for the dimpsy light, and then slink out, all alone, into

Blackslade wood with her thoughts. There's none to comfort her but Tryphena Harvey, and of course a young rich woman like her have got to put her own affairs first."

And so it happened that Elias met his old sweetheart in Blackslade wood; and before they parted they arranged to meet again. It was upon that permission to see her again that Elias left Petronell in deep excitation of mind, for nothing in the actual interview could be said to renew their former friendship. The girl was full of bitterness with life, and what young Coaker expected did not happen, for she made no allusion to her tribulations or to his part as avenger. But after an hour of desultory talk between them, in which they both censured the world very heartily and quite agreed that it was a worthless place, Petronell declared that Elias had cheered her a little, and, when he asked her to see him again, she consented.

"I'm bad company for you, all the same," she said. "I'm a sour disillusioned creature, and if you see any more of me I shall only make you hate life and everything in it, like I do myself. The irony—the irony, Elias! Here am I, young still, though only in years, and I've got to see two quite elderly people—my dear father and Mrs. Windeatt—going through the wretched farce again under my eyes! And I *know* it'll all end in dust and ashes; and they ought to know it, too, for they've both been through it before."

"You won't make me think worse of the world than I do," he said. "We agree there. Nought can deceive such as we are."

In this frame of mind they met again and yet again. Their meetings were secret and none guessed at them. Then, thanks to the man, who showed unsuspected subtlety and patience, Petronell began to feel her life at least might be useful, if nothing more.

"One has got to go on, I suppose," she said. "It's like the sky growing clouded before noon, and the rest of the day turning wet and wretched after a promising start."

"There's duty," he told her. "You'll find that hard work will help the fix you're in. After the great tragedy of my life, I worked like a team of horses. Ten men's work I did—else no doubt I'd have gone mad."

"Yes, I must work. I told Tryphena that, and she thought so, too. A nursery governess, very likely. You'll miss Tryphena sorely at Southcombe."

"She's a little wonder."

"How did you 'scape falling in love with her, Elias? "
Elias stared.

"Do you ask that? Don't you know the reason? "

This point was reached at the fourth confabulation, and, during the fifth the understanding between the man and woman proceeded.

The psychology of Petronell's spirit was laid bare. She could not choose but know what was in the man's mind, and and now, in a moment of recklessness, she revealed the contents of her own.

" I'm a wretch, and have hateful thoughts—hateful and low and mean," she said. " I'm proud, and I simply detest it when I see people finer than myself."

" What nonsense! 'Tis only a question of cash."

" You misunderstand. Not finer outside—that's nothing, and after my experiences I shall go in black for the rest of my life. But finer inside—oh, to a proud woman, to see finer souls than her own—it's gall. I love Tryphena dearly; but you don't know how difficult it is sometimes, when I realise what a poor thing I am beside her."

" Good Lord, what rubbish will you talk next? A little, happy, lucky, good-natured child—that's all she is! "

" No, no, Elias. She's a thousand times more than that. She's got a grand way of looking at everything that happens, and a grand trust and belief in her friends. And you—I'm not saying it to flatter. But you're so—great and simple, too. I'm so double and treble and horrid."

He set to work to dispute this criticism, but she would not have it.

" Just look at me," she said. " I know why you're here perfectly well, Elias; and I know what you want; and I pity you for being such a bad judge. You won't remember the truth. We loved once and then we parted—all my fault, every bit of it."

" Not at all! I won't have that. The fault was mine—a pig-headed fool! "

" Don't interrupt. We parted, and I—I found somebody else, and you didn't. And that makes the hideous gulf between us that nothing will ever bridge. Oh, why on earth didn't you find somebody else, too, and let her throw you over? Then we should have been in the same box, and you wouldn't have been able to crow."

" ' Crow '! Good Lord, Petronell, who's crowing? "

" Of course you are—inside. Not out loud, but inside you must be crowing. You can't help it. An angel would crow. And I'm not sure if it isn't rather mean-spirited and small of you, Elias, condescending to think of me any more. And— even now there's Tryphena, worth a thousand thousand of me;

and she'd be a much better wife than I could; and she thinks the world of you, and——"

Here he stopped her mouth, and it was supper-time before they left the woods.

But she would not let the man say one word for three months. "Not Tryphena, or my own father, or Sibley shall hear it yet," she declared. "It's too indecent and horrible and heartless. How you've done it, Elias, I don't know. I only know I'm not worthy to black your boots."

But he could not suffer her dispraise, and, having regained his prize, set about restoring her self-respect and happiness. She had relapses, yet in the course of months began to grow happier. And she loved the man indeed—with a fierce intensity that astonished him.

Thus it came about that, while Tryphena still strove with all her might to bring them together, and while each outwardly preserved an aloof and doubtful attitude towards the other, the old relations were secretly renewed; they were lovers, and Elias only awaited Petronell's will to make the great announcement. Tryphena was the first to hear it, and the news came to her in the company of both. Little dreaming that these two had taken the matter into their own hands, she laboured on to make them close friends again; and since both had long ago discovered her project, each took care in her company to give no hint of the truth.

But presently Petronell agreed that the girl should be left no longer in doubt. She took Tryphena for a walk, and they came to where Elias had planned to meet them. The little idyll was played without words, for when the man reached them, he put his arms round Petronell and kissed her.

Poor Tryphena nearly fainted with emotion, and the surprise was complete. Then they made confession and she frankly wept for joy.

"It's all so cynical if you don't know the secret truth about it," explained Petronell. "I simply can't tell anybody but you yet, and I won't let Elias, either. Months must go before it will be decent to whisper what I'v done; because nobody on earth but you know what Elias and I were to each other before. And to take him like this, three months after—after the tragedy—it's loathsome of me."

"Only you know it, Tryphena," said Elias, "and nobody else is to know for three more months. Then Petronell is going to let me tell it, but not sooner."

"You precious things—you distracting things!" gasped Tryphena. "I'm thankful for this, and you've both been most unkind to me, I'm sure, for you knew how I wanted—but now

—now I can say the great event in my mind. Oh, Petronell— Elias will look black, but don't mind him, and come to Australia with me! You must! Think of the lovely letters you'll be able to write to him—now you're safe and can't fall in love with anybody else! "

" Better ask me, too," said the man; but Tryphena refused.

" Not likely! Where should I come in then? I want Petronell, and only her; and the right and proper thing will be for her to come and back me up in Australia; and then I'll bring her home, safe and sound; and *then* you can announce that you and she are going to be married. I'm sure that's what ought to happen. You've had it all your own way, you two, and now you've got to listen to me, because I'm rich, and nice, and love you both."

" But how the mischief can I go and lose her for six months, now I've got her again? " asked Elias.

" You couldn't for anybody but me," answered his cousin; " but for me you will."

CHAPTER LVIII

THE spirit of compromise, which is at the heart of all British institutions and an integral factor of the national genius, would not be denied a place in the little romance of Petronell.

Elias wanted his world to know that she had promised to wed him, and he did not want her to go to Australia; while she, for her part, desired secrecy, and wished to go to Australia, deeming that enterprise exactly calculated to break her future from her past. They decided that Elias should announce the engagement, and that his betrothed should make the voyage with her friend.

But all their plans were kept secret until another summer had grown old, then the news flashed round the Vale, and the earliest to hear it hastened this way and that, that they might spread the report.

There came a day when Gabriel Shillingford rode forth by

Tunhill and the moor-edge to a destination at the north of the valley; but he was detained, for Samuel Sweetland fell in with him and insisted on speech.

" Haven't met you since the last great news, Shillingford. My word, what a whirl you people do live in! You take life too fast, in my opinion. You'll find it ageing to a man of your years."

" 'Tis life that takes me too fast, neighbour. And when you've got wife-old girls of the stamp of my daughters, I must tell you that life certainly does move. Nobody will be better pleased to sink back into peace than I shall."

" It was the same with me," declared Samuel. " Men are pretty much like what I read about comets. They blaze into the sky suddenly, after being out of sight for years. All of a moment life brings 'em to the front, and they challenge the world, and every eye is fixed on 'em. Then they fade back again into private life or the grave, and be no more heard of. And often enough 'tis the matter of matrimony that brings the full glare upon us. An everyday thing, and yet it never loses its interest to our neighbours."

" Very well said," admitted Gabriel. " In your case your bold action was a great source of wonder. In fact, anything that shows a man has got character is always a source of wonder to those who have none."

" And then your amazing discovery, and then the capture of the Widow Windeatt, and then your daughter off with the old love—or rather he was off with her and then the destroyer —I mean the man that whipped the doctor—him to come forward! 'Twas all a very romantic thing. And how d'you like it?"

" I live at such high pressure just now," answered Mr. Shillingford, " that I have no time to consider what I like and what I don't. As to Petronell and young Elias Coaker, there is more in it than meets the eye. I betray no confidence when I tell you——"

" Confidence! Good Lord, everybody's heard all about it. 'Tis quite common knowledge now, that him and her were tokened long afore that rip Grenville ever showed his nose here. And then they quarrelled over a fox's brush, or a donkey's ears, or some nonsense. They fell out, and some say 'twas his fault and some tell 'twas hers. But now they've made it up, and he's brought balm to her wounded heart. And what I ax is—how do you like it?"

" The family of Coaker is ancient, though I do not find that they were ever ennobled—not in this world, Sweetland; but as it appears no less than three of them fought and fell for

Charles under Sir Nicholas Slanning, at Lansdowne nigh Bath, we may be pretty confident that they stand high in the world to come."

"William Coaker and Grace, his wife, are very good and useful people."

"They are, and they have been my true friends for many years. I esteem them highly, and also think very well of Elias."

"You sanction the match?"

"It is impossible to do otherwise. It has helped my daughter through a very dark and sad experience. We are all prone to error, and she erred in the estimate of Hugh Grenville's character. I did myself, so who shall blame a young and inexperienced woman?"

"And how's it to be at Blackslade, if I may ask?"

"The order of events will be announced in due course. There are certain details not yet determined. I may tell you, however, that great changes are indicated."

"Of course. Whitelock Smerdon and his wife go to Kingshead after you marry."

"Is that known? It was a family secret."

"My dear man, you can't have family secrets in Widecombe! They travel on air, like seeds of grass and thistle. And Petronell goes to Australia with Miss Harvey, for the voyage; and there'll be a double wedding when she comes back And Elias will take Whitelock Smerdon's place at Blackslade, but him and his wife will live in one of them fine new houses that Arnell is building beyond the post-office."

"Really, Sweetland, one would think you'd been listening at family conferences!"

Samuel laughed.

"Not I, my dear; but so long as doors have keyholes——"

"Nobody at Blackslade would dare——"

"The ghost, perhaps?"

"Now you are jesting on a serious subject, and I will be gone," said Gabriel. "Let me ask you not to mention these matters, Sweetland. I much dislike having my affairs in the mouths of the people."

"You oughtn't to cut such a dash, then, and make such a figure in the world," answered Samuel. "Still, I'm like you; I didn't care about fame when I was the target for the nation a bit ago."

Pondering the thought of his importance, and not ill pleased at it, the master of Blackslade went his way. He designed a notable act, and made for the home of Peter Smerdon, at Bone Hill.

Here was temporary trouble, for the mother of Peter's famous family had fallen ill.

"My old woman's a thought better, you'll be thankful to hear," declared Peter, when the visitor had dismounted and entered the farmhouse. "You'll not mind the kitchen, I dare say; for it suits her best, and she can catch heat from the fire."

"I'm very glad she's better," answered Gabriel. "Whitelock brought the news last night, and assured me that she was well enough to stand a visit."

"Of course, and always glad for a sight of you, when you'm this side of the Vale," declared Martha. "You be going to be married in Spring, I hear tell. 'Tis a long ways off; but of course there's lots to do."

"Our family affairs have leaked out," explained Shillingford. "How, I know not. But it has got abroad that Whitelock and Sibley go to Louisa's farm."

"So like as not I let it out," confessed Peter. "I never could keep a secret, more shame to me. 'Twas always the same, wasn't it, Martha?"

"It was—a very open man always. 'Tis better to live without secrets, in my opinion. They be only another trouble to life."

"What I say is, there's no money in 'em," declared Peter. "I know chaps as go about big with secrets, like a woman with child. And what does it all amount to? Foolishness— foolishness, so oft as not. Honest men didn't ought to have secrets—present company excepted, of course. But, in a word I did tell my darter Emma, and she told her husband, naturally, and no doubt Young Harry Hawke have let it take wing."

"'Twill be very nice for us, having our Whitelock at Kingshead," murmured Mrs. Smerdon. "I long to see him oftener, and that precious tibby lamb, my grandchild. A sweet babe, I do assure 'ee; and the daps of what my Whitelock was at his tender age—just a wee, round face like them cherub angels on the old graves. So fat as a maggot he is, and so happy as a coney."

But Mr. Shillingford little liked these coarse similitudes.

"Fabian grows daily more to resemble his mother. He is cutting his front teeth on one of the heirlooms—a piece of choice silver and coral. And that reminds me why I am here. We have been a good deal concerned for you, Mrs. Smerdon; we have been very sorry to hear about your illness; and I only waited until you were better to come and tell you so."

"'Twas something catched in the kidneys, I believe; and you'm the kindest of men, I'm sure."

"As you know, an access of fortune has largely modified

our outlook upon life. And we naturally wish that our friends should be as happily placed as we are. In fact, I have brought you a little gift. I hesitated between an heirloom or two—to be left, under your hand and seal, to Whitelock, for Fabian in due course. But finally my daughter prevailed with me. In a word, a cheque. You have the fine common sense not to allow any feelings of false pride to come between you and your well-wishers in a matter of this kind, and you won't deny me the privilege of making a little presentation."

" Don't be uneasy on that score, Gabriel Shillingford. We meet you—we meet you in the same large spirit in which you come, and if 'tis five shillings or five pounds, we thank you without a pang—don't we, Martha? "

" Yes, we do," said Mrs. Smerdon, " and supposing 'twas other way round, and we'd found a fortune in our pigstye, you should have had your bit, shouldn't he, father? "

" I swear to God he should," answered Peter. Then he took the scrap of paper that Gabriel extended to him.

To read it he opened his mouth and screwed up his eyes; then, having mastered the figures, he nodded, smiled, and presently thrust the cheque into his pocket. Having done so he turned to his wife.

" Martha, the man has given us a hundred pounds! " he said.

" Well done him! " exclaimed Mrs. Smerdon.

" And if we can take small money in a large spirit, as we always have done, then I suppose there's no reason against this useful bit? "

They conducted their conversation as though Gabriel were absent.

" You've fought a good fight, you two," he declared, " and I'm glad to be able to show my admiration. When I consider the size of your family, and the way you have brought it up and taken it tidy to church, year after year, and put the fear of God and the love of man into it, and so on, I feel such parents have the right to admiration and reward."

" So we have," declared Peter; " but admiration be one thing and reward another. We've had a proper cartload of admiration for years—at least, Martha have if I haven't; but reward—no. There was none to reward us afore to-day. And we never expected it, and never looked for it. Still, if you can do it without hurting your own, then 'twould be proper foolish in us not to do our part. Such things don't happen by chance, and the praise is to the Lord first, since the best of us are but his stewards and bailiffs."

" I'm glad you see it so; and that's how I'd have you see

it," answered the master of Blackslade. " It has often puzzled me, Peter, that my Maker blessed me with a strong inclination to help my fellow-creatures, and then permitted the small cobwebs of life to tangle themselves round me until, instead of helping people, I actually did the reverse, and owed them considerable sums of money, which, at one time, it rather looked as though they would not get again. To put a generous heart into a very poor man seems to be wasting good material, if one may say so; yet how often it happens! And also a mean heart frequently accompanies riches."

" 'Tis the generous heart that makes a man poor so often as not, and the mean heart that makes him rich," declared Peter. " And, when all's said, 'tis only the point of view. Riches be no better than nettles, if you don't put 'em to use."

" When do you take your wife? " asked Martha.

" We wed next Easter," answered Gabriel.

" No hurry, seemingly? "

" Alliances of this sort, Mrs. Smerdon, are not entered into lightly, or completed with haste. People like myself and Mrs. Windeatt move in large orbits, and we shall wheel together, as it were, with slow and deliberate——"

Mr. Shillingford could not hit on a word.

" With slow and deliberate——" he repeated.

" With deliberate—approach."

" You be going to get the full flavour, I see," said Mr. Smerdon. " There's no doubt you be a very well-born man, Gabriel, for you look at everything in the large, bird's-eye fashion that they do. Of course, such a match ain't like the mating of a pair of hedge-sparrows—nothing to nobody but themselves."

" It modifies the careers of others, and entails reconstruction and reconsideration, building up and pulling down," declared Gabriel.

" You'll have every human eye upon you, not to mention the Lord's," said Peter ; " but," he added, " be blessed if I know anybody who's like to face it better. I've always said of you, at your darkest pinch, when you was heading straight for Queer Street, that you kept your nerve something wonderful, and went your way, like a fine ship in full sail, as if there was no such things as rocks and wrecks in the world. So, if you could cut such a solemn figure when you didn't know where to turn for twopence, you'll soar higher and higher now, and, on your marriage day, you did ought to be a sight that no man in his senses would willingly miss! "

With this great praise Mr. Shillingford departed.

His gift was not mentioned again, and he considered curiously that it had fallen much flatter than he expected.

"It is the difference between giving and receiving," he reflected. "Those who are accustomed to take, soon do so in this fashion, for gratitude grows blunt quicker than any human emotion; but giving is always fresh and stimulating, and its own reward. One is never really weary of giving. To take, deadens the pride, and lowers the tone sooner or later; to give, corrects and purifies the values of the mind. And it must not for an instant be regarded as virtuous. That ruins it. The man who gives because he thinks he ought to give —he is merely obeying a command. The thing must doubtless spring from inside to be of any worth. Yet how the lower middle class always laughs at a generous man! Is there anything more thoroughly craven, more greedy, more mean-spirited in England, or anywhere, than our lower middle-class? Probably not."

CHAPTER LIX

WIDECOMBE FAIR, while sunk from its ancient glories, yet offered opportunity for local holiday-making; and now, with its return, the life of the hamlet recognised the day from force of habit. The men were relieved of work; their masters also found themselves drifting with the throng of the fair, to see friends, mark what merriment was afoot, loiter a little, drink a little, and investigate the ewes and rams that were offered for sale.

On a sunny morning in early September few signs indicated that Widecombe intended a revel; but presently appeared men, driving, riding, and walking in from outlying villages, and the croak and rattle of heavy wheels was heard. The farm carts came from afar, and in each was a great ram—some with raddled coats; some aged fathers of the flock, gone at the knees and bent at the hooves; some sprightly, brawny, solid masses of flesh, with broad noses, curly fleeces, yellow eyes, and noble chests; the potential parents of another generation.

These great creatures, athirst, panting, and little liking their journey, were lowered from the carts and tethered under the walls of the Church-house, or in the shade of the sycamores that stood upon the village green. The horses that had brought the carts and traps were led to the hedge and fastened there, nosebag on nose; the farmers and labourers congregated together, compared notes, renewed ancient friendships, laughed and chaffed together in good-fellowship of common knowledge and common interest.

The day was hot and the sun was fierce, while on the remote Moor, westerly, darkness brooded and thunder growled from afar before noon; but no threat of possible storm frighted the people, and presently the duns and drabs of the men were enlivened by women's holiday raiment, the flash and twinkle of white blouses and blue, flowery hats with bright ribbons; here a red frock, here a green parasol.

When the children were let out of school the music of the fair awoke, and there ran laughter and spread more active movement into the increasing throng. The boys possessed themselves of paper streamers that flickered in and out among the folk, or hung on the trees round about; the girls brightened the scene with their white pinafores and sunbonnets. They ran—now to the little stall where Nanny Glubb, dressed in her gayest feathers, presided over four bottles of pink and green sweets, three dozen slabs of gingerbread, and a mound of green apples; now to another stall, where paper screens and fans and chimney ornaments were offered; now to the green, where the business of the fair was afoot.

There came a solitary Italian boy, who had tramped many a weary mile, with an accordion and a monkey. But at the first note of his rival's music, Nicky, posted under the great yew in the square, started like a terrier that smells a rat and shouted to his wife.

" What's that I hear? " he cried.

" 'Tis a hateful foreigner," she said, " a brat of a boy with a beastly ape."

" Lead me to him—lead me to him, Nanny! "

At sight of Nicky bearing down fiercely, with all his yellow tusks displayed and his blind eyes flashing, the poor interloper fled in terror, and did not slack his speed until well beyond the village.

In the shadow of the cart sat Old Harry Hawke, smoking his pipe and listening to a neighbour. It was Uncle Tom Cobleigh.

" No," he said, " no, Old Harry, I ban't very well. I was stung in three places yesterday. The appledranes* be that

* *Appledranes*—wasps.

spittish this year, along of the hot summer, that there ain't no dealing with 'em. They'll drive their spears into 'ee if you but look at 'em."

" Nasty things. Us have took three nests at Woodhayes. And no news, Uncle—no news of Christian? "

" No," answered the veteran. " No news of Christian— yet; but the time be coming round now. It can't be that us will have to wait much longer, neighbour."

Mrs. Gray, Uncle's widowed daughter, appeared.

" Be you coming along, father? " she said.

" Ah, Milly—how's yourself? " inquired Old Harry Hawke; and Milly—a woman of gentle countenance with a withered face, smiled, declared that she was pretty middling, and hoped that Mr. Hawke was the same.

" Be Young Harry and Emma and Baby Harry here? " she asked; and he answered that they were.

" They'm all on the lookout for a bit of fun somewheres," said Old Harry Hawke.

Down the lane from Bone Hill came, presently, a sturdy crowd of Smerdons. Martha led the way with boys and girls; Peter brought up the rear. He walked between Jack and Margery Mogridge, and Margery carried her third babe, while beside Jack toddled the elder child. They were proud to be seen on either side of Mr. Smerdon. Behind them walked Mrs. Reep, Margery's mother, beside Miss Tapper.

" Yes," Thirza was saying, " the fair is not what it was, Joyce. These things die out under the advance of progress."

" 'Tis they pony-races have spoiled it, my Daniel used to say," answered the old woman; " but I call home when 'twas a brighter business. Us had merry-go-rounds and a doom-show, and suchlike; now, 'tis nought but a ram fair, and the revel be died out of it."

" A good thing, too, Joyce. We gradually get a higher tone into Widecombe. I have watched it coming year after year. '

" 'Tis surprising you should come to the fair, miss, if I may say so."

" Why, Joyce? "

" I'd have thought you was above it."

" I hope you would have thought rightly. I come to see friends—not the fair. They may be at the fair; if not, I shall proceed to Blackslade and find them there."

" Mr. Shillingford will be out and about for certain," declared Mrs. Reep. " He be very set on the old customs and manners."

She was right, and the first persons that Miss Tapper met on arriving at Widecombe were Gabriel Shillingford and Mrs.

Windeatt. They stood under a tree on the Green, and Gabriel spoke—

" This is without doubt the place they called Buttes' Park in olden times. There stood North Hall, the ancient seat of the Fitz-Ralphs—but houses, courtlages, orchards, gardens, stew-ponds and moat—all have vanished. It would be a gratifying feat to rebuild them, Louisa."

" A feat indeed, Gabriel ! "

" Have you ever pictured to yourself the archers assembled at the old butts, that gave the park a name?" he asked.

" Never," she said.

Then came Miss Tapper, and they shook hands.

" In the nick of time," declared Gabriel, " for I was just about to give an idea of this place when the targets of earth, or butts, stood here for the practice of the medieval archers—a subject that one with your antiquarian tastes would appreciate, Miss Tapper. You may, or may not, know the Act of Edward II., which directed that every Englishman should have a bow of his own height—of yew, ash, wych-hazel, or amburn; and that butts should be made in every township, where the inhabitants must shoot upon every feast-day, under the penalty of a halfpenny fine if they omitted the exercise."

Miss Tapper had not heard of these things.

" No doubt the origin of our Volunteer Forces," she said, " and most interesting, I'm sure; but—Petronell—is it true that she leaves Widecombe with Miss Harvey? "

" It will happen—there seems no reason to doubt it. To return to the archers.'

Miss Tapper, however, would not return to the archers.

" Then the engagement——"

" It will happen," repeated Mr. Shillingford. " Petronell is affianced. Here are William and Lis wife—William Coaker, one of my greatest and most valued friends. He will substantiate the truth of it."

Grace Coaker and William soon joined the group; the archers were forgot, and all spoke together of affairs that more nearly concerned them. Gabriel designed to wed in the Spring, and his daughter would be married at the same time.

The company increased. Old men, in worked smocks, their limbs supported by hedge-stakes, appeared out of lonely lanes round about; and sometimes they brought old women with them. Other men arrived on horseback; some on rough ponies without saddles and only a rope for reins. They came without apparent object, and stood about listless and ignored—the subjects of an obsolescent tradition.

In the angle of a wall, not far from the lichgate, a man had set up cocoanuts upon stic's and was inviting the people to come and roll balls at them. The gayer spirits gravitated here, and Mrs. Sarah Gurney, with the doating miller and his younger children, Philip and Madge, stood before the cocoanuts and encouraged Pancras Widecombe. They paid pennies for him and Sally Turtle. Indeed, Sally proved the better shot. She was flushed with triumph. Bassett Gurney passed this group sternly. He frowned on his father and his father's wife. The laughter of Sarah hurt him, for he was growing up as serious as his sister Nelly. She had not come to the fair. Pancras, as an engaged man, now walked with his head high and patronised labourers who had not achieved his state. Sally and he presently strolled off to the Moor; while another pair of lovers had not set foot in the fair but had made holiday together far away.

By flashing watersmeet, where the Webburns come together under Lizwell, sat Elias and Petronell in perfect unity of understanding. The faithful man felt clouded, however, for a great adventure lay ahead of his sweetheart.

But Petronell's sister was at the fair. Sibley pushed a smart perambulator containing her son, Fabian, and Tryphena Harvey walked beside them. They drew up at Nanny's stall.

Whitelock was under the trees with the farmers, bargaining for a ram. The vendor held out for his price, swore earnestly that Smerdon wanted to rob him, and appealed to bystanders as disinterested parties. The ram, tethered in the shade of the cart that had carried him, lay sunk upon his side, the picture of boredom. Round about, dogs also lolled and slept. The day grew hotter, and the thunder still grumbled behind Hameldon.

At last young Smerdon agreed as to a price. Then a horse was brought to the cart; the ram was lifted until he stood erect on his hind legs, and his front feet were rested on the cart. Strong hands then gripped his fleece, and, with an unceremonious heave from behind, he was sent aloft and made fast by the head. He bleated at the indignity, and then was silent. Whitelock now proceeded to Blackslade with the carter and his purchase, and on the way, descending from Tunhill, came Samuel Sweetland; his wife, Araminta; and his sister, Harriet. They admired the ram, and passed on.

An air of high condescension sat on Samuel. He wore a blue tie and a pair of his famous bright yellow leggings. His women walked on each side of him; the sister garrulous, excitable, and amiable to all; his wife, reserved, watchful, casting quick side-glances from under her straw-coloured eyelashes. But she was well content, for Mr. Sweetland proved easy to guide, and her tact had established her in very satisfactory relations with the brother and sister. Humility was the note she struck, and Samuel found it exceedingly agreeable. He expanded into megalomania under the sunshine of her praise and worship.

Outside the " Old Inn," Mr. Sweetland stayed a moment to talk with Arthur Pierce, who had emerged from the bar in his shirtsleeves to get a breath of air.

Arthur was sanguine.

" I do believe the old fair is brisking up again," he said. " I ain't seen such a rally of neighbours for a long time. No doubt, if us could get some more fun into it, and a show or two, or one of they steam-driven roundabouts, 'twould take a greater hold on people."

" And music," declared Mr. Sweetland. " When there's music in the air it lifts the heart to gaiety, and puts a man or woman into a lighter frame of mind. With cheerfulness always comes a touch of recklessness, and then the money moves."

" Never did you say a truer word," answered Arthur. " Music would be a very great addition, Farmer Sweetland, if 'twas only something that could drown that cussed groaning of Glubb's accordion. 'Tis apt to be a wearisome torment in my opinion."

" Yes," admitted Samuel, " a great pity they can't teach him to plait withies and make baskets, and get his living in some more peaceful manner; but he's a hard case. He'll never change now."

There shrilled the tinkle of the school-bell at three o'clock, and the shouting boys departed, and the girls in white pinafores also went to work. They clustered up the flight of steps to the schoolhouse, and presently, loud enough to persist clearly through the fun of the fair, rose a steady murmur of young voices mingling through the open windows of the schoolrooms.

Figures went here and there, asserting a familiar individuality and vanishing again. Here Rebecca Cann, the parish nurse, took her constitutional and stalked awhile, oblivious of the scene about her, before returning to a sick-bed; here Faith Arnell, who had taken Araminta's place at Chittleford, walked—a drab, ill-shapen and dreary soul—beside her brother, the carpenter; here went the brothers Webber from Southcombe, with Sandy Blake and his family from Blackslade; here crept old Bell, a shrivelled shadow, crumpled with rheumatic arthritis.

Birkett Johnson was interested in a side issue, and stood arguing with Adam Sanders, the policeman, upon the question of rights-of-way. Ernest Chave, the other constable, went to stop a horseman who had tethered his steed at the village pump.

Then shone forth an ample maiden, and a married woman of like portly outlines, where Mary Hearn, with Mabel Gurney, passed through the fair. At the post-office, Mary's mother had taken her place while her daughter walked out for an hour; but the revel gave Miss Hearn no pleasure, and she and Mabel scoffed openly.

" 'Tis a thing of the past," said the latter. " We that know a little about the world, be almost ashamed to be seen among these silly creatures. My husband wouldn't knock off work for it. He flouted it. He's in the forge this minute just as if nothing was happening."

" Nothing is happening," declared Mary.

" Have 'ee heard any more of that Dexter man in Exeter?"

" I have not; and something tells me I shan't. He was an empty fool at heart, and anything in a petticoat that could get to his ear could twist him round her finger. He'd meant to come and seek me for a bit of advice as to his future line; but, between ourselves, he haven't answered my last three letters, and I've got my pride like another, and shan't write again."

" He's after something a bit younger," suggested Mabel. " Come in and see Arthur and have a drop. The heat be rolling off your face, Mary."

The sky grew dark before evening, and a storm, that had prowled like some hunting beast behind the hills, began to drift closer. The ram sale was ended; the bustle and stir upon the Green were done; the traps and carts disappeared; the horsemen also were gone.

At the " Old Inn " and the " Rugglestone," parties still lingered; but the little stalls under the yew tree had vanished, and Nanny and Nicky, the richer by some shillings, turned homeward together.

Heavier and heavier the clouds had risen and piled round the hills, while Widecombe, patient target for many a thunderstorm, waited in the gathering gloom for the lightning and the rain. Very grey into the gloaming ascended the tower, with little fingers of steel lifted above each pinnacle to ward danger. Stillness descended upon all things. Scraps of coloured paper, making points of light on the roads and grass, moved and gyrated in sudden puffs of air ; then heavy drops splashed one by one.

The form of Mr. Bell emerged from the " Old Inn " and crawled across the road like a great grey beetle. He reached the sheltering eaves of the almshouses and disappeared into his burrow.

Then came the storm, and in five minutes a hundred rivulets were running to join Webburn; lightning was dancing on the church tower and cinctures of thunder ringed the Vale with a ceaseless volley of echoes between their reverberations.

Miss Leyman, the old schoolmistress, had given the children a holiday and gone for a walk in the dusk. Now storm-foundered, frightened, and dazed by the light and noise, she turned into Chittleford for succour, and found Valiant Dunny-brig standing under his great archway smelling the savour of the storm. But his wife dreaded lightning, and was hidden within doors.

" Come in, come in, Patience Leyman," he said. " The windows of heaven be opened, without a doubt. 'Tis most blessed rain upon the roots. 'Twill beat home. The Lord hath remembered the fruits of the earth, Patience, and how much more should He remember the fruits of the heavenly harvest—the souls of men ! "

" He's forgot they people at Higher Dunstone by the look of it," she answered, shaking herself like a lean dog. " A thunder planet have fallen upon 'em, and there's fire rising."

" Then I must go up over," said Valiant. " You run in the house and call my wife and tell her to send the men. 'Tis a time to do as you'd be done by."

CHAPTER LX

Now, when October had come again and the Vale took livery of Autumn, upon a grey day, when the clouds scudded low from the south-east and the air was heavy with moisture, a man stood on the high-road east of the valley, and surveyed the fertile regions beneath him.

Upon the tawny cradle of the river he looked, and upon the uprising hills round about. Beneath, where Webburn wound, spread tracts of red sedge, and sallow still flecked with faded leaves; while the fields of the Vale shone here with stubble.

where horses ploughed, and here with bright, glaucous patches of sweed, or the apple-green of mangel-wurzel. For the rest, under this lifeless light, all tones were dim and sad, save where, about the church tower, the round heads of the sycamores glimmered with gold, and made a bossy brightness in the midst of the grey.

Beneath the watcher, and upon his right, certain lines of granite wall and earthen hedge converged finely to a clump of larches, while beyond them, far away on the other side of the Vale, loomed Hameldon through the haze, august, stern, touched with amber of fading forests darkling with spruce and pine, swept by long, dead miles of the eagle fern. Sunlight would have wakened all into one harmonious glory of colour, but to-day Hameldon was wan and sore, and soaked to sobriety by the heavy air; while above, where the mount ascended to the sky, its heights and cairns were withdrawn behind the clouds that rolled heavily upon them.

The man's eyes traversed Widecombe doubtfully and without enthusiasm. Then he shivered, turned to a vehicle that had brought him, and asked the driver to indicate the farm of Southcombe. But the driver did not know which it might be.

" I was there four years ago," said Mr. Blatchford, " but naturally on business only. This is hardly a place one would come to for pleasure."

He returned to his cab and descended into the village.

Certain details of his last experience dimly moved in memory, and when Arthur Pierce emerged from the " Old Inn " to direct his driver, Mr. Blatchford felt a vague recollection of the innkeeper.

At Southcombe the lawyer's clerk was expected. He came upon the affairs of Tryphena Harvey, and she was returning to Exeter with him.

" Dear me! Grown up! " said Mr. Blatchford, when he greeted her. " I trust that you do not see such great changes in me as I see in you, Miss Harvey."

" You are just the same," she said. " I hope your toenails didn't hurt you to-day."

" I didn't give them the chance to," answered he. " I drove."

Tryphena was tearful and excited, but she greeted her old acquaintance with friendship.

After dinner, Mr. Blatchford produced the original handbag and spread his papers.

" It lies in a nutshell," he explained, " and indeed you have already heard nearly all that I can tell you; for there is nothing like the written word. You see, this young lady's father left two trustees under his will; his brothers on the one hand, and a friend in Australia on the other. They were to administer Mr. Harvey's estate for the benefit of his wife during her life, and, after her death, to apply so much of the income as might be necessary for the maintenance of the children until they came of age, when the sole estate was to be transferred to them. You remember the dreadful misfortune that swept Miss Harvey's family out of life. She alone was left, and now she is about to become of age, and the whole estate must be transferred to her."

" We know all this, Mr. Blatchford," said William Coaker.

" You do; but it will not hurt any of you to hear it again. Thanks to the immense appreciation of the estate, the trustees have been able to allow Miss Harvey a considerable income for some time now. As her guardian, these funds passed through your hands. And now her uncles, after hearing my firm upon the subject, are of opinion that she should go to Australia, with a view to demanding all accounts from the trustee in that country. She will, of course, be in the hands of our Australian advisers, who will examine the accounts and see that she receives everything she is entitled to."

" You talk as if you were doubtful about my father's friend in Australia," said Tryphena.

" Don't think that. It is the crown and glory of British law that it is doubtful of nobody until he is proved doubtful. That is the difference between our justice and foreign justice. For in Europe, I may tell you, the law chooses to doubt everybody until they prove themselves above suspicion. Our system is obviously to be preferred from every possible point of view. Be that as it may, we feel no reason for any suspicion whatever ; but, having regard for the documents that must be signed, and a variety of business that will result when you cease to be a minor and come into your own, we are of opinion that you should go to Australia. As you know, had there been any need for it, we should have found somebody to accompany you. It is even possible that I might have gone. But in any case, you would have required independent solicitors to take the trustee's accounts."

" It would have been very nice if you had come," declared Tryphena, " but my greatest friend, Petronell Shillingford, is going with me—for the voyage and to be my companion. I hope we shall not have to stop very long in Australia, because my friend must be home again early in the Spring. She is going to be married then to my cousin, Elias Coaker. You remember him. He drove you to the station last time you came here."

" Don't be in a hurry to find a husband yourself," said Mr. Blatchford. " And now you may leave us, for there remain only certain formalities to carry through with your uncle. Your steamer is the *Ophir,* and you sail from Plymouth next Friday."

" And Petronell will meet me there on the morning we start."

At evening the girl set out for Exeter with Mr. Blatchford. She was to spend a few days with her uncles before she sailed.

She could not speak to the lawyer's clerk as they drove together through the deepening dusk, but presently, when they alighted and walked up the great hill out of Widecombe, he strove to cheer her.

" You must look forward to seeing the world again after these years in this sleepy hollow. It is very desirable for the mind to be enlarged while it is still elastic. You will be called to take your place in the ranks of a larger life than it is possible to live here. You are well-to-do, and much may happen to you of a pleasant character if you are wise and cautious."

The hill was steep, and Mr. Blatchford began to pant.

" Let us stand still a few moments," he said.

In Tryphena's eyes the glow-worm lights of the Vale were multiplied by tears as she looked down upon them; but the man only saw a twinkle of feeble brightness trailed in solitary stars around the dark cup beneath them.

" Such a sparse population is most depressing," he said. " One shivers; it makes the mind cold, Miss Harvey, to look into this place and to realise that it is the isolated abode of one's fellow-creatures. The gregarious instinct of humanity rebels at such a sight. It does indeed."

" We don't feel that here," she said.

" Because you are hardened to it. By slow degrees the mind becomes brutalised and accustomed to this dreadful, primitive silence and loneliness in the lap of Nature. But it is most unhealthy and reactionary. It should be no longer possible, in my opinion. It makes a normal intellect, such as mine, feel resentful and ill at ease. Why, good gracious, the owls might build their nests in the streets ! We might be looking down into the homes of the jackal and the pelican ! "

Then did Tryphena laugh, and the distant lights danced together in her eyes.

" Oh, no, Mr. Blatchford. The owls don't make their nests

in the streets; and if a pelican or a jackal came, I'm sure he'd very soon be shot by somebody."

"You think so? Then it is high time you were away—where events are happening and the roar of the world comes as a tonic and stimulant to the mind."

"Ever so many things happen here, too," she assured him; but he would not believe it.

"Impossible, my dear. Look down—look down! All silent, asleep. Just a mean twinkle of artificial lights—a dozen tallow candles—and that is all. Soon even they will be out, and the thing, such as it is, will have ceased to exist, until to-morrow. Now, in Exeter, if you were there at this moment, you would see brilliantly lighted streets, and hear——"

"Don't," she pleaded. "I shall see Exeter soon enough—and the world. Let me look at my precious Widecombe now."

They were silent, and he walked on while she stood still a moment. The cab had climbed to the summit of the hill and stood there waiting for them.

Tryphena traversed the Vale in thought, pictured the faces bent about each little glimmer, and then raised her eyes to the gloom of Hameldon, where dimly it hove upward into a night of cloud.

Bells from the church tower lifted a last farewell to her.

"Good-bye, dear Dartmoor—good-bye. But I'll come back to you!" she whispered.

THE END.

THE CORNISH LIBRARY

'Well-chosen works from a literary heritage which is as rich as clotted cream.'   *The Times*

The aim of *The Cornish Library* is to present, in attractive paperback editions, some of the best and most lasting books on Cornwall and the Cornish, both fiction and non-fiction.

Titles in print, or shortly to be published:

Up From the Lizard	*J. C. Trewin*
A Cornish Childhood	*A. L. Rowse*
Freedom of the Parish	*Geoffrey Grigson*
School House in the Wind	*Anne Treneer*
Rambles Beyond Railways	*Wilkie Collins*
A Pair of Blue Eyes	*Thomas Hardy*
The Owls' House	*Crosbie Garstin*
Twenty Years at St. Hilary	*Bernard Walke*
Troy Town	*Arthur Quiller-Couch*
The Ship of Stars	*Arthur Quiller-Couch*
Hands to Dance and Skylark	*Charles Causley*
High Noon	*Crosbie Garstin*
A Cornishman at Oxford	*A. L. Rowse*
China Court	*Rumer Godden*
Wilding Graft	*Jack Clemo*
The West Wind	*Crosbie Garstin*
Love in the Sun	*Leo Walmsley*
Lugworm: Island Hopping	*Ken Duxbury*
The Splendid Spur	*Arthur Quiller-Couch*
Hawker of Morwenstow	*Piers Brendon*
The Cathedral	*Hugh Walpole*
The Stone Peninsula	*James Turner*
Cornish Years	*Anne Treneer*
The Devil and the Floral Dance	*D. M. Thomas*
Deep Down	*R. M. Ballantyne*
Corporal Sam and Other Stories	*Arthur Quiller-Couch*
The Cornish Miner	*A. K. Hamilton-Jenkin*
Happy Button	*Anne Treneer*
A Short History of Cornwall	*E. V. Thompson*

All the books in *The Cornish Library* are numbered to encourage collectors. If you would like more information, or you would care to suggest other books that you think should appear in the series, please write to me at the following address: Anthony Mott, The Cornish Library, 50 Stile Hall Gardens, London W4 3BU.